POSEIDON'S PROMISE

Man is most clearly himself when he achieves the seriousness of child at play. - Heraclitus

A NOVEL

Authors: **Petros & Jer Zenieris**

WWW.POSEIDONSPROMISE.COM

LIKE US ON FACEBOOK: FACEBOOK.COM/POSEIDONSPROMISE
FOLLOW US ON TWITTER: @POSEIDONSPROMIS

Linda,
Happy Reading! Enjoy!
J. Zenieris

PROLOGUE

Cape Sounion – Poseidon's Temple and Lair

On a dark, moonless night, full of peace and mystery,
with the mythological constellations cruising overhead,
and the milky way streaming through the temple's inner
sanctum,
you stand at the foot of the revered cape hill,
surrounded by the visions, sounds, smells and feel
of Poseidon's own aqua terra, the blue Aegean.

And as you look up, you marvel at the mystically-lit,
sixteen remaining pillars of the sacred temple,
suspended in mid-air, between earth and sky,
pointing up and away, as if to another world,
another reality and dimension, defying time altogether,
miraculously shrinking the vast distances of space into now.

Pia and Pythi read the draft of their verses one more time. Sitting on a rock next to each other, they scribbled in a notebook as they watched the sun set, giving way to the dusky twilight that was rapidly enveloped into the folds of the falling night. Right on cue, the flood lights around Poseidon's Temple at Sounion came to life, accentuating the marble pillars against the contrast of the thickening darkness.

"This will do nicely," said Pythi looking into her eyes, "I believe Lord Poseidon will be pleased."

Both turned their gaze toward the top of the hill, where the majestic temple stood.

"I like it, I think it captures the mystique of this place," said Pia.

Eyes filled with the beauty of the mysteriously lit temple, so central to their own story, they let their minds wander. They were still in awe of what they had been through and the transformation of this hilltop. Two figures silhouetted against the fading light, the twists and turns of their whirlwind journey behind them.

ONE

Let him that will move the world first move himself. – Socrates

He hated flying. He hated it even more than filtered coffee served lukewarm, whole grain bread toasted on only one side, or waking up with the birds on a lazy Sunday. The thought of an engine flame out or loss of cabin pressure without the option of opening the door and feeling the assurance of terra firma beneath his feet drove him up the wall. His imagination played scary games with his mind and kept fueling his mild but ever-present claustrophobia. Despite this, even in the face of it, he had managed to log millions of frequent flyer miles. It was necessary. It was part of the job.

***

"There are things known and there are things unknown, and in between are the doors of perception- Aldous Huxley." It was the first thing that hit the screen of his smart phone as he took it off airplane mode after landing on time at JFK.

Pythi grinned knowingly as he read the text from his father and, smiling to himself, he flipped his computer bag over his shoulder, unfolded the handle of his rolling carry on and strode off the plane at a brisk pace. Pythi, short for Pythagoras, was not one to wait in queues or waste time. This made him a firm believer in never checking baggage, unless he absolutely had to, and almost never did. He loved the sensation of traveling light and never having to suffer the long waits at the conveyor belt. He had gotten into the habit of always traveling with just a small carry on in which he was able to fit essential clothing for a week in addition to the computer bag with his laptop and i-pad.

What if you wore a shirt twice, who would notice? A small price to pay for the ease of rolling free, he mused.

He walked past all the weary travelers waiting in the line for immigration, to the World Connect line, which was empty, and through the airport to the taxi stand. A tall, lanky figure in khaki pants, a non-descript shirt, and a dark jacket, there was nothing about him that stood out, until you looked at the eyes behind the dark rimmed spectacles. His eyes were mesmerizing and one could get lost in them. At times they shone amber, at times green, and sometimes a beautiful dark gold color. It was as if his eyes looked right through you, as though they were seeing into your soul.

It was a crisp, late autumn Friday evening in New York and he felt the energy of the city as he hailed a cab. His had been a long flight back, a hectic week, and he looked forward to a weekend of quiet reading and puttering around the apartment. Being a confirmed loner, he would enjoy the weekend unwinding. Especially since he never knew which part of the world he might be visiting next week. Traveling the world troubleshooting computer and internet security issues for WhiteKnight Technologies was mostly on an urgent, short-notice basis, and left him little time for scheduled rest or socializing. The few relationships he had managed to squeeze between security emergencies had ended unfulfilled because of his inability to spend time with potential girlfriends. Inevitably, they would tire of his relentless traveling and the relationship would deflate and die an emotionally anemic death.

After a desultory conversation with the cab driver, he got off outside his apartment on Chatham Square in the East Village and loped up the stairs of the four story brownstone. Pythi unlocked his overstuffed mailbox in the entrance, picked up his mail and opened the door to his first floor unit. He had been away for two weeks and the apartment smelled quite musty as he stepped in. It was a spare space. The small living room had one brown leather couch, tasteful but not really comfortable, a coffee table, and a flat screen TV on the wall. There was no dining table. In its place there was a large desk strewn with papers. The tiny kitchen, though functional, was hardly used, and the bedroom had a comfortable queen-size bed, a night stand with a reading lamp, and an arm chair as its only furniture.

One wall of the living room consisted of a large window lined on either side with shelves filled with books. Pythi loved reading, he loved books and they were everywhere. He had stacks of books beside his bed, another stack by the arm chair, and several stacks by the couch.

He dropped his travel bag by the door, the stack of mail on the coffee table, unzipped the laptop from the computer bag, set it on the desk and turned it on. As the computer screen came to life, he called his favorite Chinese take-out place, ordered a huge meal, and headed for the shower. Passing by the coffee table he noticed the new issue of National Geographic having separated itself from the rest of the mail. The magazine cover was dominated by a picture depicting the remnants of an ancient temple with the title "Poseidon, God of the Sea, at the Sounion Gate."

"There it is again," he said aloud, "Everywhere I turn these days I run into some reference to Poseidon. What's up with that?"

The thought of Poseidon brought to mind the endless conversations he had with his father about Greek Mythology and its many Gods. Poseidon was one of his favorite Greek deities from childhood.

His parents were officially retired, or so they claimed. His father had taught Classics at Fordham University for many years and his mother had worked on Wall Street. She still came into the City a few times a week, sometimes to consult, and his father taught a class every semester. They had been a close knit family and they still were.

Fifteen minutes later, his dark hair still damp from the shower, he answered the door, paid for his Chinese takeout and walking barefoot through the apartment set the brown paper bag down next to the laptop.

Ah, the civility of a hot shower and New York style Chinese takeout, he thought, *better than in Beijing and you could chat with the delivery man.*

He checked his email as he was slurping noodles, responded to a few messages and re-read a couple he had received from his boss. Seeing nothing urgent that needed an immediate response, he moved his attention to his phone. He re-checked his text messages and saw the message from his father again.

Time to respond to my Dad, he thought. It was a game they had played for as long as he could remember. He set down the food, closed his eyes and taking a deep breath, stepped inward for a few moments, letting his mind wander.

Ah, he had it. Grinning, he reached for the phone and at a rapid pace texted his father using both hands.

"Noo kallista, Father," he wrote, mixing formal and colloquial Greek. "I comprehend best, Father," toying with the dual meaning of the last word and addressing him as a son and a member of his 'spiritual flock.'

He won't miss the irony, I'm sure, and he'll love it!

"It was R.W. Emerson who said," he continued texting, "People see only what they are prepared to see."

He re-read the text. Satisfied, he hit the send text function with a crooked smile on his face. Then, stretching and yawning, he got up and walked slowly to the bedroom, feeling his eyelids getting heavy. Comfortable in bed, the last thought he registered was his mother's advice from childhood, "Never go to bed on a full stomach."

"Chinese food is exempt," he muttered jokingly and surrendered himself to the care of Morpheus.

TWO
It is a common saying and in everybody's mouth, that life is but a sojourn. - Plato

Poseidon, from his ethereal abode at Sounion, watched Pythi being attracted to the cover page of the National Geographic and smiled with satisfaction.

"Soon, Pythagoras, soon, my dear boy, our paths will cross once again, and then you will remember," he said aloud to himself, mentally addressing Pythi. Then, he sat on his rock overlooking the azure sea and let himself drift deep into a reverie of his own youth.

***

Poseidon had grown up in royal affluence under the proud eye of his father, the mighty King Cronus, and the watchful care of his mother Rhea, the divine Queen. Zeus and Hades, his two brothers, were his playmates in their youth, and, his confidants and companion trouble makers in adolescence. Unlike Zeus, the regal and amorous teenager, Poseidon, was drawn to the deep blue sea and his natural strength found early expression in the taming of wild horses, those magnificent beasts he loved dearly. Hades was the least gifted of the three, but what he lacked in physical attributes, strength, courage and bravery, he substituted with his love for conspiratorial secrecy and dark intrigue. The three of them, so different from each other, formed a formidable trio that few would ever think of challenging in power and authority, either below or above the cloud-covered Olympian heights.

The years passed slowly, spanning many mortal lifetimes, and life was good for young Poseidon. Not one to feel entirely comfortable dwelling at the royal palace, Poseidon, much like the older Zeus, liked to disguise his divinity and frequently take on a human form and mix with the mortals. . It was with excitement that he embarked on his human escapades, as the unpredictable, highly dependent and frail humans fascinated him. While amongst them, he observed the drama in their daily lives, preordained by their notions of the moods of the Gods, which seemed to change faster and more often than the playful Greek weather.

While the human form was quite a tight fit for his superior Titan body, Poseidon found strange warmth among the humans that was foreign to the impersonality of the palatial corridors on Mount Olympus. This warmth made his heart glow and ignited his many passions. This was true when he was surrounded by his many companions, drinking at the taverna, wrestling at the palestra, or hunting for pleasure. Especially so, while giving chase, capturing and taming wild horses on the forested foot-slopes of Mounts Olympus and Parnassus and the luscious green valley of Thessaly. There was an exhilarating, undeniable, earthly rush to feel his body in intimate contact with that of the wild beasts. Sensing their blood pumping through their veins, feeling their muscles fighting his in defiance, and finally submitting their freedom to his superior control.

As much as Poseidon enjoyed his companions, his great surprise and eye-opener came at the hands of an attractive, young woman. Drawn to his exceptional physique, she took him as a lover and introduced him to the feminine mysteries of the humans. Poseidon was instantly hooked. He just couldn't get enough of the intoxicating touch that awakened countless sensations within him; sensations unknown to him before. He felt his passions multiply almost uncontrollably and, having given birth to a wonderful newfound creativity, they would invent a myriad of playful ways in expressing themselves to the young woman's utter delight and adoration. It was at this point young Poseidon started to comprehend Zeus' fascination and preoccupation with the human female expression and its many mysteries, and started pitying Hades for not ever having the inclination to explore it.

His relationship with the young woman, a poetess by the name Thalia, developed and grew more beautiful and passionate, deepening Poseidon's understanding of human nature and psyche. While he was learning the secrets of physical and emotional love from beautiful Thalia, he showed her how to refine her emotions and thinking, capturing the mental and later spiritual dimensions of unconditional love. Sadly, while he remained ever young and vigorous, his lovely companion was aging. They stayed loyal and dedicated to each other into her advanced age. In the latter part of Thalia's days, she opened a school where she guided select, open minded young women in the secret knowledge that was entrusted to her by the God of the Sea. For generation after generation, this secret knowledge was passed on from initiate to initiate, and, in time this school evolved into what later became known as the Eleusinian Mysteries.

Many friendships and relationships came and went, and with each one, Poseidon grew closer to and more appreciative of human nature and the mortal way of looking at life. He felt that something had to be done to improve their lives and help elevate their thinking. Then, in time they might come to realize that fundamentally they were not that different from the Gods they worshiped, who ruled them by fear and with an iron fist.

They should really be given an opportunity to evolve, he thought, *and take more control of their own lives and destiny. They should find a way of discovering the divinity within themselves and strive to become the creators they were destined to be. They should be taught the principles of building the bridge of wisdom between the heart and the mind, traversing the great abyss in-between, and that way take flight on the wings of their divine self.*

This growing empathy, and oftentimes sympathy, with the travails of the human race, started taking hold among the new generation of Olympians and their demigod sons and daughters. When the time came for the unthinkable revolt against the tyranny of the Titans, Poseidon found himself a passionate proponent on the side of change and enlightenment, side by side with Zeus and Hades, whose motives were a little different.

The wars for divine superiority and the fate of the human race raged on and the usual peace and tranquility associated with the sacred Mount Olympus were often disturbed by stormy battle roars, thunder and lightning, sending waves of palpable fear reverberating through the hearts of the Greeks.

This lasted for a long, long time, but, finally the new order with Zeus at the helm, backed by human support, emerged victorious. A new era was about to dawn for humanity, the rise and celebration of nous, mind, and its untapped but awesome potential in transcending mortality, bringing humans and Gods closer than they had ever been before.

In this Noetic Golden Age, a powerful, wise, yet merciful and compassionate Poseidon emerged as one of the leading divinities of the transformation; his daring and far-reaching outlook, a refreshing covenant and a promise.

THREE
Girls, you be ardent for the fragrant-blossomed
Muses' lovely gifts, for the clear melodious lyre… - Sappho

Pia powered down her laptop and looked out of the window. It could not have been a more beautiful day. The sun was shining, there was not a cloud in the sky, and the ocean was a calm beautiful sapphire blue. Yet, she felt a sense of disquiet within herself, restlessness, a feeling of dissatisfaction, an emptiness.

She had grappled with these feelings for a few months now. She had given up a full-time job in New York City as a staff writer for Cosmopolitan magazine to move to South Florida to nurse her mother through cancer. Being a caregiver had left her little time to focus on her career, and, simply as an outlet for her creative instincts and to give herself something to do, she had started a blog.

That had been three years ago. Her mother had fought long and hard and was finally in remission. Career-wise, things could not have been better. "Soul Searching" her blog had become a huge success with over a million readers every day, she was now all over the Internet, Twitter, Facebook, Tumblr and Instagram. Advertisers were clamoring to place ads on her blog and webpage. The acclaim, her insightful writing, and popularity had brought requests for freelance work and her articles could frequently be found in magazines like the "New Yorker" and "O." She had become a well-known name and semi-public figure, and she didn't even have to get dressed to go to work. She had set up the extra bedroom in her mother's condo as her office space and in-between her mother's doctor's appointments, chemo, and radiation sessions, she wrote.

She wrote from her heart, reaching out to thousands of people living through the travails of a recession, to those who were either suffering themselves, or, had near and dear ones also going through life threatening illnesses; connecting on some deep level with all those living through serious life issues. To them, she was a life line, a friend, and a companion, a voice that alleviated their darkness. And yet, in spite of the accolades and thanks, she had begun to feel like the writing was getting more and more difficult each day. She often wrote late into the night but nowadays she would lay in bed wondering about her own life. Who was she? What did she want? Was she happy? And on and on.

She lived a fairly solitary life and it had not bothered her until now. She was connected to millions of people, yet, she had few close friends. Most of her college friends were either married with children or deep into furthering their careers. She was in touch with some of her co-workers at Cosmo, but there too, as the years flew by, she felt disconnected. She felt a void, a growing chasm, and knew that she needed to make a change but was reluctant to really think too deeply or too hard about it.

Shaking herself out of reverie, she realized it was time to shower and dress. She was driving her mother to meet her friends for an "early bird" dinner at the local diner. Her mother was looking forward to meeting three of her friends and enjoying a full dinner at a reduced price. Such were the joys of growing old in South Florida.

Thirty minutes later, she was dressed and ready, in a red sundress, her lightly tanned shoulders bare. Her jet black long hair framed a face with an aquiline nose, full lips, and translucent blue eyes. She needed little make up for her olive skin, just a light touch of lipstick and some eyeliner for her eyes. Slipping her bare feet into a pair of slinky sandals, she knocked on her mother's door.

Eve, her mother, was ready and waiting, sitting in an arm chair, watching TV. She smiled affectionately at her beautiful daughter and together they walked to the elevator. Eve had been born in Greece, in a small town about fifty miles outside Athens. During the summer she worked at a nearby Oceanside resort, and there she met a young and handsome American GI; they had secretly fallen in love. Much to her parents' dismay, John Hardy, had come back year after year and asked for her hand in marriage. Eve, who had been only seventeen at the time she met John, had been overjoyed and after much pleading and many tears her parents had relented. Eve had married John and come to America. Evangelia, as she had been named at birth, officially changed her name to Eve when she came to America as John Hardy's bride; she had been twenty years old then.

Forty years later, Eve, now widowed, relied heavily on her youngest child, her gift from God, as she called Pia. A year after getting married and moving to America, she had given birth to twin boys, John Jr. and Nicholas. Eve called them Yannis and Nikos. She loved her boys but wanted a daughter terribly. Twelve years later, when she thought she would never get pregnant again, she did, and was overjoyed when she had a beautiful daughter, whom she named Penelope after her mother. The boys had thought that Penelope was too long a name and they had nicknamed her Pia. She had been Pia ever since.

Pia adored her older brothers as they did her. Both of them lived in Texas with their families and Pia missed them terribly. When her mother had been diagnosed with cancer, all three of them had decided that it would be Pia who would go live with their mother and help her through the recovery process. While she had had a twinge of sadness when she left New York, she had never regretted moving to South Florida to be with her mother, until now.

FOUR

The gods did not reveal from the beginning, all things to us. – Xenophanes

Athena, the Goddess of Wisdom and patron deity of the City of Athens, observed Pia's musings for meaning and fulfillment from her ethereal abode high above the Acropolis.

"That's my girl," she whispered to herself, "It won't be long now, dearest Penelope, before your search jolts your memory and leads you to me."

Then, she turned her attention South, towards Sounion, to observe Lord Poseidon on his favorite rock, amongst the remnants of what was once one of the greatest edifices in all of Greece. Discreetly, stealthily, she harmonized her mental wave length vibration with that of Poseidon and soon she was an uninvited observer in Poseidon's review of the past.

"Poseidon's power and the grandeur of the Temple have been dormant for too long. I think it may be time for his glory and magnificence to rise again, the world needs him," she mused.

Then, in unison, they transported themselves back to the beginning, the days when the Majestic Temple came to be.

***

The era of renewed enlightenment found Zeus sitting at the throne of Olympus as the Supreme Olympian and Hades, the conspirator, in charge of the Underworld, an office that fitted Hades' dark nature like a glove, although he resented it deeply and felt cheated by his powerful brother in the shuffle of power. Poseidon was happy to be assigned the duties of the God of the Sea and he went to work with his usual enthusiasm and passion to exert his dominance and influence over his fluid element, along with the mermaids, gorgons and other fantastical sea creatures. To assist him, he initiated his tribe of Sea-Guardians, the long haired and bearded, trident bearing Beings, who protected the watery realms.

In time, he developed the reputation of a firm but benevolent ruler of the azure waters that surrounded Greece, and many were the tales told by sailors gathered at coastal tavernas of his miraculous appearances and his help at the exact moment of urgent and critical need. Just as the blue monster, agitated by the unpredictable Aegean winds and storms, was about to swallow the boat of a fisherman, or a merchant ship full of weather-beaten sailors and valuable goods, he would appear to save them. His fury with, and punishment of, the unjust became legendary and well-respected. His frequent mixing with the mortals and his passionate and compassionate nature endeared him to the Greeks, who thought of him as one of their own, but better and more powerful, a protector and divine ambassador, one they respected immensely. By and by, Poseidon won over their hearts and became one of the favorite Gods and patrons among the seafaring Greeks whose ships sailed the four corners of the known world.

Through their travels, along with the exotic merchandise that they brought back home, came colorful, strange stories and new ideas from lands and peoples around the Mediterranean. Sea travel, trade, and transport became pivotal in this cultural exchange and so did Poseidon, the Lord of the Sea. In this flourish of knowledge and creative expression, many considered Poseidon as their benefactor, and countless were the claims that he was loved, admired and worshiped even more than Pallas Athena, daughter of Zeus, and the divine patron and protector of the glorious City State of Athens.

Athena was a woman that excited him greatly. Poseidon would have loved dearly to tame her aloof, rebellious nature and make her his own, just like he used to do with the wild horses of Thessaly so long ago. But, Athena was just too smart and independent for that, although not uninterested, and the two were often at odds feeding a rivalry that became almost perpetual, leaving Poseidon to console his unquenched longing for her with women he desired less than Athena. That unfulfilled passion never really subsided, as it was meant to be self-consuming, like the ever burning flame the mortals kept burning at the altars erected for his worship. In many ways, his persistent passion for Athena, the woman he so desperately desired but would never have, formed, fashioned, and influenced his life and perspective.

There were a multitude of small altars and minor temples that the Greeks fashioned to worship Poseidon and bring him offerings in exchange for favors. As Poseidon's influence grew over the land and people, the

Athenians felt that his name should be honored at least equally to that of their patron Athena. They decided to erect a temple in his honor that would, if not rival, at least parallel the glory of the Parthenon at the Acropolis.

It was then that the king of Athens gathered his most trusted and celebrated astrologers, geographers, architects and builders and assigned them the secret task to locate the most beautiful and auspicious place and design the temple that would do justice to the Grace of the God of the Sea. It had to be surrounded by the aquamarine liquid essence of the God. It was to be the last thing Athenian sailors saw leaving home and a beacon upon their return. The search went far and wide throughout Attica and it lasted for months. Many were the proposed locations of promise but they would invariably fall short of expectations under the critical eye of the king and his advisors. The impasse was resolved during his majesty's visit to Lavrion to inspect the silver mines that were largely responsible for the Athenian wealth. While there, the king was invited by his good friend Andronicus, one of the wealthy Athenian senators, to visit his affluent farm and vineyard at Sounion, at the tip of the Attica peninsula, not more than an hour's horseback ride from Lavrion to the South.

The king loved the vineyard and greatly enjoyed the hospitality of his friend, but, mostly, he was transfixed by the wild natural beauty of the place. He was particularly enamored with the little cove at the foot of the imposing hill that formed the edge of the peninsula. The place looked and felt special, but what convinced him beyond doubt was the experience of the brilliant sunset from that hilltop. Next morning, a messenger rode hard to Athens to bring the news to the king's architects that the perfect place for the glorious temple had been revealed. The temple was to be erected at Sounion, no more than a day's ride on horseback from Athens, at the very tip of the Attica peninsula, high up on a cliff that dove abruptly into the blue Aegean, visible for miles from the sea. This would be the first glimpse of home for returning mariners, and the sunset vistas from the temple's perspective were simply out of this world.

The celebrated architects of the time were reputed to have sworn their assistants to secrecy as they begun to design a magnificent temple in the Doric tradition, consisting of 45 pillars with its altar East, into the rising Sun, and the entrance facing West, right into the fireball of the setting Sun. The Temple, dedicated to Poseidon, and also his abode, sat high upon the hill overlooking the blue waters of the Aegean. From the base of the hill to the top, a steep road was paved with white marble. Huge cauldrons lined the road, each filled with flowers of the most vivid and bright colors. Rows of olive trees were planted alongside the way so that worshipers climbing the inclined road may stop to rest or simply admire the view and take shelter from the summer heat on their way up.

In spite of the breathtaking views and the beautiful flowers and trees, it was the Temple that dominated the landscape. Visible for miles around, its splendor unsurpassed. While many spoke of the beauty of the Temple of Athena in Athens, the grandeur of Poseidon's Temple abode was beyond description. Only the best and purest white marble from Mount Pentelikon, carried on special multi-ox carts that traveled for days all the way from Athens, had been utilized in the construction and it was rumored that the Temple had been secretly designed by Ictinus and Kallikrates, designers of the Parthenon.

Perched atop the mountaintop, its white marble pillars covered in gold leaf etchings, it soared high into the sky, a beacon for weary mariners and land-bound mortals alike. Handcrafted, beautiful wool rugs by master artisans from the slopes of Parnassus lined the marble floors of the main Temple and shimmering silks from the Orient billowed in the breeze. Huge vases, intricately carved and made of pure gold and silver, from the nearby Lavrion mines, sat between the pillars overflowing with colorful flowers. Below the main temple were the many buildings, each one more beautiful than the next, which housed all those who lived and served the beloved God. On a second tier of terraces upon the hill slopes, were built numerous facilities designed to accommodate the devout pilgrims that would come mainly from the plains of Attica, but, often times would travel for weeks on end from remote parts of the known world to reach Sounion.

The Temple, its approach, and location were all selected and designed with meticulous detail and in such a way as to give a visiting pilgrim the once-in-a-lifetime impression and physical experience of ascending on, starting at the foot of the hill, a heavenly stairway. Starting as a mortal man at the bottom, by the time he reached the fabulous Temple at the peak, overlooking the sea and land as if from high up in a cloud, he had undergone his personal apotheosis and been transformed into something of a god himself, ready to merge with Poseidon and his priesthood. This slow process had the miraculous effect of shedding each visitor's particular reality and preparing him to enter the sanctuary in receptive devotion, ready to receive the God's blessings and guidance.

A high priest, hand-picked by the God himself through a series of tests, trials and tribulations, presided over the ceremonial rituals, assisted by a school of priestesses that were selected among the purest in body, heart, mind, and spirit from the Greek world. These young women came to the

Temple at an early age and dedicated their lives to the service of the beloved God. Through continuous spiritual growth and a series of initiations they would become adept in receiving and disseminating his divine wisdom.

The reputation of the Temple as a holy sanctuary and center of exceptional power and spiritual intensity grew quickly, attracting the most celebrated dignitaries of its time who came seeking the God's wisdom and advice, along with thousands of devoted worshipers. Poseidon administered his Temple faithful to his belief that divine knowledge offered to the mortals would help them develop and receive ever-increasing levels of wisdom, leading to the sacred mysteries. Thus, in essence, he established the Temple as a portal of perfected divine wisdom into the imperfect earthly domain. The classical Golden Age of the Greeks was only one of the many presents that Poseidon and the other progressive Gods gifted to the human race.

***

Eons passed, many barbarians walked the previously sacred land, and under the heavy footprint of time, the glorious Temple at Sounion was left in ruins consisting of only 16 remaining pillars and the altar stone. All this time, Poseidon and his loyal Sea-Guardians, true to their commitment, remained patiently in their dual role as gate-keepers and guardians among the ruins at the portal. They kept the divine gate open and flowing at minimum levels, hoping that the human race would overcome its darkness and find the way to their souls once again. Thus, elevating their consciousness enough to receive the blessings of the transformation this magical place and Poseidon had promised.

***

Today, it is on a dark, moonless night that the mysteriously lit ruins of the Temple, suspended between earth and the starry sky, take on their ethereal hue, bringing to mind the times of glory and grace past. It has been a long, very long wait for Poseidon and his dedicated crew, through some of humanity's darkest hours, anticipating that the most advanced of mortals will become sensitive enough to recognize the immensity of the dormant promise of Sounion.

FIVE

I cannot teach anybody anything; I can only make them think. - Socrates

The plan of the "Warriors" was about to unfold. They had worked hard to make sure that there were no kinks in the system. They had a few practice runs and all had gone perfectly. It was going to be a slam dunk. They were going to be victorious. G-Lover and his boys, "The Warriors," were pumped up and confident of their success. With the pushes of a few buttons G-Lover knew that their lives would be changed forever.

Above him, in the ethereal realm, Ares, God of War and Mischief, hovered watching, poised and relaxed. It was time.

***

It was 5:30 in the morning when Professor Harding awoke as he usually did, and quietly let himself out of the bedroom, so as not to disturb his wife, who liked to sleep in on the weekends. The kitchen was still dark and he could see his cell phone glowing on its charger. He flipped on the overhead light and walking to the phone checked his messages. The first one he saw was the text from his son.

"Very clever," he said aloud to himself, smiling.

Professor Harding was proud of his son, Pythi. They had played this game since Pythi was a child. When Pythi had been a young schoolboy, he would write a quote and set it down next to his cereal bowl every morning, before he left for school. Then, at the dinner table, Pythi would respond and they would have long discussions about the words, the writers, and their philosophies. Through the quotes he had shared his love of words with

Pythi and he had hoped that like him, his son would become a scholar of the Classics.

But, that was not to be. Pythi's logical brain and propensity for problem solving and all things electronic had driven him to become a technology expert. A Bachelor's degree from The Virginia Institute of Technology and a Master's degree from MIT had served Pythi well.

Soon after graduating, he had been offered a position with WhiteKnight Technologies in NYC and he had been with them ever since. A decade later, he was their Senior Consultant and he loved his job. t Both his parents worried about him. He was their only child and they hoped that he would marry soon and have children, or at least have a long-term relationship.

Theirs was a close knit family. The professor had met Diana when he was getting his doctorate at Oxford University and she was at the London School of Economics. Fellow Americans, together in England, they had fallen in love, had a whirlwind romance and a small, quiet wedding.

After graduating they had moved back to the States and settled into their careers. Theirs was truly a case of opposites attracting. He was quiet, introspective, and philosophical. She was a chatterbox, always having an opinion and voicing it, practical, pragmatic, extremely well organized and she had risen rapidly in her career. She had retired as a Senior VP, but still went into the City to consult.

They had lived in NYC for a few years but after Pythi was born they moved to New Canaan, CT and had bought a charming 1950's style house in which they had lived ever since. Over the years, they had added to the house, built a porch and a deck and had revamped the interior and updated it. He loved his home, it was full of memories, and the yard now had mature elm and oak trees.

He turned on the coffee pot and began to grind the coffee beans in the grinder. He made coffee every morning and it was a ritual he enjoyed. He loved the aroma of the fresh beans as they were ground and then the smell of the coffee as it brewed in his very expensive coffee maker, a Christmas gift from his wife. He loved the quiet of the morning as the day dawned around him and he contemplated the day's activities. It was his time, and in the days when he had gone into the City to teach at Fordham University every day, it had been the only quiet time he got. He had been and still was a very popular Professor, always surrounded by students and very actively involved in student activities on Campus. Now, he only taught one class a semester and usually went into the City twice a week.

On this Saturday morning, he was going to stay home and work on a paper he was writing. As he poured the coffee into his mug, his thoughts went back to his son's text, and he contemplated the words sent to him. Hearing a sound, he turned and saw his wife breeze in. She always had that effect, bright and sunny and full of energy.

"Good morning," she wished him, as she gave him a quick kiss. Then leaning over him, she reached for a mug and began to pour herself some coffee.

"I was going to bring a mug up to you in bed," he said, "So you could enjoy a lazy morning."

She smiled, "Thank you, love! I love your thoughtfulness, but I think I will go to the Farmers' Market and buy some fresh produce. Pythi is coming home tonight and will probably stay over, and, you know when Pythi comes over, we better have food, lots of food," she chuckled at her own joke.

They sat at the kitchen table, drinking their coffee and discussing what they would have for dinner. She was done before he was and briskly rinsing her mug, she left the kitchen to get dressed to go to the Farmer's Market. He sat quietly, his mind going back to the text. Then, going over to his phone, he picked it up and began texting with one finger.

Dear Lord, he thought to himself,*I will never get used to these gadgets.*

"Eleutheroo…to free," he wrote, "No man is free who is not Master of his own thoughts–Epictetus."

"Son," he continued, "Really looking forward to seeing you tonight, come early if you can."

He re-read the text, then satisfied, hit Send. It was almost seven o'clock in the morning, time to start his day.

SIX

Control thy passions lest they take vengeance on thee. – Epictetus

It was a silvery night. The full moon shone bright over the Temple, the white marble glinting in the moonlight, in relief against the darkness around it. It looked as though it rose up in the sky without any connection to the earth, floating in the darkness. White columns rising into the night, the halo of the lamps lit around the temple creating a soft, otherworldly light, illuminating the enormous structure as it towered over the landscape. It truly was an abode for the Gods, as it was designed to be.

There was nothing otherworldly about Poseidon's thoughts as he watched her from his favorite rock, perched above the ocean, in the moonlight. Ceto was one of the most graceful, accomplished Nereids, an exquisite sea nymph. The Nereids were the goddesses of the Sea, who, while they lived and played in the sea, also resided at the Temple in a special Palace on a lower slope, created especially for them.

The Lord of the Sea knew each one of them. They were beautiful nubile goddesses, who protected the sailors and seamen. Ceto was one of the most exquisite and Poseidon marveled at her beauty as he watched her frolic in the sea, the moonlight playing tricks on him as she played with the dolphins in the water.

Unaware that she was being watched, she rode on the back of a dolphin as it skated through the water; her long dark hair flowing down past her naked hips; her skin, smooth and sleek, glinted in the moonlight. He could see the lovely curve of her behind as she grasped the dolphin with her long, shapely legs.

The dolphin she was riding on turned sharply and for a moment, before she got thrown into the water, he caught a glimpse of her full, beautiful breasts and her luscious erect nipples. And then she was gone, sinking under the water…

Only to rise up again, and this time he could see her entire body as raising her arms she rose out of the water. Her lovely face turned towards the dolphins, long hair streaming behind her, her full breasts swinging gently as the sea water flowed over their curvature. She had a small waist, her flat stomach sloping into the most perfect vee between her legs.

Arms raised, she splashed the dolphins as she swam to the shore, kissing them goodbye as she waded out of the water, her fingers playing with the waves as she moved, ever so gracefully, her ambrosial body, mesmerizing him. He was enraptured by the naked vision of her, and, as she stepped out of the water, she looked up in his direction, as though she felt his stare. Then shaking the water out of her hair, she turned around and bent down to pick up the piece of white silk lying on the rocks.

He could almost feel the softness of her skin as he gazed at her. She stood up then, slowly undulating and swinging her hips as she shook the water off her body, running her hands seductively over her breasts and her entire body, almost as if she was inviting a lover to touch her.

Then, lying down on the rocks below, she spread her hair, letting the soft sea breeze dry her body as she lay in full naked repose for his eyes to feast on her. Desire flooded his entire being. He wanted to float down to the rocks below and make love to her in the most primal way. He was completely immersed in the naked beauty before him. She was truly a gift from the Gods and he was going to claim her.

He rose up to move toward her, when he saw a satyr walking toward her from across a thicket of trees. Half goat, half man, the satyrs loved to play and dance with the nymphs and were ready for any and all forms of physical pleasure.

Ceto had heard the movement too, she rose up and covered herself with the silk cloth, but, it was too late. The satyr had seen her and was moving toward her. Poseidon felt an anger burn through him and in a flash he rose up, trident in hand and moved toward them.

It was as if he had winged feet, he was beside her in a flash, his trident raised, as if to ward off the advances of the satyr. The satyr, hooves flying, was racing toward them. Ceto cowered behind a rock, her reverie broken, trembling and afraid. Poseidon rose up and raising his trident pointed it in the direction of the satyr.

There was a white flash, and it was as if a bolt of lightning hit the satyr, who fell down writhing in pain. Another bolt and the satyr went still. Turning, Poseidon picked up Ceto, and holding her close against him, he carried her in his arms as if she was a feather, striding up the mountain to the Temple.

Entering his private chamber, he laid her down on an opulent mattress covered in the softest silks. The moonlight streamed in through the columns and hundreds of stars shone in the night sky, as a gentle breeze cooled the warm summer night.

Immediately, she knelt before him, and kissing his hand whispered, "My Lord, you saved me, thank you."

"Shhh…" he whispered back, stroking her hair. He gently pushed her back on the mattress and towering above her, his piercing eyes took in every detail of her lovely body. The white silk cloth barely covered her and he could see the outline of her heaving breasts and soft curves under the damp white of the silk. Then, still looking at her, he undid the dark cloth that covered him and stood before her in his naked glory.

The breath hissed out of her as she looked up at him from the soft mattress. He truly was a Greek God, larger than life; his huge frame was beautifully sculpted. Strong muscled arms and a wide ripped chest, tapered down to a narrow waist and hips. He had strong muscled legs and as her gaze took in his beauty, she could not help marveling at the sight of his manhood.

She was trembling now, as he lowered himself and lay down beside her. Stroking her body through the silk that still covered her; he could feel her responding to his touch. Then, pushing him back against the mattress she rose up and leaning over him, reached for an intricately carved silver jar. Pouring scented oil into the palm of her hand she gently began to caress his body with it. Leaning over him, she rubbed his torso with it, very slowly and deliberately moving lower, then caressing his thighs and going down to his feet, she worked her way up again, she teased his body with her caresses and soft touches, till he felt like he was on fire with her touch. Then, very slowly, she undid the silk cloth and let it drop away from her body, forming a pool of white around her feet.

Lowering herself onto him, she slowly ran her body down the length of his. He reached for her then, and pulling her close against him began to explore her form. He trailed his hands down her face and neck, caressing her breasts as they grew heavy with desire and she moaned softly. Then, taking some of the scented oil, he began caressing her with his large hands till she was crying out in pleasure. Kissing her soft lips and moving down her body, he rained kisses on her, till both of them were drowning in sensation. Then spreading her long legs, he entered her and as she moaned in pleasure they began moving in rhythmic harmony, her legs wrapped tight around him as he moved with long strokes inside her; faster and faster. She could feel the crescendo rising in her body, and just as she felt her body fall apart in a million sensations, she heard him moan and felt him shudder as their bodies came together in a release of passion.

Above them, flying through the night sky, Goddess Athena stopped and watched the scene unfold. Then, shaking her beautiful, royal head, she moved on.....

He made love to her again and again that night, exploring her body in a myriad ways, till spent he fell asleep beside her. Ceto stroked his handsome face and sang softly to him as he fell asleep in her arms. Then, gently moving away from him, she rose, and dressing, quietly let herself out of the chamber. Dawn was breaking, soon the priestesses would be welcoming the light and warmth of the rising Sun into the Temple.

SEVEN
You'll come to learn a great deal if you study the insignificant in depth. – Odysseus Elytis

Pia was probably the youngest person in the diner. It was 5:30 on a balmy evening in South Florida and the diner was filled with senior citizens, all enjoying their "early bird" specials. She sat at the table alongside her mother and three of her friends.

Outwardly, she was a composed beautiful woman. Actually, she was stunning and her mother's friends had all exclaimed over her beauty. Her long, flowing dark hair glinted in the dim light of the diner. Her red sundress highlighted her dusky skin and curvy petite frame. Red lipstick brought attention to her sensuous lips. She could not have looked better.

The table was full of chatter, all of them catching up on the week's activities, discussing their health issues, children, and grandchildren. It was a pleasant evening and Pia had done this many times. Her mother looked forward to the ritual of this weekly meal with her friends and Pia enjoyed their, sometimes boisterous, always loud company.

But today it was different; she was just not having a good time. She had a nagging feeling of emptiness. *How long could I do this,* she wondered. Pia had been her mother's caretaker for three years now and while there were no regrets, it was obvious that she had to find a way to alleviate the emptiness she felt inside.

The feeling had been growing stronger over the weeks and she knew that she would have to do something about it soon. She was young, vibrant, her blog was doing fantastically well, and yet, there was little that excited her anymore. *Maybe I am depressed*, she thought, and promised herself that she was going to google her symptoms when she got home. Her mind began to wander as the conversation swirled around her.

Life in New York had been exciting. She worked hard and played hard, leaving no time for introspection. She had dated quite a few men while there but had never found anyone with whom she could have a lasting relationship.

Perhaps she needed a man, she thought, *or an exciting, quick, sexual relationship to perk her up?* Nah, she nixed that right away. She was not the kind to have a sexual romp with a man, she needed more and the connection among them paramount. Then, her mind began to flow to all the things she wanted to do…*write a book, travel the world, become a gourmet cook, open a non-profit organization to help needy women, have children, get married….not necessarily in that order*, she thought, as she smiled inwardly.

It would be nice to meet someone…Nice, she thought to herself. She wanted more than nice…she wanted larger than life, someone with integrity like her father, someone who was smart like her brothers, someone who excited her and brought out all the passion that lay dormant within her, someone who loved her and someone she could love back with all her being.

She sighed, and slipping back to the conversation still going on around her noticed her mother looking at her. Their eyes met and she smiled at her beloved mother. She really did love her mother and chided herself mentally for thinking the thoughts she was thinking.

On the way home, they had an animated discussion about their evening and when they reached the condo her mother said she was tired and went to bed. She stayed up late writing about emptiness and loneliness on her blog.

The next morning her mailbox was inundated with hundreds of messages. Readers identifying with her sentiments, others giving advice, still others writing about their own situations. She read through them all, responded to a few, then, decided to go down to the pool. She was sitting by the pool when her cell phone rang. It was Nick, her brother. He had read her blog.

"Pia, it's time," he said. "Mom could stay with us, she is well enough to travel. You really need a break."

"But what will I do Nick? I really feel adrift. I need a change but I really don't know what it is I want to do."

They spoke for a while and Nick assured her that whatever she decided, they would support her.

By the time she hung up she was laughing. Her brothers and their sense of humor had that effect on her. That night her mother and she spoke too. Eve was all for Pia finding the change she needed.

"I am so grateful for all that you have done for me, sweetie. Your kindness and caring have pulled me through the pain, but you must make your own life. I want to see you happy," she said, hugging her daughter. "Just think about it, no rush."

Pia thought about it, it was what she did all that week and all the next one. She knew what she wanted to do…she had wanted to do it for a while now and had even planned it before her mother fell ill. She was going to do it now….she was going to see her grandmother, her YahYah, she was going to look for her roots, find herself, visit the Acropolis and the Parthenon, her beloved Athena's temple…she was going to Greece.

EIGHT

Since we cannot change reality, let us change the eyes which see reality. – Nikos Kazantzakis

Athens, late 5th Century BCE:

Athena stood atop the glorious temple feasting her eyes on the marvels of the splendid city that surrounded the Acropolis, a city that was named in her honor, as a tribute to her divine, virginal grace and patronage by the grateful Athenians. They had done well under her protection and wise guidance and many were the flattering epithets they had attached to her name emphasizing her divine attributes of wisdom, intelligence, love of the arts and sciences. Her bravery and fearlessness in battle was exalted along with her purity, beauty and grace. Still writhing from what she had witnessed flying over Sounion, surprised that she would be upset by it, she admitted to herself that her loyal subjects had surpassed her expectations with the completion of the Parthenon, her abode, rumored to be the most glorious of all the temples of worship anywhere.

As she surveyed the mountain line surrounding Athens, opening up to the sea to the south, her mind reverted to the mental picture of wretched Poseidon being intimate with the nymph and she hissed in disapproval and dismissal. *Old goat, he cannot keep it in his loin cloth! He may as well be one of the satyrs that roam the forest around his temple!* While she was busy mentoring the Greeks to build a civilization that would help elevate the minds of the human race, and at the same time protect it from the barbarians eyeing the light that Athens had become, the God of the Sea was preoccupied chasing nymphs, mermaids, sirens and other strange and fantastical female creatures. *And what was it with those "irresistible" mermaids? How does a human make love to them anyway, as a man or as a fish?*

She calmed herself and let her eyes wander to the base of the hill, following a group of pilgrims laboring the steep climb to the top. As they reached the top, out of breath, the glorious marble-lined entrance, the Propylea, welcomed them into the high-walled Acropolis. They passed through the marble-pillared structures defining the Propylea and strolled on the gentle cobblestone slope that took them into the very heart of the high plateau, which was named Cecropea after the primordial King Cecrops.

Immediately to the right, just ahead, was the unsurpassed architectural wonder of Parthenon, the mansion of the virgin, dedicated to the Divine Virgin Athena. Its size, beauty, and intricate exterior decorations were enough to stop a first time visitor in his tracks with awe, trying desperately to breathe freely and internalize the immensity and splendor of the sight.

This was only the first of many visual shocks to come. Having crossed the threshold to the temple, one could not help being mesmerized by the attention to detail and beauty of the interior architecture, exasperated by the divine abode's magnificent opulence. The enormity of the space and the more than generous headroom made one immediately cognizant of his relative insignificance, thus awaking feelings of reverie and devotion toward the divine. But what stopped the heartbeat and brought everything into focus, was the gigantic statute of the Goddess occupying the entire far end of the temple, stretching from floor to the ceiling rafters. Regal and divine, gloriously sculpted, the helmeted Athena, holding a serpent-adorned shield in the left hand and a war javelin in the right looked straight ahead in the distance, as the gold and ivory that the statute was made of glistened mysteriously in the fleeting light of a hundred candles. Her favorite bird and symbol of wisdom, the owl, was perched beside her. The atmosphere was heavy with the fumes of burning incense. The combined effect was one of sensory overload that would lead the visitor into a trance so unique that he would recount the experience for the rest of his life, in awe and adoration.

Athena's mind drifted to the palatial splendors of Olympus, when she first laid eyes on Poseidon, as her father Zeus introduced her to the other Gods. Having being a brain child of the mighty Zeus, she never had the luxury of a childhood, as she was created in the image and likeness of the Gods but in full maturity. There were eleven Gods in attendance, many very attractive males, but her immediate attraction to Poseidon had been undeniable, electric and mutual. She liked his exceptionally built physique, emanating power, strength and masculinity and his mature but handsome face surrounded by the wild mane of dark hair. But what really captivated her were his eyes. Those deep-set blue eyes that shone with the accumulated knowledge, experience and distilled wisdom of thousands of life times that had advanced the former mortal into this present immortal status. Athena fell instantly in love with those eyes, as her female intuition told her that they held secrets that would complete her as a woman and a Goddess.

Poseidon had been equally smitten with the divine Virgin, helplessly drawn to her beauty, purity and intelligence, the attraction owing not in small measure to the prideful nature of the Goddess that he would love to tame into submissive tenderness in his favor and delight. With time the attraction had grown into a full-fledged, fiercely burning passion, as strong as their individual personalities, which would not allow them to admit their love for each other, although they were consumed by it.

"Divine brute," she muttered under her breath, rolling her eyes, as she looked towards Sounion in the distance, straight into the fireball of the setting Sun, recalling with a tingle of longing how beautiful the sunset would look from his Temple.

NINE

A man's character is his guardian divinity. –Heraclitus

Pythi took the train out to his parent's home. He always enjoyed the train ride. Leaving the hustle and bustle of the city, and getting off at the New Canaan station where his father was waiting for him.

They hugged warmly when they met.

"Glad you are back son," said the Professor, "It's been a while."

"I know Dad, I just got back from Hong Kong. It was a long trip."

Still arm in arm, they walked to the car, Pythi slinging the ever present computer bag over his shoulder.

"How have Mom and you been? Still retired?" He laughed as he said this recalling all the conversations they had had when his parents were contemplating slowing down.

"Yes, and loving it!" Said his father. "I have really made some headway with my book and now I have time for research and doing all the reading I want to do."

It was a chilly autumn afternoon as they stepped outside. The sun was shining and it was brisk and cool. Pythi loved fall, he felt invigorated. They made small talk as they drove to the house. Pythi filled his father in on his travels and the project that he had been working on. He would often post photos of his travels on Instagram or Facebook, especially for them while he was away.

Within a few minutes they were at the house and both men walked rapidly up the driveway and entered the home through the door that was always open.

Diana was in the kitchen, in her element, cooking away; Melody Gardot playing on the CD player. Diana loved jazz and she sang along as she stirred and chopped, cooking the evening meal. She enjoyed cooking and knowing that her son was going to be home spurred her to cook an excellent meal for him.

She worried about him. *All this traveling to strange places and eating different foods could not be good for him,* she thought. She had stopped at the Farmer's Market and at the butcher's shop that morning and was preparing a feast for him. Stuffed mushrooms for an appetizer, cream of pumpkin soup to begin the main meal, a fresh salad of spinach and garden greens, with baby tomatoes and red onions, dressed with her own homemade vinaigrette. She had bought a thick piece of beef at the butcher's and was going to do a roast beef au jus, along with a vegetable ratatouille; and for dessert, bread pudding. Pythi loved her homemade bread pudding with raisins and cinnamon, lots of cinnamon.

She hugged her son tightly and then holding him at arm's length gave him the once over.

"Too thin," she said, "You are too busy to eat the right foods."

Kissing her, Pythi laughed.

"Mom, I have been the same size all my life, I am just fine and I enjoy eating good food, you know that. I am never hungry."

"That I know," she said laughing out loud, "We didn't call you 'The Stomach' for nothing when you were growing up."

The banter continued as they sat at the kitchen table and watched her cook. She poured a cup of tea for herself and her boys, as she called them, and they chatted over the music, the smell of cooking filling the room. Pythi had turned on his laptop and from time to time would check the screen for messages.

"Guys," she said, "Go for a walk, enjoy the lovely weather and work up an appetite, we will be eating soon."

Going up to the room that had always been his, and which still was as his parents had changed nothing, he looked in the closet and pulled out an old sweater. Putting it on, he went back down and his father and he stepped out for an afternoon walk.

He always felt like this place was touched by heaven in the fall. The beautiful maple and oak trees that lined the street formed a canopy of the most amazing colors and with the sunlight glinting on the trees he could see every shade and hue of yellow, orange and red that nature could conjure up. They walked in silence, the leaves crunching under their feet, as both men quietly admired the beauty around them.

The professor stopped and made small talk with the neighbors, as they did yard work, and friends waved at both of them as they walked by. It was familiar, this was home and wherever in the world he was, Pythi knew there was a place for him here.

Walking back into the house he noticed that the table had been set and his mother was washing up the big pans she had used for cooking. Hugging her, he told her how much he appreciated her cooking this great meal for him. Her eyes misted over as she tried not to get emotional. "I really wish we saw more of you," she said. Then, changing her mood instantly, she told him to get washed up and ready for dinner.

Dinner was a leisurely affair. They all enjoyed good food and ate it slowly, taking breaks for conversation, which flowed constantly. They talked about the over population in Hong Kong and Pythi told them about some great meals he had eaten there and he described how exotic it was to simply walk on the streets and take in the sights. The conversation moved on to world poverty, and to a jazz concert, which the Hardings had recently attended.

Pythi enjoyed the meal and the flow of conversations with his parents. He always marveled at how well read they were and, inevitably, the discussion drifted to philosophy. Today it was Epictetus and Emerson. As father and son got deeper into the conversation, Diana got up to make coffee and serve dessert. While in the kitchen, she rolled out some bread dough for the morning. Her son was spending the night and he loved fresh bread.

As Pythi sat sipping his coffee and devouring his bread pudding, he felt his phone vibrating in his pocket. Lulled by the good food, *later*, he thought, *what could be so important on a Saturday night?* In the background, he heard his computer bling. *Another message*, he thought. Then his phone began vibrating again. Excusing himself he got up from the table, pulled his phone out of his trouser pocket and scrolled through it. Three calls from his boss and one text.

"SOS…please call right away."

Hitting the button to call his boss, he waited. The phone was answered in one ring.

"Pythi," he said, "There was a system crash in the Athens office of Banque Internationale. Their system has been compromised and the hackers have managed to siphon off and transfer millions of euro. Downloading the file for you as I speak. Treat this as an emergency. We have shut down the system, but we need you there as soon as possible. There is a flight leaving JFK tonight at midnight, can you be on it?"

Pythi looked at his watch. It was just past seven in the evening. He would have to rush if he was going to make it. Athens it was then, and he'd better be on his way. He returned to the dining room, "Sorry Mom and Dad, I need to catch a plane to Athens. It's an emergency and I must go," he said as he put his coat on and kissed them good night. "I loved the dinner and the company. Thank you!"

"Dear Lord, you need to leave tonight, right now?" Exclaimed his mother in surprised disappointment.

"Sorry, Mom, I do. Duty calls and I have to go. I do promise though to make it up to you the next time."

The Professor was already out of his chair looking for the car keys. "At least we managed to finish dinner. I'll drive you, son."

TEN

I know that each one of us travels to love alone, alone to faith and to death. I know it. I've tried it. It doesn't help. Let me come with you. – Giannis Ritsos

Athens, around 400 BCE:

A dark and heavy cloud had descended upon the vibrant and luminous city. The music and happy cheers of its inhabitants had been suddenly muted, the philosophical debates in the Agora, marketplace, had ceased. A sorrowful silence was weighing over the entire citizenship, permeating into the streets, alleys, stores, mansions and public gathering places of the glorious city, numbing the hearts of the gregarious Athenians. It was a time of despair and heavy mourning for Athens, as it was only a few days before that their beloved king, Aegeus, had jumped to his death into the depths of the blue sea below, from the high cliff at Sounion on the premises of the Temple of Poseidon. What catastrophe and curse of the Gods had brought this upon them, as they should have been celebrating the jubilant and safe return of Theseus, instead?

Aegeus, the king, had visited Sounion as the lookout point for returning mariners in the hope of catching the first glimpse of a white sail. A sign that his beloved son Theseus was returning, safe and well, as they had agreed. Instead, the tormented father had gazed in disbelief and despair at a black sail growing larger as the ship approached the tip of the Attica peninsula, a sign that his son had perished in the courageous and selfless but impossible mission to the land of the Minoans. Stricken by a broken heart and overwhelming sorrow, the enlightened king had jumped to his death, not able to bear the loss of his son and heir to the throne of Athens. What the unfortunate Aegeus did not know, before ending his life, was that Theseus, with the help of King Minos' daughter Ariadne, had succeeded in exiting the Labyrinth and escaping the wrath of Minos after slaying the monster. He was indeed alive and well onboard the returning ship. Having fallen madly in love with Ariadne, who was also onboard and under her spell, he had forgotten to switch from the black to the white sail and thus signal the success of his mission and his well-being.

As had become a painful tradition for years, the Athenians having lost the war to the Minoans of Crete, they were penalized with an unbearable blood tax. Every nine years they were to send seven of their brightest young men and seven of their purest young virgins to perish in the jaws of the monster Minotaur, caged in the Labyrinth at the palace of King Minos in Crete. The death ship that transported the sacrificial youth to Crete was always outfitted with a morbidly fitting black sail. Theseus had insisted that this had gone on long enough, and he volunteered to be one of the young men destined to die in the Labyrinth, pledging to slay the Minotaur and return safely to Athens, thus ending the blood curse that had been imposed upon them.

His father, King Aegeus, tried in vain to convince him against undertaking such an impossible mission. The Labyrinth was full of the bones of brave but desperate men that thought that they were better than the Minotaur. Even if one was successful in slaying the beast, no-one had ever found his way out of the Labyrinth. All paternal pleading was to no avail and Theseus sailed in the black-sail ship promising to return triumphant. Yielding to his father and mother, Aethra's, pleas, he had agreed to switch the sail from black to white, if he was successful. This is what he had forgotten to do being lost in the ecstatic grip of love. It had cost Athens its king and him his beloved father. When he realized the consequences of his negligence, he had fallen into a deep, dark well of inconsolable grief and depression from which even his coveted love's tender care could not lift him.

***

Pallas Athena, in a controlled fury, was pacing up and down the expanse of the Parthenon, her revered abode up in the Acropolis, feeling the sadness and despair that engulfed the people of her favorite city. *How could that happen and why hadn't she seen it coming? She could have done something to save Aegeus' life and spare her city the overwhelming grief. And that wretched Poseidon, was he asleep not to foresee and prevent the Athenian king's death in his own temple's backyard? Or, was he embroiled again to the charms of some exotic nymph and had forgotten his responsibilities? What kind of a God was he, anyway?*

She stopped her furious pacing as she realized that these feeling of helplessness did not befit a Goddess. *It was time to look at things from a calmer perspective and reassess the situation,* she thought, looking into the expansive eyes of her cherished owl. She also knew, although she would not admit it to herself, that if there was anything that Poseidon could have done, he would already have done it.

Aegeus is gone, she reasoned, *there is no coming back. Athens needs a new king to pull her out of all this despair. Theseus, the rightful and capable successor to the throne, is in a dark place where he cannot help even himself, leave alone his city, state and people. I can work in the ethereal plane with energy to lighten his burden,* she thought, *but I also need to be there, next to him in the physical to hold his hand and pull him out of the darkness. He needs someone with superior reasoning, spiritual fortitude and a fine touch. Penelope,* she exclaimed, *if someone is right for this job it is my beloved crown Priestess Penelope. I will be there through her. I hope interfering Poseidon does not take it upon himself to come calling on the distressed king to be.*

***

Mighty Poseidon was as furious as Athena and inconsolable at the death of the charismatic king, on the sacred grounds of his own Temple, nonetheless. The king had jumped to the watery depths for the love of his son, whom he thought he had lost, and he deserved to be remembered for this ultimate act of love. Thus, Poseidon proclaimed, from this day on these waters will be known as the Aegean Sea, in his honor.

But, what can be done about Theseus and his state of despair, Poseidon thought. Poseidon had to admit that he had a soft spot for Theseus and he was as proud of him as if he were his own son. He may very well have been, as Aethra, on her wedding night to Aegeus, after a lover's spat with the king, had waded through the sea waters to Spairia, an island close to the coast, and had an intimate interlude with Poseidon, simply to spite the pride of the king.

Theseus had to be shaken out of his current hellish state, freed himself from that overwhelming feeling of guilt and be brought back to his senses in order to assume his royal duties, Poseidon reasoned. He owed him that much as his probable father and he would certainly work on him from the ethereal planes, but he also needed to be there in person. He felt that transforming himself into someone with a gentle, sensitive and understanding touch, who could be close to Theseus and work with Ariadne, to salvage the grief-stricken man's heart and mind, was of paramount importance. *No better person for that than my trusted high Priest Pytheus,* he thought. *He is so finely tuned into me; it would be easy to channel my energies and personality through him.* He should travel to Athens, he decided, to represent the Temple at the funeral of Aegeus and console Theseus. *I just hope that stubborn Athena will not take offence for interfering with her city and its future king...* He caught himself smiling at the thought of a delicious confrontation with the willful divine maiden and a playful, mischievous sparkle filled his deep blue eyes.

ELEVEN

There are many wonderful things, and nothing is more wonderful than man. – Sophocles

It had been a crazy few weeks since Pia had made the decision to go to Greece. A decision that had energized and rejuvenated her....all of a sudden she felt excited and happy, and full of trepidation, it was a delicious feeling, and, she couldn't wait for this new adventure, this new chapter to begin.

Her mother had been very supportive, though Pia knew that they would miss each other. Eve too was excited about spending time with her boys and grandchildren, although she was not looking forward to the cold winter. Pia and Eve had gone shopping and both of them had bought a new wardrobe. Her brothers had sent her money and after long conversations with her YahYah, her grandmother, the plans were made and she was on her way....

On her day of departure, Eve who was now driving, took her to the Fort Lauderdale airport. Mother and daughter hugged and as they did Eve felt a moment of desolation. Pia had been her lifeline through this illness and now she was leaving her, but the moment passed, and Eve on an impulse took the chain and pendant that she always wore around her neck and slipped it over Pia's head. It was a gold chain that her grandmother had given her when she had left Greece all those years ago, telling her that the Goddess would always look after her and take care of her. The locket with the image of Goddess Athena had hung between her breasts for over 40 years. As she gave it to her daughter she said the same thing to her that her grandmother had said to her. "May the Goddess be always with you, bless you and protect you." Then, knowing that her daughter would be protected and looked after, she gave her one final hug and left, hoping that Pia would not see the tears in her eyes.

The short flight to JFK was uneventful. Making her way through the airport to her connecting flight to Athens, she felt taller, like she was alive again, free and independent...once again. She hadn't felt this happy in the last few years and she was still only at the airport. Her inner joie de vivre was reflected in her expression and energy and she turned heads as walked with a spring in her step. Dressed in tight denim jeans, a white t-shirt, and short jacket, she was comfortably dressed for the long flight to Greece, and yet, looked stylish.

It was a night flight and she stopped at the Starbucks kiosk and bought herself a caramel macchiato, sipping it as she walked to her gate. She had time and she did not need to hurry.

***

Pythi raced through the entrance of the airport. It had been a crazy evening. He had received the phone call just as he had been relaxing after an amazing meal with his parents. The food, wine and conversation had lulled him into a state of calm relaxation...the phone call had jolted him into an overdrive of adrenaline. His father had been kind enough to drive him back to the city, had waited while he had run upstairs and thrown a few more things into the case that he had not yet unpacked from his last trip; his toiletries, clean jeans, a couple of shirts, swimming trunks and he was racing back down the stairs. In less than ten minutes he had packed and locked up his apartment. He was on his way and hopefully would make the flight.

Hugging his Dad and thanking him, he strode into the airport without delay. It took him a few minutes to get checked in, one of the perks of his job, always flying business class, and, since he had no luggage to check, boarding pass in hand, he walked through security at a brisk pace. A quick glance at his watch made him realize that he was okay in terms of time; he would probably make it to the gate just as they started boarding. As he walked rapidly to the gate he felt his phone buzzing in his pocket; it stopped for a moment, and then started buzzing again. Reaching for it as he walked, he saw that his boss had sent him several emails; they were still coming in. Reaching the gate he found a seat and quickly unzipped his laptop bag. He turned on his laptop and he began checking his email, waiting for the files from his office to download.

So intent was he that he didn't notice that he was being watched. Pia observed him from where she stood. She saw him seat his lean frame and whip out the laptop, deep in concentration checking his computer and she wondered what could be so important? In brown Dockers, a dark shirt, and comfortable loafers, he looked like he was at ease in an airport. She liked his lean, clean cut look and longish dark hair and as she watched him she noticed his hands clicking away at a furious pace on the keyboard. *Nice hands,* she thought, *with long sensitive fingers. I wonder how those hands and fingers would feel exploring my body, caressing? Now where did that thought come from?* She wondered.

Embarrassed and slightly shaken by her thoughts, she mentally shook herself out of her reverie and began to look away. As she did, he looked up and their eyes locked.....his eyes mesmerizing her as she felt the intensity of his gaze, almost as if he was looking into her soul. Pia felt a small shiver run through her, like a mild electric current. Heat surged through her and she quickly lowered her gaze and told herself that she really needed to go out more often.

Pythi, satisfied that he had the files he needed, turned off his laptop and glanced up; his eyes locked with those in one of the most beautiful faces he had ever seen. There she was, in one of the most crowded airports in the world, looking straight at him, and for a moment, he felt like they were the only two people in the world, all else seemed to fade away. He felt his skin heat up at her intense look, her long dark hair framing her beautiful face and soft lips. His gaze traveled over her body....dressed in jeans and a white shirt, like a lot of other people, but on her they looked amazing, highlighting her perfect frame. There was softness in her eyes, vulnerability, and yet she stood very straight, her posture exuding confidence. It was a moment where time stood still and he felt like he was drowning in the darkness of her eyes.

I really am being fanciful, he thought to himself, as he broke the connection and looked down to put away his laptop. *I must need a woman bad, he mused.* But, he could not help himself and looked up again at the spot where she had been standing. She was gone. He realized then that the flight had been called and he needed to board too. Still thinking about the beautiful woman and the strong connection he had felt toward her, he boarded the plane.

Pia was seated toward the back of the plane, in a window seat. It was a cramped space and the flight was full but her excitement level had risen, she was on her way. For a fleeting moment she thought about the man she had locked eyes with...*Instant chemistry,* she thought....*or, I need a man more than I thought I did!* She smiled as she buckled herself and sat back in her seat, sighing with joy. She was on her way....to Greece, to freedom, to herself!

***

Pythi sauntered into the business class cabin, took out his i-pad and laptop and settled himself into the comfortable seat. The flight attendant offered him a glass of champagne, which he declined; coffee would be good, as he had work to do. Then leaning back he waited for the plane to take off as he sipped on the coffee, and smiling to himself, thought about the beautiful woman he had locked eyes with in the terminal.

"I wonder if she is on this flight," he thought. "Perhaps I need a reality check!"

Then, reaching for his phone he sent a text message to his father.

"Love is the joy of the good, the wonder of the wise, the amazement of the Gods – Plato. Night, Dad, and thank you, love P."

It was time for a nap….nine hours of flight time ahead…he was on his way to Greece…to investigate, to solve…to who knows what new adventure.

TWELVE

The chief beginning of evil is goodness in excess. – Menander

He took off his feathered, regal, shiny helmet and sat on the round rock to get some rest. The business of war was never an easy or comfortable one. Although, as War God he had never known defeat in battle, the proud, youthful and handsome Ares had been taught defeat and surrender by the charms of the Divine Maiden Athena alone. Theirs was a love like no other that had shaken and consumed the entire being of both to no end. It had burned strong and uncontrollable and in spite of Ares' initial resistance and Athena's logical and wise arguments against it, it had exploded into a giant fireball that devoured both lovers.

A typhoon of unimaginable power that had carried them in passion to places that neither lover had been before. They had been inseparable and could not find enough ways to excite each other, sharing his passionate approach to everything filtered through her meditative, careful orientation. He was battle, she was tactics. He was fire, she was wind. He was passion, she was love. Nobody knew about them, it was their tightly kept secret, but in the anvil of this passionate love, Athena had been forged into and had become a woman. She was, in name only, the Divine Princess and Virgin any longer.

Alas, it had not lasted long, and after the energy of the passionate typhoon had been dissipated, the love had gone with it. Now there was the ugly residue of mixed feelings, regret, longing, blame, humiliation and hate that had taken over Ares and controlled him. This made him even more menacing in the battlefield. Athena, although guilt and regret ridden, had managed to preserve that love and channel it into her perpetual, unfulfilled emotions for Poseidon, with a renewed strength and erotic drive that was dictated by the newly discovered pleasures of her flesh. Ares had sensed it, and blinded by furious jealousy, had vowed:

By all the Gods on Olympus, he would not be one to stand by and watch Poseidon and Athena directing their mortal marionettes, Pythi and Pia, into a happy ending. Not if he had a say about this, not as long as he was the God of War!

He had learned enough tactics from Athena herself to value the advantage of fighting the enemy undetected in their own home turf, weakening their strengths and undermining their resolve. Then, the harmony they were out to create would crumble around them leaving both gods and mortals in misery and resentment, to his utter satisfaction and triumph. Revenge would be his, he only needed to select his weapons carefully, effectively.

The internet, cyber space was where he would wage his war, intensifying the security breaches Pythi was struggling with, and by infiltrating Pia's blog, plant chaos and mayhem. Then, he would sit back and enjoy watching love and harmony flip on their side and be consumed by disruption, frustration, jealousy, infighting, disharmony and hate. He would certainly provide enough rope to the budding lovers to hang themselves at the end.

As sweet as this victory would be, what he would enjoy even more would be the deep disappointment and heartbreak of Athena and Poseidon, watching their careful plans of finally manifesting their love go up in a thick, dark and ugly smoke, offering to the very altar of the God of War. Humiliating the proud and aloof Goddess of Wisdom and the God of the Sea? That would be sweeter than nectar itself!

He let a wide, satisfying smile paint his face, as he dwelled on the mental image of the trouble he was about to unleash. It was time to summon his loyal mortal fighters and go to war. He had to select wisely. This would be a stealth war and he needed skilled fighters, imbued with ample greed and avarice to drive them to their purpose; repeat, unrepentant offenders would be perfect.

But, the business of electronics, internet and cyberspace was fairly new in this era of the planet. He needed people that had spent lifetimes excelling in electronics, became masters of the art, and then turned to the dark side. Yes, he needed fallen electronic geniuses for this highly technical undertaking. Where would he find them? He let his gaze wander for a while as his mind was running searches and permutations. Suddenly, he jumped to his feet in excitement and threw his hands in the air, knocking his helmet to the ground and startling a flock of nearby partridges that were grazing in the Sun.

Yes. Atlantis was the answer! The lost continent that had developed such an advanced and wonderful civilization. They had mastered electronics to the point of developing wireless communication and transmission of power, antigravity vehicles, weather controlling and altering machines, that led them to an unprecedented golden age. Unfortunately - fortunately for him - selfishness, greed and hunger for power had motivated some of their most brilliant scientists to misuse those wonderful inventions and cause the destruction of their own Atlantean paradise.

All he had to do was pay a visit to the Akasha, where all records were kept. As a god he had a free pass, and he could select some of the fallen Atlantean souls currently incarnated on the planet, working out their heavy karmic debt. Once he identified them, he had his ways of reintroducing them to their good-ole mischievous selves, recruit them as his loyal followers and let them fight his war. War is what he knew best and he would not be defeated at it. *By Zeus, how sweet it would be!*

Oops, did I say Zeus? Ares thought to himself. Now, that's something he had not considered at all. No matter what, the Supreme Olympian should not even suspect his carefully orchestrated plot against Athena and Poseidon. As powerful as Ares was, he was no match for the mighty Zeus and his unforgiving and punishing thunderbolts. Zeus' fondness for his beloved daughter Athena was beyond doubt, as well as his firm position against god infighting. He needed to be particularly careful not to raise the suspicions, let alone anger, of the big boss. The last thing he needed was to be spending the rest of his days, eternity, encapsulated into a mountain range like the poor Titans, planted there by Zeus, whose power they dared not respect, heed and recognize.

War it would be, but it would be a very secret war.

THIRTEEN
The most useful piece of learning for the uses of life is to unlearn what is untrue. – Antisthenes

The "Warriors" had become fast friends, over the Internet. It had been going on for years. They had first met while playing X-box games on their computers while they were still in high school. Several years later, the friendship had grown and they constantly chatted, had discussions, exchanged information and knew the minutest details of each other's lives. In spite of living in different time zones, they were in constant contact and the plan had been hatched during one of their discussions.

Zagros was from Thessaly, Greece, but he now lived in Athens, working a menial job. His family had been middle class till the crisis in Greece, at which time they had lost everything. He had gone to the local high school but being a sickly child had never made friends there and had missed a lot of school days. Epilepsy as a child had weakened his system and he walked with a limp, his left leg dragging behind his right. The kids in school had teased him and called him names. When he was ten, his father had bought him a computer and his world had been forever changed. On the computer, he was not the crippled kid, who had no friends. He was Ziggy, the whizz kid, who played games and won constantly. He had friends who he talked to, who liked him and reached out to him, who asked his advice because Ziggy was a smart, computer savvy young man, who could play X-box with anyone in the world and win. He was the kid to beat.

But, he had other problems now. His family had lost all their money in the Greek crisis. His father was without a job and in a constant state of depression, his mother cried a lot, and Ziggy was afraid that they were soon going to be homeless. He had to find a way to save his family. To pull them out of this terrible situation and to make his parents happy again. He was smart; he had to find a way. He had a plan in mind but he didn't have the courage to execute it on his own. He was going to have to reach out to his friends; he was going to have to trust, to reveal the plan in his head.

Over the years he had become friends with Yuan in Hong Kong. Yuan had grown up in abject poverty. He lived in a shanty town with his mother who worked as a house cleaner for the rich Chinese population. He had never known his father and from a young age had promised himself that he would rescue his mother from the drudgery of her miserable life. Yuan was clever, very clever. He had learned to beg in the streets of Hong Kong, he ran with a few boys who were petty thieves, and together they robbed tourists and pick pocketed people on the crowded streets of Hong Kong. He had never gone to school, but taught himself English, read the books his mother brought home, that were discarded by the rich folks whose houses she cleaned, and watched television news endlessly so that he was aware of all that was going on in the world.

Sometimes, he helped his mother clean houses. At one such time, a rich Chinese gentleman, Lin Yu was his name, had given him a used laptop. It was his prized possession and he had taught himself how to use it, how to sit outside coffee shops and banks so that he could access free internet services. Once, while he was sitting outside the local bank trying to get internet service, he realized that he had somehow accessed the bank's system at a time the security system was down for maintenance. That first time he wasn't sure how he had done it, but he soon learnt to do it over and over again, even with the system in full protection mode and the firewall activated and hot. He had found a back door entrance to the system using bank employee usernames and passwords that he had stored on his hard drive the first time. Ingeniously, he had planted a minute undetectable bug into the system and he was being copied on any username or password changes, but not through the bank security system itself, where he could be detected, but through the notifications to the employees of the change, tapping into employee emails and the general management information system.

He learned quickly that different employees had different levels of security clearance and he made it a point to learn as much as he could about everyone's duties, responsibilities and online habits. Then, in a stroke of hacking genius, he devised a way to disguise himself as anyone of the employees, as to not be identified as an intruder by the system, when the particular employee was not online and during business hours, of course. Electronically disguised as a teller, a division manager, or the branch manager himself, in time he had gained access to the bank's most coveted inner workings and accounts. It was not easy as this was a new world for him, a world he did not quite understand. However, the challenge and the thrill were just irresistible. He took a vow to himself to learn.

The next few months were a blur, as he spent endless hours at the library or online wearing out the search engines, reading up on banking and finance, starting with the technical terms that were unfamiliar to him. As his knowledge grew, so did his confidence and arrogance. A plan began to hatch in his head, but he was not quite ready and he knew it.

And then there was Andrei. Abandoned at birth into a Romanian orphanage, he was rough and determined to beat the odds. He had been educated at the orphanage that was run by nuns, and being exceptionally bright, spoke several languages. Stocky and crude, he was the leader of the kids at the orphanage. They were afraid of him and looked up to him at the same time. The nuns loved him; he was always ready to provide a helping hand, whether it was a window that needed fixing, a floor that needed mopping, or a computer that had to be repaired.

The nuns relied on him to help with all their computer related work and by the time he was sixteen, he was helping them with their accounting, their scheduling and running the orphanage. He had realized that it was very easy to siphon off small amounts of money from the accounts and he was slowly building himself a small nest egg, one Romanian leu at a time.

Andrei had free reign at the orphanage and, long after all the other kids were asleep, he spent time on the computer, playing games, chatting with friends, and in discussion groups. He had met Ziggy and Yuan in a gaming chat room and the three had become fast friends. With them, he could be honest. They knew his history and all about his life at the orphanage. He knew all about Yuan's miserable life, the poverty he lived in and his ambition to succeed. He knew about Ziggy and his family. He knew that Ziggy's family had lost all their money in the Greek crisis and that Ziggy's father had depression and his mother cried a lot. He wished he could help him, just as he wished he could help Yuan and the other kids at the orphanage. He had realized at a young age that it was all about money and he needed a lot of it to do what he wanted to do. The wheels started turning and a plan begun taking shape.

Ares, the warmonger, had done his homework through the Akasha, he had managed to hand-pick his mortal soldiers for their supreme skills and burning desire to escape the misery of their lives. He had found his team.

FOURTEEN

There is only one woman in the world. One woman, with many faces. – Nikos Kazantzakis

The royal palace occupied a central part of the city with the elevated Acropolis in the far distance. It was a typical Doric structure, massive and austere. The procession of arriving dignitaries who came to pay their last respects to the deceased King Aegeus started at sunrise and continued throughout the day. The remains of the great king had been deposited in a closed ornate coffin, befitting his high position, and placed on a marble stand at the vast main atrium of the palace. The queue of mourners extended outside the palace and it moved slowly through the palace to the atrium. Here, each visiting dignitary stopped in front of the royal remains for a few moments to raise a silent prayer or say farewell and to deposit wreaths and bouquets of flowers. A good part of the atrium was already covered in fragrant flower arrangements. The aroma of the flowers that hung in the atmosphere of the silent procession, along with the filtered and reflected sunlight that came through the windows, gave the room an ethereal, otherworldly hue.

Theseus was nowhere to be seen. He had withdrawn to his private chambers with Ariadne, refusing food and water and not agreeing to see anyone, despite the countless requests, for days now. He had only made two exceptions, admitting Penelope, Athena's Head Priestess, the day before, and Pytheus, Poseidon's Head Priest who had just arrived from Sounion. They were still with him and he had finally asked the servants to serve food and drink - a good sign.

Athena and Poseidon fully embedded in and expressed through the personalities of their chief priests, Penelope and Pytheus, had worked together patiently and diligently to bring the young king around. At first, using their own powerful energies, they started thinning out and dispersing the thick dark clouds that the emotions and mind of the sorrowful king had created under the influence of guilt and despair, keeping him captive in a self-created gloomy prison. Sending sunbursts of silver-white shimmering light first, gold later and finally a touch of pink, to start accepting himself again, worked nicely in resurrecting the spark of life in his eyes. This brought his psyche back up to the surface, from the lifeless pit of sorrowful despair, now reason and human touch could do the rest. Indeed, they worked together as a finely synchronized duet, alternating roles, as needed, using all the tricks in their considerable arsenal to convince the king that the will of the Gods was mysterious. In time, the reasons for this tragedy would become clear. Of paramount importance now was that he pull out of the misery and assume his role as the supreme leader of this city. This would help the Athenians overcome the loss of their great king and free themselves from the jaws of mournful depression and return to their normal lives and duties.

After all, he, Theseus, had managed to rid the city of its blood tax to the Minoans and in time even King Minos would overcome his wrath and become his friend, if only for the sake of his daughter Ariadne. Theseus was a veritable hero and his people had the right to celebrate this as much as they had the right to respectfully mourn their departed king. King Aegeus himself, his father, wouldn't have wanted it any other way, and from his perch in his new world, he happily looked down upon his son with extreme pride and love, anxious to see him be himself again.

Athena and Poseidon had never been so intimately close before, working for a common goal and objective. Since the days of the first King Cecrops, half human and half serpent, when they competed for the patronage of Athens, they had been bitter adversaries, although they had been harboring tender feelings for each other. The Goddess of Wisdom l had won over the God of the Seas then, by striking her spear into the earth, and after kneeling had planted an olive branch, thus creating an olive tree, symbolizing peace and prosperity. Earlier, Poseidon's powerful strike of the ground with his trident had brought to life a spring of streaming water, so needed in Athens and Attica in general. The Athenians were delighted and King Cecrops was about to declare him the winner, until someone tasted the water to find out that it was salty and of no use to the population. Cecrops impressed by Athena's gift, chose her to lay claim to the city. Poseidon peeved with Athena and in anger for the defeat, cursed Athens to never have enough water for its needs. The Athenians have lived with that curse ever since; water shortages being common place.

But this new experience at the Athenian palace, disguised behind the physical forms of Pytheus and Penelope, had brought about a harmonious but intense chemistry between each other, an unforeseen but delicious connection that left both gods stunned. Ariadne had caught sight of Pytheus and Penelope in private exchange, more than once, when they thought that they were away from prying eyes, and she had thought to herself, "These priests seem to be passionately in love with each other. May the Gods they serve help them with their vows of purity and the forbidden fruit of their love." Little did she know that the Gods themselves, acting through the priests, needed someone much more powerful to bless them.

FIFTEEN
Know how to listen, and you will profit even from those who talk badly. – Plutarch

Athens was just glorious. Pia was in love again. In love with life…her life, and this city, to which she somehow felt so connected. It was as if the heartbeat of the city was in synch with her heartbeat. The pulse of this city reverberated through her. It was so familiar, and yet, so different, and she reveled in all of it.

She had been here three days. She was going to stay in Athens for a week and then head to Sounion to be with her YahYah, her grandmother. And she was going to enjoy every moment, she promised herself. She was going to discover this country, the country of her mother's birth, and hoped that she would also discover herself.

"I am on the path of self-discovery," she wrote in her blog, "And I invite you, my friends, on this journey as I find myself, my path, and my home. My spirit is alive and well in this place, which I know so little about, and yet feel so connected to. Who am I, and why do I feel this connection to a place I have only ever visited as a small child? It is as if I have been wandering all my life and am only now finding my way home!"

Her blog had gone viral and in a matter of a few hours she had gained thousands of new readers. She promised herself that she would stay connected every day, reaching out to those who read her blog, and maybe, at the end of this trip, she would write a book about it.

Her hotel was in the heart of Plaka, the old part of the city, connected to the downtown areas and within walking distance to all the museums and ancient sites. She had spent the first days just wandering through the streets, taking in the color and chatter all around her. Everywhere, were narrow cobbled streets winding up and down the steep roads. Crammed alongside the streets were stores, every kind of shop, selling wares from all over the world, Greek artifacts, souvenirs, olive oil, statues and paintings. To anyone else it may be overwhelming, to Pia, it was pure exhilaration.

She walked the narrow streets, exploring the beautiful old buildings, taking photographs to put on her blog. She sat at the little cafés, drinking endless cups of coffee watching the locals and tourists interact. She listened to the myriad languages around her. She swore to herself that it felt like every language in the world was spoken here. She laughed at the handsome Greek shop keepers when they asked her out and she answered them in her broken Greek.

And through it all, wherever she was, all she had to do was glance upward and see the majesty of the Acropolis, its beauty drawing her attention, time and again. She felt as if she knew this beautiful monument, as if she had known it in all its splendor, as if she had lived in another time, when the city of Athens was alive with the magnificence of the living Gods and Goddesses.

"It must be jet lag," she told herself. "How fanciful of me to imagine that I may have lived here at another time."

And yet, time and again, a feeling of déjà vu swept over her.

***

Pythi had landed in Athens, checked into his hotel and gone straight to work. He had landed on a Sunday night and after a quick meal had spent the rest of the night reading the files that he had downloaded. He had to be ready for Monday morning when he would go into the headquarters of Banque Internationale and begin to address their security issues.

Three days later, bleary eyed and completely exhausted from working non-stop, he decided to take a break. He had asked for a team of their young computer geniuses to be flown over to assist him. They were to join him at the end of the week. Pythi felt grumpy, alienated, and very tired. While the employees at Banque Nationale had been very polite, they had not been very helpful, and he was frustrated that he could not work faster.

"But enough," he said to himself, "Time to clear my head and let go, at least for an evening." It was already eight o clock when he stepped out of the beautiful old three story building that housed Banque Nationale in Syntagma Square. The city was bustling and full of life and traffic was backed up as far as his eyes could see.

I may be better off walking, he thought as he strode through the doors and began the short walk to Plaka. *A cold beer and some good food will definitely help my grumpy mood.*

The streets were full of people, tourists milling around, cars streaming in every direction along with motor cycles and buses. He tried walking briskly but soon gave up, just ambling along, watching the sights as he walked.

It was a pleasant evening, almost cool and he enjoyed the cool air on his face as he weaved in and out among the crowds of people walking on the sidewalks. He passed the McDonalds and Starbucks and smiled at himself, as he glanced in. They were both full of tourists. He walked past the boutiques and banks, smiling at the vendors selling their Chinese made wares on the street. He passed several booths where fresh corn was being grilled on the street and he enjoyed the aroma of the grilling corn as it crackled on the coals.

His stomach growled and he realized it had been hours since he had eaten. He stopped at Monasteraki, outside the metro station, and watched some local mime artists perform and then turned his attention to finding himself a taverna, to get some food. With the same meticulous detail he applied to everything, he checked out all the menus displayed at the entrance to the tavernas before deciding on the one he thought had the best food. The street was thronged with walking tourists and Pythi tried to make his way to the only table still vacant at the taverna.

Pia, after having enjoyed her evening wandering around Plaka and Monasteraki had decided it was time to eat. She made her way to the taverna with sure steps in spite of the almost mob like crowds around her. She had eaten there before and enjoyed the food and the live bouzouki players. As she walked toward the taverna, she realized there was only one table left. Quickening her stride, she walked as rapidly as she could toward the one empty table at the taverna. So focused was she to get to the table that she did not see the man walking toward her, and, without any notice, they slammed into each other.

It was the absolute end of a lousy day and when Pythi collided with Pia, he dropped his computer bag. Reaching down to pick it up he let loose on the hapless tourist he had collided with, not even glancing at her.

"Why can't you look where you are going, are you blind?" He thundered, then, realizing that he had spoken too harshly, and also that the person he was speaking to may not speak English, he glanced up.

Pia was really annoyed. Not only had she lost the table but her umbrella and jacket were now all over the sidewalk and this rude man was berating her when he had walked right into her.

"I am not the blind one here," she bit back. "If you weren't in such a hurry, you may have seen me, I am not invisible."

Irate at his rudeness, she glanced up, and the breath was knocked out of her. She knew him, he was her airport reverie, the man she had locked eyes with at the airport in New York. He was looking at her too, with a strange look, as if he too knew her, his eyes flickered with recognition. Then, picking up his bag, and muttering under his breath, he moved on.

Still fuming, she bent down to pick up her belongings. Pythi walked to the table in shock. He had felt it again, the heat, the electricity between them. It was her, his girl from the airport. And he had been so rude.

"Stop it," he said to himself. "She is not your girl, she is a stranger, a silly tourist who doesn't even see where she is going." As he seated himself, he felt a twinge of guilt at how he had treated her. But, if he had stopped, he would surely have lost the table.

It took Pia a few minutes to pick up her things and calm herself. Composed, she walked slowly toward the table. And as she did she felt her anger rising again. The cad had seated himself at the last vacant table at the taverna. This was the man she had fantasized about? Shaking her head, she turned and walked away fuming.

SIXTEEN

It is hard to contend against one's heart's desire; for whatever it wishes to have it buys at the cost of soul. – Ephesus

Poseidon sat on his rock at the Temple of Sounion, overlooking the beautiful sapphire ocean, deep in thought. He had a sense of disquiet within him. Something was not right in the world. It was as if there was a sense of doom building in him. It was the same sense of doom and helplessness he had felt during the last days of Atlantis. It was as if time and space were spinning out of control, as if the Universe was being pulled into a vortex, like a hurricane that was whirling, building up speed and intensity. He knew it, and he also knew that he had to do something to stop it, but what? Where would he start? And who was responsible?

Over the centuries, after the debacle at Atlantis, he had lost the sense of his own power. He had trusted then, but his trust had been betrayed and the world and he himself, had never been the same. His power had remained dormant for too long and now, he didn't really know if he had the strength or the ability to fight whatever was coming next.

His beautiful abode at Sounion had been his home and dwelling place over the millennia. After Atlantis, he had sought refuge there, going dormant for ages. But, now he felt that he was needed, his power and strength were what the Universe needed to bring the world back into balance. Maybe, this time he would get it right.

So deep in thought was he that he did not see her approach. He felt a movement, like a soft gush of air and there she was before him, Athena, his secret love, the image of all his desires. Knowing that she could sometimes read his thoughts, he quickly banished them, raising his eyes and taking in her beauty.

"Well, well," he said. "What brings you to my humble abode? It has been ages since you have visited."

"Cut the chit chat," she snapped, "We have things to discuss and much to do."

"Really? With that attitude, do you really think I even want to hear what you have to say?"

Softening, she sat down next to him. He could smell her intoxicating scent and feel her soft skin as she touched his hand.

"I apologize, but I am really worried. I know that Ares is up to his old tricks again. I know on good authority that he is set on domination once more. He is going to try to wreak havoc on Earth and through the process gain power and ultimately destroy all of us and reign supreme."

Poseidon laughed.

"Athena, how is he going to do that? The world is already in chaos, it is spinning out of control, how much worse can he make it? Plus, who gave you this information, and why? We, you and I, have really not been very active for a long, long time; what makes you think we can still wage such a battle and win?"

"Poseidon," she said, straightening up and looking at him with haughty pride, "Since when have you believed that your power has diminished? You are one of the fiercest warriors I know, your power is legendary and your intellect and planning skills unsurpassable. You are stunning in speed and stealth and your courage is mythical."

Poseidon felt himself respond to her praise. Did she really think of him in this way? Or was she just praising him to get him to do what she wanted? Athena was immensely skilled herself and he knew first hand that she was a formidable opponent. What she lacked in physical strength she made up in mental agility.

She leaned into him.

"We have often been on opposite sides and we know each other's strengths and weaknesses, but this time, we will have to work together, in unison, to stop Ares. Poseidon, I promise you, this is not a lover's tiff; I am not trying to make him jealous or involve you in some tawdry affair. It has been a long time since we have had a relationship, though I know that our meeting would enrage him. This is about stopping him, once again, and this time, we will do it together."

"Why me, Athena?"

"Because, we almost triumphed the last time. We lost because we did not trust each other, you and I, and because your love of the female form enticed you to trust the wrong ones; we were all betrayed. This time, we trust and stick close together."

The thought of sticking close together with Athena was alluring. She read his thoughts and laughed, shaking her head.

"Poseidon, Poseidon…this is serious. This is not about your attraction for me or mine for you."

Oops….had she really admitted that to him?

Poseidon caught it immediately.

Well, she was attracted to him. He was feeling better and better. *First, she had praised him and now she was attracted to him. Could this day get better?*

"What is this about, Athena, and once again, I ask you who gave you this information?"

"This is about finally getting it right. This is about bringing the world back into balance and harmony, it has been too long. This is about creating a world of beauty, health, and abundance once again. And, who knows, it may also be about you and me, for together, I think we are unbeatable."

"I should go," she said, "We don't want Ares' spies to know that I was here. Think about it."

Then, leaning forward, she did something she had never, ever done; she kissed him softly on the lips.

As she disappeared, she looked back at him, smiling:

"Father," she said, "Father, told me."

Poseidon sat there, reeling from the meeting and lost in the promise of the kiss.

SEVENTEEN

And a soul
if it is to know itself
must look
into its own soul:
the stranger and enemy, we've seen him in the mirror. – Giorgos Seferis

It had been a fun few days for Pia. Sightseeing, walking all over Athens, visiting the Port of Piraeus, and eating…eating…all that delicious Greek food. She felt as if she had discovered herself. She was blogging about her journey and wonder of wonders had begun to meditate again after many years.

During the years that she had lived and worked in New York, she had met Shanti, who became her good friend and house mate. Brilliant, smart, and extremely hard working, Shanti, who came from India, balanced her frenetic life with yoga and meditation and gradually Pia too had begun to meditate. It balanced her and helped her quiet her over active mind. Meditation had been the soothing balm in her crazy lifestyle.

She had lost the practice when she moved to Florida to look after her mother. Caught up in the day to day activities of being a caretaker, she had stopped meditating, she had stopped yoga; she had stopped a lot of things that brought her enjoyment.

One evening, in Athens, she had climbed the steep hill to go up to the Acropolis yet again, and, as she sat there under a tree waiting to watch the sunset, observing the few tired tourists begin their descent down the steep steps, she had felt the urge to meditate again. Releasing all tension, as she sat under the tree, she felt a calm come over her, a peace, she had not felt in a long time. It was as if the Gods had conspired to bring her to this place, to find her Soul. Sitting, Buddha-like, her limbs crossed, she gradually silenced her mind and let go of all thought. It was as if she was immediately transported to another dimension, stars and planets unfolding a beautiful pathway….She sat under that tree for a long time, till it became dark and the guard came and told her she had to leave. It was, as if the presence of the beautiful Goddess Athena, who had lived and ruled from the Acropolis was all around her, bringing her to this place of solitude and peace.

As she walked down the mountain, she thought, *I really am getting imaginative; the Goddess Athena would not bother with someone like me.* But, the feeling stayed with her and she beseeched the Gods to bestow their blessings upon her, as she left Athens and went to be with her YahYah.

***

Pythi had had a nerve racking few days. Exhausted from the long work hours and the non-stop problems, he had had no time to do any exploring, or even get a straight nights' sleep. He was spending all his waking hours at Banque Nationale with the newly arrived team and all his nights on his laptop with his team back in the States. The weekend was just ahead, he was going to take a break. He needed to get out of Athens. He stopped at the concierge desk at the hotel and asked them to help him get a room at a place outside the city.

"Don't worry, Sir, we will send you to a beautiful place not far from here." Pythi didn't care where he went, as long as it was away from Athens, the bank and work.

***

Pia caught the bus to Lavrion, the nearest town to Cape Sounion, the next morning. It was only a couple of hours away from Athens, by slow tourist bus, but it was a completely different world. The bus station was in the center of the town of Lavrion, right across from the port, and she stepped off the bus, breathing in the fresh air and the smell of the sea. It felt glorious! She walked across the road to a café and sat at a table facing the water, sipping her coffee, waiting for her ride. Time meant little here, and she knew that her YahYah's neighbor would come by to pick her up eventually. In the meantime, she would gaze at the blue waters, sip her coffee, and have a conversation with the waitress who had little to do.

Her YahYah's neighbor drove up as she was finishing her coffee and after much hugging and exclaiming over how grown up she was, they loaded her bags in his old car, and began the short trip to her grandmother's home.

Pia remembered the drive from her earlier visits as a child. The road was narrow and winding, going up and down the mountain, and suddenly, after a sharp turn, the beautiful temple of Poseidon appeared, perched on the mountain top, overwhelming the landscape with its beauty. It took her breath away as it always had and she smiled happily to herself.

Her YahYah's little house was nestled in a small plateau up the slope of the mountain, overlooking a small bay which housed a couple of tavernas and which was walking distance from the two hotels that serviced the tourists who visited the Temple.

Very little had changed, the white washed house stood facing the ocean, its doors and windows open, white lace curtains flapping in the breeze. A small table with two chairs was placed right outside the front door at the elevated porch, and fuchsia colored bougainvillea covered the side wall of the house. It was a simple home, small and neat, but Pia had the happiest memories of being there as she jumped out of the car as soon as they arrived.

Her beloved grandmother, her YahYah, was sitting on one of the chairs outside, awaiting her arrival. She looked much as she had all those years ago, her white hair in a bun under a scarf, her lined face beaming, and her arms outstretched in a welcoming embrace. Pia rushed into her embrace. She smelled of garlic and lavender, of olive oil and baking bread. She smelled like her YahYah had always smelled…she loved it.

"Koritsaki mou, my little girl," she exclaimed, as she held Pia at arm's length and examined her head to toe. "You beautiful," she beamed in her broken English, "I missed you so much."

Then, she launched into rapid-fire Greek, little of which Pia understood, but she didn't care, they were words emanating love, misses, longing, delight, happiness and the warmth of family.

She lugged her suitcase into the house and waited for her eyes to adjust to the dim light. The house was as it had been all those years ago. The same velvet sofas, covered in plastic, the same kitchen table with the handmade table cloth, the kitchen with its stone counter tops and pots and pans. She noticed that her YahYah had a new stove and a new refrigerator, but other than that little had changed.

She put her luggage in the bedroom and went into the only bathroom to freshen up. By the time she came out, there were coffee and fresh cookies on the table outside for her and the neighbor. Giorgos, the neighbor, also had a cup of Greek coffee before him and soon his wife strolled over and joined them, once again exclaiming over Pia and hugging and kissing her. They sat at the little table overlooking the water, with the beautiful temple towering over them, enjoying a leisurely cup of coffee, chatting, and laughing. Pia felt at peace, it was a good feeling.

***

Pythi felt the tension drain out of him the further he got away from Athens. He had rented a small car and had the navigation system set, so he could enjoy the drive as he tuned in to the latest Greek music on the radio. He liked the lyrical sound of the music and the bouzouki sound, even though he did not understand all the words. He knew, intrinsically, that most of the songs were about love; Greeks are very romantic and their lives revolve around love and loving.

He drove out of the city, driving through the arid countryside, covered by olive groves, their silvery leaves glinting in the sunlight. He drove through small towns and villages, and stopped at one to get some Greek coffee and bougatsa, a delectable pastry filled with custard and topped with powdered sugar and cinnamon. It was still warm from the oven and so fresh.

It was a little over an hour later that he drove around a bend in the mountain. In front of him, on a mountain across the blue water, sat the ancient columns of the Temple of Poseidon. It took his breath away and he almost lost control of his car, so mesmerized was he by the view. Its marble columns glinted in the sunshine, as it stood lonely and unfettered, a beautiful relic from another time.

Pythi, was always extremely pragmatic, even sensible. But, here, he felt a pull; something drew him to this beautiful vision. He was not sure what, but he felt it. A strange connection to this ancient place, this home to God Poseidon.

Dropping down off the mountain, his mind still enthralled by the view of the beautiful Temple, he turned into the narrow road that took him to the Resort where he was staying. Sitting in a secluded bay, the resort was a two-story modern building that somehow blended with the landscape of the mountains behind it. The strip of beach in front of the Resort was dotted with umbrellas and lounge chairs. He was enchanted.

It took him a few minutes to check in and quickly changing into his bathing suit, he went down to the beach. The water was spectacular....blue, blue water, glistening in the sun as seagulls skimmed the top. The water was so clear that he could see his feet when he stepped into it. Ahead, a dark rock arose out of the water, menacing and beckoning at the same time. Pythi was a good swimmer, and he swam out to the rock, climbing on it for a few minutes to get a seaward view of the Temple, towering above.

He swam back to the beach at a leisurely pace, lay back in his lounger and ordered a beer. *Ah*, he thought, *this is the life!* Completely relaxed, he took a nap, woke up, and ate a sandwich, that he bought at the little beach bar of the Resort. All the tension had left him. His mind was clear once again.

Clarity, he thought, *how can I ever live without it?*

He checked his cell phone…no messages.

That's a good thing, he thought to himself, *but I do need to send my dad a text.* Then, gazing out at the blue ocean he began reflecting on the past weeks. He ran the problem issues in his mind, going over them, slowly, trying to find the details that he felt he had been missing. So far, after the first time the security walls had gone down and Banque Internationale's system had been hacked, it had not happened again. But, that did not mean it would not. He had to ensure that the system was completely safe.

The afternoon stretched into early evening and Pythi decided it was time to stop being a beach bum and go back to his room. He took a leisurely shower, dressed in jeans and a soft cotton shirt, grabbed a sweater and headed to his car….it was time to go visit the Temple and watch the setting sun from there.

It was a glorious evening, cool and bright. There was not a cloud in the sky as Pythi tore up the mountain in his little rental, the window down, Greek music playing on the radio. A sense of well-being pervaded him, how could it not? He had had a lovely relaxing day, the swim, the nap on the beach, the beer had all added to his sense of relaxation and ease.

He parked the car, bought his entrance ticket at the kiosk and began climbing the smooth marble steps up to the Temple. All of a sudden, he was overcome with a deep sense of the antiquity of the area. He was walking on steps that were thousands of years old. "Who else had walked the same steps? Man or God?" He wondered.

Pythi had grown up steeped in the classics. While other kids were being read bedside stories at night as children, Pythi's father had read him Greek and Roman mythology. As a child and a young man, the family had traveled every summer and Pythi was used to seeing ancient relics and ruins, but somehow, this place spoke to him. He felt as if he knew it, as if he had been here before, as if it was familiar. All too familiar…almost a sense of homecoming. *Déjà vu they call it*, he thought. But, he felt more, he felt as if he was being welcomed, as if he was home. *Oh boy*, he thought, *the beer or the sun must be affecting me. I have never felt like this before. I have been all over the world, why would an ancient ruin on a mountain in rural Greece affect me so?*

At the top of the mountain, the ancient ruin stood silent and strong, steeped in history and its own secrets, each rock polished smooth from the elements and from the constant wear and tear of people walking on them. Pythi lovingly touched a marble pillar, wanting to feel its texture and warmth, wanting to somehow connect with this beautiful place, to know its secrets, to become part of its story. He touched the pillar, stroked it, almost with a sense of reverence, and all of a sudden as he looked up, he saw the sky open up and rays of golden sunlight streamed down on the Temple, enveloping it in their golden-red radiance, and in that moment enveloping Pythi into their fold as well. Pythi felt as though he was at one with the pillar, with the Temple, and for a moment, time stood still, and he was one with Poseidon, the Lord of the Temple.

And then, it was gone, and he stood there, with his hand on the pillar trying to re-orient himself. He looked around bemused, where was he? It was as if everything had changed…and yet as he looked around, nothing had changed. It was still so.

I should go sit down, he thought, *maybe the sun is getting to me.*

***

Pia, had spent the day in quiet relaxation with her YahYah. It had been wonderful. They had spent the afternoon baking, stopping to chat, drink coffee, and just enjoy each other's company; they even did a little gardening. She could not have felt better. She felt as if she was strong again, and full of energy and life, bubbly and joyous and yet, she felt calmness and a sense of peacefulness she had never felt before; not quite like that.

It must be the blue water and the fresh mountain air, she thought with a smile. *I could live here forever!*

She had also re-discovered her love of cooking. Ever since she had been a teenager, she had cooked and loved it. Her mother had been a great cook too, but, not as fantastic as her YahYah. The two of them had spent the afternoon in harmony in her little kitchen making spinach pies- spanakopita, and koulourakia- little Greek cookies with egg glaze. Pia had kneaded the bread that YahYah would bake in the morning. For lunch, there was a lovely fish stew, with warm freshly baked bread, and a crisp green salad. Life couldn't be better, she mused.

It was early evening and she decided she would take a walk up the mountain and visit the Temple. *Time to go there again,* she thought. She had always loved the Temple and had often played there as a child when she visited.

Putting on a pair of jeans and sneakers, she began the long trek up. She enjoyed the activity, and the mountain was so familiar. She stopped to look at the view as she got higher, smell the scent of the beautiful pine trees mixed with the lingering aroma of wild thyme and simply enjoy the hike up the mountain.

The lady at the kiosk, Thea-Olga, Olga-auntie, recognized her, came running out to give her a hug and waved her on. She was family, no charge for her. Smiling, she climbed the marble steps to the Temple. She loved this place and as a child had imagined being a Goddess living at the Temple. Still smiling, she looked around observing the few tourists who were up there that evening. Not too many, she thought, just a few stragglers.

Very little had changed, the beautiful marble columns still rose up into the sky, elegant and grand. Bathed in the evening light, the white marble had warmth and a softness as it stood there, an edifice to the ocean, to the sea nymphs, to sailors, and to love.

Oh my, she thought to herself, *I really had forgotten how much I loved this place. Could I really have forgotten the spectacular view and the beautiful light up here? I should go sit on my rock.* Laughing to herself, she remembered the rock that was poised in front of the Temple, hewn out of the ground, and worn flat from the easterly wind. She and her brothers had fought over who would sit on the rock. She smiled at the memories, thinking that today she would have it all to herself; her brothers were not there to fight with her this time.

Looking down from her vantage point, she saw the rock, still there. It was the perfect place to watch the sunset. She began walking down the stone pathway, moving toward the rock, the bright light of the setting sun blinding her as she made her way to it. Just as she found herself sliding safely onto the rock, she felt the presence of another body and movement beside her.

Heck, she thought, *now I have to share 'my rock' with some stranger.* Turning her head she looked at the person now sitting on the rock beside her.

Pythi staggered to the rock, slightly dizzy. He had felt the need to sit down really bad, and had almost slid down the rocky hill side to get to it. At the moment when he sat down breathing hard, the sun in his eyes blinding him, he realized that someone else had got to it at the same time. Turning his head, he looked at the person beside him.

"You!" They both yelled at the same time.

This was too bizarre, thought Pia. Of all the people in the world why would luck conspire to seat her next to the boorish man she had encountered in Athens; that ungentlemanly person who had knocked her down, and, then taken her table at the taverna in Monasteraki, with no apology. Since that night and until this moment, she had not given him another thought. Now, here he was seated next to her.

Still dizzy, Pythi glanced at her again. *Oh no*, he thought, *the woman who ploughed into me and turned an already bad day into a disaster.*

Neither of them spoke, they just glared at each other. Pia's awareness was heightened and she noticed the lightness of his eyes as he stared at her, the chiseled features, wide mouth, and rough skin, where he had not shaved. Once his vision cleared, he noticed her beauty; she really was beautiful, beautiful like a Greek goddess.

Abruptly, he got up to leave and the movement made him feel dizzy again. Reeling, he plunked back on the rock, trying to steady himself.

From a distance, he heard her ask if he was okay. He nodded but could not reply. She leaned over and pushed his head down between his legs.

"Breathe," she said, "Take deep breaths."

He did, and after a few moments, when he felt better, he lifted his head.

"Thank you," he said finally, breaking the silence between them.

American, she thought, *like me*, recognizing the accent.

They sat in silence for a few more moments. It was not an uncomfortable silence, it just was. "I'm Pythi," he said, "And before I say anymore, I would like to apologize for the other night. I had a terrible few days and I took it out on you."

She listened quietly and nodded. Then after a few moments, she reached out her hand, smiled the most luminous smile, and said, "I'm Pia, let's start over." Pythi held his breath as he shook her hand, a small current of electric shock running through him as their hands connected.

Extraordinary, he thought, *that's never happened to me before. But then, I have never felt dizzy before either.*

They sat there on the rock, watching the sunset, two strangers, yet not strangers at all, chatting away. Pia told him about her grandmother and her blog. He told her a little about why he was in Athens, about his parents, and why he spoke and read classical Greek.

The sun had almost set and the few tourists that had been there had departed. They were almost alone in this magical place, sitting in the shadow of the Temple, quietly gazing at each other, talking, and both of them reluctant to get up or move, for, they both understood, then, the magic of the moment would be broken.

Finally, Pythi got up, dusted his jeans, and reaching out his hand to help her up, asked her if she would like to have dinner with him. She agreed. He was enchanted, she mesmerized.

EIGHTEEN

Not what we have but what we enjoy constitutes our abundance. - Epicurus

Pia was excited, excited like she had not been in a long time. The drive back from the Temple had been a pleasant one, both of them sitting in silence. It was a silence of understanding, there was nothing awkward about it, as often happens between two people that click. It was simple, uncomplicated, and very comfortable. It was as if their energies were in synch and they both knew it.

Pythi had dropped her off at her YahYah's house and simply touched her hand before he left. Pia had felt a tremor run through her at the contact. His touch felt good, she wanted more.

She told her YahYah about her meeting with Pythi. YahYah had smiled and told her to go get ready. Pia was in a conundrum, after taking a shower and spraying herself with a soft perfume, she had spent a long time trying to decide what to wear, discarding outfit after outfit, as she wanted to be perfect. Eventually, she settled on a black lace dress with a nude under layer. In the front the dress was demure and the three quarter length lace sleeves hinted at her arms. The back plunged down almost to her waist showing off her tanned skin and the curve of her body. The dress fit her perfectly and the color complimented her honeyed complexion. The dress was both feminine and sexy, showing off her tanned legs and svelte figure. She put on her makeup skillfully, glossing her lips with a soft pink color. Picking up a black wrap to guard against the evening chill, and slipping into very thin, high heeled shoes, she glanced at herself in the mirror and smiled. She looked good and felt great. YahYah smiled at her as she stepped into the small living room, looking up from the TV show she was watching to gaze with pride at her beautiful granddaughter, whose hair shone and face glowed with excitement. She mentally crossed herself and asked God to look after this child.

A few minutes later there was a knock on the door and Pia walked over to open it. Seeing her standing there in the soft evening light, silhouetted in the doorway, took his breath away. *Could he be so fortunate?* He thought to himself. Pia was the most beautiful woman he had ever laid eyes on, and standing there gazing at each other, not touching, just looking, a current passed between them, a connection, a bond; they both felt it.

Pia broke the connection by inviting him in to meet her YahYah. He was enveloped in a warm hug and rapid fire Greek which he did not understand. Smiling he responded in classical Greek, promising to bring Pia home early. He saw the surprise in YahYah's eyes.

"This boy speaks Greek?" She asked Pia in amazement. "It's strange, ancient Greek," she told Pia, "But I do understand what he is saying."

"Classical style Greek, YahYah, his father is a Professor and taught him," she responded.

YahYah was happily impressed. The accent was not very good, but he already knew some Greek. She would trust her granddaughter with this man, she decided.

Pia kissed her YahYah and they stepped out in the evening air. Pythi opened the car door for her, and made sure she was comfortably seated in the small car. It was a short ride to the taverna. There were only two tavernas in this area, near to each other, almost side by side.

The location of the tavernas could not have been more magical. They were both situated by the water, in a small bay, with large open terraces overlooking the water. They parked the car and Pythi helped Pia up the short path to the taverna he had picked. He held her elbow to make sure she did not slip in her high heels on the rocky path. Pia was completely aware of his touch. She loved the feel of his hand on her elbow, the way he grasped her arm, gently and yet with a firmness that made her feel safe…he would not let her fall.

They walked into the taverna and were seated at a table in a corner overlooking the bay. The owner, who was a longtime friend of YahYah's, greeted them exuberantly. The waiter leaned over and lit the candles on their table and brought them a carafe of red wine. It was a small table and their knees touched under the table. They were both aware of their knees brushing and the secret connection it gave them.

Above them, in the moonlight, loomed the lit Temple, a beacon of light in the otherwise darkened sky. It shone, white in the night sky, large, almost overpowering, a symbol of all that had gone before and all that was yet to come.

Pia felt like her senses were in overdrive. *It must be because I haven't been on a date in years*, she thought. But then, she had never felt like this, ever, not with any man she had ever dated; ever.

The wine tasted sweet on her tongue and she moistened her lips with the taste of it. It was perfect; sweet, yet not too sweet, with a slightly dry aftertaste. She sipped on the wine as they waited for their appetizers, her fingers playing with the glass, twirling the ruby liquid in it. Pythi, took her hand and turned the palm up, then ran his fingers gently up and down her palm. Pia was filled with sensation, shivers running up her arm, her senses overpowered by his light touch.

As they sat there, conversation flowing between them, the cool night air swirling around them, she could smell the ocean and the night jasmine that grew in pots around the balcony, the fuchsia bougainvillea, gleaming brightly in the moonlight. The food began to arrive. Elias, the taverna owner, had promised them a great meal, and it was…

He served them fresh bread toasted with oregano and olive oil, the freshest green salad, eggplant dip, fried zucchini, and gavros, small fried fish that he promised he had caught that morning. In addition, they were served tzatziki, the traditional yogurt-cucumber sauce laced with garlic, more fresh fish cooked in a tomato based sauce, and fried kalamari. They ate, enjoying the food, Pythi always making certain that her glass was full and her plate heaped with the delicious food. There were others around them, the taverna was full, but it was as if they were the only ones present. They were absorbed in each other and the magic of the evening.

He fed her fish with his fork and she felt as if she was drowning in his eyes and his touch. Pythi never thought himself to be romantic or emotional but Pia took his breath away and he wanted her to himself, to immerse himself in this beautiful, intelligent, spirited woman. They gazed at each other as they ate, slowly, enjoying every morsel and every moment of pure delight. They had both lived long enough to know that such moments were rare and precious.

Soon, it was time for dessert, and the waiter brought them a huge slice of galaktoboureko, a traditional custard filled Greek phylo pastry topped with a honey sauce and cinnamon. The honey was sweet and sticky on her lips and as she ran her tongue over them, Pythi felt an overwhelming urge to reach over and kiss her, but he stopped himself. *Not now, he would hold her and kiss her in a place where he could have her all to himself.* He contented himself, by reaching over and running his fingers over her sticky lips, then slowly licking the honey off his fingertips. Pia felt her breath hitch and her eyes grew wide as she gazed into his. She felt intoxicated and it wasn't the wine!

When they got up to leave, he wrapped his arm around her and pulled her close. She felt his breath fanning her hair, as they walked, bodies touching, out of the taverna. They were the last to leave, the meal had lasted almost five hours but Pythi felt it had passed too fast. He did not want to let her go, he wanted more….more of her…more of her time….her touch…the feel of her body….her soul…

They sat in the darkened car; he turned to her and ran his fingers down the side of her face as if he was learning the contours, feeling her soft skin, intent at how she felt under his touch. She sat very still, completely engulfed in the feel of his touch, light yet intense, blazing a trail of heat as his fingers ran down the side of her neck, playing with her collar bone, and nestling in the small sensitive cavity at the base of her throat. She trembled and he felt her tremor. Breaking the contact, he took her wrap and covered her with it. She sighed, not a word had been spoken since they had left the taverna, and yet, much had been said between them.

He put the car in gear and drove the short distance to her YahYah's home. It was dark now, the house shrouded in silence, a single light shining dimly by the front door. He walked her to the door, up the short flight of stairs, and, reluctant to let her go, he wrapped his arms around her. She was glad; she didn't want him to leave either. He pulled her even closer, till the full length of their bodies was touching. She trembled again as he lifted her chin up slowly, and gazing deep into her eyes, he lowered his head and kissed her. It was a slow, sensuous kiss. Her lips felt soft and warm and oh so pliant. She entwined her arms around his neck and pulled him closer, making small sounds deep in her throat as the kiss deepened…till sensation after sensation swept over them. Pythi ran his fingers through her hair, stroking the back of her neck and running them down her back, pulling her even closer, till they stood there as one, entwined in a kiss that neither of them would ever forget.

It was as if the Gods had descended to create this coming together…this moment of magic.

NINETEEN

Love
bittersweet, irrepressible,
loosens my limbs and I tremble. –Sappho

It was happening literally under the moon-shadow of his temple, at that little taverna by the waves, and he witnessed it all from his lofty abode. Through the sands of time, after so many lifetimes had rolled by, Pytheus, his high priest of the past, and Penelope, Athena's trusted priestess of long ago, both imbued with the unfulfilled passion of their respective Gods, had finally found each other as Pythi and Pia and were falling in love. *If only Athena could see this,* he thought, *perhaps she would abandon virginhood for the sweet, ripe fruit of womanhood.*

Athena felt the familiar tingle which she had learned to interpret that Poseidon was thinking of her, and she afforded herself a smile and a frown:

He is thinking of me, I can tell. Who knows what machinations go through his lustful mind again? Perhaps the nymphs, the mermaids and the other exotics do not satisfy his fancy any longer and he is looking uptown for some classy excitement. He has another thing coming, if he thinks that I'll give in to his crude advances and not demand the respect I deserve. I do wish, though, that he would submit to some serious charm lessons from Aphrodite and discover his romantic nature once again. It's high time that he learned how to treat a sensitive, intelligent, real woman, which knows him only too well and has no fear or patience for his fierce outbursts! It would be a cold day in Hades, the day that I would permit him to treat me like he treats his horses, the wretched Barbarian!

Then, she turned to her trusted owl.

"Go my beloved bird, fly under the cover of night to Sounion and see what is going on that has the divine Water Stirrer polluting the ether waves with his lustful thoughts of me. Be quiet and discrete, I don't want him to know that I react or even give a moment's thought to his imaginations."

When the owl was gone, she undid the brooch of her fine peplos tunic and let it slide onto the floor revealing the magnificence of her figure with the alabaster skin that looked almost translucent. She stepped out of her sandals and, totally naked, walked a slow sensuous walk to the pool of warm water covered with rose petals that her maids had prepared for her. She slowly slid in, closed her eyes and, enveloped by the liquid warmth, let her mind drift to unfulfilled female pleasures.

Let's see what the owl brings back, she thought, and let a mischievous smile paint her lips.

TWENTY

I speak of lives given to the light
of serene love, and while they flow
like streams, they keep that light inside
eternally inseparable, just as
the sky glints in rivers,
just as suns flow through the skies.
I speak of lives given to the light. . . – Kostas Karyotakis

Pia awoke the next morning with a sense of wonder. It had been a magical evening; it was as if the Gods were smiling on them. She made herself a cup of coffee and, picking up her laptop, went outside to sit on the small patio, breathing in the cool morning air and gazing at the ocean.

"Friends," she wrote on her blog, "Here in the country of the Ancient Gods I feel as if I have been re-born. The sun, the sea, the beautiful ancient temples have all added to my wonder! I am awe-inspired by the beauty of it all and words are not enough to describe the feeling. It is as if I have been engulfed by magic, a sense of awe that envelops me, fills me and makes me whole. Here, in the shadow of the beautiful temple of Poseidon, I have re-discovered not only my roots, but my wholeness, the sense of who I truly am, this joyous person....whose eyes cannot take in enough of the beauty around her and whose soul sings a melodic song. I know that you are here with me in spirit as I share the wonderment and discovery of a whole new me, inside and out."

Then, she continued, "And, if I haven't mentioned it yet....I met someone with whom I feel I have a very deep connection. More on that later..."

Smiling to herself, she clicked the post button. Almost immediately, she began to get responses from all over the world. She had thousands of followers, and comments began to pour in….some wanting to know more, many wishing her well, others posting comments about their own path to self-discovery, and of course, the few trolls, the creepy ones, especially the one called G-Lover, who always made lascivious comments. But today he wrote, "I am with you, body, mind, and spirit, and await the day when we become as one. Remember, I am watching you, always."

Ooh, creepy, she thought, but decided to ignore the comment. No one was going to spoil the perfect morning. After a while, she stopped responding, and closing her laptop, decided to go for a walk.

Should I walk over to the hotel? She wondered. *Hmm…maybe that would be too pushy; after all, it had just been one date, albeit a magical one. Maybe, I am over-thinking the chemistry and the attraction, what if he didn't feel anything? How foolish would I look then?* She thought.

She spent a few minutes having an argument in her head about what she should do, then decided she would change and go down to the beach by the resort where Pythi was staying. She might bump into him.

The morning had turned warm, and wearing a soft sundress and flip-flops she began the short walk to the hotel.

***

Pythi was awakened by the buzzing of his phone. He really didn't want to open his eyes and face the day, he just wanted to revel in his memories of the most perfect evening and think about Pia, who he couldn't get out of his mind. He could still smell her soft flowery perfume, and feel the touch of her skin.

Mmm…I think I will just lay here and relive the whole evening, he thought.

His phone buzzed again, and again. Reaching over, he picked it up and squinted at the screen. Three calls and as many text messages. *What could be so urgent on a Sunday morning?* Then, he saw the 911 text…all thoughts of Pia left his mind as instinct kicked in and he leapt out of bed, phone in hand, reaching for his glasses.

"Banque Nationale system hacked again last night. Need help, please advise."

The next text was from one of his team, who were already at the Banque's headquarters, as was the next.

"On my way," he responded, "Be there as soon as I can."

Pythi pulled on a pair of jeans and a sweater, threw his belongings into his overnight bag, grabbed his laptop and headed out. *He really needed to call Pia,* he thought as he raced down to the reception, paid his bill and rushed to his car. Throwing his overnight bag onto the back seat and his laptop on the passenger seat, he swung the car out of the parking lot and raced back toward Athens. He called his team, and for the next hour, while he drove back, he was on the phone.

How could this happen? He thought. *The system was fairly foolproof; the first time the hackers probably just got lucky, but this time?*

His mind racing with the issues ahead of him, he pulled into the Banque and ran inside, going down to the basement of the building where the rest of the team was assembled. Every few minutes a thought would pass through his mind, *I really need to call Pia and let her know*, but he was so caught up with the emergency at hand, he never did.

***

Pia walked over to the hotel, smiling to herself as she strolled. It was a perfect day. She clambered down to the beach and put her beach bag on the sand beside a lounge chair. Taking out a novel, she thought she would read for a while, but, her mind kept wandering…taking her back to the lovely evening she had spent with Pythi. She wondered what he was doing. *Was he thinking of her too?* She scolded herself mentally, and told herself to stop being naive and impressionable.

A couple of hours went by, it was now lunch time and Pia could feel her tummy rumbling. She put away her book and decided to saunter up to the reception area. Eleni, the owner's middle aged daughter, was at the desk.

"Koukla mou, kala ise?" She asked as she leaned over and hugged Pia. Then, in a conspiratorial tone, winking at Pia, she asked her about the dinner last night.

Of course, thought Pia, *this is a small town; everyone knows I was on a date last night. They probably know all the details as well!*

"The dinner was great, Eleni, the food was very good."

"Ah, how was the young man? He is okay?" She asked in her accented English.

Pia smiled back, but before she could respond, Eleni continued, "If you are looking for him, he is not here. He ran out of here about an hour ago, like demons were chasing after him. He was supposed to stay till tomorrow, but he is gone."

Gone, thought Pia. *Really…gone?*

Still smiling, she exchanged a few more words with Eleni, then left the hotel and began her walk back.

She felt like the wind had been taken out of her sails. Her mind whirring, she walked back at a brisk pace. And, as she walked, she got angrier and angrier…first at herself and then at Pythi.

How naive I am, she thought. *It was just another dinner for him, a way for him to pass the evening. After all how well do I know him? He may be married for all I know!.. But, he was so charming and sweet*, another part of her brain responded…..*so charming and sweet that he left without saying anything…* her brain whirred on…thoughts ebbing and flowing.

I do have his phone number, I can always call him, she then thought, *but, why would I want to do that? He obviously didn't think I was important enough or he would have called me*, her thoughts continued.

By the time she made it home, she was deflated and feeling sorry for herself. *I need some food and a nap.*

***

She was woken up from her nap, when she heard her phone beeping. A text message had just come in.

"Had an emergency, and had to leave"…it was Pythi.

"Really?" She responded.

"Really…work related," he answered. "btw, I had a fun evening, thanks," he continued.

A fun evening, she thought, *that's all it was for him?*

"Me too"…she wrote.

"Will call you later tonight, after I get done," he said.

"Ok"…she responded.

*Hmm…*she thought….*he had fun; how about that?* If she didn't need her phone as much as she did, she would have hurled it at the wall!

It was after midnight when she got another text.

"You have your brush, you have your colors, you paint the paradise, then in you go - Nikos Kazantzakis. Thank you for allowing me into your paradise and sharing it with me. The beautiful painting that was last night will forever live in my mind's eye, sleep well."

TWENTY-ONE
Most men are within a finger's breadth of being mad. - Diogenes

The moon had travelled all night through the sky and just after daybreak the faithful but exhausted owl, Glauki, arrived at the Acropolis to take a brief rest before her mistress' rise. It was a long round-trip flight from Athens to Sounion and back for a heavy bird, and she was surely heavy on the way back. With her mission to spy on Poseidon, Pia and Pythi completed, the hungry bird had gorged herself on the succulent rodents frequenting the seashore round the Sounion Temple. The flight back had been slow, tiresome, and with frequent stops for rest. Thankfully, she did not have to worry about predators too much as she was in her element at night.

As the veil of night was wearing thin, though, she had started being concerned about the hungry falcons and eagles that would soon be gliding the air currents looking for food for their young ones back at the nest. The silhouette of the Temple of Athena in the distance, just as the day was breaking, could not have been timed any better, and the tired bird was beyond relieved. She made a mental note to be wiser and not overeat and fly the next time.

By sunrise Athena was up and walked out to the high terrace of her palace where a lavish breakfast had been prepared. She loved getting up early in the morning, from the high vantage point of this terrace that was facing south, and observe the early activity of mariners and ships in the port of Piraeus in the far distance. Down below, the city of Athens was waking and slowly coming to life and it would not be long before the faint voices of vendors promoting their goods at the marketplace reached the heights of Cecropia.

She finished her leisurely breakfast and then asked for the owl; had she returned? She was told of the poor bird's arrival in exhaustion and that she was resting. She decided to let her rest some more and attend to her business at the Temple. When the Sun was at mid-sky she sent her servants to summon the owl; she was curious to hear her account of the events at Sounion.

The owl, well refreshed and nourished, gave her a vivid account of the budding romance between Pythi and Pia at the little taverna. Outlining their link with the past as Pytheus and Penelope, and the true fuel of their developing attraction traced back to the unfulfilled desires and passion that resided in her Lady's heart and that of Lord Poseidon's.

Athena was as dumbfounded as she was fascinated, but what really rocked her divine world were the carefully selected words of the owl, struggling to hide her surprise, when she described how Lord Poseidon was observing all this with moist eyes and a tender look in his eyes.

"I am telling you my Lady, the Lord of the Sea is truly in love with you and it was like living it through those two young people at the taverna. They were your priests in the past after all, divinely imbued by your forbidden passion," said the loyal owl. "And what a handsome and powerful man he is, that Lord Poseidon!"

Athena, with a wide sweep of her arm knocked the impertinent but beloved bird off its perch.

"How dare you, you white feathered blob!" She exclaimed pretending to be angry, as she turned away to hide a happy tear from the owl.

So, at last and for a change, it was not just lust that was motivating the thoughts of the beloved brute toward me. We really have a chance this time, she thought, as an ethereal calm took over her face and her glance became unusually soft.

TWENTY-TWO
Blushing is the color of virtue. – Diogenes

Pia lay in bed, wide awake; phone in hand.

Wow, she thought, *no one has ever sent me a text so meaningful. Such few words were used to say so much.*

How do I respond? She wondered. *I do not want to sound sappy or too over the top, but on the other hand, I don't want him to feel that I am blowing him off. And,* she thought to herself, *no icons…definitely no icons…too trite!*

***

She awoke with a start….she had fallen asleep, phone in hand, and never responded. The sun was streaming in through the window as she got out of bed, pulled on a warm hoodie and carried her coffee outdoors.

Checking her phone and her email, she settled herself on a wooden chair, under an arbor of bougainvillea, reading through the comments on her blog. There were hundreds of them and she scanned through each one. She enjoyed her readers, as they did enjoy reading her blog. They had journeyed with her through her stay in Florida and the ups and downs of her mother's cancer treatment and care, and now here, in Sounion. She felt safe on her blog, safe to reveal how she felt and what she was going through. It made her feel connected….connected to all those out there who were also on a sojourn of discovery…like beings, like her, and it gave them all a kinship, no matter where they lived; they were only a laptop, or a smart phone away.

Thoughtfully she began to blog.

"Hello Friends, I wish you well on this beautiful day. As I sit under a vibrant, fuchsia bougainvillea tree, overlooking the blue, blue sea, under the spell of the beautiful Temple of Poseidon. I feel as if I am far away, far away from all the trials of the life I lived yesterday. Although each day brings with it an upside and a downside, it could not happen in a more surreal setting. I do feel as if I am living in a picture postcard (photos to follow).

Yet, in a deep way, I feel connected to each one of you. It is no longer necessary to be in physical proximity to have a deep connection, our thoughts and our words connect us and I do believe that those with like thought flows or similar energies, come together on some universal plane to tap into the flow of each other's energy field. And, as I sit in this idyllic setting, I feel your energy and your presence; Divine Mind connects us, we are One."

Turning off her laptop, she sat gazing out at the blue sea, in quiet meditation, thoughts flowing through her mind, some painful, some pleasant. She let them flow, releasing them, quietly aware of the ebb and flow.

I am in a place of peace, she thought. *Everyone should have such a place. Hmm…I think I need to blog about that. Maybe later…*

***

Pythi's entire team was assembled in the basement of the Banque Nationale. He looked around and smiled grimly. Some of the best brains in the computer business were here with him and they had been working feverishly round the clock. Coffee cups and food cartons lay over all the desks, the room smelled of stale cigarette smoke and old food. They had been here for almost twenty four hours, trying to ensure that the system was secure again.

Sam, a young bearded Dutch encryption specialist, was bent over several monitors. Derek, had flown in from the States a few hours ago and was reading code on another monitor. A genius at fire walls and internet security, he was enraged at how easily the Banque's system had been compromised.

And then there was Tanya. Born of a Swedish mother and a Jamaican father, raised in London, Tanya had worked with Pythi on many projects. Dressed in jeans and a t-shirt, her hair in a ponytail, with shiny gold hoops in her ears, Tanya with her beautiful brown skin and bright blue eyes, walked around the room, stretching and trying to shed her tiredness. Her buoyant gypsy-like looks and personality hid a tragic past and deep intelligence and tenacity. Tanya, the anomaly, with a brain that was extremely logical and very sharp, she was also immersed in New Age philosophy and 'mumbo jumbo,' as they teased her.

Her mother had died of cancer when she was young and her father had abandoned her soon after. Raised by a relative, she had triumphed over her past, gotten a degree at the London School of Economics with graduate studies at Yale, and enjoyed a job where she had no roots and nothing to keep her in any place. Terrified of commitment, she was content to move from project to project, her work being her salve and her wall against the world.

She crossed over to where Pythi was working and perched on the desk next to him, legs dangling above the floor.

"I'm tired," she said, "I need to go out and clear my head, I feel like I have been in this room too long, brain getting fuzzy!"

Pythi looked up from his computer, not quite focused on what she was saying. He saw the tiredness in her eyes and was about to tell her to go to the hotel and get some rest, when her laptop across the room, pinged.

Tanya jumped down from the desk and strode across the room.

"It's her," she exclaimed.

All three men got up from their chairs and began to walk over to her desk.

"Her?" Asked Sam.

"It's G2, the blogger, I follow. She has not been on for a few days. I love her blogs and so relate to her writing."

Both Derek and Sam said in unison, "G2?"

"She sounds like she is a sci-fi character," said Sam.

"No silly, she calls herself Greek Goddess, G2," went Tanya.

Then looking at her screen, she began reading. The other three were crowded around her now, all curious about this blog and G2.

"And you are not going to believe this," she exclaimed excitedly, "She is here in Greece. She is blogging from the Temple of Poseidon at Sounion."

Pythi's interest was now piqued. Could it be? Was it simply a coincidence? Could Pia be G2?

Tanya was reading aloud now as the others listened. Sam and Derek began rolling their eyes as she finished.

"Just as I thought," teased Sam. "New Age stuff," Derek agreed.

"You guys…I love her blogs, she speaks to me, she is very real and there is nothing new age-y about her writing. She constantly reveals her own experiences and shares her life with the readers in a very real way, I really like her!" She said.

Pythi listened silently. He promised himself that he would read some more of G2's blogs when he had a chance.

Tanya was happily back at her laptop, her tiredness gone as she resumed working on the problems. Sam and Derek went back to their desks and Pythi kept checking his phone to see if she would text him back. The Gods were not on his side today.

TWENTY-THREE
Seek not, my soul, the life of the immortals; but enjoy to the full the resources that are within thy reach. - Pindar

The Gods are simply not smiling on me today, thought Pythi, as he walked out of the Banque's building a day and a half later. They had managed to secure the system once again but still had not figured out how the hackers had breached all their firewalls. He was baffled. He was even more baffled because Pia had not responded to his text or called him.

Maybe, she didn't feel the connection as deeply as I did, he thought. Shaking his head, he continued walking to the hotel where he was staying. He had spent one evening with Pia but felt like he had known her forever, how could she not have felt that too? And the kiss…He thought about how he felt as he had held her and kissed her. It was as if he had felt paradise for those moments. Sheer heaven!

I really am turning fanciful, he thought, giving himself a mental shake. He needed to get a grip. But he needed a shower and bed first.

A few hours later, refreshed from the shower and nap, he stepped out on the small balcony of his hotel room. The evening sky was glowing, the street below was busy with traffic and people walking and talking. It was bustling and full of activity. Athens was a city that came alive at night and he found it enchanting. *I wish Pia was here.* He pulled out his cell phone and dialed her number…

Pia had spent the last two days trying to forget Pythi. It had been a tough couple of days and she was upset and angry with herself for seeing so much in the one evening they had spent together.

I simply haven't been on a date in a long time and because I enjoyed it so much I thought he did too. It was just another date for him and now he has moved on. I must too, she thought. But, there was little to do in Sounion and her thoughts seemed to engulf her. She had spent the last day with her beloved YahYah, cooking, drinking coffee, and enjoying a late afternoon visit with the neighbors. On the outside all was tranquil and peaceful, on the inside, she was nervous and jumpy.

Time for some meditation, she thought as she clambered down the rocks to the beach to find a quiet spot. Looking out at the ocean, she took a few deep breaths and closed her eyes, trying to let go and quiet her turbulent mind, when, all of a sudden, her phone, which had been quiet all day, began to ring.

She pulled it out of her hoodie pocket and looked at the screen. It was Pythi. For a split second she thought of letting it go to voicemail, but she answered.

"Hello," she said.

"Pia, its Pythi, how are you?"

"I'm doing very well... you?"

"It's been a tough couple of days," he responded.

Hmm, she thought, *not just for you*.

"It's been quiet here," she said.

"Am I calling you at a bad time?" he asked, "I can always call you back."

"Like you said you would a few days ago?"

Whoa, she thought, *too intense, I need to lighten up.*

After a pause, he replied, "I am sorry, we had a terrible emergency at work and I could not get away, even to make a phone call. My team and I have worked non-stop. I really did want to speak to you."

"That's okay, you don't have to explain yourself to me," she went.

"But you sound upset at me."

"No, not at you," she said.

"Who, then?"

"At myself."

"Why?"

"Because I had a really great evening and I thought you did too and then you were gone."

"Pia, I did, I really did. I wanted to see you again, I want to see you again, but I had to leave because I got called in. Please try and understand."

"Hey, it's okay. No problem. Nice text though, thanks."

And before he could respond, she hung up.

He looked at his watch; it was seven in the evening. He knew what he was going to do....he was going to Sounion, for dinner...

Pia hung up on Pythi, took a deep breath and calming herself closed her eyes and lost herself in meditation. Time for a peaceful evening. After a while she walked back up to the house as it was beginning to get dark. Dinner was not for a few hours yet, they ate late at YahYah's. She picked up her laptop and sat by the fire, while YahYah cooked and watched TV. The little house was filled with the aroma of fresh baking bread in the oven and the large pot of "stifado," the Greek style stew that was cooking on the stove. It smelled delicious.

TWENTY-FOUR

It is not he who reviles or strikes you who insults you, but your opinion that these things are insulting. – Epictetus

Pia was deep in thought when she heard the knock on the door. YahYah was hard of hearing and Pia was sure that she had not heard the knock. The TV was on in the living room and YahYah had her transistor radio playing Greek music in the kitchen.

Pia got up and straightened her sweats as she walked to the door. *It must be one of the neighbors*, she thought. *Someone stopping by to visit YahYah, as they often did.* No one ever called here, in Sounion, they just came by. It was part of the culture, the way of life here. You always had time for friends and family, it was never an imposition, and they were always welcome.

Still deep in thought, she opened the door…and she could not hide her expression of shock. There, silhouetted in the dim light was Pythi, dressed in jeans and a sweater, he stood indolently against the door jamb, watching her reaction.

Pia began to smooth her hair and straighten her bangs as she forced herself to stop staring at Pythi. He took her nervous fingers as they stroked her hair and held them in his, intertwining his fingers with hers. Then, with his other hand he raised her chin so that she was looking straight at him.

The moment their eyes connected, Pia felt a ripple of energy run through her, as if they had connected in some way. His beautiful eyes looked right into her as he said, "I'm sorry, I had to come apologize in person. I want you to know that I feel the same way as you do about our first night out and I was really looking forward to seeing you again but had to rush back to

Athens to deal with an emergency at work. I know that you are angry and want you to believe me."

Pia was about to answer when a shadow fell over them. YahYah had come to the door to see what was going on.

"Pia tha mou kriosis, come in from the cold," she said. Then, seeing Pythi at the door, she beamed at him and pulled them both inside.

Before Pia could object, or actually before she could say another word, YahYah had pulled wine glasses from off the shelf and was pouring wine for all three of them.

"Get warm in front of the fire," she told Pythi, "While I serve the dinner."

Pythi thanked her and apologized for coming uninvited to see them.

"In my home, no one ever needs an invitation, the door is always open, you are always welcome." Then, still smiling, she asked them to come to the table for dinner.

YahYah's kitchen was small and the kitchen table even smaller. It was a tight squeeze for Pia and YahYah alone. Now, with a third chair drawn up to the table, Pia could really feel Pythi's nearness and sense his desire to speak to her. She felt overwhelmed in a happy kind of way. She had been mad at her perception of how he had treated her, but maybe, just maybe, she had misinterpreted the situation. She was going to give him the benefit of the doubt.

Conversation at dinner flowed, mostly in a question and answer format. YahYah asked Pythi questions about his family, his life, and his travels. Pythi answered in his accented Greek as best he could and Pia helped him along. YahYah made sure that their bowls were always full of steaming stifado, the Greek stew with meat, vegetables and whole small onions, which had simmered on the stove all afternoon.

There was warm, crusty bread, plenty of feta cheese and a salad to go with it. It was a delicious, simple, hearty meal and Pythi enjoyed it as if he were eating in a gourmet restaurant, savoring every bite and asking a lot of questions about the food. By the end of the meal YahYah was completely charmed by the Amerikanaki, as she called him.

Somewhere, during the meal, Pythi had found Pia's hand under the table, and he quietly stroked it while he ate and spoke with YahYah. Pia tingled at his touch and had to force herself to stay focused on the conversation.

"Come walk with me," he said after dinner was over and they had cleared the table. She pulled on a jacket, as they stepped out into the chilly night air. They climbed down the rocks to the water edge, where they sat on a couple of big rocks.

After a few minutes of silence, Pythi asked, "Am I forgiven?"

Pia slanted her face as she looked up at him and smiled, "For now," she said, laughing.

He pulled her close and they stayed like that for a few minutes. Then he lifted her face to his and began kissing her lips, deep hungry kisses that set her on fire; kisses that consumed her. Kisses, that made every nerve in her body tingle. Kisses that made her run her fingers through his hair and pull him closer. Kisses that made her want more…

The headlights of a passing car brought them back to reality and Pia found herself on Pythi's lap, being held tightly by him. They drew apart then, and getting up, walked back up the hill.

"I must go now," he told her, "But I promise you, I will be back. You and I have unfinished business."

Laughing at his words, she challenged, "And what happens when our business is finished?"

"My heart says that it will be a long time before our business is finished, if ever." Then, looking at her seriously, "I feel as if I have known you before and just found you again…to continue our… unfinished business."

This time Pia didn't laugh, she just leant in and kissed him. She had expressed the same feelings on her blog a few hours ago….she understood.

TWENTY-FIVE

Anybody can become angry - that is easy, but to be angry with the right person and to the right degree
and at the right time and for the right purpose, and in the right way - that is not within everybody's power
and is not easy. – Aristotle

G-Lover had been following her blog since she had first started posting. He was obsessed by her. It was as if she wrote to him alone, expressing his feelings in her thoughts. He had cyber stalked her for a long time and knew all there was to know about her in cyberspace. She was his passion and his obsession and he was usually one of the first to respond to her posts.

"She will be mine," he promised himself. "All mine."

His bedroom and study walls were lined with pages from her blog posts, pages that he printed and marked up; words that he felt were written by her to him. After all, he had little to do all day. Brought up in immense wealth, the son of a wealthy socialite and a father whose money had come from a family alcohol business, he spent his days in isolation and quiet loneliness.

He had converted the basement of his opulent house into an electronic command center, never failing to upgrade to the latest electronic gadgets available in the market place. In the semi-dark, the place looked like a space station cockpit, full of glowing screens, keyboards, and high-end electronic toys. The atmosphere was ripe with the sounds of rock music; heavy metal was his distinct preference. The internet was his backyard, cyberspace his world, and hacking his hobby. Breaking into domains he was not supposed or allowed to enter was his life challenge and spice. Impossible was a concept he refused to acknowledge when it came to breaking through complex defense systems to gain access. He would always triumph, thanks to his supreme skills and ingenuity; it was only a matter of time and perseverance.

Although generally impatient with people, when it came to repeat efforts to infiltrate a presumably "secure site" nothing phased him, not even time. Sometimes it took weeks and even months, but who cared, it was the victory that mattered in the end. He had even developed a celebratory routine for the time of triumph, the conquest of the firewall, the gain of forbidden access. He would play Wagner's Ride of the Valkyries at a thundering volume, his only deviation from heavy metal, and throwing his arms in the air he would exclaim, "I'm good, I'm so good!"

Having being raised by a series of nannies, he had little contact with either of his parents who had divorced when he was two. He rarely saw his father and his mother spent her time between rehab and her latest husband. He had been exposed to drugs when he was ten years old and it was very easy for him to walk into his mother's room and help himself to the drug of his choice. Right now it was cocaine.

And then, it was that strange hallucination that felt so real last night. Riding high on cocaine he had visions of a strange land surrounded by waters, an anachronistic world that felt very futuristic, judging from the advanced machines used by its people. In the midst of it, he had recognized himself leading a group of scientists in wonderful discoveries and electronic applications that gave them unfathomable control over the very forces of nature. In awe, he had witnessed the appearance of an imposing, god-like warrior stand before him, praise him for his intellect and genius, promise him return to his past glory and prominence, to fantastic power and influence. All he had to do was open up to him and follow his instructions. Then, all he ever wanted and desired would be his.

He had been an intelligent kid and done well at school. He had managed to hide his drug use from everyone, and while he had been a loner at school, the girls had run after him and he partied a lot in his youth. His family money had gotten him into Yale, but he had dropped out after a year and come back home. He had little to do all day but watch TV, play video games, and spend time on his computer, on Facebook and Twitter. He had first heard about her from one of his Facebook friends (no one he knew in the real world), and ever since had been hooked on her blog and obsessed with his G2. His online pseudonym was G-Lover, short for Goddess Lover; after all she was his.

But now, for the first time, she had mentioned that she had met someone in Greece…she was in Greece, and was blogging from there. He was filled with anger. How could she betray him by talking about some other guy?

He remembered going to Greece on vacation as a kid. In fact, if he remembered right, his mother had once been married to a Greek industrialist. He had enjoyed his time there. She was there now and he felt that he had to join her there, to convince her that he was her man. There was nothing else to do but go to Greece, he had the money and the time, nothing was going to stop him from making her his. He was going to Greece to find her, and he had the Warrior-God on his side…

TWENTY-SIX
Beauty of style and harmony and grace and good rhythm depend on simplicity. - Plato

Pia woke up to a chilly morning. Snuggling under the covers to stay warm, she smiled to herself as her thoughts flew to the night before. Once again, it had been magical. She knew that she was getting more and more enraptured by Pythi. She loved that he had taken the initiative to come and see her, that he understood her anger, and that it was important enough for him to drive all the way to Sounion to see her and make things right between them. More than anything, she loved his touch and the way he made her feel when he was close by. She loved, loved, the tingly feeling she got when he touched her and the way her senses heightened when he looked at her. In fact, she had begun to love everything about him, especially the silences between them. It was as if they did not need words to communicate…

Throwing the covers off, she got out of bed, ran to the bathroom and took a quick shower. Then, donning jeans and a warm sweater, she went into the kitchen, kissed YahYah and made herself a cup of Greek coffee. She liked it thick and strong with a touch of condensed milk to sweeten it. YahYah had plenty of koulourakia, Greek cookies that can be dipped into coffee or tea. She powered up her laptop as she had her breakfast.

Checking her email, she decided to write on her blog:

"Friends," she wrote, "Life is always interesting, never boring, especially here in Greece. Sometimes, we need to re-think our perception of a situation, and give ourselves the chance and time to see things differently. Our own minds and our vulnerabilities often allow us to think the worst of a situation, but sometimes that is just not so. Allow the situation some space and time…let it unfold and you may be pleasantly surprised as I have been, that life has one more surprise in store for you.

I had a surprise visit from a person and relationship that I had written off and it turned out to be a magical night full of promise for what might be. I hope that you too will allow yourself a second chance and take the risk of being vulnerable and emotionally open again. The results may just well surprise you.

I love you all, and wish you well on this beautiful day! Let me know your thoughts. Signing off with hugs!"

Closing the laptop she looked over at YahYah, who had changed her clothes and was wearing a thick sweater over her black dress, along with the shoes she wore when she was going out. With a start Pia remembered that it was time for the weekly visit to Lavrion, to go to the Layki, the Farmer's Market. She had promised YahYah that she would take her.

Her grandfather had owned an old Peugeot car and it sat by the side of the house, covered by a canvas tarp. Pia had asked YahYah if she could drive the old car and YahYah had agreed. No one had really driven it since her grandfather, her Papou, had passed away. The neighbor kept it running by turning it on and making sure that the battery did not die. They went outside, removed the tarp and Pia looked at the thirty year old car. In America, it would be considered an antique, but here it was serviceable and it worked.

Pia was a little nervous about driving in Greece and it took all of her attention and focus to drive on the narrow mountain road to Lavrion, but she knew that it was only her fears and that she would soon get used to driving here. They pulled into the town square in Lavrion and after parking the car and unloading the folding shopping cart from the trunk, she followed her YahYah into the thick of the Farmer's Market.

Pia loved visiting the open air market. The whole area was set up with open booths and vendors were selling everything imaginable at the market. There were vegetable stalls, fruit stalls, a fish monger, several butchers, clothes, toys, house wares, furniture, shoes, handbags, curtains and table cloths, and several stalls of homemade knitted sweaters and blankets. It was enthralling and Pia wove her way through the crowd following YahYah, taking in the sights, sounds and smells.

Soon, YahYah had filled her shopping cart with fresh vegetables, fish, fruit and meat. They stopped at the bakery and bought fresh bread, then checked out the table cloths which were finely crocheted. All the while, YahYah stopped and chatted with the vendors, running into friends and neighbors. Finally, they stopped at a mobile food truck and got a cup of coffee and Pia got herself a Greek style hot dog. They sat down at a small table and soon several of YahYah's friends joined them and there was much laughter and conversation. No one hurried or rushed, it just wasn't part of the culture here. Things happened at their own pace and Pia relished that, remembering her harried and very rushed lifestyle in New York. She made a mental note to blog about that later that day. The joy of enjoying the moment, of spending time with friends and family, and the simplicity of enjoying a cup of steaming coffee with friends and acquaintances in this beautiful seaside setting. Pia felt at peace, she was happy.

She felt her phone buzz in her jean pocket as she sat there. Pulling it out of her pocket she saw that she had a text message. It was Pythi, her heart began to race.

"Enjoying your morning? Back at work, but thinking of you, hope you are thinking of me too."

She was even happier now.

"Yes, enjoying the morning, at the layki with YahYah…not thinking of you!" She teased.

"Then I am glad I txted you, you have to think of me now!"

Pia laughed when she read that.

"Banish the thought. YahYah has me busy helping her to get the best prices and to carry her shopping, lol"

"Enjoy the morning! Will call you later, running off to a meeting, btw, free for dinner this weekend?"

Pia smiled, she sure was. Life was good!

TWENTY-SEVEN
It's not what happens to you, but how you react to it that matters. – Epictetus

They were practically brother and sister, Ares and Athena. They hailed from the chief Olympian couple, Zeus and Hera. But, were they? This relationship was not your everyday brother-sister one, since both of them had been immaculately conceived by the all-mighty and habitually philandering Zeus. Athena was born as a thought out of his head and Ares was incubated in his thigh, following yet another clandestine affair with a mortal woman. Cunning Zeus would play endless games to keep suspicious Hera off his tracks, so he may have free range. He even charmed nymph Echo, one of his old but still burning flames, to cover up for him by befriending and flattering his wife so she stayed occupied and uninvolved.

This worked for a while, but following Athena's and Ares' immaculate conceptions, Hera felt neglected and grew more suspicious. She started investigating and before long she had numerous reports of the head God's infidelity, including the pretenses of Echo. In an outburst of jealousy and rage, she vowed to punish the deceitful nymph and cursed her to never be able to hear the voice of anyone else, except reflections of her own. And thus, poor nymph Echo became the source and very definition of the word "echo."

Ares, a true product of this deceit and subterfuge, ranted at Athena:

"I gave you my heart, my passion...everything that I ever was. You became a woman in the caresses of my fervent love and in return you gave me nothing but humiliation. I, who have never been defeated, proud master of the art of war, brought to my knees by the First Maiden, well...what used to be a maiden. How will I ever be able to correct such an injustice, insult and offense... becoming the laughing stock of mortals and immortals alike?

And what did you do, instead? You ignored my love and conspired with the... First Sailor.

Together, you are manipulating your earthly marionettes in modern day Athens, trying to find relief for a slow-burning passion that the two of you have been harboring for centuries now. A passion that neither of you has the courage to acknowledge and admit openly. Or did you think I am blind and cannot see what you two are trying to do? Well, let me tell you, so long as my name is Ares and war is my craft, war you will harvest, and I will make damn sure that none of your clandestine earthly plans come to pass!"

Ares, red-faced from rage, was almost shouting to a composed Athena, while he was gesturing wildly.

Athena kept silent for a few moments, allowing Ares to calm down and find his composure. Then, in a soothing, almost maternal voice, she addressed her former lover.

"My beloved Ares, love is a wondrous thing, the magical glue that holds this magnificent Universe and many others together, and you, as an advanced divine being, know it better than most. Know and revel in that knowledge, that I loved you well, deeply and passionately and it is on the wings of your wonderful, powerful love that I discovered my womanhood and the pleasures and ecstasies of the physical form. This is your everlasting gift to me and I will always cherish it beyond any other, being eternally grateful. The unforgettably passionate memories of our love will forever stay etched in my mind and heart. This heart of mine that you helped blossom has reserved a very special place for you and the love you brought me.

I would like to think that in some small measure, I have also helped you get beyond the limiting confines of your deservedly proud male ego. To help explore the generous, outwardly gifts that the soul reserves for those that approach it with the surrender and abandon of unconditional love. Your generous love was the stepping stone to this harmonious feeling of being one with everything and everyone that ever existed or ever will, being both the Creator and the Creation, in perfect harmony and indescribable joy and bliss that transcend any physical ecstasy or pleasure that one can ever experience. It was through loving you so deeply and freely that the gates to that paradise of perception opened to me and I was admitted into a brand new world of indescribable beauty, awe and wonder. Having discovered it, all I want and desire anymore is to become a more intricate part of this reality and serve it to the best of my abilities. How would I ever be able to thank you enough, my beloved, for bringing me to this realization, for offering me such a very precious gift?"

Athena took a few steps, collected her thoughts and she continued:

"I responded to your summons to meet at this neutral ground of Delphi, at the ruins of the temple of Apollo, under his loving, sunny gaze and in the ancient mist of the inspired fumes of his Oracle, engulfed in the powerful energy of the vortex of this holy place. I came hoping that time had deepened the understanding of what happened between us, and together, the two of us, elevate it to its rightful place and once and for all erase any tension between us. I was thinking, beloved, that you have elected to take the best and leave behind the rest of our love. I was hoping that you have decided to let go of trying to recreate the past or trying to keep the bird of love locked in a cage that your desires have created. Love, dearest, knows no barriers, limits or borders; it is born of free will and lives, expands and grows free; it knows no other way. I fervently wish, beloved, that you will use the beauty of this love we shared as the stepping stone to move on to a love so much greater, wonderful and expansive, as I have done."

Athena stopped talking, visibly spent by the emotional effort her words had exerted, and raised her head to look into her former lover's eyes. She hoped to see the light of understanding and agreement in them. Instead, she saw the lightning of anger and the storm of rage and she backed off a step or two in fright. Ares, with the frozen expression of hate on his face, turned abruptly on his heels away from her, and in a stern, defiant voice he uttered:

"Never! Never will I let you go! And if I cannot have you, then no-one will! You, your loved ones and your mortal pawns will soon feel the fruit of my wrath!"

TWENTY-EIGHT

Nothing exists except atoms and empty space; the rest is opinion. – Democritus

"Friends, life is good. As I continue my journey of discovery, I find myself drawn to someone who has awakened something in me I thought was long gone. I feel excitement, happiness, and have a sense of expectancy as my life unfolds. I look forward to the next minute, the next hour, the next day…It is a wonderful feeling and I hope that all of you find that something or someone who creates that sense of joy and happiness within you. For me, today, it is gazing at the sapphire ocean, watching my beloved grandma bake fresh bread and cookies, sipping on a delicious cup of coffee, meditating with the sound of the waves in the background, and the breeze over the azure water cooling my sun drenched skin. It is a feeling of contentment in this moment that I wish for all of you. Off to meditate and prepare for a wonderful evening…more later!" She signed off her blog.

Pia was filled with anticipation. Pythi and she had texted back and forth and Pythi had asked her to come to Athens for dinner. He had offered to come pick her up but she had decided to drive herself in her Grandpa's old car. It was time for her to get over her fears, and driving in the crazy traffic of Athens was one of them.

She spent hours dressing very carefully; she wanted to look her best. The evening was cool and she wore a short black mini skirt with knee high suede boots, a soft black sweater with lace trim, and patterned hose. Her hair had grown longer; she had washed it and left it loose and she needed little make up as her skin was sun kissed and glowing. She felt happy on the inside and her happiness shone through her eyes making them bright. She looked lovely and YahYah crossed herself several times when she saw her beautiful granddaughter, asking the Gods to keep the evil eye away from her.

Pia climbed into the old car, set the map up on her GPS of her cell phone, sent a text message to Pythi to let him know she was on her way, said a little prayer for safety and put the car in gear…she was on her way. She felt proud of herself, she was facing a fear! The old radio in the car played music from a Greek radio station and she hummed along as she made her way to Athens.

***

Pythi was deep in discussion with his team when he got her text. He smiled, then got up and told them he was leaving. Tanya, Sam, and Derek, all looked up at him.

"You are leaving? Now?" Asked Tanya.

Derek and Sam just watched with questions in their eyes.

"I need to leave, I have a meeting tonight," he replied.

"A meeting? With whom? It's almost seven o' clock," she responded.

"I'm meeting a friend," he said.

Tanya let out a shriek, "I get it. Guys he's going on a date. Oh my, you are a dark horse. How do you get to meet anybody when you are working the hours we are working?"

Pythi just smiled.

"I'm off," he said.

The other three were now teasing him and talking amongst themselves about following him on his date. It was all friendly ribbing in the spirit of their camaraderie. Tanya was a free spirit, though Sam secretly had a crush on her, Derek had a girlfriend who he was constantly texting and chatting with. It was Pythi's love life that was often the topic of their conversation. They were all curious. Pythi was not about to reveal anything.

Whistling to himself, he picked up his jacket and walked the short distance to the hotel, where he took a shower, changed his clothes, made some phone calls and went downstairs to wait for Pia.

TWENTY-NINE
The most difficult thing in life is to know yourself. - Thales

It was almost two in the morning and G-Lover was wide awake. The cocaine and the alcohol helped him and he felt as though he was indomitable….he was a God, no one could deny him. His plan had been set in motion and all was good. He was the Mastermind and he had thought through every move. His friends had been great, and together they had triumphed. Things had gone according to plan and had been so easy that for kicks they had repeated the plan…but he knew that Lady Luck should not be pushed anymore and he had told his buddies to lay low. No point in taking unnecessary chances, plus they were all very rich already. Money did not interest him at all, he had had plenty of it all his life and he knew he would never have to worry. His trust fund would provide for him till the end of his days.

His friends were another story….they were really poor and he knew that the money would change their lives forever. They had been friends for years now, Internet friends, loners in the real world but brothers on the Net. They chatted incessantly and had set up a secure chat room just for each other. They knew each other's life stories, the pain, the deprivation, the hardship, and the horror of their days. He never told them that he came from money, just that his mother was a drug addict and his father a depraved womanizing alcoholic. They understood and empathized. They were the Warriors and they looked out for each other.

The money was sitting secure in several accounts in the Cayman Islands….no questions asked. He had set up the accounts well in advance. But he had told the others that they needed to wait a few weeks before they moved it again. He was in the process of setting up accounts for Ziggy and

Andrei in Switzerland and for Yuan in Dubai. Then, he would move the money in small amounts to each of the accounts. His friends would be rich, they would have the means to triumph over their miserable beginnings.

Ziggy would save his family and their home, his parents would smile again (of course, they would have much more than that!). Andrei could set up a trust for the funding of the orphanage and then get a place of his own. If he lived carefully, he would never have to work again. Yuan could actually buy his mother and himself a real home and start his own company. His mother would never have to work a menial job again.

And all this because of him….he had made it all possible. He had convinced them that it would be easy, they would never get caught. And that their lives would be changed forever. It had taken some convincing, but once they were all on board it had been fairly easy. Working together, over a period of months they had worked through all the issues and problems that they might encounter to ensure that the operation would go without a hitch….it had.

But now he had another problem that he had to take care of. His girl in her daily blog was indicating that she had met someone. He had followed her from her days in New York. Then, she still worked for Cosmo and he would often go stand outside the Cosmo building in New York City and watch for her. Sometimes, he followed her at a distance. Once he had even followed her to her apartment so that he knew where she lived.

But then she had moved to Florida to look after her mother and he loved her for that. Not only was she beautiful and smart, she was a loving daughter and, if she was so loving and caring about her mother, he could only imagine how loving and caring she would be toward a lover, toward him.

While she had lived in Florida, he had visited his family estate in Palm Beach several times and driven to Delray Beach, where she lived with her mother. He parked his car across the street from their high rise building and watched for her. He had seen her taking walks on the beach, sitting on the balcony, or by the pool and he felt that he was part of her life. He knew her, all about her, her likes, her dislikes, her life…she was his….now all he had to do was go claim her.

Tomorrow he would buy a ticket, go shopping, get a new haircut and new wardrobe and fly to Greece to claim his love! The Greek Gods had better be on his side!

THIRTY

Appearances are a glimpse of the unseen. – Anaxagoras

Things were going according to plan. All was well and Goddess Athena was feeling smugly happy at the success so far. Poseidon and she had called a truce, and after eons of time they were working together again for the betterment of their mortal followers. She had sensed a change in Poseidon. While he was still the charming cad, there was quietness about him; his arrogance seemed to have subsided.

The centuries had not been exactly kind to him and since the glory days of Atlantis, Poseidonia as the Greeks called it, his power had dimmed and he had been relegated to the legends of the Greeks that gradually became myths. The mortals living today knew little about his immense power and strength as it had lain dormant for the ages. They also knew very little about his thousands of years of glory in Atlantis, as the only quasi-historical facts preserved were the written words of Plato relating the stories about Poseidonia.

Plato had heard these stories in Egypt from the lips of the priests of Ammon Ra, when he visited there so many centuries ago. These stories were told by the Ra priests as tales of legend and amazement. It was high time for Poseidon to come forth, bring back his power and influence, let those around him feel his strength and benevolence. But, he knew that he could not do it on his own. He needed the other Gods on his side, especially Athena.

She had beaten him before with her skill and quiet strength. Plus, mentally, she was stronger and smarter that all the other Gods together. He needed her, just as he knew she needed him. Together, they could guide the world again; they could change it completely and bring it back to its glory days when all was blessed, peaceful and abundant. There was too much war, too much pain and suffering these days. Ares had been given way too much of a free range and by the looks of it the planet was going from disharmony to disaster and catastrophe. It was time for them, Athena and him, to rise up…together. Thus far, they seemed to be in accord. Things were going according to plan with their little scheme with Pythi and Pia. They would need their mortal skills to overcome some of the evil in the world.

Elsewhere, Athena mused, she needed to take care of Ares. He was a wily one and he knew her like no one else knew her, just as she knew him inside out. She sensed that he was up to his old tricks and she knew that he sensed that she was creating her own plans. She would have to make sure that he did not have any inkling about her doings, he thrived on conflict and he certainly would do everything he could to stop her. Plus, she knew how jealous he was and if he had even a smidgeon of a certainty that she was conspiring with Poseidon, his rage and jealousy would know no bounds. She would have to be very careful this time around if she was going to have any success, he would most certainly step in and create even more destruction and turmoil.

***

Ares watched her from a distance. He knew her and realized that she was planning something. Somehow he was not convinced that her romantic ploy with the God of the Sea was the only or main thing the two were working on. He was going to make it his business to find out. No one was going to get the better of him. So far, he had managed to remain powerful and he enjoyed wreaking havoc in the mortal world. He thrived on conflict and destruction, that was his forte, and his cunning ways had helped him have the upper hand so far. Of course, he had to thank the weak and easily corruptible nature of men, as well for all his successes. He would find out what Athena was up to and stop her.

The last thing he needed right now would be some immortals taking the side of men and guiding them from weakness to strength to realize their great potential. Ares liked men just as they were; foolish, opinionated, judgmental, egotistical, and ready to be insulted and offended at the drop of a hat. With these "qualities" sensitized to the extreme, the seeds of disorder had been planted in fertile land; sowing the ripe fruit of war afterwards was just child's play for someone with his skill and cunning.

***

Poseidon gazed out over the ocean from his Temple in Sounion, bearded chin in hand, deep in thought. The time had come and he knew that he had a hard battle ahead of him, but his people were suffering, the world was in a terrible state and all the dormant energy within him and around him needed to be released to create a whole new world. It was time to release the deep vortex's powerful energy, filled with amazing light, which had been dormant and buried for so many millennia.

It was time to open up the world to the new energy and start the process of the race of men reinventing themselves…..just like the old days in Atlantis and the more recent "ancient" days in Athens and Sparta. It was time for men to come back to the light where they came from and truly belonged, and it was time to put aside his past rivalry and animosity with Athena and ask for her help. She would be an invaluable ally and perhaps...maybe... working in harmony together could be the prelude of personal, tender admissions to come.

Nah, he thought allowing a crooked smile on his face, *now I am thinking like a mortal. I need to stay focused on the task ahead, not on the allure of the beautiful and oh so intelligent Athena. But,* still musing, *I will have to watch out for Ares. Otherwise, we may have destruction the like of which we have not seen in a long time. I was careless with him in Atlantis; I cannot afford to make the same mistake again.*

THIRTY-ONE

Friendship is a single soul dwelling in two bodies. – Aristotle

Pia felt a real sense of anticipation as she drove the long drive to Athens. The old car was easy to drive; the Greek music on the radio put her in a great mood as she hummed along. Soon she would be approaching the turn off to the City and all the traffic would begin, but she was ready for it. She had driven in New York, though infrequently, and this could not be much worse.

It was not long before she was caught up in bumper to bumper traffic, all heading into the center of the City, just as she was. "Patience," she told herself as she was cut off by yet another cab driver and stalled at yet another traffic light. She knew that Pythi would be waiting her at the end of the long drive.

***

Pythi had moved heaven and earth to set up the date. He wanted it to be perfect and had pulled every string in the book to create the perfect setting. The concierge at his hotel had helped, as had a chance meeting a few days before with the Director of Antiquities for the Acropolis Museum. The concierge had a friend who ran a taverna in the Thesion area, above Monasteraki, and his services had been employed as well. He was ready and waiting.

When she pulled into the hotel, Pythi was waiting in the lobby and he stepped out to help her from the car. The concierge looked over the old car with a raised eyebrow and a smile in his eye and wondered how this antique had made the distance. But, smiling politely, he welcomed Pia and ushered her into the foyer.

She had taken Pythi's breath away…more beautiful than he had imagined in his mind's eye. He had watched her step out of the car, straighten her short skirt, and push her hair back as she looked up at him. Their eyes locked and the rest of the world stood still.

Her beautiful eyes looked directly into his as she walked slowly up the stairs; her long legs encased in soft knee high boots, the patterned panty hose shimmering in the dim light. Her dark hair shone and as she walked, her hair moved with the movement and he caught a glimpse of long shimmering gold earrings sparkling in her ears. She was simply lovely and for tonight this loveliness would be his.

He had to mentally shake himself as she moved to the top step, her gaze still locked with his. As if in slow motion, he reached out to her and she stepped into his arms. He could smell her heady perfume and feel her soft skin as he held her close with one hand, reached out and moved her hair away from her face and kissed her lips. It was a lovers' kiss, soft and slow, but he was aware that he was standing in a public place and quickly pulled his mouth away from hers. Taking her hand in his, he led her inside.

They exchanged pleasantries and she commented on how charming the hotel was. It was very quiet in the lobby, a safe haven away from the noise and bustle a few steps outside. He asked her if she needed to freshen up after her long drive. He asked her if her boots were comfortable as they had a walk ahead of them, but he would tell her little else. It was his surprise.

Soon, they were walking the streets of Monasteraki, stopping to look at all the little shops, laughing at the boisterous shop keepers, observing the passerby's as they meandered up the hill. In what it seemed as a minute, they had left the hustle of Monasteraki behind them as they continued to climb toward Thesion. Hand in hand, they stopped to kiss in the darkness, and then walk, and kiss again, over and over again. He did not seem in a hurry, though, she could sense something more in him, and she was not sure what.

They passed beautiful tree lined streets with old Athenean mansions and soon were walking in an area that seemed to be a park. He took her hand and led her through a small gate and once again they were climbing. This time, though, they climbed stairs that felt like they were centuries-old, long wide marble stairs, and there were few trees, only bushes as they climbed and the air seemed to get thinner.

They took a turn up the stairs and there….a short distance above them, in all its splendor, lighting up the night sky was the Acropolis and the majestic Parthenon. It took her breath away and she stood there looking at it in awe and admiration. She had been to the Acropolis many times, but never in the dark as it closed at sundown and never, ever in the quiet of the night when they seemed to be the only people there.

She was amazed and questions flooded her mind. How had he swung this? No one was allowed up here except during visiting hours? Who was this man that she had begun to care for so much?

He put his fingers to her lips, "No questions now, sweetheart, just enjoy this moment," he said.

She agreed.

She let him lead her higher, up through the beautiful pillars and ruins, the whole of Athens spread before her, lit up and twinkling with lights. The city was enchanting, but her sense of wonder at being in this space, one of her most favorite places in the entire world...the Temple of her Guardian Goddess Athena, with the man of her dreams, took her breath away.....and it was all his doing. He had heard her, he had listened....and she began to love him for that.

Her reverie was broken once again as she saw a movement in the corner of her eye. Looking in that direction, at the foot of the Temple, with all of Athens laying out before it, stood a table with two chairs, laid for dinner, a bottle of wine chilling in a silver bucket and a young man standing beside it.

Pia felt as if she was in a dream, this was unreal. Yet, there was a part of her that insisted that it was reality and that she should enjoy and remember every moment. This was special, she acknowledged, and surrendered herself to the experience.

The young man withdrew a chair and invited her to sit down. It felt good to sit after the long walk and as Pythi seated himself, the young man poured the wine, after which he disappeared behind a workman's shed, where she now noticed that he had set up as a make shift kitchen with a small barbeque and was cooking lamb chops on it.

"Pythi, I am speechless. This is simply amazing. I want you to pinch me to make sure that I am not dreaming all this."

"I won't pinch you," he said, "But I will kiss you," and he leaned forward in his chair, pulled her close and kissed her slowly till all thought left her and she was drowning in sensation.

The young man served them lamb chops with salad, warm bread and lemon and oregano potatoes and then he disappeared, leaving them alone. They ate slowly, feeding each other, drinking the wine, savoring the moment and each other. It was the best meal Pia had ever eaten in the most romantic spot in the entire world. Pythi told her that the concierge had helped him set up the date and then laughing he said, "If you hear police sirens…run." Pia looked alarmed at that and he laughed and assured her that he had permission for this date. He continued to tell her that he would have loved to have candles on the table but it was not permitted as it was a fire hazard. Small concession for such a fabulous evening!

After dinner, they walked around the Temple, took pictures of the view and of each other. They took a selfie together and laughed at Pythi's funny expression in the photo. They went back to the table and sitting close to each other, sipped on the wine and looked into each other's eyes. The energy was explosive and soon she was sitting on his lap and he was kissing her passionately, his hands running up and down her body, moving under her jacket and sweater, feeling her bare skin, igniting his passion and exploding hers till both of them felt as if they had burst into flame, together!

They had been there for over three hours before Pythi drew her away from him and suggested they begin the long walk down. She took a few more pictures and spent a few moments taking in the entire panorama, as if to imprint it in her mind's eye and then, with a shake of her head, she leaned in and kissed him ever so gently, thanking him for the most beautiful evening of her life. Then, taking his hand they walked down the stairs hand in hand.

On the way down, they stopped at a small café and got some hot coffee to warm themselves as the night had turned chilly and to prolong the time together, as neither of them wanted it to end. A small group of musicians was playing on the street and they stopped to listen, still hand in hand.

Soon they were back at the hotel and for a while they sat in the lobby drinking more coffee and talking and touching. Pythi invited Pia up to his room and when he saw her eyes widen he assured her that he simply wanted to spend some more time with her, in private. Trusting him, she went up to his room, they wrapped themselves in a warm blanket and sat on his small balcony talking, touching, and kissing.

It was past three in the morning when she got up. She really did not want to leave but she knew that YahYah would be waiting for her and she needed to make the long drive back. Pythi offered to take her after he tried to convince her to spend the night, even offering to get her a room, but she declined.

He took her downstairs to her car, where kissing her again, he let her go. He really didn't want to see her leave. She understood him, his jokes and his love of the Classics and Greek antiquity. She admired his intelligence and was interested in his job. They shared a love of reading and books and throughout the evening, he had not felt an awkward moment. Plus, the chemistry was explosive. It was perfect.

She glanced at him one last time as she pulled out and blowing him one last kiss pulled into the street and disappeared down the road. On the drive back she reflected on the most perfect evening of her life. This is what she had been waiting for all along, this feeling of being swept off her feet by a man she had begun to love. He was perfect. No one had ever planned a date with such attention to detail. He listened to her; he understood her and her culture. He got her strengths and insecurities and he was really great looking! She loved it when he touched her, the chemistry, the sexual tension, the longing, it was all there, and yet, she felt safe. She knew he would protect her, she was in love.

Goddess Athena had showered her blessings upon her and she felt her presence strongly when they were up in the Acropolis tonight. It just could not have been a coincidence that this perfect evening was spent at her Temple, where she had presided for eons.

The Gods were smiling…and watching. All was well!

THIRTY-TWO
Love is composed of a single soul inhabiting two bodies. - Aristotle

"Dear Friends," she wrote on her blog the next morning, "I have spent a day and night of enchantment. In a country where there is a huge financial crisis and where people are suffering terribly, where many are without jobs, a future or any hope, there is still a sense of joy in the simple things that bring happiness in life. In this lies the greatness of the Greek culture, the ability to live in this moment, to enjoy a simple cup of coffee, or a walk on a beautiful beach, to spend long hours overlooking some ancient monument, while whole heartedly and passionately discussing the current political situation, or the price of food in the supermarket. It is this ability to enjoy each moment to the fullest, regardless of life's circumstance, that gives one the strength to go on in spite of the darkness that surrounds the country. This strength and passion inspires me and makes me believe that no matter what the circumstances today, tomorrow may be better, but it is this moment, this NOW that I must enjoy and cherish.

Cherish the NOW moments of your life, feel the joy my friends….and may you too have days of enchantment. More later!"

The sun had begun to rise by the time she made it back to Sounion and quietly crawling into bed, she laid there for a few minutes reliving all the precious moments of the most memorable date she had ever had. It had been perfect. She smiled happily as she fell asleep for a few hours.

***

Pythi had gone up to his room with a sense of loss; he really had not wanted to let Pia go. Lying in bed, he too relived the date. It had been perfect; he had never felt like this about anyone. He had dated a lot and had several relationships, but, he had never felt this sense of longing to be with someone like he did with Pia. It had always been easy for him to disconnect from a relationship, especially since he traveled as much as he did. But Pia filled his thoughts and he felt a sense of longing to be with her again, to know her in the most intimate way, to touch both her heart and her soul.

Restless, he reached for his phone and i-pad, checked his email and his Facebook page; not much going on there. He scrolled through his messages and saw one from his father that he had not responded too.

He wrote, "Love is the joy of the good, the wonder of the wise, and the amazement of the Gods. – Plato. All good here Dad, hope all is well, kalinihta!"

Then, he hit send.

***

It was late in the evening in New Canaan, CT, when Professor Harding heard the familiar tone of a message from his precious son. It had been a few days since he had sent his son a message. The older couple was watching the late news, sitting hand in hand on the couch, the fire burning in the grate, relaxed after a nice dinner.

He got up from the couch and crossed over to the small table where his phone sat. Picking it up he scrolled through the message, then re-read it. He walked back slowly to the couch, re-read it again, deep in thought.

"Diana," he said.

"Shh…" she shushed him, she wanted to hear the weather for the next day.

"Diana," he went again, ignoring her response. "I think you should read this."

"Read what?" She countered, still focused on the TV.

"I believe that your son is in love," he went on.

"Really," she said. "Why is this such great news? He's been in love before. Did he tell you he met someone? Is that it?"

He handed her the phone. She read the message, then, looked up at him.

"This message tells you that he is in love? Really? How?"

"We have played this game since he was a kid and he has never in all these years sent me a quote about love. I know Pythi, he has found someone special."

"Robert, you are just being fanciful. I know, we both want him to find that someone special, but this….it's just another quote," said the ever practical Diana.

The Professor was thoughtful for a moment, then picking up his phone he typed, "At the touch of love everyone becomes a poet – Plato. Glad to know all is well; tell me more when you have time. I love you, son."

He hit send.

Pythi was almost asleep when he heard his phone buzz; he picked it up from the bedside table, read his father's message and laughed aloud. His father was amazing, he understood, somehow he knew.

Rolling over he fell asleep.

THIRTY-THREE
An honest man is always a child. – Socrates

Things were not going according to plan at Banque Nationale. In fact, chaos reigned. The team had been working round the clock with other staffers all around the world and they were at a dead loss. They had a two-fold job…the first was to make sure that the system was secure again, and, the second was to track the money and find it. So far they had not been able to do either.

It was obvious that there was a glitch in the system that allowed the hackers to get in, but after days of working on it they had no idea how it had been transgressed. They had been running diagnostics for days and still had nothing. They were constantly in touch with National Security agencies, and financial institutions around the world to track any movement of a large sum of money, but so far, here too, it had been a dead end. No movement of money anywhere. It had just disappeared…poof.

Tanya sat at her desk, a sense of foreboding building in her. The logical side of her was staring at the computer screen, watching the diagnostics, trying to find anything unusual in the algorithms. Meanwhile, instinctively, she felt that something was terribly wrong. She felt a sense of danger and a shiver of fear ran through her. She shook her head, telling herself she was over thinking things. But Tanya had grown up on the streets, in a crime ridden ghetto, and she had learned to trust her instincts. Something was terribly wrong, she just felt it, but could not put her finger on it.

She looked around the room, it was late afternoon and the others were working quietly in their own spaces. No one else seemed bothered, and they were all intently trying to solve the problems at hand. Derek was on the phone with one of their security experts in New York, Sam was bent over his laptop and he kept looking over a pile of papers at his side. Pythi was staring at a bank of computer screens but his thoughts were elsewhere.

After he had left early last night, the other three had had a short discussion about his leaving early. It was very unlike Pythi to ever leave his team and he was being very tight lipped about it, but somehow Tanya knew it had to be because of a woman. And, if that were true, she was happy for Pythi.

They lived lonely lives, and, while their friends thought that it was so glamorous to travel all over the world and live in different countries, in reality, they were often alone. Flying from one crisis to another, they rarely had time to enjoy any of the places they visited.

Tanya didn't mind at all. She had decided at an early age that she was never going to make the same mistakes as her mother. Her parents' relationship had been a mess and she had promised herself that she would live a life without all the drama and abuse. She was going to focus on her career, build up a nest egg and then find a quiet corner of the world to retire to. No relationships, no complications. So far, she had done just fine. Life had been very good these past few years and immersed in her work, she had found a semblance of happiness. She enjoyed working with the 'boys' as she called them, too.

Derek was young and exuberant. She enjoyed his enthusiasm and had worked with him on several projects. They had often traveled together and she enjoyed hanging out with him after hours. Uncomplicated and fun loving, he was also a computer genius, with a very sharp brain. She teased him endlessly and they often had a friendly competition going as they pitted their brains against each other.

Sam was the quiet one, the numbers genius. Sam was amazing, he listened, he watched, he observed, he played scenarios out in his mind, patiently and quietly, till he got the answers he was looking for. Tanya often marveled at how tirelessly he worked. When she had first met him, she had pegged him as too serious, almost grumpy, but he turned out to have a funny sense of humor and he was very thoughtful, always making sure that the other members of the team were okay. She liked him, but Sam had walls and it was difficult to penetrate them. Of late, she had noticed that he was opening up to her and sometimes she felt him watching her.

Pythi, she knew and loved. He was the big brother she had always wanted. Smart, real smart, but never cocky, she really looked up to him. She had met his parents as well and enjoyed them. He was one of the lucky ones, she thought, as she glanced at him. A loving, supportive family was something she had always craved and he had that. They had all laughed and made comments about Pythi's long line of ever revolving girlfriends. *It was hard to keep up,* she thought, with a small chuckle.

Shaking herself out of her reverie, she decided to get her coat and go for a walk. She needed some fresh air to shake the cobwebs out of her head. They had always solved the security issues that came up and they were going to win this one as well. She proudly told herself that the best brains in the business were in the room, they were just missing something and they would find it soon. Then, grabbing her coat, she asked the others if they needed anything, and using her secure key, stepped into the elevator and went upstairs, through the service entrance, and out on the street.

As soon as she stepped onto the busy street, she felt that sense of foreboding again. She began walking slowly, and felt the hair on the back of her neck stand up. She knew she was being watched. She had felt this feeling so many times before, she never questioned it. Someone was watching her, but who and why? No one knew who she was, especially here in Athens. She stopped and turned around slowly, but the street was too busy and there were people and cars everywhere. There was no way she would ever be able to pinpoint someone following her. She ducked into Starbucks, bought a caramel macchiato, and then walked back to the bank at a brisk pace. She had the same feeling again, she was definitely being watched. This time, she went in through the main lobby and then took the service elevator down.

She was going to have to tell the others. They may not believe her, but she had to tell them. Her instincts had never been wrong, she had grown up in danger and her senses had been sharpened by it. She had to warn them that something was askew.

THIRTY-FOUR

A few vices are sufficient to darken many virtues. – Plutarch

He sat at the little café across the street from the entrance of Banque Nationale, drinking a cup of hot coffee. He looked like any other tourist in the area. Blue jeans, a sweater with a light jacket, his blond hair cut short, a shadow of growth on his chin. He chain-smoked cigarettes and wished that he had some of his mother's stash of cocaine with him. He needed a hit, his hands were beginning to get shaky, but he had been afraid to carry any with him in case he got caught at the airport. He would have to score some soon.

It was late afternoon and he had arrived the night before. He was here to claim his girl but he was also here to find out all about his enemy, the man his girl claimed she was charmed by. He was here to get even. No man was ever going to get his girl. He knew her, and everything about her, he checked his i-pad, which sat on the café table in front of him, to see if she had posted anything on her blog. She had not. In fact, she had been quiet for a couple of days now. He wondered how she was doing. It wouldn't be long though, before they would meet in person and then he would be the man in her life, her Man!

But, he had other business at hand too. He was also here to check out the bank and to make sure that all was going according to plan. He had transferred small amounts of money to each account and he continued to do so every few days. No large sums, just enough for his friends to know that it was coming. They had agreed to do it slowly and they would have to trust him to do it. But already, his friends were richer than they had ever been.

And it had been easy, too easy. So easy, that another plan was formulating in his head. If they could do it at one bank, they could do it at another, and then another. He could take his share and buy an island somewhere in the Indian Ocean, and then no government or country would ever be able to find him. He could spend his life away from the family he hated, with his beloved Pia.

***

It was late afternoon when Ziggy clocked into work. He always worked the late shift at the Banque.
Finding a job, any job, was very hard in Greece with the poor economy, and a neighbor of his who worked at the Banque had helped get him the job. Ziggy hated working at the Banque. He thought it was very demeaning but his family needed money and he was their only means of support. He limped into the Banque, clocked in, and changing into his work clothes, picked up the large bucket, mop and trash can on wheels that he moved around the Banque. The Banque closed at four to the public, and by five all the employees were gone. He went from floor to floor, mopping floors, emptying trash cans, arranging the chairs in the reception area and cleaning and polishing the brass on all the doors. It was menial work and he hated it.

He had no friends at work. No one ever spoke to him and if they did, it was to order him to do something or the other. He was invisible. Slowly wheeling his trash can, he began emptying the waste baskets in every room.

"These people are pigs," he thought to himself, "So much trash, every day. And they leave the bathrooms in a disgusting state."

He went about the business of cleaning. It was tiring and tedious. Soon the Banque began to empty as it always did. He went methodically from floor to floor, cleaning, mopping and emptying the trash. While he did this he thought about his future. He would not have to do it much longer. As soon as they felt that it was safe, he would go to Switzerland and bring some of the money back to his parents. A fraction of his share would keep his parents for the rest of their lives. He would wait a few years and then buy himself an apartment, somewhere far away from the city. He wanted to live on a quiet beach, in a place where no one knew him and where he could begin again, not as the school cripple but as a man of means, to be respected.

But right now, he had business at hand to take care of. He knew that the Banque had a security team in the basement. He had watched them and knew who they were. He had reported back to the others every night about their activities but he had still not been able to go to the basement by himself. The security guard outside would escort him down to the basement and he was given a few minutes to pick up the trash and clean out the space.

Sometimes, he went down when the team was there. Working quietly and invisibly, he would walk around their computers trying to get a glimpse of what ever was on their screens but he had been warned over and over again to be very unobtrusive and so he didn't linger.

At other times, he heard snippets of their conversation. He knew the girl, Tanya, was very frustrated. He knew that so far they had found nothing. He knew that Derek liked to drink beer at night and often worked late with a bottle of beer on his table. He knew that Sam, the quiet one, was very careful and that Sam watched him and when he came close to his space he often closed his laptop or changed the screen on the desk top. Sam was suspicious of everyone, and he knew he had to be very careful around him.

He knew that Pythi, the American, was the team leader and that he was often on the phone talking to people in the United States. No one ever spoke to him and so none of them knew that he spoke, wrote and understood English. They just presumed that he didn't and continued their conversations around him. But, thus far he had heard nothing that would alarm him or his friends. Things were going as planned.

***

Outside, at the café, G-Lover watched her going down the street. Ziggy gave them an update about each one of the team every night and they had done their own research. He knew all about Tanya, or at least whatever he could find on the Internet. He knew she was really smart, that she had gone to the premier schools and excelled and he had a real respect for her intelligence.

She wasn't bad looking either, he thought to himself, as he watched her saunter down the street. He saw her stop and turn as if she was looking for something, then duck into Starbucks. A few minutes later, she stepped out again and this time she walked back to the Banque at a brisk pace, her long, wild hair flowing behind her. She was casually dressed and as she walked closely by him, he noticed that her eyes looked tired and that she emanated a nervous energy.

An interesting mix, he thought, *intelligent, energetic, yet nervous.*

It was time for him to go back to the hotel and find some food and some drugs. He had a phone number of a dealer he remembered his mother using a few years ago, when they had holidayed in Greece and he needed to contact him soon. He was beginning to really feel shaky and he only had a few Ambien in his bag in the hotel. He needed something stronger, and he needed it soon. Picking up his i-pad, he began walking the short walk back to his hotel.

THIRTY-FIVE

...in a single day and night of misfortune, the island of Atlantis disappeared into the depths of the sea. – Plato

It was in a conversation he had with Apollo that Poseidon learned in passing about the meeting of Athena and Ares at the sacred grounds of Delphi. The two Gods in charge of the major energy vortices in the Greek land, Sounion and Delphi, they would meet from time to time to assess the energy levels and act accordingly. The current major concern had been the financial crisis that kept the entire world in its grips and had crippled Greece. They both agreed that drastic measures were needed to address this problem and had concluded that intensifying the output of the two Greek energy centers was now a necessity. As was the connection of them to the global network of the other fourteen vortices at different places on the Earth, if humanity were to stay on course for the new epoch. And, if the Greeks were to be helped to find the way back to their collective soul.

As he heard the unexpected news of the meeting, his left eyebrow sprung instinctively in an upward curve and he fought hard to hold back a blade of jealousy.

What does Ares want with Athena? I hope he is not making any amorous plans for her, he thought to himself. And immediately after, *What is Ares really after this time? I hope we are not heading for a second Atlantis.*

It had been some 350 centuries ago, yes - 35,000 years ago - *how does time fly...* - that the glorious civilization of Poseidonia, Atlantis, had flourished under his patronage and protection in the now lost island continent in the depths of the Atlantic Ocean. This had been the golden age of humanity. For millennia on end that civilization had advanced in knowledge, both scientific and occult, wisdom and innovation, in peace and harmonious coexistence with other civilizations on the surface of mother Gaia, Earth. It was a heady time and Poseidon had really been honored, glorified and worshipped by the Atlanteans in a truly inspired way. Memories of that sweet and glorious epoch started flooding Poseidon's mind, as he was bidding Apollo farewell on his way back to Sounion.

Poseidon himself had worked closely with their advanced elders to design a magnificent city of five concentric circular islands separated by an equal number of sea channels. Each such ring of land was at a higher elevation than the previous ring, as one moved toward the center of the circle. The piece of land at the center was circular and, forming the apex, was the crowning jewel of Atlantis. This is where he had built his palace in the early days to share with his mortal wife Cleto, create the laws of the land and rule the infant civilization that was destined for unimaginable glory.

As the centuries rolled by, he passed the governance of the budding empire to the Atlantean Rais, emperors that were selected on the strength of their wisdom and benevolent occult powers to rule and care for the people, and lead the empire into the future. The Rai's palace, and seat of government, situated in the central island, overseeing the entire city unfolding in terraces below, was a monument of magnificent architecture, which got more and more impressive with each successive Rai.

Having achieved an admirable balance between science and spirituality, they had developed a terrific understanding of the laws of nature, which in turn led them to spectacular discoveries and inventions. Suspended electrical cars were used for transportation throughout the city, while their cigar-shaped airships could take them to the four corners of the known world at speeds similar to those of modern airliners. The difference was that their engines used almost no fuel, as they were built to manipulate the Earth's gravity, riding on the planet's magnetic lines. At antigravity mode, the vessels were airships and by reversing the engine mode to flow with the gravity, they could become submarines. The heaviest of storms were of no threat to aviation as the airships had no wings.

All common minerals used in industry and construction were available from the mines in Atlantis or the colonies in what is today North and South America. The most common among them was aluminum and they would build their vessels, cable cars, and entire architectural mega structures out of it. The abundance of the metal was primarily due to an ingenious process they had developed to create aluminum out of simple and abundant clay. They would elevate the atomic energy of clay to a very high degree, and then, they would gradually reduce it to the level where aluminum and other useful metals would crystallize.

Knowledge and wisdom were revered, as were integrity of character and the adherence to the laws handed down by Poseidon himself, which were in direct harmony with the cosmic laws. Benevolent spiritual powers, developed over long courses of study and adeptship, were held in high regard, respect and admiration. Their civic leaders and servants were selected early in life on their strength with these abilities and for service to the community as a whole. Books were viewed with high respect and were classified as being in the food category, as mental food.

It was a civilization based on beauty and harmony, and it was in very close contact with nature. You could experience this in their daily surroundings, from the architectural beauty of their homes and city, where elaborate landscaping of all types with exotic plants predominated, to the magnificence of art, sculpting, painting and architecture everywhere. Having developed advanced tools of stone-cutting allowed them to sculpt shapes in such intricacy and size that would be unthinkable in modern times. The greatest of their architectural and artistic creations, a true testament to their devotion and gratitude to the God that they had named Poseidonia after, was the magnificent Temple of Poseidon at Atlantis.

Built of white marble in a style that became typical later of ancient Greek temples, it was gigantic in proportions and dwarfed anything around it. A humongous statue of the God was presiding over the entrance to the temple and smaller but still gigantic statues of lesser deities were used to decorate the grounds around the temple. The temple compound was a piece of art of unimaginable proportions that left the visitor and worshipper, even the frequent ones, out of breath and in total awe.

Poseidon stopped the reverie of those wonderful times for a minute, as a dark cloud passed over his gaze at the thought of Ares, the sworn enemy of harmony and monster of destruction.

For millennia on end, Poseidonia had flourished and prospered in close cooperation with the other two developed civilizations on the planet at the time, Suern (modern India) and Necropan (modern Egypt and North Africa). They enjoyed continuous technological advances, including advanced electronics that allowed them instant communications by voice and image anywhere on the planet. The epitome of their technological marvel came with the development of technology that could influence and control the weather. The early uses of those weather changing machines were strictly to boost agricultural productivity. As a result, Poseidonia became a dominant exporter of grains and cultivated food to the other two civilizations that were at the mercy of unpredictable weather and droughts that depleted their food supply. That is when Ares stepped in sensing fertile ground for corruption, self-interest and power, and of course disruption, destruction and war.

Ares worked patiently, generation after generation, on the most gifted of scientists and men of power, boosting their importance and personal egos away from the common good, igniting and fueling a thirst for power, enshrouding everything under the veil of pride and grandeur of Atlantis. In a few short centuries, what used to be a benevolent empire was turned into an intolerant and domineering nationalistic force that started using their advanced technology as weapons against nations that would oppose them or fail to yield to their will. It was not uncommon, for instance, if some local tribe in North America was to revolt against the Atlantean mine exploitation, for Atlantis to manipulate the weather there with their machines and literally drown the revolution in flood waters or burn it in amplified sunbeam fires.

But, it did not stop there. The overfed egos of the most powerful of Atlanteans reached a point that could not tolerate instruction even from their formerly revered Rai. Thus, factions were created, conspiracies were planned, and soon enough the blessed and privileged continent found itself being ravaged by civil war, where all the advanced weaponry was used by Atlanteans to destroy Atlanteans.

This had been Poseidonia's gravest hour and merciless Ares, who had planned all this methodically, reserved his triumphant celebration for the moment of final destruction and annihilation. He did not have to wait long. The blind hatred between factions led them to use the awesome technology they possessed with no regard for anyone or anything, so long as their enemies were destroyed.

Soon, the climate became unstable, the forces of nature were polarized to the extreme and, in a final crescendo, powerful, long lasting earthquakes rearranged the crust of the Earth under Atlantis. The continent was broken up in pieces that were swallowed then by the waters of the Atlantic Ocean some 9500 years ago, never to be seen again.

Poseidon shook his head in profound sadness at the memory of all the destruction and loss.

What a terrible pity, he thought to himself.

I hope the warmonger monster is not up to his old tricks again, but even if he is, I will not stand idle this time round!

THIRTY-SIX

Every heart sings a song, incomplete, until another heart whispers back. – Plato

Pia felt very good when she woke up late that morning. The drive back from Athens had been wonderful. She had rolled the window down and let the cool air in as she sang along with the radio, reliving the entire evening. It had been the best date she had ever been on. She had smiled to herself the whole drive back, thinking of Pythi, and the things he had said, the way he looked at her, his touch…that sent shivers running through her. It had been perfect.

She had tip-toed into the house and quietly changing into her pajamas, so as not to wake her YahYah, had crept into the bed and cuddled under the covers. Before she fell asleep, she texted Pythi, "Made it back, thanks for one of the best evening this girl has ever had, nite, xox"

A few seconds later he texted back, "Thanks, your spending it with me made it truly special. I miss you already! Sweet dreams!"

Smiling to herself, Pia fell asleep.

It had been past ten in the morning when she had woken up. She could smell food cooking, cookies baking, and could hear her YahYah bustling around the kitchen. She stepped out of the bed and pulling on a warm hoodie, went to brush her teeth. By the time she came out of the bathroom, her coffee was being brewed in the briki, the small saucepan in which Greek coffee is made. Brewing Greek coffee or Elliniko Café, as it is called in Greece, is an art. YahYah had a small gas burner which existed purely for the purpose of making coffee. The water was added to the briki after which she spooned a heaping teaspoon of coffee into the mix. The coffee brewed on the burner. It is never allowed to come to a boil; when it starts to simmer and build a layer of foam and bubbles at the top, it is ready. YahYah made it especially for her and knowing her sweet tooth, after she poured it into a cup, she always added a spoonful of condensed milk to sweeten it.

In Greece, coffee is not just a beverage, it is a social occasion, and so it was that morning. YahYah loaded up a tray with two cups of coffee and a plate full of koulourakia, the Greek cookies she expertly baked, along with some fresh bread and feta cheese. She carried it outside to the little table with the magnificent view of the ocean and the temple of Poseidon.

They sat there, sipping their coffee, and Pia began to tell YahYah all about her date. Soon, they were joined by Yannis, the next door neighbor and his wife, and other friends of YahYah, Spyros and Maria. They all wanted to hear about the date and while at first Pia felt really awkward telling all of them about her date, she soon realized, as she wove her tale and described the charm and beauty of the Acropolis, that they were enthralled and that sharing stories and discussing each other's lives in great detail was very much part of the culture in Greece. Here, they didn't call each other on the telephone and keep each other at a distance. They shared their lives, their pains and their joys, with each other, and it was usually done in an unhurried manner over a cup of coffee.

She was careful to omit the parts she felt were between Pythi and her alone, but she described in great detail the beauty of the city, all lit up at night, and the amazing feeling of having a meal in the shadow of one of the most beautiful structures in the world, just Pythi and her. The women were charmed and they all had an opinion about Pythi, which they voiced without rancor. Maria thought it was the most romantic thing she had ever heard, and then turning to her husband Spyros demanded that he do something romantic for her. They all laughed, it was light hearted and fun, and Pia could not remember a time in the last few years when she felt so at peace in that moment. Just happy to be sitting there, in the middle of the morning, relaxing and sharing stories.

Soon, the neighbors drifted off for lunch and a siesta and Pia and YahYah went inside too. YahYah went to take her nap and Pia picked up her laptop and walked the short walk down to the beach, where she sat on a rock, looked out at the ocean, contemplated her life, and began writing.

"Friends," she wrote, "Sometimes the Gods conspire to create the most perfect situation in the most perfect place and I was fortunate enough to be part of that conspiracy. Having spent the most delightful evening at the Acropolis on a perfect, clear night, sipping wine, enjoying the amazing setting, and I am truly grateful. Thankful for the thought and planning that went into creating what has to be one of the best evenings of my life. All this, in the company of someone who has my head spinning and my heart beating at a faster rate!

A year ago, I would not have believed that this would be possible and that I, who has lived through enormous turmoil, am now in a place of peace and enjoyment. I want to thank you, my friends, for staying by my side through the years where, as a caretaker, I had no time for myself, and through the dark times, where not knowing who I was, or where I was heading, I was groping for a sliver of light. I feel that I have come out on the other side that the Light shines bright and I am hoping that you will walk this journey with me too. Let's walk in Lightness together! My friends, I wish you peace and a perfect day or night, wherever you may be. More later!"

It was late afternoon, when she signed off and clambered up the path to the house. YahYah would be awake by now and together they would cook the evening meal! She looked forward to the simplicity of cooking and spending time with her beloved grandmother.

THIRTY-SEVEN

Nothing is more active than thought, for it travels over the universe,
and nothing is stronger than necessity for all must submit to it. - Thales

Ares was satisfied. His network was already in place and G-Lover was getting more and more under his control. His drug addiction had made it so much easier for Ares to enter his mental body and imprint his desires on the unsuspecting addict's brain. His "Warriors" had been carefully selected after a thorough study of the Akasha. Although G-Lover, Ziggy, Yuan, and Andrei did not know it, they had lived several lifetimes in the 25,000 year span of Atlantean dominance, mostly as highly regarded scientists that had gradually drifted to the dark side, contributing to the demise of the great civilization. Their present incarnation on Earth was one of many lives of atonement in the immutable wheel of cause and effect. They had been together before and mostly on the same side, usually under the guidance of the one that called himself G-Lover.

G-Lover himself had not disappointed Ares, as he had done well endearing himself to the others through his care for them, money and initial success. Their trust for him was growing by the day at the rate of the deposits into their bank accounts. Nobody in their lives of pain had offered them that much money before, no-one had promised them riches in their gloomy and misery-ridden lives, and no one had ever delivered on promises.

G-Lover was different, he understood them, and he really cared for them and treated them like brothers. He was the big brother that they never had, who was there to support, motivate and encourage them. To help them reason out of their hesitations and doubts, to push them to believe in themselves, their talents and dormant greatness. To lift them when they were down, to rein their enthusiasm into balance when it was getting out of control and bordered on arrogance.

He was a true leader, a master planner who had brought the best out of them and united them under the common goal. To become fabulously wealthy and live a life of ease, comfort, and privilege. It was their birth right, he had told them, to strive for the best and get it no matter who was to stand in the way. Life had served them nothing but pain, bitterness, poverty, and cruelty thus far. It was high time they changed all that.

"It is time to realize your potential, grab life by the horns and not let go until you milk generous riches out of it. Money is power and we need plenty of it. Your destiny is to be served by others, not to be in the service of others as you are doing now, and in a menial way. I am here to reassure you that you have what it takes and lead you to find and manifest that greatness and wealth. The world owes us and all we are doing is planning to collect on that debt. But we need to stick together as a team, like modern musketeers, one for all and all for one. Alone we are nothing, together we are everything. With our combined talents, smarts and expertise, even the most sophisticated of security systems are vulnerable.

It may take time and effort, but, believe me, there is no system designed by human beings that we cannot hack, penetrate or infiltrate. We just need to be patient enough to search for the weak links; they always exist and most always are linked to petty human vanities. Then, we need to be careful to infiltrate undetected, become part of the system itself, so it does not recognize us as intruders, but as friendly users. Once in, any bank's security system, we will have control over it, but then we need to remain patient and very careful, control our rightful pride and the need for triumphant celebrations, bragging and pounding our chests to the hacking world for empty glory.

We are not hackers, we are businessmen using hacking as a tool, and our business is to become rich beyond our dreams. But, it has to be done with mastery, expertise, and under the veil of non-detection so we can do it again and again. Pride and greed have no place in our brotherhood, if we are to be successful in a sustainable way. There are thousands and thousands of banks all over the world and many of these would make worthy targets for us. Soon, it will be harvest time my friends, my brothers, soon will be harvest time for the 'Warriors.' In the meantime work smartly, diligently, and patiently and follow my lead. This much I do promise you, I will lead you to your promised land and your life will be nothing but honey."

The cocaine-boosted confidence had done the job and G-Lover had certainly inspired his team, his Warriors, to a wealthy vision. The many months that followed found him working closely with them, researching, investigating, planning, and going over exhaustive details, organizing, evaluating targets and zooming into the most vulnerable ones. He boosted their esteem, pulling them closer and closer into the common goal. In the process, he had won their trust and at times they would confide in him their most intimate thoughts and secrets. If they had any lingering doubts, they were surely convinced when they started seeing their accounts swell. He had broken no promise made to them and had delivered in the most convincing way. It was him that had identified Banque Nationale in Athens as a highly vulnerable target and the hard work on this project over the past three months had already paid off handsomely.

Yes, G-Lover was family to them by now, he was a teacher, the General that lead them into battle and they would win too. He had become their guru, and they would follow him to the end of the Earth, no matter what.

THIRTY-EIGHT
Modesty is the color of virtue. – Sinope

It was well after midnight when Tanya and Sam had decided that enough was enough. Everyone else was gone by then and the early-to-bed Protectors, that is what the team called itself, were probably already dreaming away in lala land.

Tanya and Sam had been running diagnostics and checks on the main security system and its branches all day long, glued to their screens. Disappointment after disappointment, none of the diagnostics raised any flags or sounded alarms, and all the checks came back negative. No visible sign of an intruder, no evidence of violation or trespassing, but it was an indisputable fact unearthed by the Protector team that money from many of the accounts, all the very busy ones, was siphoned away to accounts that seemed to vanish into cyberspace. They were not big amounts of money, small amounts hidden here and there, that looked like just another ordinary payable entry to an outside account, and they would not have noticed, until Pythi came up with the idea to select the three busiest corporate accounts of the bank.

He assigned one account to each member of his team and told them clearly, "Go back a week and scrutinize any and all outgoing payments from the account and follow them all the way to their conversion to cash, no matter where in the world it may be. Look for patterns, repetitions, unexplainable transactions. Don't leave a stone unturned. At the end of the day, you should be able to explain every single outgoing transaction and follow it to its resolution. Anything unusual, anything out of the ordinary, I want to know about it. We need to find out how did these hackers do it, how did they get into the system and how did they manage to stay invisible. Once we have these answers, it will be easier to track them down and find out who the hell they are."

They went at it with zeal and dogged determination, to spot discrepancies and outliers in their assigned accounts, to identify the footprint of the intruders. This was patient, tedious, detailed work that had them follow each transaction to its final resolution. They worked at it for long days with the discipline of trained CIS investigators and the methodical rationalizations of little electronic Sherlock Holmes'. They were instructed to work independently and only get together every few days to compare notes.

They did that and at the first meeting there was nothing noteworthy to report. Tanya even expressed the opinion that this may be yet another wild goose chase. At the second meeting Derek reported a couple of transactions that led to accounts that he could not reconcile and he vowed to revisit and try again. At the third meeting both Sam and Tanya had identified irreconcilable transactions as well, all to different accounts that they did not seem to have a real home and they started calling them 'ghost' accounts. A pattern started to emerge and after a month of hard work, they had a map of footprints on the three accounts. "My friends," Pythi said, "This is a break through! The ghosts have left us a faint footprint to follow. Now, it is our job to put our noses to the ground and like well-trained hounds, follow the scent of the beasts to their lair."

That night they celebrated and went out together to an outdoor taverna in the northwest suburbs of Athens. Situated at the foot of Mount Parnis, in the pine tree studded yard of the taverna, they feasted on delicious grilled lamb chops, horiatiki and marouli salads, different grilled mezehs, artisan bread toasted on the spit and sprinkled with olive oil and oregano, and plenty of Attica dry red wine and tsikoudia, moonshine, from Crete. That was a night to remember, as the wine and moonshine fumes helped bring out the true personalities of the individual Protectors. It was also the first time that Tanya felt that strange chemistry with Sam and started questioning the hard line, almost monastic rules of her life.

Reacting to the memory of that connection of many days before, Tanya was looking for an opportunity to spend time with Sam.

"We have become almost cross-eyed by looking at flickering monitors all day," said Tanya, "I am hungry and exhausted. What do you say about a late gyros sandwich before going to bed? I know just the place about a block from here. Are you game, Sam?"

Sam's growling stomach quickly convinced him to agree and soon they were busy shutting down their machines, turning off the lights in the bank basement and securing the building. Once out on the street, they took a deep breath of fresh air and exhaled with delight. The street was quiet and deserted with the exception of a limping kid lugging grocery bags.

"There goes another insomniac Greek," commented Tanya cheerfully. "Let's go, Sam. I'm starved!"

Across the street, Ziggy carrying his supermarket bags, limping slowly, heard the comment and smiled a sneaky smile.

Foolish, naive Americans, he thought to himself, *I'm watching you and so are G-Lover and the Warriors.*

Once again, Tanya felt that terrifying feeling that she was being watched. She moved closer to Sam, as though he would shield her. Sam sensing her disquiet looked at her quizzically.

"What's wrong?"

"I am feeling it again….remember, I told you guys about the feeling I get when I am being followed or watched? I spoke about it a few days ago, when I came back from the coffee shop. The feeling has not left me, I feel it often. Right now, I am almost freaking out. Someone is watching us, Sam, I know it. My instinct is never wrong; I grew up with this feeling. It is innate, a sense of danger and knowing that I have to protect myself."

Sam looked around. The street was empty, except for the cripple and his shopping bags, limping slowly away, and he was not looking at them. The street was lined with parked cars but they were all dark and silent.

He pulled her into the light and the warmth of one of the only tavernas still open, and still shielding her with his arm, helped her to a chair. Then sitting down next to her, he pulled her close. She did not resist. It felt good to both of them to just sit there, close to each other. They ordered souvlaki and fries, and sat silently for a few more moments.

Then Sam looked at her and said quietly. "Tell me about your childhood, why did you feel in constant danger?"

Tanya felt safe with Sam; she had begun to trust him. In low tones, she told him about growing up in a ghetto, in East London. Her Jamaican father had deserted them and she lived with her white mother and Jamaican grandmother in a one room apartment. Her mother had been a drug addict, going from one man to another. Everyday living was a nightmare. Her grandmother was fierce and none of the neighborhood gangs dared mess with her. Her mother was another story, often beaten up because she did not pay the drug dealers, trying to keep one menial job or another, she was never home.

Her grandmother and her aunt had raised her. They had instilled in her a sense of pride and not only encouraged her to study but pushed her to do well in school, so she could escape the poverty and grime of Brixton. They had also protected her, helping her develop a constant sense of awareness of her surroundings and an instinct to ward off danger. She had rarely been allowed to go out without either her grandmother or aunt accompanying her and she had had no friends in school, none were encouraged to come visit their one room shabby apartment.

She had done exceptionally well in her A levels, getting into King's College at Oxford, and then into Yale with a full scholarship for her Master's. Her beloved grandmother had died when she had been at Yale and she had grieved quietly, not being able to go back for the funeral. Her mother was long gone, and only her aunt remained. She refused to leave the neighborhood, but at least Tanya could help her by sending her money every month. She really had no place to call home or go home to, and no one either.

Sam listened, not speaking. He was beginning to understand her, at least a little. Too many walls, too much protection, he would have to be careful not to hurt her. He had really begun to care for her and for tonight at least, to protect her.

Outside, on the dark street, in a dark car, G-Lover sat slumped, in a drug induced haze, watching them.

THIRTY-NINE

There are only two people who can tell you the truth about yourself - an enemy who has lost his temper and a friend who loves you dearly. – Amfisthenes

Ares watched patiently from his abode. His plan was being set into motion and so far all was going well, but, he knew that he had to be careful. He was dealing with mere mortals and things could go wrong very fast. Plus, he had to watch the other Gods. They better not get any inkling of what he was up to. So far, all was quiet. His spies reported nothing. Athena was still floating around and Poseidon had retired to Sounion. They were still asleep as far as he was concerned.

It had been fairly easy. His gang had performed well and their greed had worked to his advantage. He had not calculated that they would try it twice, but even the second time all had gone well. And, he figured, if they could do it twice, they could do it again and again.

Banque Nationale was only small fry and just the beginning of his entire plan. He could only imagine what would happen if they managed to do this to all the large banks in the world. Wreak havoc on the entire financial system, bring it down. The entire world was connected through money and if he could control it all, he would be able to reign supreme. This was the new mode of warfare as far as he was concerned. Controlling the monetary system of the world would give him control over countries, states, people, industry…it was limitless. And who was going to stop him?

He had already created disruption and war, the world was in turmoil, it was going through very dark days and he was pleased. The plan was beginning to unfold. His mortal team, filled with the victory of the first round would be ready to go again soon, and as long as he controlled them and their base needs, all would be well.

FORTY

If you want to improve be content to be thought foolish and stupid. - Epictetus

Pythi had been feeling very frustrated. When he had first come to Athens, he had thought that he would be there for a few days, work through the glitches in the system, secure it, and move on. It had been over a month now, and he felt as if they were nowhere closer to finding either the stolen funds or those who had done it. They had recovered a faint footprint, but once again, the trail seemed to lead nowhere. He knew that Sam, Derek, and Tanya, were working overtime to uncover something, anything.

And then he saw it. It was almost three in the morning, unable to sleep, he had gone back to the basement and in the quiet of the night he saw it. A small deposit from a bank in the Cayman Islands deposited into an account at Banque Nationale. He flagged it. *Strange*, he thought. *Why is money from the Cayman Islands being deposited into a bank in Greece?* It was only a deposit of $5000, and it had been deposited yesterday. *Hmm*, he thought. *Let's check it out.* He began going through the history of the account. It had been opened several months ago, dormant until yesterday. $5000 deposited and withdrawn. *Stranger still.*

Like hundreds of other accounts they had checked out, nothing had really stood out, but now, he wanted to know more. The account had been opened in the name of Universal Alliance LLC, a Cayman Island entity. Why would they deposit and then withdraw money from a bank in Greece? He needed to know more but looking at the time realized that he simply could not wake the others, it would have to wait. Meanwhile, he was going to find out all he could about the Bank in the Caymans and this company. He told himself not to get too excited. It was probably some rich Greek person hiding their money off shore and bringing it back in small amounts to avoid paying taxes. This was not unusual. He knew that and tried not to get his hopes up.

**

G-Lover still sat in the cold car, grumbling to himself.

These people were crazy, he thought.

He had been sitting outside all evening, watching the bank. Why, he did not know, he just felt compelled to see in person, the people he was up against. Ziggy emailed them an update every night, letting them know what was going on. Ziggy was the perfect faceless, nameless, invisible person to watch them, plus he worked at the bank. He had described each one of them in detail and he had been spot on.

G-Lover had watched Tanya and Sam just a few hours ago, and then he had seen Ziggy exit the bank too. What was that all about? None of the others knew where he was and they didn't really need to know. He was really here to see Pia and tomorrow he would. He would make his way to Sounion and his future.

Especially now that he had managed to get himself enough cocaine to last him for a few weeks. It had not been easy and drugs here were very expensive, much more than in the States. The doorman at the Grand Britannia, where he was staying, had finally come through for him, but at a price, at a huge price. He had not carried that much money with him and eventually had given in and transferred money into an account he had opened a few months ago at Banque Nationale. The money had bought the drugs he so needed. He was happy now.

But, just as he thought it was safe to go back to his hotel, he saw the team leader, Pythi, walking toward the bank. *It's past one o clock and he is still working,* he thought to himself as he watched him greet the guard and go in.

He contemplated sitting there for a few more hours, but deciding against it, waited for the guard to go into the bank before he started the car and drove to the Grand Britannia hotel. The hotel was one of the oldest and most beautiful and luxurious in all of Athens. He had stayed there with his family when he was younger. The beautiful lobby was lit up with chandeliers, the marble tile floors and red carpet gleaming in their glow. But, tonight, as he got out of the car and stumbled up the stairs, the lights hurt his eyes and seemed too bright. He just wanted to get up to his room and get some rest. He felt very, very tired.

FORTY-ONE

Opposition brings concord. Out of discord comes the fairest harmony. - Heraclitus

It was past four in the morning and Pythi was still awake. Being Sunday, he decided to take the day off. He had been working too hard and in the few moments of time that he was not thinking about the problems at work, he was thinking about Pia. They had texted and spoken on the phone but he had not seen her since the amazing evening they had spent together.

On an impulse, he dressed, putting on jeans, a warm sweater and a jacket. Then running a comb through his hair, he left the spare hotel room and going down to the garage, got into his rental and drove to Sounion. He was going to meet Pia.

He stopped on the way to get gas and a cup of coffee. It was early in the morning and in Lavrion a bakery had just opened. He bought some warm croissants and then drove on to Sounion. Parking by the beach, he texted Pia.

"You awake?"

Pia was fast asleep, but slept with her cell phone right next to her. She heard the ping and was up instantly. It was a few minutes before five. She squinted at the screen and saw Pythi's message.

"I am now," she replied.

"Then get dressed and meet me at the cove by the beach."

"What beach?" She responded.

"The beach at Sounion, silly, I am waiting for you."

"Be there in a few," she replied.

Pia jumped out of bed, changed into warm sweats and a hoodie, thought for a moment about putting on a bra, then decided against it, and quietly crept to the bathroom and brushed her teeth and putting her hair up in a ponytail, grabbed a warm blanket, and quietly left the dark house, so as not to wake YahYah.

It was really dark outside, as she clambered her way down the rocks, using the short cut to the cove. He was waiting there, seated on a rock, watching her. Their eyes connected and Pia felt her knees tremble as she almost threw herself at him. He caught her and pulling her to him, kissed her soundly.

"Did you miss me as much as I missed you?" He asked.

"Did you miss me?" She asked back smiling.

"Every minute that I wasn't with you," he said.

She giggled.

"Liar, you are too caught up in your work."

"Don't remind me," he replied.

He continued to stroke her hair and her face as they gazed at each other and bantered back and forth. She was breathtaking and he could not get enough of her. Without any makeup, her lovely dark hair up in a ponytail, her beautiful eyes shining, and her soft mouth warm and trembling with his kisses, she looked lovelier than he ever could have imagined.

Picking up the coffee and croissants, he led her down the steep rocks, around the cove to the sheltered cave that the tides had battered into the rocks. It was quiet there and much warmer; the cave was sheltered from the wind. They set the coffee and box of croissants down and spreading the blanket they sat down on it.

Pythi pulled her back into his arms, till she was sitting on his lap, she did not resist. He continued kissing her, deep sensual kisses, which set her aflame as his hands sought her bare skin under her hoodie. Her skin felt warm and smooth and as his hands moved to caress her, he touched her breasts, first one then another, stroking them gently, then, increasing his touch. He felt her shudder and tremble as she moaned softly.

Unzipping the hoodie, he gazed at her beautiful bare breasts, her dark nipples erect with excitement. He stroked one breast with his hand and he bent his head and began licking and kissing the other one. Pia was moaning louder now, a deep throaty moan, her eyes closed. He moved his mouth to the other breast sucking and swirling his tongue over the hardened nipple. She trembled at his touch and he could feel the tremors running through her. She stroked his head and pulled him closer, moving back and forth on his lap, arching her back in excitement and passion. He felt her long fingers searching for his skin under his sweater, and ran her fingers along the belt of his jeans, he felt as if he was on fire, he could not get enough of her.

Still kissing and sucking on her breasts he ran his hands down her back and into the waistline of her sweat pants. He felt the curve of her soft, rounded buttocks, and the silkiness of the thong that she had on. Cupping her, he pulled her even closer, till she was on top of him; they were now lying on the blanket. She moved his head and pulled his mouth to her, stroking his face with her hands as she kissed him, deeply and with sexiness that was almost his undoing.

Her hoodie was long gone, and topless she arched over him, her lush breasts swinging as she moved on top of him. He felt her tremble uncontrollably as he slid his hand inside the thong, touching her and feeling her wetness. She was on fire as she slid his jeans and underwear down to his knees and off his legs, stroking him, till he felt like he was going to burst.

It was as if they were alone in the entire world, caught up in the sensual temptation of their desire for each other. And then, suddenly, voices broke the quiet of the early morning. The fishing boats were coming in and suddenly Pythi realized where they were and that someone could walk up to them or see them. A sense of protection poured out of him and he stopped, pulling her close and reaching for her hoodie.

Still holding her tight he continued to stroke her hair and face as she caught her breath and her heartbeat slowed down. He could feel the chill air on his naked torso and knew that she was probably getting cold too, as she lay there in the aftermath of the most erotic touching either of them had encountered. He helped her sit up and slide into the hoodie, while he zipped her up and then watched her as she slid the thong over her legs and thighs and put on her sweat pants. He then pulled on his own clothes, while she watched, her knees pulled up to her chin to stay warm.

He kissed her nose. "Thank you," he said quietly, as he pushed her hair behind her ear. Somewhere during their loving making her ponytail had come undone and her long hair now cascaded down her back, making her look even more vulnerable.

She watched him quietly, a soft smile around her lips as he brought the coffee cup up to her mouth. The coffee was cold now, but it didn't matter, it was the gentle, thoughtful way he held it to her that made her heart feel full. They sat there in silence, eating the still slightly warm croissants, sipping on the cold coffee and watching the sunrise. It was a magical moment.

Pythi knew that something had changed within him forever, Pia felt it too…

Flying above them, Athena smiled in satisfaction. She was happy; her plan was unfolding.

***

Pythi spent the rest of the day with Pia. They walked back to the house, had breakfast with YahYah, then he helped Pia load up the fresh bread and spanakopita she had baked for the restaurant atop the Sounion mountain, and together they drove it up there. After they delivered it, they walked around the ruins, hand in hand, stopping to kiss and touch frequently. It was as if they couldn't get enough of each other and couldn't bear to be apart.

Pythi pulled out his phone and took many photos of Pia as she giggled and posed for him. It was a delightful morning and for a brief time Pythi let go of all the worries and cares of his job. Soon, the tourists and tourist buses started driving up and the beautiful Temple began to get crowded with people.

They left the Temple and drove along the coast, stopping to enjoy the view and getting a warm drink. When they got back to the house, YahYah had lunch ready, fresh fish fried in a batter along with a lentil soup and salad, feta cheese and olives.

After lunch, YahYah said she was going to walk over to one of the neighbors to visit with them. Pythi and Pia cuddled on the rug in front of the wood burning fireplace, wrapped in blankets and took a nap, holding each other.

When it was time for Pythi to leave, they stood by the car, holding each other, as if they couldn't let go. It was hard for both of them. Pia knew that her feelings for him ran deep but she was afraid to say anything, not knowing how he felt about her yet. Pythi knew he was in love, deeply in love, he had never felt this way before. He wanted to hold her and protect her, to love her and make love to her, and never let her go, but he didn't want to scare her with the intensity of his feelings. He hoped that in time he would be able to bare his soul and let her know exactly how he felt. For now, he hoped his kisses and caresses told her how he felt about her.

Giving her one last kiss, he let her go and stepped into the car, waving as he drove away. Pia felt a real sense of loss as she saw him leave. She felt, almost….empty.

Going back into the house, she decided to do some writing and go to bed early.

Poseidon, sitting on his favorite rock, watched all the activity and smiled to himself. Love, loving, and being loved was something he knew a lot about.

FORTY-TWO

Happy is he who has gained the wealth of divine thoughts,
wretched is he whose beliefs about the gods are dark. – Empedocles

When he finally woke up it was late Sunday evening. He had slept through the entire day. He remembered sitting in the car all afternoon outside the Banque. He remembered coming back to the hotel, doing some cocaine and then crashing; he had felt so tired, bone tired.

But, he was up now, and after calling for room service and doing some more cocaine, he was invincible. He was ready to implement the second phase. After checking in with the others and making sure that they had all executed their tasks and that all was secure, he logged into the Banque and the accounts...and watched with deep pleasure as he saw the numbers roll by on his screen. It only took a few minutes.

Then, checking all the bank accounts to make sure that the transfers were done, he logged onto the secure Cloud that they had set up and sent them a message, "My friends, I just played the game again and won! Looking forward to the next round. Take care." Logging off and turning off his computer for safety, he took a shower and began to dress. He was hungry again. It was time to go out, get some food and prepare for his visit to Sounion.

In the Banque basement, Tanya and Sam were working side by side. They had not heard from Pythi all day and didn't want to bother him. He really had needed a break. Derek was out on a date with a girl he had met at the hotel bar. He had called Sam and told him that he was going to take the day off too.

They had both received secure emails from Pythi to track the account activity, the Cayman account at the Banque. They had worked at it all afternoon, wondering why Pythi would be interested in an account with no money in it. They were looking for large amounts of money, millions of dollars, hundreds of millions of dollars, and they were feeling really frustrated about having to spend a Sunday afternoon researching an account that seemed to be going nowhere.

Sam was convinced that the account belonged to some Greek seaman, someone who probably worked in the merchant marine, who had stopped in the Cayman Islands, opened an account there, deposited his paycheck, and was now cashing it in since he had come home to Greece.

Not much here to worry about, he thought to himself, *Pythi is wasting our time.*

***

Pythi drove back at a leisurely pace. He enjoyed the cool air and sang to himself as he drove along. Soon, he was caught up in the bottleneck of Sunday night traffic in the city. Athenians leave the city in droves on the weekend to visit nearby towns, beaches, and islands and, on Sunday night when everyone is returning, traffic can be horrendous. But, Pythi thought to himself: *I am not in a hurry, I am not going to let sitting in traffic bother me today.*

He thought of Pia and the lovely day they had spent together. They had talked a lot during the day and he really felt he was getting to know her. He was learning her expressions, the little furrow in her eyebrow when she was thinking, or when she bit on her lower lip, deep in thought. He loved the look of her glazed eyes, wide with passion when he made love to her, or the soft look of her face when she closed her eyes as they kissed. He admired how bright and intelligent she was and so articulate. *Hmm,* he thought, *I am really into her, like I have never been with any other woman.* He missed her already. He had never really missed any other woman, work had always come first, and while he worked, he had the ability to put all other thoughts aside. But, somehow, Pia kept floating back into his thoughts and his mind. He smiled to himself, feeling content.

Suddenly, he felt his phone go off in his pocket. Pulling it out, he saw it was a call from the States. The traffic was moving now and he couldn't answer the phone. He would call back as soon as he reached the hotel. The phone went off again. This time it was not the office number, it was his boss' cell phone, and then the text messages began to flow in. It was a 911 situation; he knew what that meant. There was a crisis and he needed to get to his computer as soon as possible and wait for further instructions. In between texts, Tanya and Derek called and by the time he reached the hotel, dropped off the car and ran up to his room to get to his computer, the sense of peace he had felt all day had completely vanished. Some new development or something big was going down and he had to get to a secure line as soon as possible and wait to be contacted.

FORTY-THREE

Reserve the right to think, for even to think wrongly is better than to not think at all. - Hypatia

Late into the night, early morning really, Pythi was laying on his bed, hands behind his neck, going over the day's events, waiting for the communications to come in. All these endless days of work followed by nights of worry over the Banque Nationale security breach had left him drained and disheartened. But now, there was a dim light at the end of the tunnel, there was a faint trace of the perpetrators, that although it did not lead anywhere at the moment, had the hidden promise of discovery. Thank God for Pia. She had brought magic into his life and gave a truly unreal twist to all this.

Pythi paused to go over what they knew so far. The firewalls of the bank system had not been breached; no signs of intrusion were detected by any of the myriad diagnostics he and his team had run. Whoever these people were, had found an ingenious way to either bypass the system, or infiltrate it undetected and they had managed to gain access to the bank's accounts and inner workings. But how did they do it? The bank's system was quite robust and there was no record of previous violations or trespasses. It would take some real detective work to unravel this one.

The phone rang pulling him abruptly out of his reverie. *Who in the world is calling at this ungodly hour,* he thought to himself, *I hope it is Pia.* He glanced at the screen of his smart phone to recognize the personal number of his boss in New York City, the call he had been waiting for all this time.

He answered, "For God's sake, we get precious little sleep as it is, and now you have me stand by for hours into the night as well?"

"Take it easy, Pythi. There is news that I think you need to know, but I had to do some cross-checking first and settle arrangements. Switch to the secure mode on the computer and we will talk there." Once on the secure line, Pythis' boss continued, "This thing seems to be spreading over into the Middle East. My connection at the Bank of Dubai, Ahmed, a long standing client, called me. They have detected transactions they cannot explain and they suspect infiltration. Their resident IT and security people cannot spot anything wrong or unusual, but large amounts of money have started disappearing and they are very worried. Ahmed is desperate for help. They have a good crew that can do the leg work but they need a security expert to lead them. What do you say spending a few days in Dubai?"

"But," said Pythi, "We are buried here in Athens; you want me to drop this, leave my team alone and go chasing mirages in the desert?"

"These two incidents, Athens and Dubai, may be connected. If so, a visit to Dubai may give you a valuable insight into the perpetrators' minds that will help to connect the dots. Plus, a change in locale may clear your head and help you start seeing things differently. I think it will be good. In addition, we will strengthen our ties with the Emiratis. There is an Emirates Airline flight from Eleftherios Venizelos airport in the afternoon tomorrow. It's only a four and half hour flight to Dubai and flying business on Emirates is a treat in itself. You'll like it."

"I suppose I can meet the team in the morning," said Pythi, "Set priorities and fly over to Dubai in the afternoon, but..."

An idea started developing in his head and taking form and shape by the second, a beautiful form and prettier shape. He was already missing Pia and wanted her to go along with him.

"I'll need a generous budget and some flexibility," Pythi continued.

"That should not be a problem and I believe I can work it out with Ahmed, so long as we keep him happy," said his boss, "Now get some sleep, you have long days and possibly nights ahead of you, You'll need every ounce of rest you can get. Good night, Pythi, and be good...or, at least be careful."

Pythi hung up and immediately dialed Pia. A few rings later a sleepy Pia answered the phone to hear that she was being invited to go with Pythi and that they were to be flying together tomorrow afternoon to Dubai for a few days.

"But..." Pia started saying not entirely sure if this was really happening or it was part of her interrupted dreams.

"Don't argue with me, love. Trust me on this, you will love it. YahYah will approve, I have no doubt. Just pack for a few days in the morning and meet me at Venizelos airport. I'll call with the timings. Sleep well...and dream of me."

"I was," said Pia, "And you were naughty. Good night, we'll talk in the morning."

She turned over, hugged her pillow tightly and went back to her dream with a wide smile on her relaxed, happy face.

FORTY-FOUR
Wisdom begins in wonder. - Socrates

Pia waited after the morning coffee and koulourakia to announce the Dubai plan to YahYah. She did it hesitantly expecting objections from the old lady. To her surprise, YahYah's face lit up and she exclaimed, "Pia mou, Pia mou, and you are not packing yet? I like that boy!"

The rest of the morning had been a blur of excitement and activity.

She got online and made plans with zeal and enthusiasm. A few hours later she had filled several pages of notes that formed their plans for good times to come in the Emirate of Dubai. Then, she called a taxi cab, kissed YahYah goodbye and settled in the back seat for the half hour trip to the airport, making mundane conversation with the taxi driver along the way.

When she arrived at the airport, Pythi was already waiting at the Emirates check-in counter. They kissed lightly and checked their luggage to a smiling and very courteous ground crew. Then, Pythi took her by the hand and lead her to the open café 'Grigoris' just outside the check in area. "Come, I want to introduce you to my favorite Greek drug," he said with a mischievous smile. They took a table and he went to the kiosk type bar to place his order. A few minutes later he returned with two cappuccinos and two pieces of some kind of pastry pie. "The Greeks call this spanakotyropita, spinach and feta cheese pie, and it is baked in thick phylo pastry crust, the peasant way, as they do it in the villages. I warn you, once you taste this, the craving of it will be imprinted on your taste buds and there will be no relief, unless you bite into it again and again. Think twice before you accept this addiction." She laughed a happy, playful laugh and took a bite.

"Yummy," she exclaimed, "This is really, really good!"

They ate and sipped on their cappuccinos for a white chatting and sharing ideas about the next few days in the desert until boarding time. They avoided the long line at the gate going through the VIP check-in and before long they were seated in the comfortable easy chairs of the business class section of the airplane, a brand new Airbus 380. They were welcomed on board with a glass of champagne and moist warm towels, and throughout the flight the refills kept coming, with a selection of cheeses first, a luxurious elegant meal, and a lovely arrangement of dessert bites afterwards. It was the first time that Pythi was not hit with the all familiar feeling of claustrophobia he usually felt when on board a plane. When the pilot announced the beginning of their descent to Dubai International airport, Pia leaned tenderly toward Pythi and with glazed eyes, whispered in his ear, "I can really get used to this." He laughed, kissed her on the lips, and faking a stiff demeanor, "This is only the beginning of an unforgettable adventure, my lady!"

Landing at concourse one at Dubai International at a little after eight pm, they wasted no time at lengthy passport and immigration control lines thanks to their business class fast-track passes. However, the immensity of the terminal and the great number of passengers going through it left them in amazement. "No wonder this is the second busiest airport in the world," mused Pythi, "The gateway between Asia and the Western world!"

Once they finished with the formalities and found themselves outside the terminal, they looked for the shuttle to 'The Address,' the five star hotel near Dubai Mall where they were staying. It was then that she noticed the two rows of waiting taxis. One featured regularly dressed male taxi drivers, but the other row consisted of cabs with a pink sign on the roof and the drivers were women in uniform and with a pink scarf.

"I want to ride in this," Pia exclaimed, jumping up and down like a little girl, "In the pink one," pointing to the first pink cab in the line. "My lady's wish is my command," replied Pythi laughing. "I think these are for conservative local ladies that do not want to ride in a male-driven taxi, or they feel safer with a female driver. Whatever tickles your fancy Pia, habibti!"

"I see you have been brushing up on your Arabic, Pythi, habibi; I have too. I'm impressed, and shukran - thank you - for going along with my wish," said Pia. They teased each other as they rolled their luggage towards the waiting pink taxi.

FORTY-FIVE
Youth is the best time to be rich, and the best time to be poor. - Euripides

The taxi driver, a Moroccan woman with charm and accented but good English, helped them load their luggage in the 'boot' of the car and took it upon herself to become their tour guide during the drive from the airport to the hotel 'The Address'. Once on Maktoum Bridge, she pointed to the right and explained that they were looking at the Dubai Creek waterway which connected to the Persian Gulf, known locally as Khaleej al Arabi, the Arabian Gulf. This has been the heart of maritime commerce with Iran and the neighboring countries since the days Dubai was a fishing village, not so long ago. The world class port in Jebel Ali, outside the city to the south, fills this role now, although the Creek is still commercially active in addition to being an entertainment hub with water activities and is bustling with night life.

"To the left is Festival City, a fairly new addition to Dubai, and ahead is the majestic Dubai skyline which is famous, at least in this part of the world. That lit needle-like, very tall building in the distance is Burj Khalifa, the tallest building in the world. It took five years to build. The Saudis are building an even taller one, one kilometer high, as we speak, can you imagine? You see, Arabs love to outdo each other, especially the ones with money," she said laughingly. "Arabic ego is a stout motivator...and an annoying hindrance, sometimes," and she laughed louder.

They had left the bridge and to the right a pyramid like structure with an illuminated cornerstone caught the attention of Pythi."I thought we were in the Emirates not Egypt. This is a beautifully decorated pyramid complete with hieroglyphics and Egyptian statutes, exclaimed Pythi. What is it?"

"Ah, this is the luxurious Raffle hotel and the attached mall at different levels is called the Wafi. I like the Middle Eastern restaurant, coffee and shisha bar in the basement. I go there sometimes for shisha and mezeh. It has a retractable roof that they open in good weather and although you are in the basement of the pyramid, you look at the sky overhead and have the impression that you are at an astronomical observatory on some mountaintop. It's nice and the cuisine is from all over the Middle East and the Mediterranean."

"What is shisha," asked Pia, "And what is mezeh?"

"Shisha is a Middle Eastern past time," laughed the driver. "The Iranians call it hookah and in Turkey it is known as nargile. Now, for mezeh, these are the little plates with different types of prepared food that you pick and choose from. We, Arabs, are not big on individual main dishes, we like variety and we like to share. We are a very hospitable people and eating is a social event to share with family and friends," continued the gregarious Moroccan.

By that time they had entered a well-lit highway lined with skyscrapers on both sides.

"Wow," both Pythi and Pia marveled. The driver laughed her hearty laugh and remarked that it is a typical reaction of a first timer to Dubai. "Some of the most famous Architects in the world have designed these building that give Dubai its unique and famous skyline.

Pia and Pythi were all eyes and ears taking it all in, reading the signs on the facade of the buildings that towered over them. The Shangri La hotel on the right, the Dusit Thani on the left, and "What are those sea shell type structures every so often along the road to the left, in front of the buildings," asked Pia.

"Oh, these are the metro stations. The Dubai metro is the first one in the region and its line is designed on monopiles, the large pillars you see running parallel to the road. Everyone wants to come and live in Dubai, a haven of peace and prosperity in a region that has suffered so with the Arab spring turmoil."

"This is the Dubai Mall," pointed the driver soon, "The biggest in the world, and your hotel is part of it. Burj Khalifa is also here and construction of the new Opera house is also underway. You'll enjoy staying in this area; so much to see and do. Make sure not to miss the fantastic dancing waters show. Dubai has spent two hundred and fifty million dollars to design and build those dancing fountains. Also, the huge floor to ceiling aquarium in the mall; the whole world is talking about it."

With that, she navigated the taxi up a marble rotary ramp and brought it to a stop at the lavish entrance to the hotel. A well-dressed valet was waiting to help them out of the taxi, welcome them to The Address

Downtown, and help them with their luggage. They thanked their talkative taxi driver cum tour guide and Pythi paid for the fare leaving a generous tip.

"Shukran, shukran," she said bowing to Pythi. Then turning to Pia with a mischievous smile, she said, "Enjoy Dubai pretty lady, but be careful of the Moroccan women. With such a good looking and generous man as yours, they wouldn't be able to help themselves. We do have a reputation in these parts, you know..." She winked at Pia and she was off, down the ramp and into city traffic.

FORTY-SIX

Time is the most valuable thing a man can spend. - Theophrastus

Pia and Pythi checked in and spent some time getting used to the space and opulence of their suite on the eighteenth floor. From this height, they could see the lights of Dubai stretching all the way to the sea. Also visible was Palm Jumeirah, the artificial island in the shape of a palm tree, like it was flowering from the land into the water. It was as if they were living a wonderful dream and neither was too eager to wake up from it. Security problems, work, hackers and troubleshooting all seemed so distant to Pythi at this moment. He knew that all this would come rushing back in the morning, but tonight it was the beginning of a magical trip and he was planning to miss not a single moment of it.

"The dancing water show is at ten and the terrace overlooking the huge pool is the best place to view it from," the concierge had said and they were planning to be there. After freshening up, they took the elevator to the lobby and, stepping out to the terrace in the back of the hotel, they picked a table at the edge with a peripheral view of the pool and in full sight of the well-lit Burj Khalifa towering over them. The place was filling up quickly as the hour for the show was approaching. They ordered cappuccinos, with cinnamon for Pythi and chocolate for Pia, sat next to each other and quietly took in the view in front of them.

"This is beautiful," said Pia, "I'm so glad you asked me to come on this trip." Pythi squeezed her hand tenderly and before he could say another thing, the flood lights in the pool and around it, as well as the lights of the Burj Khalifa went out. There were a few moments of expectant silence and then from myriad loudspeakers the melodic notes of Swan Lake filled the air of the outdoor area of the Mall. Immediately, and on cue, the hidden under water fountains came to life shooting their waters in artistic formation and in synch with the music; paired with synchronized flood light displays. It was a beautiful audiovisual show of beauty and harmony as liquid beams of light danced around to the music through lows and highs, coming to a glorious crescendo at the end. As the music stopped, Pia jumped to her feet and clapping enthusiastically, she exclaimed, "Bravo, bravo, that was just beautiful, wasn't it Pythi?"

"Magnificent", he replied, still mesmerized, "That was a thing of beauty!"

Many more water dances followed and they watched them all with occasional breaks to sip on their cappuccinos and the refills that followed, totally into each other, awed by the show, the surroundings and each other. It was as if the rest of the world did not exist, just the two of them and their budding love in this majestic little world of music, light and water.

FORTY-SEVEN

...There is the heat of love, the pulsing rush of longing, the lover's whisper, irresistible – magic to make the sanest man go mad. - Homer

Thus far the evening had been magical. Once again, Pia marveled at how much she enjoyed being with Pythi. They were really comfortable with each other, the conversation flowed easily; she loved the sexual tension between them and how they constantly had to be touching each other, a brush of the hand, his fingers stroking her face, or playing with her hair, the deep longing look in his eyes. All of it gave her butterflies in her tummy and made her heart beat faster. She was not only mesmerized by him, by his intelligence, but also by his thoughtfulness. He had gone to great lengths to make sure that she was okay and that sharing the same suite did not make her uncomfortable.

While she had showered and dressed for the evening, he had sat outside on the spacious patio, overlooking the city and the Arabian Sea, giving her the space she needed to get dressed, and he had not been disappointed. When she had emerged on the balcony in an ivory sheath with lace trim, silver stiletto heels and a cloud of soft perfume around her she had taken his breath away. He wanted to love her...to protect her, forever.

But, putting those thoughts aside, he had pulled her into his arms and kissed her with a fervor that took her breath away and made her feel like taking him into the bedroom and pulling him onto the bed and forgetting all about their evening plans.

He had pulled away, and taking her hand, led her out of the suite, so that they could go see the Dancing Fountains. The balmy evening, the beauty of the fountains and the swish of the water had set the mood for the rest of the evening. In the Middle East, dinner is a late affair and after watching the fountains, they walked to a nearby restaurant with delicious

Lebanese food and music. The music added to the mood, it was at first soft and lilting but as the evening wore on, and the excitement of the on-coming belly dancer began to grow, the music got more sensuous. Pia and Pythi ate the delicious food and sipped on the wine they had ordered, while nibbling on the kebab, kibe rolls (balls of deep fried meat), baba ghanoush (eggplant salad), and hot, freshly made flat bread. Pia was enchanted; the colors, the flavors, the music, all made the experience very exotic and with her heightened senses, she was even more aware of Pythi's presence beside her.

She felt him watching her as she enjoyed the dancing and swayed in her seat to the music. She knew that he was not looking at the dancing; it was her that he was interested in, and she relished the moment. After a leisurely dinner, the waiter brought out the shisha, which initially she was loathe to try, but after some persuasion and picking an apple flavored one, she agreed to try it. At first, it wasn't very pleasant and she had to keep herself from choking but she soon got into it and enjoyed how relaxed it made her feel…or maybe it was the wine, she wasn't sure.

Pythi was enjoying every moment too. He was mesmerized by Pia. He loved her reactions to all that she was being exposed to and she seemed to be really happy to try all the new experiences and enjoy them. He thought how much more fun and fulfilling his life would be if she could always travel with him. He could not get enough of her and reached for her hand under the table, intertwining his fingers with hers and stroking her thumb. He felt her quiver at his touch and at that moment he wanted to grab her and run up to their room, but she was enjoying herself too much and he sensed that she was not ready to leave.

It was almost an hour later that they decided to go to their suite. The tension between them was palpable. He had played with her fingers under the table, she had stroked his thigh with soft brushing strokes and they had spent long minutes gazing into each other's eyes, not speaking, just looking, devouring, and enjoying.

For Pythi, the walk back was almost unbearable. He knew that he was in the Middle East, where there was a different sense of decorum and as much as he wanted to pull her against him and hold her, he couldn't as they were in a public area. They walked into the hotel and made it into the elevator, where he pulled her close and held her to him. On reaching their floor they walked hand in hand to the door of the suite, which Pythi unlocked swiftly and let them in.

Locking the door behind them, he pulled her close, kissing her, running his hands down her back, as he entwined her fingers around his neck. In a tight embrace, bodies touching, they kissed as if they could not get enough of each other. He picked her up easily and carried her to the bedroom and laid her gently on the bed, running his fingers down the length of her body as she lay on the bed looking up at him, her eyes dark with passion.

He reached down and pulled off her shoes, one by one, then ran his hands up her long smooth legs, caressing her calves, and stroking her thighs. He could feel her body tremble but she did not stop him. She reached up and stroked his face and neck and slowly began to unbutton his shirt, running her fingers across his chest, stroking him. He turned her over and unzipped her dress, sliding it over her shoulders and down her body, looking at her beautiful body in the soft light and taking in her curves as he stroked the swell of her full breasts still cupped by her lace bra. He ran his fingers and then his lips down her neck, caressing and kissing her breast through the bra, till she was moaning, her eyes closed, as she stroked his hair and pulled him closer.

She helped him out of his shirt and watched him unzip his pants. The bed had been turned down for the night and on the soft pillows the night staff had placed delicious heart shaped chocolates. Pythi, fed her the chocolates and watched her tongue and her lips sensuously lick and taste the chocolate, then he kissed her again, and leaning over unhooked her bra, caressing her naked breasts, sucking on her nipples till they were hard and she was crying his name, wanting more.

She reached down and slid his underwear off him, feeling his hardness against her, stroking it, playing with it, as he continued his exploration of her body, kissing, licking, and touching every curve, her legs parting for his touch, her thighs trembling with anticipation as his tongue kissed her tummy and went lower. He slid her thong off her easily and played with the inside of her thighs till he touched her and began to stroke her in that most intimate of places.

Bending his head, he began to lick her and he could feel her breath hitch as he continued licking and playing with her. She was calling his name and he could feel the tension building within her as he placed his body over hers and parting her thighs, felt himself enter her moistness. She cried out, begging for more and together, they began moving in rhythmic harmony. She ran her hands down his muscled back, pulling him even closer into herself. They began to move in unison, their hearts beating as one, aware of nothing but their deep desire for each other, moving faster and faster, till in an unstoppable crescendo, they reached the pinnacle. She felt every nerve and cell in her body ignite and carry her on the wave of love as he let go and joined her, together, coming together as one.

Eventually, he rolled off her and still holding her close, he asked her if she was okay. Sensuous and slow, in the aftermath of their passion, she reached for him too. He asked her if she would stay with him and nodding her agreement, she rolled into him, entwining her legs with his. He kissed her slumberous body and still holding each other, they fell asleep, naked in each other's arms.

FORTY-EIGHT

Observe due measure, for right timing is in all things the most important factor. - Hesiod

It was not easy for Pythi to wake up after all that happened the previous night. More so that it was Sunday, a day of rest for the western world, but not in Dubai. Sunday was the first day of the working week here and it was as bad as Monday elsewhere.

He finally forced himself out of the bed careful not to wake Pia and stepped into the shower for a cold one. By eight thirty he was on the ground floor of the hotel and walked into the restaurant, marveling at the buffet breakfast that was available covering just about any taste from the West all the way to the Far East. *Nah,* he fought back the urge to gorge, *coffee and a croissant will do just fine. I need to get going, Ahmed should be waiting for me.* Banking hours were short in this part of the world, eight to one only. He needed to talk to people, assess the team on the ground, check their systems out, coordinate with Ahmed and set up a systematic evaluation before one o'clock.

I hope Pia will find something interesting to do while I'm gone, he thought to himself chewing on his last bite of his almond croissant. He asked for a cup of coffee to go and approached the valet desk for a taxi.

The Filipino valet was quick to explain that the Central Office of the Bank of Dubai was only ten minutes away on foot and with this nice weather it would be very pleasant. However, if 'Sir Pythi' was in a hurry, there were always two to three taxi cabs standing by outside. Pythi opted for the ride and four minutes later was entering the bank building.

"Mr. Ahmed Dajani, please," he inquired, "He is expecting me," and he handed his card to the uniformed doorman. "Just a minute, Sir. May I offer you some Arabic coffee while you are waiting?"

"No, thank you, as you can see I brought my own," said Pythi pointing to the cup he was holding. The doorman smiled and disappeared in the back offices to announce Pythi. A minute later, a jovial, mustached, middle aged man arrived and introduced himself as 'Mr. Ahmed, Director.'

"Welcome, welcome to Dubai, I hope your flight was uneventful and you had a chance to get some rest last night. Please come back into my office. What can I offer you? Coffee, tea, some sweets, perhaps?" Pythi declined politely and apologized for being direct, but he had little time and he wanted to do the best with it.

"We are very concerned," started Mr. Ahmed, a dramatic expression taking over his face. "The account of one of our most influential clients seems to have been compromised and we don't know how or to what extent. It came to our attention only because his accountant is a very diligent one and he noticed irregularities during reconciliation. We do not know if this is the only account affected or if there are more. Obviously, it is a matter of trust with our wealthy clients, many of which are part of the royal family, so our Management was quick to ask for your services. Your company has served us well in the past and I hear that you are one of the best in the field. I am glad you are here and hope that you detect the problem very soon and fix it. The last thing we need is nasty rumors to spread that this is an unsafe bank. It would be a disaster."

"I'll do my best, Sir, but I will need your help," replied Pythi.

"Anything you need, my friend, just ask for it," reassured the bank executive. "Where do we start?"

"First off, I need you to introduce me to your IT and security teams and put them under my direction. I am alone here and I'll need every skilled man you have available to help me. There is a lot of tedious work that needs to get done. They need to be prepared to work long hours for a few days, until we get a handle on the situation. Everything needs to be questioned, doubted, tested, and evaluated. In situations as this, we assume the worse and allow ourselves to be surprised pleasantly by the not-so-bad. Would that be a problem?"

"Walah, not a problem at all, habibi! I'll call an emergency meeting in the conference room right away. Inshallah, with your guidance, we will solve this embarrassing problem and go about our routine very soon. Nothing more reassuring in the life of a banker than boring routine!" With that, he picked up the telephone receiver and in a stern voice he placed orders in Arabic.

"Done," he said, "They will gather in twenty minutes. Let me give you a quick tour of our premises in the meanwhile."

FORTY-NINE
God loves to help him who strives to help himself. - Aeschylus

Director Ahmed, like a good host, walked Pythi through all four floors of the bank building, stopping to introduce him to division managers and explaining that Pythi was a well reputed expert that would be with them for a few days on a routine security check of all systems.

"Nothing out of the ordinary," he explained, "Just to make sure that all systems are a go and there are no glitches. Please extend the gentleman our traditional Arabic hospitality and any assistance he may require or need. Mr. Pythagoras has the trust of the bank and please deal with him as you would deal with me. We have afforded him full and complete clearance of the highest level."

On the way to the Conference Room, to meet the bank team entrusted with security and information technology and management, Ahmed asked him to try and keep a low profile with his investigation. "Only people that will work closely with you need to know the real reason of your presence here, Mr. Pythagoras. There is no reason to raise suspicions, anxiety and brew panic prematurely. That way it will be easier for you and things will be calm for us as well."

Pythi agreed, and they walked into the Conference room where half a dozen people were waiting for them. There were two IT employees, Sabu and Joyson, Indians from Kerala, who appeared to be well experienced about information technology. The head of security, Mr. Ghazi; Rodrigo, the security booth operator (cameras and other security equipment), and two Pakistani security guards.

After the introductions, Mr. Ahmed proceeded to give the story of regular inspections and checks and asked everyone to cooperate with Pythi without any reservation. At the request of Pythi, Mr. Ahmed dismissed the security guards to return to their patrol duty and kept Ghazi, Rodrigo, Sabu and Joyson for deliberations.

"Gentlemen," Pythi addressed the team, "I'm here alone. My team is in Athens addressing a serious bank security issue, not unlike yours, so I'll need your help and dedication to try to get to the bottom of this. But, first things first. This is highly confidential and it goes beyond what Mr. Ahmed said. It is very important that you do not talk about this to anyone. As a matter of fact, Mr. Ahmed will ask you to sign non-disclosure agreements. If you accept to sign them and you talk to anyone about this you will be legally liable, meaning you can end up in prison and then be deported from the UAE, if you break your promise. Is that clear and are there any objections?"

"What happens if we refuse to sign?" Asked one of the Keralites.

"You'll be asked to go on a leave of absence until the investigation is over, and then you can return.

This is very serious and the reputation of the bank is at stake," jumped in Mr. Ahmed.

They all signed the NDA's Mr. Ahmed put in front of them and Pythi continued:

"There are large sums of money withdrawn out of an important client's busy account but they do not seem to reconcile at a specific location or in a particular way. The money seems to have vanished into cyberspace. We have faced the same problem in Athens and we have started calling them ghost accounts. Our experience there has taught us a few things and we'll try to use those lessons to cut down on the time of the investigation here. Our objective is to find out where does this money go and how do these people do it? If we answer these two questions correctly, the answers should lead us to the perpetrators."

Pythi took a few gulps of water to clear his throat and collect his thoughts and then, he continued:

"Since we know so little we have to be systematic, thorough, and we will try to narrow down our targets by elimination of non-possibilities. We are shorthanded, so we have to be efficient. Sabu and Joyson, I want you to start scanning the entire bank system of electronic security and all its branches, intra- and inter-net based, using your standard diagnostic tools. Test everything. We are looking for breaches, intrusions, infiltrations, by passes and anything unusual; anything at all strange that comes up on your screens, I want to know about right away. How long do you think it will take you?"

"Sir," Sabu volunteered, "If both of us work long hours, and ignore our regular duty, we should be able to complete everything in about three days. If we have to perform our daily functions as well, we probably need ten days, minimum."

Mr. Ahmed jumped in, "You two are dedicated to this investigation starting tomorrow. I'll bring replacements from the not-so-busy branches to take over your duties, with some direction and guidance from you, of course."

"Very good," noted Pythi, "So you, Sabu and Joyson, may go tie up any loose ends and I expect your undivided attention and dedication by tomorrow morning."

After the Indians had departed, Pythi turned to Rodrigo. "Rod, I need you to go back to your hard drives with the video recordings of all the security cameras for the past month. I want you to scrutinize them for anything unusual, out of the ordinary, even suspicious looking people and action. Are we clear?"

"But, Sir," Rodrigo started protesting, "This is a lot of work and I have my regular duties..."

Before Pythi could respond, Mr. Ghazi jumped in this time, "Just do as Mr. Pythagoras asks, I'll get you help tomorrow." Rodrigo nodded and left the room as Mr. Ghazi was reassuring Pythi that he would be personally involved in the recordings evaluation.

"Two pairs of eyes are much better than one, no?" Remarked Mr. Ghazi, as he was exiting the room.

Mr. Ahmed and Pythi were left alone; Pythi turned to him and said, "Mr. Ahmed, we now need to start looking at your big accounts. I don't believe these people have hit only one account. Please pick five of your most important and busy accounts and have a competent accountant assigned to each. Have them trace every single transaction to its resolution and if there is not clear and complete reconciliation, have them mark it as irregular. The more often they siphon money to a ghost account, the higher the possibility they will be careless or make a mistake. This sweeping of select large accounts should help us assess the extent of the infiltration and damage, and if there is a mistake, I want to latch on to it and ride it all the way to its source."

"Consider it done, I'll put my best people on it," said Mr. Ahmed, "And Mr. Pythagoras…I am glad you are here, habibi!"

"Shukran, Mr. Ahmed. Please call me Pythi. Pythagoras sounds so...ancient," and he smiled.

FIFTY
You cannot teach a crab to walk straight. - Aristophanes

Meanwhile, in Athens, Tanya, Sam, and Derek, continued the tedious work of tracking the "ghost" accounts. It was as if a tornado had hit and simply sucked the money out of the bank, with no way to track where it went. They saw it over and over again. They now had dossiers full of accounts with funds not reconciled, and they were working hard to find a pattern.

Tanya had gone back to the account that Pythi had flagged over and over again. A Cayman island account with a small deposit and a quick withdrawal. This was the only account that did not seem to have a pattern or fit the other "ghost" transfers.

Derek checked on the account information. If anyone could track down information on the web, it was Derek. But once again, he found a dead end. The company, Universal Alliance, LLC, had been incorporated over a year ago but beyond that there was no more information. He tried pulling up the incorporation papers, no, nothing there. It had been incorporated by a legal entity but when he followed that lead it turned out to be a legal mill run on the Internet; no leads there.

The three of them were feeling really frustrated and being Monday morning in Athens had recently heard the news of the Bank in Dubai and Pythi's hasty departure to Dubai. It was spreading and they had no clues. But, as they discussed, there were always clues, they just had not found them yet. They also understood now that whoever was doing this had a plan and was extremely knowledgeable. They were also in agreement that it had to be more than one person, a group? A pair?

Tanya sipped on her coffee, and the three of them made desultory conversation as they continued looking at their computer screens.

Come on, she thought, looking at her computer screen, *show me who you are, give me a clue?* Following Pythi's instructions, she had the Cayman account tagged; any activity and she would know within minutes.

At approximately 10:30 in the morning the flagged window started beeping. Tanya sat up in her chair, clicked over and opened the window. There was an eight thousand euro deposit from the Cayman account into the Greek account. *Whoa.* She called out to the others, they came running over and looked at it. Both Derek and Sam still believed that it belonged to a Greek seaman who was transferring his money into Greece in small amounts so as not to be detected. The Caymans were a tax haven and this way whoever it was could avoid paying taxes. In the normal course of banking business this account would never have attracted any attention. The three of them would not have paid it any attention had it not been for Pythi. They all knew to trust Pythi's instinct. He had often been right and if he felt that there was something odd with the account and that it needed to be tracked and watched, they would do it, even against their own doubts.

The account went dormant again, and Tanya sat back in her chair, going back to the tedious work of examining the accounts. Sam was checking all the security filters to detect the breach, and Derek was working with Pythi on a long distance call, discussing accounts in Dubai.

About two hours later, the account went active again. Tanya clicked over and sat up. There had been a withdrawal of seven and a half thousand euro. She continued to read the detail and then with a yell, knocking over her chair, she ran to the stairs, racing upstairs as fast as she could. She had to go faster, but her knees began to feel weak as she raced up the stairs to the lobby. She burst into the Banque's administrative area racing toward the Teller stations and then stopped dead in her tracks. There were long lines at all the Teller stations. She ran to the Manager's office and burst in.

"Please," she said, pulling at his hand, "I need you to go with me to teller station no. 10. It is very urgent."

The manager was already rising out of his chair, keys in hand, as they raced out of his office toward the locked door that led to the teller stations. He unlocked the door and Tanya ran to the teller station no. 10, shouting to the manager as she ran to lock down the Banque. The Manager started yelling to security and people began to start scurrying and moving sensing an emergency. Tanya almost pushed the Teller aside as she took over her computer and began pulling up the previous transactions.

She got to the one she was looking for.

"Did you see this person?" She asked the teller.

The teller nodded.

"Was it a man?" She asked.

"Yes," the teller responded, nodding her head, sweating and alarmed.

"Did you speak to him?" Tanya demanded.

"Yes," nodded the teller. "He no Greek, maybe tourist," she added in broken English.

"Do you still see him?" Tanya demanded. "Look around, is he still in the Banque?"

The teller craned her neck and looked around.

"No, he not here, he wear cap like American tourist. He say thank you and leave."

Tanya looked toward the door. The Banque was in lockdown and people were gathering on both sides. She led the Teller through the Banque, making her look at each person closely. But no, the person was gone.

***

G-Lover had seen Tanya come racing up the stairs and had hurried out minutes before the Banque had gone into lockdown. He wondered what she had been looking for. There was no way they were looking for him, he had covered his tracks well and no one knew he was in Greece. Now that he had money, he was going to take a shower and head to Sounion. He blended into the street like any tourist on the busy streets of Athens; no one gave him a second glance.

Inside the bank, Ziggy had just clocked in when the lockdown had taken place. No one knew what it was about and some of the employees complained that they could not go out to smoke. Few of the Banque workers actually knew what was going on. They had heard of the team of Americans working in the basement but they did not know why. The Tellers had all been briefed to report any unusual transactions or people that they felt were suspicious, and so far, the breach had not been reported outside the confines of the Banque. The Management was hoping to get it solved soon and have the perpetrators brought to justice.

The lockdown was soon lifted and Tanya frustrated and angry went back down to the basement. She explained the whole situation to Sam and Derek.

"Whoever it was, he was right here at the Banque withdrawing funds, I missed him by a few minutes and guys, it is not a Greek seaman. The Teller said over and over again that it was a foreigner, a tourist, she thought. So let's drop the seaman theory, Pythi may be right, let's follow his hunch."

They conference-called Pythi and told him about the activities at the Banque. Tanya described in detail the information provided by the Teller. As they were about to hang up she said to Pythi, "I want you to do me a favor. Please check and see if the Bank of Dubai has an account opened in the same company name, Universal Alliance; just curious."

Pythi said he would before he hung up.

Three hours later he called back. Universal Alliance, LLC had an account at the Bank of Dubai. It had five million dollars sitting in the account. The money had been transferred in many smaller increments and he needed Derek to track the transfers. Five million dollars in a Bank in Dubai was not unusual, what was unusual was that it had been transferred over the last month. What was even more unusual: the trail to every transfer seemed to lead nowhere.

Another clue or another dead end?

FIFTY-ONE

I both love and do not love; and am mad and not mad. - Anacreon

Pythi had been working hard all day. It seemed as though the problems and issues were pouring in and he was feeling a lot of pressure from the Bank of Dubai's management to find a quick solution. Dubai was considered a Banker's haven and the National Bank was rich and full of money siphoned into accounts from all over the world, no questions asked. Now, it seemed that their own system was operating against them and they had to find a solution soon and as secretly as possible. Word of the breach could not get out; it would scare away the rich of the world and stop the deposits of large amounts of money from flowing in.

Throughout the day Pythi focused on the tasks at hand. He had the team organized, he had given each one their specific tasks, he went over hundreds of accounts himself and then after the call with Sam, Tanya, and Derek had taken on the task of tracking the Universal Alliance account himself.

He had hoped to take some time off and meet Pia for lunch but as the day progressed he realized that it was going to be impossible. They had texted throughout the day and she was never far from his thoughts. In fact, she intruded at the most inopportune times, making it quite difficult for him to concentrate sometimes. Thoughts of the previous night kept intruding and in his mind's eye he saw her beautiful naked body, he could smell her fragrance, and feel the soft touch of her. He could hear her passionate moans and feel her lips all over him. He had to constantly shake himself to stop daydreaming and focus on the emergency at hand.

Lunch had been a shawarma sandwich at his desk. While the delicious grilled lamb and warm Arabic bread really helped appease his hunger, he ate hurriedly. The Bank had an employee especially at hand to provide tea or coffee, water or soft drinks and the young man was kept busy all day.

Finally, at about seven, Pythi realized that it was time to end the day. All the other team members were waiting for him to let them go for the evening and he began to feel bad about keeping them late. As they were leaving, the bank manager took him aside and thanked him for his hard work and proceeded to let him know that the Bank had arranged the evening's entertainment for him. A car would be waiting at his hotel.

Pythi rushed back to the hotel. He had already called Pia and asked her to be ready. Pia had had the best day. She had taken a taxi to the Gold Souk, the Gold market, and spent the day wandering around the shops, looking at all the amazing handmade jewelry. Then stopping at a nearby clothing souk, she had bought beautiful pashmina shawls for herself and her family, and an exotic long sleeved fuchsia silk blouse embroidered with gold and embellished with sparkly stones.

She had gone back to the hotel, taken a nap and shower and was ready for Pythi when he walked in. Dressed in the fuchsia shirt, and slinky black pants, long shimmering ear-rings dangling in her ears, and gold bangles jingling on her wrists, she looked beautiful and oh so exotic. Pythi almost wanted to cancel going out but he didn't. Kissing her and holding her close he realized that he had really missed being with her all day. He had a strange look on his face as he stepped away from her and Pia wondered what thought had passed through his mind? But time enough for that later.

Downstairs, a car and driver were waiting for them and as soon as they climbed into the back seat, they were whisked away. Soon, they had left the city behind and they were driving out in the desert, into the stillness and darkness of the desert night. Pia was awed by the emptiness and vastness of it all. She had seen pictures of the Arabian Desert before but had never experienced it first hand and she found that she was enthralled by it. The ride out to their destination took over an hour and after a while they left the main highway and rode on a dirt road. They could see lights in the distance, but she still had no idea of where she was going or what to expect.

The dirt road ended abruptly in an area that looked like a parking lot where other cars were parked. The driver helped them out of the car and Pia realized that before them, in the sand, was a red carpet leading to an entrance of a group of buildings. As they walked down the red carpet, a lady in traditional dress came up to them and offered her a warm, fragrant, cleansing towel. A group of Arab men in traditional outfits with scimitars welcomed them and they stepped into an area that, to Pia, felt like she was part of the Arabian Nights.

"Pinch me," she whispered to Pythi, "is this real?" He returned a warm smile and kept quiet.

The cluster of buildings shielded a large open area that had tables all beautifully laid with red velvet tablecloths. Around the periphery of the open area were large cooking stations where food of every variety was being cooked and served in beautiful earthen ware, brass and rustic cooking vessels. There were tables piled high with fruit and flower arrangements and as they stepped on the beautiful rugs that adorned the floor, they were led to their table. Pia was absolutely enchanted. The setting was simply magical. Large brass lamps provided the lighting and there were candles on every table. The scent and smells of the exotic food was intoxicating.

"Even if I were not hungry, the sight of all this food and the lingering smells make me feel famished. What is this place?" said Pia with a little giggle.

"To tell you the truth, the drive here and all this food in display made me realize that I'm quite peckish myself. Let the feast begin. We'll eat well tonight!"

Soon they were seated at their table and had ordered their drinks. It was only then that Pythi told her that they were at the Bab Al Shams Resort in the Arabian Desert. It was going to be an extraordinary evening and Pia was filled with anticipation. In the center of the space was a large stage and there were musicians playing Arabic music.

"Let me show you around," offered Pythi. They walked around, hand in hand, taking in all the sights. There was a tent with falcons and Pia loved having them sit on her gloved arm while Pythi took a lot of photos. Then, the ancient Arabic village with the small homes, tents, and art displayed, from the history of the nomadic cultures of the Middle East. They took their time walking around the food stalls, looking at all the exotic foods. There were huge grills piled high with lamb and beef, large vats of rice pilaf being cooked, tables laden with salads, hummus, baba ghanoush, stuffed grape leaves, and so much more.

It was overwhelming, the variety of food, and filling their plates high to get a taste of it all they went back to their table. Sipping their wine and feeding each other, they were lost in the awareness of the fantastic food and their sensual pleasure.

The music began to get louder and soon the stage was filled with handsome young men in traditional Arabic dress doing a ritual dance with their swords. This was followed by belly dancers, their voluptuous bodies swaying at first in slow sensual movements and becoming more and more erotic as the music rose to a crescendo. All the tables were full by this time and the patrons clapped in sync to the music, enjoying the energetic dancing full of lusty innuendo.

But, it was what came next that completely enthralled Pia and drew her attention; the swirling dervish, who danced for over a half hour. It was hypnotic and mesmerizing and Pia clapped her hands and whistled in complete abandon. She loved the graceful movement and admired the control and agility of the dervish, who danced himself into frenzy. She was absolutely amazed, never having seen anything that compared and Pythi was delighted at her joy.

All of a sudden, all the lights went out and the whole Arabic village was shrouded in darkness. This lasted for a few moments, the quiet of the stunned, anticipating crowd being broken by occasional nervous laughs. First, there was lingering middle-eastern music and then, in the distance, on the sand dunes outside the village, a slow-moving caravan appeared in torch and moon light making its way towards the village. Riders on horse and camel back, sheep, goats, donkeys, were almost outside the village when they were abruptly ambushed by a gang of bandits on horseback, hidden in the dark. Swords in hand, they fell upon the caravan yelling and shrieking in Arabic at the bewilderment of those dining in the dark. The make believe sword and hand-to-hand fight that ensued lasted for a while, only to come to an abrupt end by the extinguishing of the torches and the turning of the electrical lights back on inside the village.

It had been an amazing magical evening and as they walked back hand in hand, Pia thanked the angels for bringing Pythi into her life. He fascinated her, he complimented her and he had become very precious to her. She loved him.

They stepped into the back of the waiting car and he pulled her close putting his arm around her back as they were driven the long ride back to the hotel, discussing the dancing and the food.

At the hotel, they climbed into the big bed together. This time Pia fed Pythi chocolates and he licked her fingers slowly as he nibbled on them. Sensing his tiredness, she kissed him slowly, working her way down his lean body, learning its secrets, listening to his breathing hitch and change, and feeling his pleasure. It was a slow, sensual coming together, full of tenderness, till passion overpowered them and, in spite of his tiredness, they made love over and over again, till satiated they fell asleep, the darkness of the desert night enveloping them.

FIFTY-TWO

The difficulty is not so great to die for a friend as to find a friend worth dying for. – Homer

In her lair high above the city of Athens, the beautiful Goddess Athena watched the going-ons with interest. She had heard snippets of information about some calamity at the Banque and then she watched the lockdown as it took place. She saw a young man leave the Banque in a hurry, and quickly walk down the street. That in itself was not unusual, but, what was unusual was that for a quick moment in time she saw Ares hovering over the young man, before he disappeared. What was more, she sensed that he was angry.

An angry Ares was not a good omen.

Why was he around this young man? She asked herself. *And what was really going on at the Banque?* It was time for her to pay attention and find out.

Before long, she had her answers and knowing Ares as she did, she also began to see his hand in the unfolding events. *It's time to bring in Poseidon,* she thought. Checking to make sure that Ares was nowhere around she embarked on a quick trip to Sounion. *I hope that Poseidon is not bedding some young maiden and will be available,* she thought, *I really do need his help.*

Poseidon, she realized when she got to Sounion, was still sitting on his rock, deep in thought.

Appearing before him, she signaled him to move over and sat down beside him. Quietly, she told him all that she had found out and surmised. Athena was extremely clever, and reading between the lines, she explained to Poseidon what she believed was Ares' plan: to eventually rule the world by controlling the flow of money.

"Money in this world is power, and if he controls its flow, he will control the world. He's using a young American mortal to manipulate the system. I don't know yet who else he has targeted as part of his scheme but I will find out. We have to make sure that we are ready to combat his efforts and having watched this whole scenario play out, we already have a head start. We know his plan, he doesn't know ours. Seriously, Poseidon, he will follow through, you know he will. He always wanted to rule the world and this time with the growth of technology again, he will. We have got to stop him."

"Athena, I am good at warfare, I can use a sword and shield very well, what am I to do here?" He asked.

"This is not very different from Atlantis," she mused, "Atlantis was not destroyed by swords, it was destroyed by evil thoughts, manipulation, and greed of power. It is the same today. Only this time we need to align with those who will not betray us, and, Poseidon, this time, we work as one, you and I. So get your sword and shield if you have to, but bring your mental powers with you too, as you are going to need them. I know exactly which mortals are going to assist us in this fight and we are going to help them overcome Ares' evil.

Well, come on, stop sitting there and gazing out at the ocean, it's time to get your house in order and get your disguise on. You are coming with me, let's go."

Laughing now, he said, "You always were bossy, but I will come with you. I do trust you and your goodness. Ares does need to be stopped. This world is already in chaos and we, you and I, have been remiss. It's time to let go off the past and restore order and harmony. Okay, let's do it…together."

Then, hand in hand, they stepped into the Temple, Poseidon rising tall and strong beside her as he gave orders and prepared himself and his abode for the coming events. Athena stood beside him, watching quietly, marveling at the change in him, towering above the others, so strong and virile, so much a God… once again.

FIFTY-THREE
Men are the dreams of a shadow. – Pindar

It had been a grueling few days, Pythi was exhausted. Yet, he felt energized. Pythi's instincts were very well honed and he felt that they were about to make a break through. Patterns were beginning to emerge, both in Athens and Dubai.

He had had long conference calls with Tanya, Sam, and Derek. Tanya had interviewed the teller at the Banque and the lady was insistent that the person who withdrew the funds from the Universal Alliance account was not of Greek descent. She thought he was American, the way he wished her and his accent, he wore a golf hat with lettering on it but other than that she had little to describe him, just like any other tourist. He had asked for the money in 100 euro bills, had counted it, thanked her and left.

What was worse was that Tanya and Sam had found hundreds of accounts with small amounts of money withdrawn, not reconciled, and simply gone…just disappeared. It amounted to millions of dollars. Interestingly, the money had disappeared at almost the same time from each account.

In Dubai, the team worked hard and they were uncovering the same pattern, only here it seemed to be on a much larger scale, hundreds of millions of dollars gone. The Bank Management was panicked but working hard to keep everything under wraps. Pythi began to realize that if this could happen at two banks, it could happen to many more…it could jeopardize the entire banking system, worldwide.

***

Pia had spent the morning at the hotel pool, then, going up to their room had sat down in quiet meditation, bringing herself into balance, retreating into the silence within her, her place of love. She truly felt that her meditations were a salve and she wished that she could show others how wonderful and life changing they were. She quietly beseeched the Goddess Athena to look after her man and provide him with her help and protection as she meditated.

Stretching, she got up of the floor where she had sat during her meditation and walked over to the little hotel desk where her laptop sat. Opening it up decided to blog. She had shown Pythi her blog page and he had begun to read her blogs. Laughing, he had also told her about Tanya's obsession with her blog and how Tanya followed her writing. It had made Pia very happy to hear that. But, Pythi had asked her to be careful and while he had not asked her to refrain from blogging, he had requested that she not mention where she was or with whom. Pia knew that Pythi was in Dubai for a security breach but she knew few details about the real problems he was facing.

"Friends," she wrote, "Life is full of strange twists and turns and often times we are not prepared for the changes and fight them. Instead of the fight and the fear, I am finding it so much easier to simply flow with the changes, to open my heart, and allow life and its beauty to reveal itself. Not knowing what the next minute or hour may bring I am truly being mindful of living in this moment, enjoying what I am given now and not worrying about what is to come next or allowing myself to be hampered by what has come before. It has been truly freeing and I beseech you, my friends, to try it, even for a little while. Quit worrying about what has been or what will be and enjoy what is…right now, for, life has a way of working itself out whether you worry about it or not. Allow yourself the freedom of living in the moment, being grateful for all that this moment provides you.

Wherever you may be right now, I send you love and light and hope that you have many moments of joy. More later. Much love and light."

Then checking to make sure that her location settings were off, she signed out. Stretching, she walked over to the balcony and looked out over the tall palm trees. It was a very hot afternoon and the sun was beating down over the desert landscape in the distance.

Below her, the hotel pool shone glittering blue in the sun light and the fronds on the palm trees swayed gently in the breeze. As she gazed at the beautiful palms, deep in her own thoughts, she spotted a bird, just sitting on the top of a palm frond. She blinked…it could not be…it looked like an owl, looking directly at her. *An owl?* She thought. *How strange, in the middle of the desert afternoon. Could it be? Maybe she was hallucinating?* She looked again…it sure looked like an owl…and again she felt as if the bird was looking directly at her. Maybe the heat was getting to her; she needed to get back into the air conditioned hotel room.

As she opened the door to step back inside, she turned once more to look at the tree….the bird was gone. *Strange,* she thought to herself, *I must google owls to see if they even exist in desert habitats.*

FIFTY-FOUR

No one can hurry me down to Hades before my time, but if a man's hour is come,
be he brave or be he coward, there is no escape for him when he has once been born. – Homer

Ares reached the banks of the Acheron River, dividing the Overworld and the Underworld, on a rainy afternoon. He flipped a coin into the dense fog covering the waters and within moments a grotesque ferryman emerged from the mist poling his dilapidated boat toward Ares. "What do you want?" Shouted the ferryman, "You are no mortal needing help to cross into the afterlife. What business do you have here?"

"Take me to your master, Hades, the Lord of the Underworld," shouted Ares back. "We have business together. I have paid you the toll you require."

From eras past, Hades had been Ares' confidant in times of trouble. Whenever Ares was in need of advice and consultation, he would visit with his dark fellow god and relative. Ares had respect for Hades' cunning mind and his ability to contrive diabolical schemes to serve Ares' plans. And, if those plans happened to make the life of Zeus difficult, so much better, as this fed the growing hatred Hades had for his ruling brother. Ares knew that his plans were safe with Hades, as Hades had little interest in controlling things happening above the Acheron, where the mortals lived their lives before submitting to him at death - although Hades remained well-informed. The wars and loss of life that Ares often caused had been a generous source of new souls, which endeared Ares to Hades.

"Welcome my dear fellow," Hades received Ares in his chambers, "It has been a long time since you last visited me. What brings you here?"

"As usual," said Ares, "I come seeking the advice of my wise uncle. You alone among the Olympians understand my nature and you accept it without criticism. It is easy to discuss things with you and get perspective. You have empathized with my primal need for instigating wars in the past and you have even supported it at times. During the Trojan War, for instance, you agreed that I should help the Trojans against the invading Greeks, in support of Aphrodite. You understood that my passion for Aphrodite at the time left me no other choice. And when cursed Athena and her conspirators managed to wound me, you gave me shelter in your kingdom to recuperate and become invisible to the wrath of the other Gods. I was thankful for that."

"Ares, Ares,…what is it with this belated expression of appreciation and gratitude? It's no secret that you are my favorite nephew. I never developed warm, fuzzy feelings for aloof Athena and I was only too happy to assist balance the powers in Troy."

Ares nodded and paused for a moment to collect his thoughts. Then, he continued, "It goes beyond that, uncle. You are the only one that acts like true family to me. I will never forget your stance at my trial at the Aeropagus Hill in Athens, the first trial to ever be held, with the jury being all the Olympians. Wretched Poseidon had the audacity to accuse me of murder for killing one of his sons, whom I killed in just revenge for raping my daughter Alcippe. Then, I was tried before the Gods. You were the only one sympathetic to my case from the beginning; although at the end they all saw my just rage over the rape and acquitted me of all charges. But, the humiliation of being put on trial by my fellow gods for defending my own was unbearable, something for which I will never forgive Poseidon." Upset Ares paced up and down lost in the details of those memories.

"Come, come now nephew," Hades extended a calming hand over Ares' shoulder. "You're acting like an old man, reminiscing of old glories and tragedies. I think you are still sore at Athena's victory in Troy. As for your anger for my brother Poseidon, how could I blame you? But, why are you dredging up all these old stories? Surely, this is not the reason you came to see me, to reminisce about the past, and you don't need to butter me up, you know I'm on your side. Go ahead, speak your mind. What is it that really bothers you, what have you done, what's the trouble?"

"Uncle, I cannot hide from you, you know me only too well," Ares started slowly, "I am involves in a battle with Poseidon and Athena who interfere with my plans to bring great disharmony to the world and start the elusive World War III. I have never disguised my antipathy for those two, especially now that they seem to have formed an alliance against me. This is where I need your perspective and wise advice." Ares took his time to unfold the story of Pythi and Pia, G-Lover and his Warriors, the computer security team Pythi had assembled, and the defenses Athena and Poseidon had created to put obstacles in Ares' path.

"I am so close I can taste it," said Ares with fervor, "If G-Lover and his group manage to destabilize the global banking system, on the heels of a multi-year economic crisis that has drained the world of patience and hope, then revolt, chaos, anarchy and war will be almost a certainty. But, Poseidon and Athena stand in my way and their combined strength is too much for me to face."

"The legendary bloodlust of my warrior nephew!" Hades exclaimed with excited laughter. "Two great wars in the past century and so many smaller ones since then have not satisfied your thirst for blood, and want more, don't you? At least you are wise enough not to challenge Athena and Poseidon directly. Deceit, my nephew, deceit should be your greatest ally in defeating combined strength. Deceive, divide and conquer. Learn from the history of the mortals, it is full of such examples."

Hades walked thoughtfully to a lounger and made himself comfortable in it. He pointed to another one close by and said, "Sit down, Ares. Patience was never one of your virtues and I have plenty of that to spare. Let us review the fairly recent events and see what we can learn from them to help your dilemma. I warn you, though, mine is a lonely life down here and I do not get too many visitors. Whenever I do have a chance to talk and present my views, I tend to get winded. Stop me if I go too far."

"But that's what I came for; your views, opinions and perspective. Talk away..." Said Ares.

"World War II was a major accomplishment of yours and brought a lot of death and destruction to the human race," started Hades. "My Underworld was flooded with boatloads of new souls every day for nearly five years, and my courts of last judgment were working overtime to process all those miserable souls.

"It was a great time, but it produced an unanticipated side effect: the rise of the United States, as the apparent white dove that, thanks to Athena's influence, would bring peace, justice, equality and prosperity to the world. In spite of their many internal and external problems, they were perceived as the hope that will re-orient the world to shy away from its corrupt ways of the past into a new order of things, led by the empowered individual.

"It worked for a while, to the exasperation of one of your favorite and equally bloodthirsty honorary sons, Stalin, who in despair proclaimed, 'America is like a healthy body and its resistance is threefold: its patriotism, its morality and its spiritual life. If we can undermine these three areas,

America will collapse from within.' Stalin certainly did his best to achieve this, including the cold war that survived him."

"Yes," interjected Ares. "The cold war kept polarization and tensions high for many years and gave me time to work on that hope perception. By using deception, avarice, and fear I started undermining the foundation from within."

"And you did a good job of it," said Hades, "In time the capitalist system managed to exonerate greed and elevate it to the status of an ideal, which in turn resulted in the de facto legalization of corruption in the name of special interests and lobbying. Pair that with the fear that followed the events of September 11, 2001 and the rise of the fear mongers that tightened their grip on the hearts of the Americans, and in a few short years you had the harvest of the financial crisis that started on Wall Street and spread around the globe like the plague. This is the new battleground of the world today, nephew; the banks, the financial institutions, the sources of wealth and the few that control them."

"But uncle, there more than seven billion people on this planet. Are you implying that they are slaves to the few that control wealth?" Asked Ares.

"Not quite," answered Hades, "But, they are greatly influenced and certainly affected. Physical slavery has to a great degree been abolished, but the financial slavery through debt in the name of progress and prosperity is spreading wider and wider and the new slave masters are far fewer than before. If you want a great new war, try to hurt the slave masters and deprive them of their power; their wealth. That should start the rockets flying. In spite of the pain and suffering the economic crisis has inflicted, the 'slaves' are not yet desperate or hungry enough to revolt. They still have things to lose."

"There is also a shift that seems to be taking place," said Ares.

"So true," agreed Hades. "This crisis has shifted wealth from the West to the East, the Orient; in many cases in the hands of previous slaves that now are masters and very hungry to exercise their newfound power. There is no going back to poverty and servitude for them, whatever the price they may have to pay. Furthermore, these new lords do not have the impediments of consciousness, morality and the value systems of the Westerners. They are ruthless and any and all means are justified so long as they achieve their desired end, their objective of controlling power. These are your unreliable but valuable new allies, Ares. Identify and befriend them. Your interests are moving in parallel courses."

"This is a good analysis, Hades. Any particular advice about my team of hackers and strategy?" Asked Ares.

"Yes, definitely." Said Hades, "Bring your team of mortals to military-type discipline. Do not allow loose cannons to undermine your efforts. Keep an eye on the leader of your team, G-Lover, is he? He doesn't appear all that stable. Also, open new fronts of conflict to distract Athena and Poseidon from your true objective of world domination. Deception, use it to its full potential. And when everyone is satisfied that you are occupied in local, trivial conflicts elsewhere, have your team strike one sudden and massive attack on both the financial system and the lords of wealth and power. The lords will start fighting each other for superiority over the collapse of the system and the slaves will be caught in the crossfire. You'll have your global war, I'll multiply the ranks of my dead, and the planet will solve its problem of overpopulation and global warming. Everybody wins!" Hades burst into thunderous laughter that echoed throughout his cavernous chambers.

He walked over to Ares who was starting to reply and said, "No, no arguments, and no further discussion. Just go and think of what I have said. Let the purity of your heart lead you to your choices and actions. My servants will see you out." And with that, the Lord of the Underworld disappeared leaving behind a cloud of foul smoke, his last words still echoing:

"I warned you that I tend to talk too much, didn't I?

FIFTY-FIVE

The gods envy us. They envy us because we're mortal, because any moment may be our last. –
Homer

The day was wearing thin at the Bank of Dubai. The regular employees had left a long time ago. *You've got to love those banker's hours*, thought Pythi and checked his watch. *Wow, it is after six. Where did the day go?* Surprisingly, Pia had not texted for a while now. *Then again*, he thought, *she must have been busy with the research I gave her to do. But, I do need to make arrangements for our evening.* With that, he went to his computer, googled 'Time Out Dubai,' and after checking, pulled out his mobile phone and dialed a number he read off the computer screen to make reservations for two.

At seven o'clock he decided to wrap up, packed his laptop, wished good night to the team that was staying to burn the midnight oil and exited the bank, hailing a taxi cab. As he was seated in the back of the cab his phone buzzed.

"Where are you?" Read the text from Pia.

"I'm coming to you, baby," he typed back, "Are you ready for me?"

It took a minute and the mobile answered back, "I was born ready for you! But don't take your time, my biological clock is ticking! lol"

He burst out laughing as he read, something that alarmed the Pakistani taxi driver who turned around and asked with real concern, "Sir, you ok, sir?"

"I'm fine," Pythi reassured him, "Just take me to The Address."

Five minutes later the taxi door was opened by the valet at The Address. He was greeted and he stole a peak at the Dubai Mall before entering the hotel. The Mall looked brilliantly lit in the falling dusk and the outdoor restaurants in front of the fountain pool were already busy with relaxed diners.

This is going to be such a delicious evening, he thought to himself as he was entering the elevator, punching the floor number on the control panel. Then, a thought occurred to him, and he jumped out of the elevator as the doors were closing. He run to the concierge desk, "I need a red rose," he said to the concierge, with embarrassment. "No problem, Sir," responded the concierge, "We always keep an emergency supply for such situations."

"Thank you," said Pythi, "You are a life saver!"

Red rose in hand, computer bag over his shoulder, he entered the elevator again. At the suite door he did not use his key, but rang instead. It took a minute before Pia opened the door in a simple off-white silk baby doll with thin straps, which looked as if it had been designed to showcase her beautiful thighs and legs. All kinds of primal desires were awaken in him.

"Oh, my Prince has arrived bearing a red rose," she teased as she kissed him tenderly on the lips.

"Thank you," she curtseyed playfully and accepted the rose graciously.

"I would love to take hours to show you my love and appreciation, my Princess," he said, "But I need to take a shower to wash off the grind of the day, and then take you out to Dubai by night."

"Should I dress to kill, charm or just entice divinities?" She laughed. "You just dress," he laughed back, "All else will fall into place naturally."

He stepped into the shower and let the lukewarm water massage and cleanse his tired body for a long time until he felt all the fatigue of the day wash away, leaving him renewed and refreshed. He put on an off-white shirt, comfortable but stylish pants and a pair of soft, dark tan loafers with no socks. Pia stood in front of the mirror adjusting her pearl earrings, a match to the single string of pearls around her neck that accentuated her simple but very elegant dark dress. She looked lovely.

"And now the shoes," she said, "My Prince gets to choose; I hope he chooses well," and laughed. She tried on a pair of low-heeled golden sandals, avocado green medium heel pumps, and red leather platforms with high heels. She posed for him with every trial and then she walked up and down the room as if on a fashion runway. He liked them all, but finally settled on the golden sandals.

They left the hotel in a taxi cab all laughs, flirting and teasing.

"To the Dubai Marina, Grosvenor House," Pythi instructed the taxi driver. Soon, they had merged into Sheikh Zayed Road traffic, leaving the Dubai Mall, Burj Khalifa and The Address behind. Pythi pointed ahead to the right, where an illuminated building in the shape of a sail emerged out of the darkness of the night.

"This is the famous Burj Al Arab," said Pythi. "I love that building at night, all lit up and blowing in the breeze. Next to it is Madinat Jumeirah, a souk (market place) that combines the charm of Arabic Architecture with the watery appeal of Venice, as there are canals that run through it and electrical dhows (local fishing boats) that tour them. I spent time in this area on a previous trip and I just love it. From here going south there is a string of royal palaces along the beach before you come to the entrance of the Palm Jumeirah, the famous artificial island in the shape of a palm tree, and then, farther south, is the Dubai Marina, one of the newest developments in Dubai, where we are heading."

"This sounds wonderful," chirped Pia, "But what is that lit bell tower in the distance to the left," she asked.

"Oh, that is the Kempinsky hotel tower which is part of the Mall of the Emirates with its famous indoor ski slope. Yes, you can ski in the mall, with the desert all around you," he laughed.

"My Prince has a talkative, easy side, then? Is the Dubai allure or the presence of the Princess that brings all this out?" She teased him. He laughed expansively, leaned over and kissed her.

"Definitely the Princess, unequivocally the Princess, you bet your bottom dollar the Princess," he mimicked in a semi-serious tone.

FIFTY-SIX

Faults are beauties in a lover's eyes. – Theocritus

Holding hands, they walked the long stretch of the Marina Walk people-watching, checking the slow parade of Lamborghinis, Ferraris, Bentleys, Aston Martins and other exotic cars. The Marina Walk cafés and restaurants were full of people. Paul's, Roma Café, Starbucks, Lebanese, Thai, Mexican, and Chinese restaurants, fast food joints, were all busy. As were the hotels: the Hilton, Ritz Carlton, Sofitel, Le Meridien, Rotana,… The retail stores, mostly fashion ware and jewelry, competed with each other to attract attention and catch the eye of the passerby. A colorful sea of people was everywhere, in varying attire, strolling along, chatting happily, and taking in everything. This was probably one of the best people-watching venues in the city.

When they reached the end of the long Marina Walk stretch, Pia exclaimed:

"Wow, hthat was exhilarating!"

They walked another few minutes along the central road connecting Jumeirah to the Dubai Marina, when Pythi pointed to a high rise across the street with its top lit in electric blue.

"This is us, my sweet," he said, "The Grosvenor House hotel!"

"And I'm taking you to a place you may be tempted to do something you like a lot…meditate," he continued. "I think you will really like this place," said he, as they passed the fancily dressed people entering the hotel and walked down a staircase to the north end of the building towards the water canal.

They followed the carpeted corridor marked by thick, luxurious red ropes on brass stands to the heavy wooden double door with rich carvings. A tuxedoed doorman greeted them cheerfully and respectfully, "Welcome to the Buddha Bar," as he pulled the heavy half door open for them to enter. Pythi guided Pia gently to enter first, and she looked back at Pythi with surprise, "Buddha Bar? What…" The ambiance of the interior left her speechless as she took it all in. "Oh my God!" she whispered slowly, "Pythi habibi, you did very well!"

The dimly lit interior, accented with the light of a few strategically placed candles that enhanced the carved, dark wood wall panels gave the place an otherwordly feel, like that of entering a holy shrine. But, there was no chanting here, only some upbeat, haunting music coming from somewhere deep in the interior, muted by the walls in between. She looked to the right where a door led to a well lit room with a small statue of Buddha and a fountain in front of it. Rose petals were floating in the pool water and there were dozens of glass containers spread throughout the room with burning aromatic candles that were flickering with a sense of reverence, serenity and mystery, filling the room with the fragrance of blooming flowers.

The hostess smiled at the surprised expression on Pia's face, "Welcome to the Buddha Bar, madam. I take it this is your first time here. We are happy to have you." And, turning to Pythi, "Would the gentleman have reservations for dining with us, or are you visiting for music and drinks at the bar?"

"We do have reservations," answered Pythi, "And I asked for a table at the edge of the room, near the glass paneled wall overlooking the water and in full view of the Buddha statue, if possible. I hope they reserved it." After taking his particulars and checking the well concealed computer, she answered, "Yes, sir, we have, and madam will be very pleased, I am certain." Then, pointing to her left she explained, "This is Mariam, your hostess and waitress for the evening. She will show you to your table."

Mariam, bowed bringing her palms together in front of her torso uttering "Namaste" and asked them politely to follow her. She guided them past the Buddha shrine into a long corridor lined with Tibetan prayer wheels, thangkas, and small wood statues in wall recesses. In between those decorative ornaments were entrances to private rooms where small groups of people were dining or socializing over drinks on comfortable sofas and heavy pillows. The music got louder and louder as they were approaching the end of the corridor and they could see a large group of people standing in a well-lit area in front of them. Mariam pointed to a wide staircase to the left, "This leads to our lounge area on the upper floor, where you can enjoy appetizers and drinks in comfort as you wait to dine, and the music is louder up there," said the hostess.

"We are too hungry for that," returned Pythi.

"Then, perhaps a drink at our bar?" Said Mariam gesturing in front of her as the corridor opened to a sizeable bar with extra tables in front. The bar area was quite full and very lively with people standing, sitting on high bar stools, chatting loudly, and swinging to the rhythm of the music in between sips of their drinks.

"This looks like a lot of fun," said Pia, "But we are not here to socialize, not really. I hope our table is not as loud, and we can really talk."

"Of course, ma'am," returned Mariam, "Please follow me," and she pointed to the left where the monastery-like corridor opened up to a great, huge room with high ceilings. Dimly lit by low burning chandeliers, the room was studded with white tablecloth covered dining tables, each with a red candle holder in the center. The wall at the far end was dominated by a huge, three story-high, golden statue of Buddha seated cross-legged in his usual peaceful meditative position. The wall in the distance in front of them, also three stories high, was all glass, reflecting the canal waters outside, the lights of the distant sky rises, and the starry night sky above. Mariam pointed to the middle of the glass paneled wall and said, "Your table is over there, a very special one!" Pia caught her breath, and snuggling up against Pythi, she whispered in his ear, "I love, love this!"

They wove through situated diners to reach their table and after they were comfortably seated, Mariam asked if they wished to start their evening with a cocktail.

"Of course," volunteered Pia, "But no appetizers. I'm really hungry and my Prince promised me a feast. I'll save my appetite for that. A white Russian for me, please, and let me see if I know my Prince well...Sapphire Bombay gin martini, well shaken with ice and chilled to the bone, dirty, and with a generous portion of Spanish olives. Am I right?" She teased playfully.

Pythi laughed, "Always right my sweet, only they may be hard pressed to find Spanish olives in these parts. Jordanian or Egyptian olives is common fare in the Middle East."

They spent the time waiting for the drinks to arrive by taking in the unique ambiance, noticing the details, absorbing the music and touching each other in a myriad of different ways, between tenderness and teasing. When the order arrived, Pythi tasted the drink and exclaimed, "Not a bad martini in the middle of the desert. My compliments to the bartender!" They continued their flirting which got more tender and intimate with each successive sip of their cocktails and they decided to transition into wine for the second round. She picked a California Chardonnay and he asked for an Australian Shiraz.

Two hours went by and it felt as if they had walked into the place just five minutes earlier.

"I don't hear any protests of starvation and I am worried," said Pythi, "Is it time to order?"

"I thought you will never ask," said Pia, "Getting away with a cheap date," as she kissed him playfully on the lips. They asked for menus, but very soon Pythi put his down, "I know what I want. We need to find something exquisite for you to match your beauty and spirits tonight," he said. It took a long time for her to decide from all the delicacies on the menu, but finally, after lengthy conversations, she settled for lobster bisque, Thai salad with mandarin slices and nuts, and grilled hamour fish with peppercorn sauce. Pythi had to explain that hamour is the Middle Eastern cousin of the Western grouper and is delicious.

Pythi ordered a sushi and sashimi platter, and warm sake to compliment his meal. Pia stayed with her Chardonnay and for the next two hours they delighted in each other's food and drink, feeding each other with tender fingers, being lost in the awesome music and their budding love. It was as if they had no care in the world, as time had stopped ticking just around the space of their table, as there was just the two of them, no-one else in that fabulous environment with the exceptional food.

With their hunger more than satisfied, they declined desserts and it was then that they realized that only a handful of tables were still occupied and the waiters were making preparations to close the restaurant for the night. They paid the bill and left a more than generous tip for Mariam, who had been spectacular. Wishing them good night, she said appreciatively, "Madam, sir, please come back. You are my favorite customers!"

They left the restaurant well after midnight, holding hands, and took up the valet's offer to call them a taxi. "To the Jumeirah Beach, next to Burj Al Arab and the Jumeirah Beach hotel," Pythi instructed the driver.

"I need to show you Burj Al Arab at night and get your feet wet," said Pythi to Pia. When they arrived at the beach, there were a few stragglers still left, mainly groups of teenagers coming from some party or the other; the beach was largely deserted. They sat on the wall, close to the road, and with arms linked watched the magnificent architectural sail, the Burj, change colors with the gentle splashing of the water in the quiet of the night.

"I just love the shape of this building," said Pythi, "It does touch some inner chord of mine."

"It's beautiful," said Pia in a low voice, "And how can I thank you for this fantastic evening? Although, it is not over yet. You promised to get my feet wet…"

Pythi smiled, leant down, rolled up his pants, and removed his shoes. "Take off your shoes and follow me," he said.

Holding hands, shoes dangling from their free ones, they walked the width of the sand, down to the shallow water, lightly splashing their way along the length of the beach, away from the lights and the grandeur of the Burj, into the dark and mysterious Dubai night…to that secret place that only lovers can reach and no-one else can follow.

FIFTY-SEVEN
It is said that wrath is the last thing in a man to grow old. – Alcaeus

He had showered, dressed, and done some more drugs before he got into his rental car and began the drive to Sounion to find his girl. G-Lover was pumped up, full of energy and enthusiasm. This was going to be the greatest day of his life. He had followed her posts and stalked her for years, now he was going to meet her and claim her as his own. They were going to live a life of perfect togetherness, forever.

***

Ziggy had been following the activities at the Banque closely. He sensed trouble. He had seen the girl from the basement, the foreigner, run up the stairs and rush to the teller. He, of everyone at the Banque, had some idea why they were holed up in the basement and he wondered what she had found. Word was already traveling through the employee grapevine and rumors were flying all over the Banque. In addition, Ziggy had noticed that there were more security personnel at the Banque and he could feel the tension. Many employees, in small groups, were gathered in the break room discussing what they thought was going on. Someone mentioned that they thought it was a terrorist they were after; others thought that there was bank fraud or the possibility of theft.

Ziggy, the faceless employee of the Banque, continued his job of emptying trash cans, cleaning counters and mopping floors and bathrooms as the rumors swirled around him. He waited his time, he knew the habits of every employee of the Banque and when he saw the teller of window number 10 go outside for her break and her smoke. He made her a cup of coffee and followed her out.

She was a middle-aged mother of three, who had worked for the Banque for a long time. Short and stocky, she often wore the same dress for three or four days, her graying hair pulled back in a bun, ugly comfortable shoes on her feet. They had often shared smoke breaks outside the Banque together and today was no different. Ziggy handed her the plastic cup and asked her if she was okay.

That was all he needed to do.

"Kala, kala," she began, and then she launched into the drama, telling him in great detail about the tourist who had withdrawn the money and then disappeared. She still didn't understand what the whole incident had been about. Tourists come into the Banque every day and withdraw money. In a low tone she told him that she was upset at how the girl from downstairs had pushed her aside and grabbed her computer, as if she was a common criminal. She had been at that Teller line for over ten years, there was nothing irregular about that account or the withdrawal, and she, Maria, was not going to lose her job over it. After all, she had three kids to feed and raise.

Ziggy listened to her ranting quietly, letting her know that she would be okay. They were probably mistaken and the tourist was long gone by now. When she stopped to take a sip of her coffee and light her cigarette, he said, "Maria, they must know his name by now and if he is a criminal, the police will get him, his name must have been on the account."

"That's the problem," she replied. Then looking around to make sure no one could hear her, in a whisper, she said, "The account did not have an individual's name, it was set up in the name of a company, Universal Alliance, or something like that, and there was no contact information when the manager pulled it up."

Ziggy froze.

She continued, "Please don't tell anyone I gave you the name, the Manager and the girl from downstairs made me swear I would not say anything to anyone."

"Don't worry, I will not," responded Ziggy absent mindedly, his mind going over what she had just revealed. It couldn't be. He knew the names of all their accounts and he himself had set up the Universal Alliance account. And, why would someone withdraw money from that account, in person, here in Athens? There must be some mistake, he thought, or maybe it is a similarly named account. He would have to check and do it soon. His next break was at least two hours away.

***

G-Lover drove his rented BMW through the traffic, zigzagging and maneuvering expertly through the chaos that was traffic in downtown Athens. Then, he picked up the coast road and drove, enjoying the scenery and thinking of his Beloved, imagining her delight at seeing him. He stopped at a gas station after an hour, and going into the bathroom did a round of cocaine, before he got back into the car and continued his drive to Sounion.

Sounion is a small village and he drove right through it before he realized that he needed to turn around and go back. In the distance, he could see the magnificent Temple. High up on the mountain, its marble pillars standing tall and stately. At another time he may have stopped and visited the Temple, for he had a love of history and architecture, but today, he had more important things to do.

He stopped at the little grocery store cum bakery at the bottom of the mountain and went inside.

"Anyone speaks English here?" He asked as the bell on the front door jangled.

A young lady at the counter replied, "A little."

"Good," he said, using the most charming smile he could muster. "I am looking for my girlfriend, a beautiful American, who is here to visit her grandmother."

"She is here in Sounion?" Asked the girl behind the counter.

"Yes, her grandmother lives here, and she has come from America to live with her. Her name is Pia, do you know her?"

The girl stared at him, hesitating. Then, shrugging her shoulders, she gave him directions as best as she could, telling him that the only American she knew lived in the little cottage over the beach.

Thanking her, he rushed out of the store. This had been easier than he thought. He would be at her home in a few minutes…

***

Ziggy waited for his next break. Pulling on his jacket, he left the Banque, shuffling along the street to the Internet Café a few blocks down. Paying for half an hour, he went into the darkened, smoke filled room and sat down at one of the computers. He knew what he was doing was dangerous and he knew the others may be angry at him for the possibility of jeopardizing the security of their operation but he had to know, it would be hours before he got home and could use his securely encrypted computer.

He justified his activity. He was only going to check a bank account, no more, no less. It took him seconds to log into the account and within a minute he realized that someone had used the account to withdraw money from it. But who? He was the only one who lived in Athens. He took out his cell phone and took a screen shot of the account, then quickly logged off. He had to contact the others and let them know. He was filled with fear, and as he shuffled back to the Banque to finish his shift, he felt sick to his stomach. Something was wrong, he felt it. He had been promised a lot of money but so far he had seen very little of it. He felt his limbs begin to shake and he had to stop and regain his composure before he could go back into the Banque to finish his shift.

FIFTY-EIGHT

Bad company corrupts good character. – Menander

It was late in the afternoon, Tanya was feeling very tired as she continued staring at her computer screen, the events of the morning running like a movie in her mind. It was a tape playing over and over again, as she tried to sort and make connections. She was hungry too and her mind began to wander as thoughts of food began to take over.

Derek, Sam, and she, had discussed the happenings and they all had the same questions. Why would someone withdraw money in person from an account that seemed to come out of nowhere? Why were they here in Greece? What was the connection of this person or persons to the missing funds? Could this account in the name of Universal Alliance lead them to the stolen money or were they barking up the wrong tree?

As she pondered these questions, absent mindedly staring at the screen, she heard the now familiar ping. Someone had accessed the account again. She called out to Derek, who came running and almost pushing her aside he started running his encryption program. It took him only a few seconds.

"Son of a bitch," he exclaimed, "Someone is accessing the account from a computer right up the street from the Banque." Leaning over to the computer next to him he punched in the address.

"It's at the Internet Café up the street."

And before he could finish his words, Tanya and he, were running out of the basement, yelling to Sam to cover for them. They ran up the stairs and then walked through the front of the Banque at a brisk pace so as not to attract any untoward attention. They weaved through the afternoon pedestrians at a very fast pace, making it to the Internet Café in a few minutes.

Pushing the door open, they rushed inside. The Café was empty. They looked around again…no one. Going by the description of the tourist at the Banque, Tanya asked the young man at the counter if an American tourist had been in the café a few minutes ago. Shaking his head, he replied that he had not seen anyone like that.

"But, he just emailed me, telling me he was here a few minutes ago," Tanya improvised.

"No," he said, "No foreign tourist in here all day. Very slow day, very few people in here today."

They walked back in silence, feeling completely deflated.

At the Banque, they found Sam still staring at the screen.

"No activity on the account since you guys left here," he said, "Someone logged in and then logged out within a minute."

Derek was frantically working on his computer, re-confirming that whoever it was, had logged in from the Internet Café.

Why? He kept asking himself, *Why would they use a computer at a public Internet Café?*

* * *

It took G-Lover a few minutes to locate YahYah's house; it wasn't difficult to find. Parking his car on a little ridge, he looked at himself in the make-up mirror of the car, then, stepped out straightening his shirt and clothes. All of a sudden, he felt a wave of nervousness flow over him. He almost stepped back into the car to compose himself when the front door opened and YahYah stepped out. She had seen the car coming up the hill, and curious, had come out to see who it was.

G-Lover walked over to her and looking straight at her asked her if Pia was around.

"No," said YahYah, not providing any more information, waiting for the young man to speak again. She felt a small shiver run through her as she continued looking at him. Something was not right here, her instincts were telling her to be careful.

Smiling, he put out his hand, to introduce himself. "I am Pia's boyfriend from America. I have come to surprise her."

YahYah held his gaze steadfastly but refused to shake his hand. She waved him away, telling him that Pia was gone.

"She not here, she gone away," she told him.

G-Lover began to feel anger building in him. This old lady was being unreasonable and where was Pia?

He tried asking the old lady where Pia was but she would not give him any more information. He tried looking over her shoulder to see if he could spot her in the small house but he couldn't see inside. He thought of pushing the old lady aside and going into the house himself, but realized that if Pia was indeed in the house, it would not be a good beginning for him.

He tried asking the old lady when Pia would be back, but she shrugged her shoulders and said she didn't know.

"I'll wait in my car for her," he told her.

"She not coming back here," responded the old lady.

"What do you mean she is not coming back here? She lives here."

"No, she gone, no coming back," said the old lady stubbornly.

Then she started yelling in Greek and before he knew it an older gentleman cleaning fishing nets at the beach below began walking up with a younger man by his side. They walked up to them and YahYah continued talking to them in rapid Greek.

G-Lover attempted to introduce himself and charm them with his smile but they stared at him stoically and finally giving up, he went to the car. Taking a deep breath, he tried to calm himself. He was really angry; so angry that if he had had a gun, he might have shot the old lady. She had dashed his hopes. How dare she not tell him where Pia was? Why was she so rude to him? His heart was beating really fast and he hit the steering wheel in anger.

Outside, the three of them watched him, and YahYah told the others that something was very wrong. She felt evil when she had seen the young man and she wanted him to go away, to leave her granddaughter alone. She crossed herself and thanked God for protecting her lovely Pia and she thanked him again for making sure that Pia was not here today. Now she beseeched the Gods to remove him from her property. This man was trouble, she could feel it in her bones; she knew it. Just like she knew that he was lying when he said he was Pia's boyfriend. Pia had never mentioned anyone nor had the rest of the family.

He backed the car slowly, then spinning his wheels drove away, still furious. His plan to meet his Beloved had not worked. He had come all the way to Greece and she was gone. Where could she be? He needed to get to his computer to try and find her and go to her, but before that he needed to stop somewhere so he could snort some more cocaine, he was beginning to feel very low and depressed, he needed some to lift his spirits. He would find a way to reach Pia, he knew he would.

FIFTY-NINE
Man is a measure of all things. – Protagoras

From his lair, high above the clouds, Ares watched the going-ons with some misgiving. He watched his principal mortal player and realized that he needed to act fast if he was going to strike. He understood the human needs of G-Lover; he knew all about his addictions and his obsessions, he knew all about his constant need for cocaine, and his inability to function without it. He knew all about his obsession for Pia. That, in his estimation was an added bonus. Pia, due to her involvement with Pythi, had now become one of the players in his battle for dominance and he would have to consider how he could use her and the relationship she had with Pythi. He realized that she could possibly be the weak link that he may need as this battle progressed.

His mortal team was performing as he had wanted them to. He had not accounted for G-Lover actually going to Greece to meet Pia, but he figured, that would be a small hurdle. He had been very irritated though, and he really had little patience for human error, when G-Lover had actually gone into the Banque to withdraw funds and nearly been caught. That had caught his ire. He realized he would have to exercise more control and make sure his mortal team did not make stupid mistakes.

***

From his perch at the Temple in Sounion, the mighty Lord Poseidon watched over the unfolding drama. Seated next to him, the divine Goddess Athena watched as well. Looking at each other, they smiled grimly. Ares had misstepped. They had seen him following G-Lover. They now knew that somehow, in some way, this mortal was involved in Ares' game plan. They watched him too.

Athena was alarmed when she saw him drive up to YahYah's home and was even more alarmed when she saw the hate and anger in him. And why was he seeking out Pia? Pia was her ward. She, Athena, watched over Pia, she was Pia's guardian angel, and she was going to find out what he wanted with her child. Poseidon sensed her restlessness and curiosity and with a look beseeched her to be still and silent.

Ares did not need to know that they were on to him. They were only now beginning to find out about Ares' plans and they needed to know more without alarming Ares or raising his guard.

***

G-Lover pulled over by the side of the dark road on his way back to Athens, leaned over and with shaking hands, pulled out his little bag of cocaine and snorted some as quickly as he could. He leaned back in his seat, taking big gulping breaths to steady himself, and calm himself down. He was angry, very angry. His plan to finally meet his beloved Pia had been foiled and now he was going to have to re-group and try and find her. He had to get to his computer but he needed to get back to Athens first. Eyes red with anger, he checked his mirrors and almost recklessly pulled back into the traffic lane. Lucky for him there were no other cars on the road.

Ares, watched, satisfied. He was going to have to find a way to fuel that anger to make G-Lover act quickly. He had to infuse some urgency into this weak human.

From the safety of the Temple at Sounion, Poseidon and Athena watched too. Ares was using this mortal pawn, of that they were sure now. They just had to figure out why and how.

Athena watched the anger swirl around G-Lover, a dark red cloud engulfing his drug induced mind, she watched him drive the car in an aggressive and erratic way, she listened to him ranting to himself and realized that she was going to really protect Pia. This man was evil and with the help and power of Ares on his side, he could really harm her.

Closing her eyes, she summoned her trusty owl, her constant companion, and often, her quiet watcher and spy.

"Glauki," she ordered, "Watch him, follow him, be discreet, but never leave his side. Let no one know where you are, and report to me directly. Go now, koritsi mou."

A fluffy shape flew way over the car, following it at a safe distance but making sure it was always in sight, as G-Lover made his way back to Athens.

SIXTY

Quickly, bring me a beaker of wine, so that I wet my mind and say something clever. - Aristophanes

Ziggy had had a long and very stressful day. His body hurt, especially his leg, and as he finished his shift and signed out his limp was more pronounced. His brain had been running on overload. His mind kept going over the day's activities. Why would someone withdraw money from their account? Who would do it in person at the Banque's teller counter? No one except the four of them knew about the accounts, so it had to be one of them, but why were they in Greece? And why were the others not notified?

G-Lover had told them that he would take care of all the transfers. That he had set up all the proxy accounts and that once he transferred the funds, they would all have access to the accounts to withdraw money as they needed. But, he had ensured that no one had access till he said it was safe. Ziggy had not heard from him in a few days. In fact, he had not heard from anyone in a while. They were all lying low, but he had to get hold of them, to let them know what was going on and figure out what was next. This was not part of the plan. They had gone over their moves and their roles many times; withdrawing money from the Greek account was not one of them. Plus, the Greek account had been set up for Ziggy. He had to get to the others; the uncertainty was making him crazy!

It was past one at night when he finally left the Banque. Limping out of the Banque, he walked slowly, the cool air hitting his face and slim body and making him shiver. Hunched up, he focused on walking, his leg dragging behind him as he made his way through the narrow streets to the tiny basement apartment he shared with two others. Usually, it took him about twenty minutes, but tonight, it seemed to take longer, his tired body unable to move any faster and his fatigued mind not able to focus on anything but the crisis he felt was brewing.

Finally, he walked past the overflowing garbage bins lining the street he lived on, past the stores and tavernas, which were now closed, to the brick building in which he lived. The building was old and very rundown. He pushed opened the entrance door and made his way down the narrow stairway to the wooden door of his apartment. He paid for a room in the apartment and when he went inside, he saw one of his roommates asleep on the couch in front of the TV, which was still playing, in the tiny living room of the apartment. It was a small, dark, airless apartment. In reality, it was more of a cluster of rooms than an apartment, a tiny living space consisting of a counter, which served as a kitchen, with a sink, a stove and a very small refrigerator. The living area boasted a couch, a chair and a narrow table on which the TV was placed. It led to Ziggy's room.

As soon as he had moved in, he had installed a lock on the door of his room so that no one but himself had access to it. It was a tiny room, with a single mattress on the floor, a narrow cupboard that housed his clothes and meager belongings, and a table against one wall which served as his desk and eating space, all in one.

On the table sat his laptop and several monitors, along with a desk top computer that he had put together. They were his most prized possessions and he had installed the lock on the door to make sure that no one touched his computers. The room had a tiny, barred window, which was at street level. The window was permanently closed. Ziggy had never tried to open it. There was no other way to get in or out of the room. Spartan and small, it was Ziggy's haven. In spite of the smallness of the room, it was very neat and clean, Ziggy liked everything in its place.

He went into the room, locked the door behind him and turned on his computers. The room lit up as all the monitors began to turn on. He had a small table lamp set next to his computers and he turned that on as well. Then, changing his clothes, he waited for the computers to boot up. He checked for messages, and seeing none, sent out one to the others, requesting a call-in in fifteen minutes.

Then going out of his room, he walked quietly into the kitchen area and made himself a cup of coffee. Carrying it back to his room, he locked the door again. Ready, he waited for the others.

Andrei was the first one to log on. His face came on the monitor, at first very grainy and unclear and then in focus. They greeted each other and made small talk. A few minutes later, Yuan logged in. They greeted each other, and each one made sure that the security and encryption was working before Ziggy relayed the activities of the day. They waited an additional ten minutes for G-Lover to log in, but he did not.

Ziggy outlined the incident at the Banque and what the teller had told him. He told them that he had checked the account, leaving out the information about going to the Internet Café to do it. He knew that would anger the others. It was against their rules. He showed the screen shot of the account, which showed the deposit and withdrawal of funds. And, he conveyed to them that he was incredibly worried about what he felt was a breach of security among them.

Andrei had listened quietly, trying to piece together what may have occurred. Andrei trusted no one, never had. He had seen terrible things in his short life and he began to feel the same sense of disquiet he felt when his instinct kicked in and told him something was not adding up.

He asked Yuan, "Brother, where are you, still in Hong Kong?"

"Yes, still here," was the reply. "I was waiting for G-Lover to tell me it was okay to go to Dubai to pick up the money. You still in Bucharest?"

Smiling, Andrei replied that he was. "Still in my little office at the orphanage, but hopefully not for long. Anyone heard from our American friend?"

Both Ziggy and Yuan replied that they had not.

They could not understand why G-Lover had not logged in. He usually called the meetings and told the others what was going on and what to do next. The three of them were not sure what to do till they heard from him.

"He may be asleep, and missed the message to call in, after all there is a time difference," said Yuan.

"He never sleeps," countered Andrei, "But let's wait for him to check in, maybe he has an explanation."

"Maybe he decided to take a vacation in Greece?" said Yuan.

"Nah, too far-fetched," said the other two.

They spoke for a few more minutes, deciding to wait for a response from their American friend. Maybe he would have an explanation. Till then, they would do nothing. They signed off agreeing to get together to play Call of Duty in a few hours.

Andrei sat in front of his computer deep in thought after the others were gone. Something was not right and he was not about to get caught, he needed to act now. This was his only way out of the turgid circumstances of his life and he was not going to let anyone ruin it. He sent a private text to Yuan, "Take care of yourself, brother." Then, using the secure encryption codes that each one had set up, he transferred the money out of the Romanian account into several private accounts he had set up himself. It took him awhile. Transferring small amounts from one account to another till they were untraceable, from the Caymans, from Dubai, through the Swiss accounts, into those in Luxembourg, to Argentina, to Russia, moving some of it back to separate Romanian banks, others to accounts he had set up all over the world. Same method, different accounts. He had to ensure his security. It had taken him many hours to make sure there was no trail. Finally, he turned off his computer and, still sitting in the chair, fell fast asleep.

***

In Hong Kong, Yuan was still on his computer. He had heard Andrei and he had listened. He was going to act, he was pulling out, now, and he was calling Lin Yu, for protection.

SIXTY-ONE
It is not living that matters, but living rightly. – Socrates

Ares was absolutely incensed. Things were falling apart. His team was rife with mistrust, and deceit. If he did not act soon the situation would quickly get beyond his control. But before he could control the mortals, he would have to control himself.

He was puffed up with anger and was himself fast losing control. He stormed around his heavenly abode, yelling and shouting, his minions scurrying away in fear. He railed against Athena and Poseidon, he screamed at his Father and picked up large marble urns and hurled them into the air. This time he was not going to let go. He was going to win. Domination of the Earth would be his…his victory. He was going to rule the Earth, and then move his conquests out throughout the Universe. He had almost prevailed in Atlantis; almost. This time he was going to be the absolute victor.

Hidden behind the rocks at Sounion, high up in their lair, Poseidon and Athena watched Ares' angry outburst. Ares was quick tempered and his meanness often bordered on violence. They knew Ares, they understood him, they had been around him for centuries, and they knew that he was coming unhinged. In this state, he was capable of anything. His desperation would drive him and they could only imagine what he would do next…

Athena closed her eyes and began to breathe deeply. She focused her thoughts and zeroed in on her trusted friend and advisor, her Owl, Glauki. The response was immediate. In her mind's eye, she saw the Owl. Communication was easy and fast. In a matter of moments, she waved her hand and opened her eyes. Then moving close to Poseidon, she began whispering in his ear. He listened quietly, and when she finished, he sat in silence, deep in thought. Things were worse than he imagined, he was going to have to move fast.

SIXTY-TWO
God has entrusted me with myself. - Epictetus

Pia felt as though she had been living in a dream. The past week had been absolutely perfect. She sat by the pool musing about her good luck. A few months ago she could not have imagined that she would be traveling the world with someone like Pythi. He was charming, considerate, educated and more than anything else, he was genuine. There was nothing false or fake about him. She admired his work ethic and marveled at how hard he worked, always making sure that he gave her his full attention when he got back.

When he spoke to his team members, she noticed that he never raised his voice and usually listened patiently, even if the call came in late at night. He was a problem solver and he took his job seriously. She loved him for that. She loved his ability to adapt to new cultures and people from all over the world, never condescending or judgmental, simply curious about the paradigm in which they functioned. She loved how much he loved his parents and that he was constantly texting them and in touch with them through social media. She liked that he had emotional connections and was not afraid to show them.

More than anything, she liked how she felt when she was with him. He made her feel safe, secure and loved. She could be herself with him. He understood her insecurities and fears, and when he held her, she felt them all dissipate and disappear. He had a quiet quality, a sense of stillness, that emanated from the inside out and that touched all those who crossed his path. She couldn't quite figure out what it was and where it came from, but it was integral to whom he was and she was really attracted to it.

The past few weeks had been very revealing. While she had spent a lot of time working with Pythi, she had also spent a lot of time alone, by herself, walking on the beach by the hotel, or taking their rental car out into the desert by herself. She loved the desert on the outskirts of Dubai. The vast expanses of ever changing sand dunes, their color and shape, changing with the light and the wind, enthralled her. She loved the sense of isolation and was not afraid of it, though she was careful not to go too far off the main highway.

She spent hours, taking photographs and sitting in her car writing about the landscape and her heightened sense of feeling while she was there. The desert enchanted her and in it she was able to weave a tale in her mind's eye, which she knew one day would become her first book. It was an exciting possibility and she was thrilled at the course her life was taking.

On one such afternoon, after a particularly lovely ride into the desert, she sat at the desk in the hotel room and began to write her blog.

"Friends," she wrote, "At the point in my life when I had given up on everything, had no sense of my future, was not interested in re-living the past, and was simply content to enjoy the present moment bestowed on me, did my whole life come together again.

As you know, the past few months have been an amazing journey and I have shared it with you. I left all that was familiar, to move to another country, in the hope that I would find that integral part of me that would be essential for my growth and future. Not knowing if I was going to find anything or even get to know myself any better, I simply enjoyed the times I spent with my beloved grandmother in Greece, immersing myself in the excitement of discovering a new culture and place. Make no mistake, the simplicity of life in my grandmother's world was at first hard to take, having lived in large urban metropolitan areas with all the amenities at your fingertips.

But, I soon began to realize that there was something very special about sipping a cup of coffee, mid-morning, without having to rush off to an appointment, or being able to simply enjoy the company of friends in an unhurried atmosphere, with the most breathtaking ocean views laid out before you.

It was in those simple moments that I began to breathe again, to listen to myself once more, not the jumbled non-stop dialogue of my mind, my self-talk, but the quiet stillness within, that gradually began to emerge. And, while I still do not have a sense of my future or the direction that my life should take, I have been imbued with a great sense of peace.

Ironically, while I was neither looking for, nor interested in a relationship, I am now in what I call, a perfectly complete relationship with a truly amazing man; a relationship that has shown me how wonderful life can be when it is shared. A quiet unfolding of the wonder that I never imagined I would experience. Life is wonderful…..wishing you a life full of wonder….more later."

She re-read the blog and hit post. Then, she waited for a few minutes till the responses started coming in.

***

In Athens, it was late afternoon at the Banque. Tanya had spent a desultory few days working at her computer. All the indications seemed to be pointing to the Cayman Islands. She was waiting for a call from Pythi to discuss what their next step should be.

Her computer tinged. It was a new blog post on "Soul Searching," her favorite blog. Tanya read it with interest, sighing as she finished reading. Over her shoulder, Sam read it too.

"Come on," he said, "Get your cell phone and let's get out of here. We have been here for weeks and not seen anything of this country; let's spend an afternoon away from this basement."

It took Tanya a few minutes to decide, picking up her phone, turning off her computers and making sure all the others were off, they left the basement a few minutes later.

Also in Athens, in his hotel room, G-Lover read the blog post too. Livid, he swore vengeance. He was going to do something big, he had to get revenge….he needed to clear his head and hatch the biggest plot yet.

It was time to call the others…

SIXTY-THREE

There is no pain so great as the memory of joy in present grief. –Aeschylus

It was a blustery evening, when the Professor got off the train. It had been a busy day in the city, and while he enjoyed the hustle and bustle of New York City, he was always happy to get off at the train station in their little town.

His office hours had gone longer than usual and he had had to take the later train back. He had taught a morning class, then had lunch with another Professor and attended a seminar in the afternoon, after which he had held office hours for his students. He always enjoyed office hours and encouraged his students to come see him. He liked getting to know his students, he was old school. Over the years he had stayed in touch with many of them, and was often surprised, pleasantly so, to hear of their successes and their need to keep in touch with him.

He had climbed on the train, pleasantly tired, and soon was immersed in a book of poetry on the ride back. He had remembered to call Diana, his wife, and let her know that he was taking the late train. She had offered to pick him up at the station, but he had turned her down, saying he preferred to walk the short distance home.

The ride to New Haven Union Station took an hour, and it was almost dark when he got off the train. He felt a shiver run through him as he walked briskly down the station platform to the gate leading to the street. Smiling to himself, he thought it may have been a good idea to have let Diana pick him up. Then giving himself a mental shake, he stepped out of the station on to the street and began the short walk to their house. It was a busy evening for New Haven; lots of cars and traffic moving along Church Street. He cut across a small park to Orange Avenue and continued his walk at a good pace to Crown Avenue. It had begun to drizzle and the air was definitely getting chillier. He would be home soon.

He hit the button on the pedestrian crosswalk and waited for the light to turn. When it did, he stepped off the sidewalk and began to walk across the street on the pedestrian crosswalk. He looked to his left and saw bright headlights bearing down on him. It was the last thing he remembered before the world went black.

Way up in his lair, Ares, smiled grimly to himself. His plan was unfolding.

***

It was three in the morning when Pythi was woken up with the news. He had worked late. His team in Dubai was doing very well and they had begun to uncover a pattern. Encouraged by their success, they had worked through dinner till Pythi had finally told them to go home. He had called Pia and told her that he was going to be late. Pia had told him not to worry, that she would get something to eat at the hotel restaurant.

Pythi marveled at how low key and accepting of his situation Pia was. He loved that she was so self-sufficient and that she did not cling or demand more of his time than he could give. She understood and he had begun to love her for that. He felt like he had finally met someone who accepted the importance of his work to him, and was not threatened by it. Plus, having her there, waiting for him at the end of his exhausting days was something he really looked forward to. It was the high point of his day and he could not wait to spend time with her, to hear about how her day went, to watch her describe her latest trip around Dubai or the desert and to discuss her discoveries in the City.

He loved her independence and her honest revelations about herself. He loved how animated she could get and yet he knew that she was immensely introspective. He loved holding her and making love to her. He loved waking up next to her. In fact, he loved everything about her.

Whoa…he stopped dead in his tracks as he crossed the lobby to the hotel restaurant. Was he actually admitting to himself that he was in love with Pia? In the past, the thought of being in love and loving someone made him decidedly uncomfortable and too vulnerable, but somehow with Pia it felt right. He was not afraid, just happy that she was with him.

He found her at the hotel bar, drinking a glass of wine and having a conversation with two British tourists. They seemed to be having a fun discussion and he watched her as he walked across the room, a beautiful smile on her face. She was the loveliest woman in the room and he wanted her to be his.

She was waving the others goodbye when she saw him and crossed the room to meet him half way. Dressed in a long white flowing skirt and lacy shirt to match, she looked stunning, her long dark hair flowing down her back. Being mindful of the cultural mores of the country, she gave him a quick hug and laughing told him how hungry she was.

They walked across to the pool area and decided to have dinner sitting by the pool, the cool evening air fanning the breezes around them. He had had a sandwich at work, but ordered again with Pia and they had a leisurely dinner discussing their day.

When they went up to their room, they made love. Still holding her in his arms he fell asleep exhausted. Pia had lain awake, listening to his breathing and watching his handsome face in the dark. Pythi had become a major part of her life and he meant a lot to her. Cuddling into him, she had fallen asleep too.

The phone had woken them both. The ring tone was different; it was the ring tone Pythi had set for phone calls from his parents. He rolled over and grabbed the phone, sleepily answering, "Hello, did you forget the time difference?"

In an instant he was up and Pia could sense the tension in him. In the quiet of the room, she could hear his mother sobbing on the phone. Getting out of bed, she pulled on a robe and waited for him to end his conversation. When he hung up, he sat on the bed, his head in his hands, very quiet. Pia went to him, holding him, waiting for him to speak.

"It's my Dad, he had an accident. It was a hit and run. He's in hospital in serious condition with a punctured lung and many broken bones. I need to go home."

"You should, your family needs you. I'll help you make the arrangements and will start packing."

And without any drama, quickly and efficiently, she packed first his things and then hers. He was really grateful to have her there with him. He wanted her to go with him but felt that it would be unfair to her. She would be much better off going back to Greece to her YahYah. She quietly agreed. His parents needed his undivided attention.

He called New York and spoke to his boss. Then he called Tanya, Derek, and Sam and had a long conversation with them. After that he called the team in Dubai and explained his need of an emergency leave for a few days to be with his father.

Pia called the airport and booked them flights after which she called a taxi. They held hands in the taxi, not saying much. Pythi was constantly on the phone and Pia sat quietly, praying inwardly that his father would be okay.

Dubai airport is always a frenetic mess, one of the busiest airports in the world, and once the taxi dropped them off, they were caught up in the hustle of checking into their flights and moving through passport control. Pythi's flight to New York left first and she walked hurriedly with him to his gate. His flight was being called and boarding had already begun when they got to the gate. All around them were other passengers and travelers. Pythi pulled her to him and kissed her quickly. Then, looking into her eyes, he stroked her face and arranged a strand of hair behind her ear. He raised her face to look into his eyes. "I have to go now," he said, "But I want you to know I love you and I will be back."
Then, pulling her close, he whispered in her ear that he loved her, again.

Letting her go, he stepped away and got pulled into the crowd moving toward the gate. Pia watched him leave, her heart breaking. In an instant her life had changed again.

What next? She wondered as she walked to a coffee bar to get herself an early morning cappuccino and wait for her flight to be called.

SIXTY-FOUR

When you set sail for Ithaca, wish for the road to be long,
full of adventure, full of knowledge. – Constantine Kavafis

Pia sat in the Costa Café bar for a while, sipping through her cappuccino, tasting the cinnamon in the froth, mindlessly watching the passenger traffic, letting herself relax, while she was recapping the recent developments. She loved her cappuccinos and she loved Costa Café, the British chain with the Italian taste. The coffee was good, roasted with traditional Italian mastery, and their large size cappuccinos were served in a bucket-size cup with two handles, it was that heavy.

As calmness started taking over the tension of the past few hours, she felt that unfailing warning signal coming again from her inner guidance system, the "Pia Compass," as she had playfully named it. She had learned to trust her inner compass and she was slowly applying it to every aspect of her life. It had proved itself to be true, time and again, so long as her mind was not influencing its direction. It was a rather complicated system and she had a hard time explaining it in words, but its signals were loud and clear: "feeling good," meaning this is in harmony with what Pia is, and, "feeling not good," meaning disharmony with inner core. In due course, Pia had noticed that the more she paid attention to her compass, the more sensitive and receptive she was becoming to its signals. The compass beacon was active right this minute, and it was beeping a constant red alert signal that gave her anything but a good feeling.

"The clouds are gathering and the storm is approaching," she whispered to herself, "I hope it is just a tropical storm and not a hurricane this time." She was not one to run away from the fury of a storm, but she was well-trained by now, and wise enough in spite of her young age, to take all necessary precautions in weathering it.

She checked her watch. Three hours left to her flight, a generous two hours before boarding time. "Plenty of time to go inside and check what is on the agenda," she whispered to herself, winning her a curious look from the stiff British lady sitting nearby. "I said it is time to get away from this circus and find me a quiet spot where I can collect my thoughts," she said to the Brit with a smile.

"Oh dear, the absolute insanity of Dubai Airport," returned the old lady, "I wish I had a pass to the VIP lounge and get away from all this madness while I am waiting for my flight."

It was like a light went off in Pia's head. *But of course, how could she have forgotten?* Pythi, using his gold frequent traveler status with the airline had gotten her a pass. "Use it," he had advised her, "It's much nicer than the public cafés, the service is great and time passes much more pleasantly." She touched the old lady's arm thankfully, and with a smile she wished her safe travels. Then, picking up her carry on, and having spotted the sign for the VIP lounge, she walked toward that direction.

The staff at the Marhaba VIP lounge was friendly and after they checked her pass, passport and boarding pass, they welcomed her to the lounge by giving her a small tour of the facility. All she wanted was a private corner away from intrusive, curious eyes.

The lounge was nicely appointed, comfortable, and best of all, it was not crowded. She picked a high back easy chair at the quiet far corner, and with the help of an attendant she turned it to face the wall, leaving enough space for a coffee table in between. The puzzled Nepalese attendant asked if he could bring her anything to drink as she deposited her belongings by the side of the chair. He returned with a clean glass and the requested bottle of Evian water. She took the glass of water he served her, thanked him, and made herself comfortable in the chair, as she slowly enjoyed the chilled liquid with eyes closed.

SIXTY-FIVE

I said to the almond tree, 'Sister, speak to me of God.' And the almond tree blossomed. – Nikos Kazantzakis

She sipped the water as she alternated tensing and relaxing her major muscles, slowly rotating her head to release all accumulated tension. At the same time she started slowing her breath, breathing in and out in a more aware, controlled manner. Soon, the events and thoughts of the day faded away, leaving her relaxed, with the mind focused on her breathing and not much else, selectively blocking out the sounds in the room.

She went through her aura cleansing exercise, removing any remnants of lingering tension, and started running the pineal gland exercise, stimulating the one organ in the head that acts as the doorway to the infinite. The pineal technique along with the accompanying deep breathing had her soon merging into the golden light circles of the passageway to deep meditation. She rearranged her posture to make sure her spine was straight, crossed her legs at the foot of the chair and rested her hands on her thighs, thumb and index finger touching, closing the circuit, and she was off; "wheels up," as she used to joke.

Many years ago, unexpectedly, she had run into her teacher, soon after she had been introduced to meditation by her roommate, Shanti. Some people call them gurus; he preferred to be called a wayshower. A kind, unassuming man without funny robes, throngs of devotees, or glistening halos, he looked and behaved like everyone else, until you looked into his eyes.

He had told her that people search for gurus all their lives, running to ashrams in India, monasteries in Tibet, shrines in Japan, cathedrals in the western world, and mosques in the East, hoping to find the secret to a miraculous transformation. Most returned disappointed and many were deceived by false teachers and prophets, who profited handsomely from the spiritual yearning and naivety of the seekers. "All this searching outside and in strange places, when the one true teacher is within one's self," her guru had said.

"The unselfish teacher or wayshower," he told her, "Will help you open the door to the inner part of you and, then, that higher self will become your one and true guru forever. Gurus that draw attention to themselves are not true teachers and their motives are selfish," he had said. "Do not trust them, as you should not trust me or believe what I say. Instead, you should strive to find out for yourself." She had lived by those words ever since.

He taught her how to relax, quiet and then focus the mind. Then, he showed her how to go into her subconscious, and sweep it clean, before programming her own thoughts, in full awareness this time. Finally, he taught her a special yoga meditation technique. He told her that this was an invaluable gift, which if developed properly, would help her find herself and take her to the gates of Paradise. He also warned her that it was very powerful, and if used improperly, much harm can come from it.

"Keep your heart pure and be of service," he had said, "Your higher self will lead you back home to the Promised Land, where you came from and where we will all return some day. You are ready for this journey back home." That had been the last thing she remembered him telling her, before he disappeared from her life, as suddenly as he had appeared.

In the years that followed, meditation became a daily routine for her and a central part of her life. There were times that her busy life would drive her away from this established routine, but, discomfort, and lack of focus and clarity always brought her back to reestablish balance. Especially in times of unrest and turmoil, as now, or times of anguish and loss of perspective, she reached to her higher self for advice and guidance through her meditation.

Eyes closed, relaxed and well-focused, oblivious to the going-ons in the room, she centered at the top of her head, seat of the crown chakra, gathered energy at the base of her spine, and ran it up through her body centers, fountaining it out at the top of the head. Her heart center felt tender and sensitive, in need of balancing. It was no wonder with all the sad news and abrupt separation from Pythi. She continued running the energy methodically, until all obstructions were dissolved, feeling more fatigue-free and rejuvenated with every breath, until she was part of the current floating along effortlessly.

Oftentimes, all she had to do is thinking of a place during her meditations and she would be instantly transported there, leaving her inner vision to do the rest of the exploration. Today, she was not in the mood for adventure and exploration. Today, she wanted answers and the best place for that was her inner abode, her place of peace and tranquility, where she could pose questions and receive answers, if she was quiet, focused and centered enough.

In her meditations, she had created a place of peace for herself, her inner abode. Just above the high peaks of the Himalayas, with spectacular views of the snow-covered mountain tops, white as purity itself. Inside her abode it was warm and cozy. She sat on her favorite wing chair near the glowing fireplace, as she let the pristine mountain views fill her eyes through the expansive picture windows. Then, she turned to the stone wall above the fireplace where she was usually projecting her questions and, as on a computer screen, she mentally typed: "Beloved One, please grace me with your wisdom. Why do I feel this unrest and sense of danger? Am I or Pythi in harm's way?"

Normally, there would be a small delay and the answer would appear as typed text on the same screen. Not this time. She tried again, thinking that she had not concentrated enough. Again, no answer and the screen started blurring and slowly dissolving into the stone wall that it really was. As she was getting ready to ask for a third time, a mist appeared on the other side of the fireplace. Light at first, it was becoming denser and denser, shaping into a human form, a female form. When the process was completed, Pia looked at a woman in full ancient war regalia, wearing a high helmet and holding a spear in one hand and a large round shield in the left. It was an imposing, regal presence.

"You have developed the gift your teacher gave you well, little one," said the warrior woman. "Your powers are getting stronger and more focused. You no longer need to project your thoughts as words on a screen. This is a rather primitive approach. Instead, just project your thoughts as vibrations and the answers will return to you the same way. Simply, mentally ask and you will mentally receive."

The regal presence moved a little closer and continued, "I am Athena, daughter of the almighty Zeus and Goddess of Wisdom. You are one of mine, and thus, you are under my care and protection. Your developed intuition has warned you well; there are dark forces moving against your loved one and threatening you as well. We are monitoring their movements and we will do our best to stop them. However, these are powerful forces and you need to protect yourself as well. Make sure that every day, before you leave home, you build the force field of protection your teacher taught you to build around yourself. In addition, take this shield and use it as protection, if and when you are under attack. All good energy will go through it to reach you, but no evil force will ever penetrate it. However, remember that you have to deploy it mentally; you have to sense the evil force coming and deploy the shield, which will serve as a fortress around you. You may do that by calling my name. Do not neglect my advice. You are strong and sensitive. I have faith in you. Go with my blessings and know that I am here to help and support you."

Pia almost jumped out of her seat as a hesitant finger was tapping on her shoulder. "I'm sorry to wake you miss," said the lounge receptionist standing over her chair, "But, your flight has started boarding. You need to get going." She thanked the woman in a misty daze, collected her personal items on unsure legs and slowly headed for the security check, trying to regain composure.

SIXTY-SIX

*If all misfortunes were laid in one common heap where everyone must take an equal portion,
most people would be content to take their own and depart. – Socrates*

The last few hours had been a complete nightmare. The flight back had been simply horrible. Usually, after take-off, he would open up his laptop and work, or have a beer, watch a movie and fall asleep.

On this flight he was restless; he knew he was disturbing the lady in the seat next to his. He couldn't sit still, his mind was racing and he mentally willed the airplane to make it to New York as soon as possible. The beer did not relax him either; he couldn't focus on work or a movie, and he kept getting up and walking up and down the aisle trying to calm himself. He was on a twelve hour flight with no way of knowing what was happening to his father.

The brief conversations he had had with his mother had not helped. He knew her well and had never heard the level of panic in her voice that he had heard in their last two conversations. They were wheeling him into surgery just as he got on the flight and he prayed that his father made it. It had been difficult to find out from his mother exactly what had happened and what the level of his injuries were. All he had heard her say, over and over again, was that his father was horribly injured and that they didn't know if he would make it. He needed to know more, his logical brain could not handle not having all the facts.

He leant back in his seat, closing his eyes for the hundredth time, trying to calm the frenetic thoughts racing through his mind. It was cold on the plane and he felt shivery, he wasn't sure if it was the cold or simply shock from the news. He reached for a blanket, covered himself, then closing his eyes one more time, he began to take deep breaths, focusing on the breathing.

Breathe in…hold the breath….release it, he mentally repeated over and over again, till, after a few minutes, he began to feel a little of the tension seep out of him. In a few more minutes, he began to feel his racing heart slow down, and gradually he felt some semblance of calm overcoming him.

Hmm, he thought to himself, *This whole meditation and breathing thing is not bad, I should have paid more attention when Pia was trying to show me her meditation techniques…*

Pia…Oh no, he had forgotten to call or text her before his plane took off, he had been so worried about his dad. He sat up again, heart racing, wondering what Pia was doing, his mind running amuck again.

"Back to the breathing, focus," he told himself as he tried to calm down once more.

And so it went, breathing in and breathing out till he finally fell asleep, deeply exhausted.

***

He had made it to the New Haven hospital, tired and blurry eyed, to find his mother looking frail and diminished. His mother had always been a strong woman, practical and stoic, the voice of reason in the family. It hurt him to see her so vulnerable and racked with worry. There was little they could do but sit in the waiting room and wait for him to come out of recovery.

He had found out that the car had hit his father head on. He had rolled onto the front of the car and then rolled off of it, while the car was still in motion. Luckily for him, the car had not rolled over him. But, it had kept going, and the passerby's and people in the cars behind had stopped and called 911. He was also lucky that the ambulance got there in record time and transported him to the hospital. His injuries were extensive. Broken ribs with punctured lungs, legs and arms broken, and that was only the obvious, easy part. The doctors had no idea of the extent of the head injury. They had done their best to stabilize the internal hemorrhaging, before they wheeled him into surgery to save his lungs and drain the fluid building up in his brain.

Pythi stared blankly out of the window of the waiting area. Like most hospitals, it was full of people sitting on the uncomfortable plastic chairs, sipping insipid hospital coffee, the smell of fear and sickness pervading the room. His mother sat next to him, and he could sense the tension and stress seeping out of her. He held her hand and stroked it in an effort to calm her down, there was little else for him to do.

It was hours before the doctors came out to speak with them; two of them. They were ushered into a small office where the doctors explained the professor's condition. They also told them that they had put him in an induced coma, as his body had gone into shock and they would keep him that way till he stabilized. He was currently out of recovery and in intensive care. They were allowed to go see him through the glass wall of the intensive care room in which he lay.

Mother and son walked hand in hand down the endless hallway, past the darkened nurses' station, to his room. They looked in to see his frail body covered with blankets, his head swathed in bandages. There was no light in the room, except the bank of machines that he was hooked up to cast a grayish pallor over the part of his face that was not bandaged.

Pythi, put his hand up against the glass as if he was reaching out to touch his father and willed him to get better.

"Don't go, Dad," he beseeched, "We need you, and we love you."

Then, standing there, in that bleak space he remembered the words of Socrates that his father had often quoted, "The hour of departure has arrived and we go our ways; I to die, and you to live. Which is better? Only God knows."

God knows that we want you to live, God knows that we cannot live without you. May God bring you through this, he prayed.

Mother and son stood there for a long time, watching him, till a nurse came over and ushered them out. There was little for them to do but wait. Pythi was not a patient man; the waiting was going to be agony. He convinced her that it was time to get back home to rest and they drove home quietly. Lights were still blazing in the house as his mother had not had a chance to turn them off and she had forgotten to close the garage door in her panic and hurry to get to the hospital. Pythi wheeled his bag in and took it upstairs. Then he came down and made his mother a cup of tea as she sat at the kitchen table, where the table was still laid for dinner.

"Mom, get some rest. It's going to be a long few weeks and you are going to need your strength."

Shaking her head, she looked at him, "He was on his way home, just like any other day. I should have gone to the station to pick him up. If I had, this wouldn't have happened."

"You can't blame yourself," he admonished, "It's absolutely not your fault. The guys who hit Dad will be caught. I will go to the police station tomorrow to get an update. In the meantime, you need some sleep. Come on, let me help you up."

"Pythi, I am not an invalid. I am perfectly capable of climbing up the stairs, which, mind you, I have done hundreds of times before, and putting myself to bed," she said with vehemence.

Pythi smiled. For with that, his mother was back; the lady he knew and admired, her strength flowing out of her again.

Before she went up, she walked over to him and hugged him for a long time.

"Thank you for coming as fast as you could. I really needed you to come home. I feel so much better now," she said softly.

"Of course mom, no thanks needed. I love you both, we are family, and I'll always be here for you."

She hugged him again and, as she turned to go up the stairs, looked at him and with a sparkle in her eyes she said, "Tell your lovely lady that I am sorry you had to suddenly leave her and come back here."

Pythi looked at her with surprise in his eyes.

"I know," she said, "A mother always knows. I hope I get to meet her soon, son." Then, climbing up the stairs she disappeared into her bedroom.

He knew his inbox would be full by now but he did not want to deal with work issues. He turned on his phone and saw two text messages from Pia. One message before she boarded her plane for Greece and another when she landed. She was hoping to hear from him.

"Pia," he wrote, "Made it back. Dad is in critical condition. Hoping for the best. Glad I came home but miss you and hoping you made it back okay. Too tired to talk but will call you in the morning.
And I mean what I told you before I left; I love you, S'agapo, agapi mou."

Then, turning off his phone again he went up to the bedroom, took a quick shower, and fell into a deep dreamless sleep.

In Sounion, it was late morning when Pia heard her phone buzz. She read the text and smiled. She loved him too.

SIXTY-SEVEN

Time is the wisest counselor of all. - Pericles

Ares was watching his evil plan unfold with great interest. *So far so good,* he thought, perched high over the Santorini volcano looking into the boiling lava. The professor was mortally wounded and Pythi had already abandoned Pia and his team of bank sleuths and had rushed to New York to be on the side of his dying father. The Warriors could breathe now and G-Lover would have a chance to recover and assume leadership of his group. Or would he?

Ares had developed serious misgivings about G-Lover. *His truly evil nature and cool demeanor were ideal for leading this operation,* Ares had thought. But he didn't count on him being such an easy victim to his vices, and he had not foreseen his obsession with Pia developing to the uncontrollable level it had reached. G-Lover was a time bomb that could derail his plans, and that he could not afford. G-Lover had to be reined in and refocused, if his plan were to grow roots and spread.

The banks and financial turmoil would only be the beginning, his target and grand prize was the world at large. Ares concluded, "I simply need more diversion, more confusion, I must inflict more personal pain and suffering, more collateral damage to keep them all running like chickens with their heads cut off, instead of them focusing on how to find and defeat G-Lover and his team." With that he picked up a boulder and hurled it into the volcano crater.

The explosion that followed, the thick black smoke spewing out of the mouth of the volcano, the lava that fountained and started running down the mountain slopes, the panic that this grand spectacle caused in the villages nestled at the foot of the mountain did Ares' heart good and he started laughing, a roar of a laugh that rose above the roar of the volcano. "They are so weak, so helpless," he managed between his chortling, "And they will be mine."

***

Both Athena and Poseidon saw the volcanic eruption at Santorini and felt the dark presence of Ares. He was up to no good again. They had relaxed their defenses way too much and Ares had already surprised them by hurting the professor. They knew him well enough to be certain that there would be more.

The smoke rising from Santorini and the gathering dark clouds were enough of a confirmation to set things in motion and they agreed to meet on neutral ground on the island of Aegina. As it were, Aegina, the Parthenon, and the Temple at Sounion, were the apexes of a perfectly formed equilateral triangle. No unfair advantage there for either of them, it was neutral ground, although, there was too much at stake here to allow themselves to be consumed by petty rivalries.

Pythi, Pia, and their loved ones, were in danger and the fate of the world at stake. They talked for a while and quickly agreed that they needed to move and protect their own and their loved ones from the evil plans of Ares and his Warriors. They had no doubt that Ares and his cohorts would try to hurt YahYah and possibly Pythi's mother next. They had to provide protection for them and they had to help the Professor stay alive and be given a fighting chance to recover and heal. They didn't think that Ares would try to hurt Pythi and Pia, as he knew full well that they were under their protection and it would draw the combined wrath of Poseidon and Athena, something Ares could ill-afford at the moment his team seemed to be falling apart. They both conceded though, that, protection must be provided for both Pia and Pythi too.

"You must warn your man Pythi of the danger," said Athena to Poseidon, "I have already done it with Pia. And get your Sea-Guardians busy; protection around the clock. The Warriors are getting desperate and Ares will not hesitate to resort to despicable measures to recover and regain control. We need protection."

"Yes boss, General," joked Poseidon. "I'm off to Sounion to summon my Sea-Guardians and assign them duties. Why don't you visit with your priestesses who specialize in healing and see what they can do to improve the survival chances of the poor professor?" With that he leaned over and landed a tender kiss on her cheek, "By the way, you look stunningly beautiful today."

There was a gentle smile on Athena's face and a sparkle in her eyes as she watched Poseidon disappear high up in the ether, before she turned northeast and headed to Athens.

SIXTY-EIGHT
The test of any man lies in action. – Pindar

While the grounds at the Temple at Sounion were no busier than any other day the Temple was open to the tourists, the ethereal plane above was teaming with action. Poseidon, sitting on his majestic throne, was addressing his troops of Sea-Guardians in military arrangement in front of him. Grouped in teams of one dozen, each with a leader, they looked imposing, fearsome, and huge. Spear or trident in one hand, shield in the other, dressed in simple short tunics with their panoply and high helmet, they looked as war worthy as anyone could imagine.

"Our mission is to protect, not start a war," said Poseidon in his stentorian voice. "You will be warrior guardian angels and you will allow no harm to come to the person you are assigned to protect. Under no circumstance will you be allowed to take physical form and reveal yourselves. The only exception will be if your protected person is in mortal danger and no other option is available to protect their lives."

Then he went on to explain the situation and identify the persons to be protected: Pythi, the Professor, the Professor's wife Diana, Pia, and YahYah.

"I want protection round the clock until further notice," said Poseidon, "You never know when and how the dark forces may strike." Then, he went on to assign a regiment of twelve with their leader to each person.

"Four of you should be with your person at all times. Four will scout the perimeter that this person is in at any time, and four will wait in reserve, but not far away. There will be frequent rotations, as I want everyone to stay sharp; your leaders will brief you on the details. I cannot stress enough the importance of this mission and I am counting on you and your superior skills, my trusted Sea-Guardians, to keep everyone you have been assigned to safe. Go now and see to your duties."

Athena had summoned her priestesses in the middle of the Parthenon, all devoted virgins who had dedicated their lives to the Goddess and had specialized in different areas. She took her time to explain the objective of their mission, stressing the importance of it. The ailing professor was the target of their attention and their mission was to save his life. Things looked pretty grim at the moment and they had to go to work immediately, if they were hoping to succeed in keeping him alive.

Then, she proceeded to lead a team meditation where their combined energy was focused to build healing patterns of vibrant, electric green light energy around all of the professor's damaged organs, to speed up recovery and healing, but also focused on building a dome of sparkling white energy around him to sustain him. When finished with the meditation, she addressed her priestesses again.

"Once again, I am proud of your spiritual development, as your purity of thought, devotion and dedication have given you formidable powers, as I have just experienced once more. The Professor's life force is very weak and he will not make it without our help. Let us all meet at this main Hall every day and focus on enhancing the Professor's life force. Let's put him on a life force I.V., so to speak, until he has built enough strength to do it on his own. Those of you that specialize in the healing arts, please form a separate group and work methodically in identifying the most vital of the Professor's organs which have sustained damage and work diligently in restoring functionality and health to them. We need to save the professor. Now, go my Beloveds and tend to your daily duties."

After the last of the priestesses had gone, Athena stayed in silent reverie for a while, pondering what had been set in motion and was unfolding. Poseidon had telepathically messaged her that the Sea-Guardians had already been deployed, and not to worry. Between Poseidon's guardian angels and her priestesses' restoring powers, they had built a pretty good defense. Was that enough? She knew only too well how crafty and cunning Ares could be. They all needed to stay on their celestial toes and be as alert as they could. Who knew, but evil Ares himself, where he planned to strike next?

SIXTY-NINE

Nothing is harder to direct than a man in prosperity, nothing more easily managed than one in adversity. - Plutarch

The last rays of the setting Sun disappeared behind the substantial relief of Makronisos, the long island which acts as a natural breakwater for the Port of Lavrion, providing protection against the winds that come from the open expanse of the Aegean Sea. Unpredictable are these winds, known from antiquity to bring the wrath of Aeolus, the God of Winds, to bear upon the unfortunate mariners that happen to be sailing during the temperamental God's moody outbursts.

A lone figure stood in the twilight at the Lavrion Marina, just a few kilometers from Sounion, with the open cafés and tavernas to his back. He looked beyond the berthed sailboats and pleasure motor boats, at the thickening shadow of Makronisos, that island of pain and suffering during the seven dark years of dictatorship that had befallen Greece in 1967. The statue of the mother/wife/sister in the small square behind him, looking out to the island with outstretched arms trying to reach her beloveds, was a stark reminder of that grim period, when the island was used as both prison and exile for political decedents and prisoners.

The lone figure was a middle-aged man, well dressed, with an air of superiority and arrogance in his poise. It was no coincidence that he carried the name "Aris", short for Aristotle. He looked to the right, towards the newer, northern part of the Port, where cruise and passenger ships docked. "No, not desperate enough," he muttered to himself. Then, he turned to the left, toward the old Port to the south, where cargo and mineral ore vessels load and unload. "Yes, indeed," he smiled to himself, and he slowly started that way.

When he reached the poorly lit main entrance, he found the rusting metal gate locked and chained with no security guard around. "The economic crisis is taking its toll," he said to himself, "And poverty and despair will be my recruitment agents."

It was a good thing that there was no security guard around to witness what happened next, as he would have questioned his own sanity for days to come and been the scorn of his friends at the taverna, as he recalled in amazement that, "The damn man just dissolved himself, passed through the bars, and materialized again inside; the damndest thing, I tell you, and I kid you not!" There was no question that his buddies would have teased him that after all these years his wife had finally managed to drive him bananas and he was losing his marbles.

Once inside the Port, Aris headed for a dark, single story, out of the way building in obvious need of maintenance and repairs. In a recess sheltered by the wind, along the northern wall, he found what he was looking for - three men in soiled worker's outfits, crouched around a low cut 55-gallon drum with a fire burning inside, trying to warm themselves against the evening chill.

"Who are you and what are you doing here?" He addressed the men in an authoritarian voice.

"Boss," squirmed one of them, "We are port workers, but without much business we cannot pay rent and live here. Once in a way we catch a few hours of work, helping the docked crews. Sailors are kind that way and give us food too. The crisis is killing us. Please be kind and don't report us to the harbor master. Ok, boss?"

"Ok, I'll pretend I didn't see you this time, but you need to do something for me and you'll be paid well," replied Aris. "How would you like making a quick five hundred euro each for a few hours of work?"

"Boss, five hundred euro is a good month's salary these days! You don't even have to ask. What do we need to do?"

Aris sat with them and explained that at Sounion, a few kilometers up the coastal road, there was the house of an old lady who had been particularly stubborn. She was refusing to sell her property to his very wealthy and influential boss that wanted to build a Bed & Breakfast there, as the views of the bay and the temple of Poseidon were great. The old lady needed to be convinced to change her mind.

"Give her a good beating and send her to the hospital, but don't kill her. I want her alive to sign the bill of sale. A couple of weeks of recovery at the hospital will give her plenty of time to reconsider."

When the three desperate men started protesting that dirty work was one thing, but beating up an old lady would put a curse on their souls, Aris was quick to remind them that there was a lot riding on this for them. The old lady was really a witch of a woman that nobody liked and his boss was one to value and reward loyalty. "Do right by him with this, and all three of you will end up with money in your pockets and a regular job at the B&B during construction and after it is built."

"You can get your lives and dignity back for just a few hours of work that may even be fun. Imagine her being your mother in law," he joked with a grin, "And let yourselves express your long overdue appreciation."

The money and the promise of a regular life to the desperate men proved too powerful to resist and the homeless men soon agreed to go ahead with it. Then, all four started planning the operation. The local tavernas at Sounion close at midnight and the place becomes dark and deserted. The plan called for the three porters to catch a taxi from Lavrion to Sounion after one in the morning and arrive at the Aegeon Hotel, looking like they were guests returning from a night of fun at Lavrion. Then, under the cover of night, they would take the path up the slope to YahYah's house, break in quietly, and teach the old lady a lesson, before leaving quietly.

"Leave the old lady well beaten but alive," emphasized Aris, "And leave the front door ajar. I want her neighbors to find her in the morning when she does not show up for the ritual of the Greek coffee and call for an ambulance. Is that clear? Then, walk to the other hotel in the area, Porto Sounion, and take one of the stand-by taxis to Lavrion town. Nobody will think anything of it."

He gave each two hundred and fifty euro upfront and money for the taxi rides. "The rest in the morning," he said, "Meet me at the Marina Café at eight to report completion of the mission and you'll get the rest of your money. Do this well and your life will change forever." He got up and started walking away, then, he stopped, turned around and said, "Fail and this town will be too small for you, way too small. You understand me?" They were still shaking their heads in scared agreement as Aris disappeared into the darkness of the Port.

***

It was one thirty in the morning when the taxi arrived at the rear of the sleepy Aegeon hotel, near the closed, darkened tavernas. Nobody saw the three men getting out of the taxi, crossing the hotel parking area and slowly, carefully, heading up the steep path towards YahYah's house.

It was the roaming sentries that noticed movement first and alerted the four Sea-Guardians in the house. The reserved four were also notified to join the group and all twelve took defensive positions around the house. YahYah was fast asleep inside and peaceful as she could be. Lately, her female intuition was giving her signals of increased safety and security, which she welcomed and made sure to thank Virgin Mary and the Goddess in her prayers for this added blessing.

The invisible roaming sentries let the three vagabonds pass without incident and followed right behind them in defensive alertness. The three reached the yard in front of the few steps that lead to the elevated porch and house entrance. They stopped, listened carefully and looked all around. All was quiet, no signs of life, whatsoever.

Slowly, quietly, they started ascending the small staircase, careful not to trigger any unwanted squeaks that would be compounded by the stillness of the night and alert YahYah and the neighbors. All was going according to plan. That was until mid-step they ran into an invisible wall that seemed to block their way up. Puzzled, they instinctively tried to push through it but it would not yield. It felt as if it was made of metal, and it moved as they changed positions trying to bypass it. As the vagabonds intensified their efforts to penetrate the invisible wall, the shields of the Sea-Guardians became offensive weapons hitting them in the face and pushing them back.

That brought them into the shields of the roaming sentries behind them. The tennis game that ensued between the invisible house sentries and the roaming ones with the vagabonds as tennis balls in-between left the vagabonds badly bruised, with bleeding noses, and horrified to the point they soiled themselves. The minute the shield onslaught stopped and they were able to gather their fleeting courage, they burst into a mad run, to get away from the haunted house, thinking they were being chased by horrible, blood-thirsty ghosts.

***

The morning coffee was a lonely affair for Aris, as none of the vagabonds showed up to claim their reward money. By noon, there was a rumor spreading that a certain part of Sounion was haunted and superstition took over from there. By nightfall, there were several stories circulating among the café- goers. Some had Poseidon as the main protagonist, others the spirit of dead king Aegeus, even the tragic story of the local Romeo and Juliet from the 1920's was brought back to life. The versions were endless and some entrepreneurial minds had started thinking about setting up a haunted house at Sounion to give the tourists thrills. The vagabond porters that had started the rumor chain were never seen again in Lavrion, but no one missed them, as very few knew of their existence.

***

Similar attempts to harm Pythis' mother in New York City with hired hoodlums met with the same failure due to the diligent defense of the alert Sea-Guardians. Ares got the message loud and clear; Athena and Poseidon had guessed his moves and had prepared for them. The element of surprise was not his advantage any longer.

SEVENTY

He fashions evil for himself who does evil to another, and an evil plan does mischief to the planner. –
Hesiod

Ares was brewing anger and releasing rage. "Bloody Athena and Poseidon and their pawns! They are everywhere, stopping me and I cannot fight them. It is time to revisit my evil-inspired uncle and see what we can cook up."

With that, he set course for the Acheron River. The grotesque ferryman, uglier than ever, was already waiting for him. He pocketed the handful of coins that Ares handed him and without uttering a word, rowed his boat to deliver Ares to the gates of the Underworld. To Ares' surprise, Hades himself was there to welcome him.

"I saw the clouds gathering nephew and sensed you coming," he said with a crooked smile. "I take it things are not going according to plan? It looks like the tactical wisdom of my niece Athena and strength of my sailor brother Poseidon have gotten the better of you. Fret not, come in and let us do some creative brainstorming. We have an axe to grind you and I, and by all the fires in hell we will," as he roared in malicious laughter at his own joke. Ares felt his helplessness abate as he followed Hades to his chambers with a newfound spring in his step.

Once comfortably seated, Ares updated Hades on the recent developments, not failing to mention the shortcomings of his team and his failed attempts to inflict more harm to the ones protected by the Poseidon-Athena duo. Hades listened carefully and after a thoughtful pause, he said, "You underestimated everyone and your attempt to distract by hurting the professor was detected too quickly and they sprang into action. But, what is most worrying to me is the falling out within your own team. This is not good, definitely not good. The vices of your leader, the G-Lover, which made it easy for you to recruit him, are turning against you now and are undermining the team. Discipline must be restored, if you are to succeed.

Also, you did not heed my early advice to deploy deceit to your advantage, to make yourself visibly involved in many smaller conflicts, and to unleash threatening attacks on the wealth lords. You need a multi-front attack to have a chance to succeed. Attack on a single front, the banking system, allows them to concentrate all their efforts there. I warned you before, together they are a formidable foe, if not impossible for you. You need to redraw the plans, nephew, but this time I will help you do it. But let us have supper first, I think better with a full stomach. You'll find my ambrosia to taste unlike any other on divine tables. The former chef of King Minos himself is in charge of my kitchens and his inspired cooking has my palate anxious with gastronomical anticipation every single time."

Their dinner was a lavish affair over a truly regal spread with happy chats, catching up on the latest news in the corridors of the Olympian Palace and gossip on the private affairs and intrigues of the other Gods. This helped Ares let go of his gloom and be really attentive to his uncle's advice when they reclined on comfortable couch-beds after dinner, still sipping on their spiked nectar.

"Now, now," started Hades, "We need to make you invisible and introduce new players that are not on their radar. There is plenty of unrest and conflict in the Middle East to keep you busy. That is what you will do and do it very visibly, making everyone believe that you are up to your eyebrows in trouble there. Then, bring your trusted and equally as evil divine sons from your union with Aphrodite, Phobos (Fear) and Deimos (Terror), into the game. Assign Deimos the task of scaring the daylights out of G-Lover, rein him in, restore discipline to the Warriors team and refocus them in taking down the system.

For Phobos and his dark diplomatic talents I have thought of a very special, deliciously diabolical mission. Let me keep it to myself for now as I develop its details, but I assure you, it will be effective and lethal in its impact. I am planning to use my well-placed connections on that. I just hope we are not too late; you should have come to me earlier. In the meanwhile, talk to your sons and I will send for Phobos when I am ready to discuss details. Go now my nephew, as the hour is getting late, and stop worrying. Things will be alright."

SEVENTY-ONE

The only thing I know is this: I am full of wounds and still standing on my feet. – Nikos Kazantzakis

Pythi felt like he was living in an alternative Universe. It had been a few days since his return home and he spent his days sitting at the hospital or rushing back to his parents' home to catch up on his work and email.

It had been a waiting game; endless days, hours, minutes of simply waiting to hear of some progress. It was very tough on Pythi. He was a problem solver. Patience was not his forte. But, in this instance, he could not solve the issue of his father's health and he could not leave his mother alone and go back to Athens to take care of the issues at the Banque. It frustrated him, but there was little he could do.

Once again, he sat on the little plastic chair in the hospital waiting room, hoping to hear of some upbeat news regarding his father. His mother and he kept a vigil at the hospital, and they were there around the clock, just going home to shower, rest a little, and in Pythi's case to catch up with ongoing developments at work.

The news on his father was neither hopeful nor grim, it just was. They were waiting to see how he would come out of the series of surgeries and the terrible injuries he had suffered. His mother had reverted to her stoic practical self again, and was hoping for the best. They were often visited by neighbors and friends and that kept her in good spirits. The Professor was well loved, and there had been an outpouring of support for his family.

Pythi would often leave his chair and walk down the long corridor to the ICU room in which his father lay. From time to time the nurses allowed him in. Then, he would sit by his father's bed and talk to him, stroking the feeble arm that was ensconced in tubes and bandages. Over and over, he told him how much he missed him and that he, Pythi, was not ready to let him go. He told him all about Pia and their trip to Dubai. He told him about the wonders of Sounion, and sometimes he recited his favorite poems to him, in Greek of course. At other times, he would just sit quietly, stroking his hand, watching the nurses and doctors going in and out of the room, tending to his father; it was part of their daily routine. To him, all of this seemed unreal.

He sent his mother home every night, so she could rest, while he stayed at the hospital, keeping watch over his father. It was the night times that were the most peaceful and yet the most excruciating. The lights in the ICU were dimmed; he could hear the humming of the machines and the soft voices of the nurses and doctors, as they walked by. The hospital slowed down for a while and he became a part of that rhythm. Not wanting to disturb his father, he would stand for long periods of time outside the room, looking through the glass wall at him.

On the second night, in the early morning hours, when all strength had abandoned his body and
there was no resistance to anything, Pythi laid his head back against the sofa of the waiting room, and closed his exhausted eyes hoping for a short, refreshing nap. It was at that moment between conscious and subconscious that an imposing figure with long dark hair, naked from the waste up and holding a large trident, appeared in his mind's eye. The image was very clear.

"I am Poseidon," he said in a deep, thundering voice. "You are one of my own, as you will come to realize in time. I take care of my own and that is the reason I appear to you. I am here to warn you that there are dark forces that are moving against you and your loved ones. We will do everything we can to deflect and neutralize the evil these forces intend to cause, and protect you and your loved ones, but you need to be extra vigilant. The accident of your father was not an accident at all and we are working to restore his strength and keep him alive. When you wake, your mind will try to convince you that this was a dream. It is not; keep your eyes open because the danger is real."

Right on cue, when Pythi woke up an hour later, he remembered the dream and was amused at how vivid it was. *I need to stop reading Greek mythology*, he noted to himself, *it has started messing with my reality*, and he headed for the coffee machine, for the caffeine shot that would help him see his vigil through.

***

With all the time Pythi was spending at the hospital, he soon begun to know all the nurses and the doctors by name. They knew him, as well, and liked him for his personable style. Thus, a few nights later, when he noticed a new male nurse, he was surprised; then, he clearly remembered Poseidon's warning and tensed. He was a big, burly male nurse, dressed in his scrubs, going from room to room with his cart and his computer on it, checking the patients. Pythi had not seen him before. He watched him, wheel in his cart, open the door to each room, step inside and come back out a few minutes later. He continued down the corridor, methodically going from room to room. Pythi thought nothing of it, till he saw him go to the door of his father's room. He turned the handle on the door and it would not open. He tried again, jiggling the door.

From where he was sitting in the waiting room, Pythi watched him and as soon as he realized it was his father's room, he got up and strode down the hallway toward the nurse, a question in his eyes. He knew the hospital routine. His father has already been checked on; he had stood by the nurse while she had monitored him. He, Pythi, sat in the waiting room in a spot where he could see the monitors at the nurses' station and could keep an eye on any changes or fluctuations in his father's vitals.

The nurse looked up as Pythi strode over to him.

"Just checking on the patients, as I do every hour. This door seems to have caught, it won't open," he said in accented English.

Eastern European, thought Pythi.

Pythi checked his name tag; it read 'Grigory H.'

"That's my father's room," he responded, "I was just in there."

The nurse tried again.

"It feels as though there is some resistance, the door won't move."

The nurse at the monitoring station watched the interchange and quickly walked over. She asked them to step aside and gently turned the door knob. It opened without any resistance.

"I think I will just sit with my father, in case this happens again. Do you mind?" Pythi asked the night nurse, "I promise to sit very quiet and still, right beside him."

Smiling, she told him to go ahead.

Pythi went into the cold room, zipped up his jacket and seated himself in the chair by the Professor's bed. When he looked up he noticed that Nurse Grigory was no longer there and that he had not come into the room to check on his father.

Odd, he thought as he settled himself in the chair and looked up at the T.V. that was showing the News, but was muted.

That night, he dozed sitting by the bed, in the sterile hospital room. Several times through the night as he dozed, in that place where he was not fully awake yet not deep in sleep, he felt as if the room, the small hospital room, was full of beautiful beings in long gossamer gowns and flowing hair. The vision would wake him, and he would look around and seeing nothing would fall back in his dozing state, only for it to happen again….and again.

"I'm either truly very tired or turning delusional," he said to himself, "But I must remember to mention it to Pia tomorrow."

So saying, he fell back to sleep again, and this time when he woke up he found doctors and nurses scurrying in and out of the room, the bank of monitors behind his father's bed showed a slew of movement and he sat up, jerking himself out of his deep slumber, his sleepy eyes focusing on the activity in the room, his heart racing and a feeling of panic beginning to spread within him.

He had fallen asleep holding his father's hand, and it was at the moment when three physicians strode into the room that he realized that he was not holding his father's lifeless hand, his father was clutching his…and it was a tight clutch, Pythi's fingers hurt.

He looked at the hand in surprise and then looked up at his father, his eyes were open. Pythi felt the tears rushing and blinked hard to hold them back. What was more, in the split second when their eyes connected; he saw recognition and a softening. His tears flowed quietly, but he did not let go of the hand.

The doctors were in there for a long time, trying to determine the extent of the injury on his brain and his body. Through it all Pythi and his father continued to hold hands. He could not speak…. yet, and because of his extensive physical injuries could not move but could slowly and minutely nod, or shake his head and blink in acknowledgement.

When asked if he recognized Pythi, he nodded twice and squeezed his hand tighter. When asked to move his fingers and toes, he understood and did…and so on it went for a long time. Soon, tired, he closed his eyes, and the doctors and nurses, with their boards, and additional equipment, left the room.

Pythi waited till his father loosened his grip on his hand, and then went out to meet the doctors. The news was good. It would be a long recovery but he would recover. They had not ascertained any extensive brain damage. The Professor had understood and responded to their queries appropriately. His broken bones would heal and once the tubes were taken out of his throat they would be able to tell if there was any speech impairment, but so far it was all looking good. The Professor would live.

As he walked down the hall to call his mother and Pia, the images of the night before flashed before him. The beautiful beings in the room, full of light, the incident with nurse Grigory, and he rubbed his fingers as he once again felt the warmth of his father clenching his hand. He smiled happily as he thought of his guardian angel watching over him and his loved ones. Then his smile widened.....he, Pythi, was getting mushy and fanciful. In that moment, it felt right.

The Sea-Guardians and Athena's priestesses had done their job and they had done it well.

Up above, Poseidon and Athena, watched with smiles on their faces, their hands gently linked.

SEVENTY-TWO

We can easily forgive a child who is afraid of the dark;
the real tragedy of life is when men are afraid of the light. - Plato

It was an unexpected turn of events for the Warriors but order had to be restored. Their faith was shaken by the departure of Andrei and the capricious behavior of G-Lover, but help was on its way. Deimos was to be deployed soon and that's all that mattered; he would rein in G-Lover, and get the remaining team back together. Phobos, on the other hand, had been prepared by his father Ares, but was not aware of what his mission was supposed to be. That was until he received word from Hades and he was on his way to the Acheron.

He dealt with the greedy ferryman and soon he was standing in front of his uncle. "Welcome son of my nephew," he was greeted by Hades. "Times are difficult for your father and we need to help him. This is the reason I called you here, as you probably know. I have an idea and I would like to discuss it with you."

"I am listening," said Phobos. "I know the fervent desire of my father to involve the world into a global war and I'll do whatever I can to help."

"As I explained to your father, destabilizing the banking system is a very good first step. Ares has a team working on it already and I understand Deimos has been recruited to help and discipline them. In parallel, I think, we need to feed the ambitions of the newly rich for unlimited power. The combination of the two should start things rolling in Ares' desired direction. That's where I need your help," said Hades.

"Tell me how I can help," said Phobos.

"Well," started Hades, "As wealth is shifting from West to East, many Asians have become millionaires and billionaires. While the Indians want to be rich to improve their standard of living, the Chinese see wealth as control and they want to rule the world. Top among them are the heads of the powerful triads, the crime syndicates, and top among the top ones, and Tai-pan Supreme, is Lin Yu, head of the Hong Kong based triad with tentacles throughout China and around the world. He controls gambling, prostitution, drug trafficking, arms dealing...you name it. If there is a large profit to be made and it is risky or illegal, he is into it. Of course, he has built his empire of legal fronts, legitimate business to hide and support his illicit operations. Rumors have it that the Chinese Government is in his pocket and the Premier does not make a major move without his approval. He likes to be invisible and control his marionettes from behind the scenes. But his ambition is monstrous and only the whole world would be enough of a trophy to satisfy his hunger for power.

He is a strict disciplinarian; discipline that he exercises with his large private army of devoted street soldiers. Anyone that opposes or betrays him ends up enjoying my hospitality in the Underworld after he has been brutally murdered. No one can touch Lin Yu. As you understand, I have a special fondness for the man and he knows it too. I want you to go see him, as an emissary from me, and I want you to get Yuan, from the Ares' Warrior team, in touch with him as well. I think the two will find a lot in common that will serve Lin's ambition and ultimately Ares' plan. Go see Lin Yu, he is expecting you, and there is no time to be wasted."

***

Phobos did visit Mr. Yu, as Mr. James Chang, a well-connected Chinese-American businessman. He flew from Dubai to Hong Kong and then he chartered a boat to Kowloon. From there, one of Mr. Yu's boats, with the appropriate security detachment, took him to the private island of Mr. Yu and his palatial compound. Private guards and security personnel could not be more plentiful and elaborate, if they were protecting a head of state. His private radar system on the island could easily detect anything approaching the island by sea or air for miles, and his defense arsenal included vertically taking off Harrier jets, Apache helicopters, interceptor gun boats and even submarines. By all accounts, the island was impenetrable to the many enemies of Mr. Yu.

Mr. Yu received Chang in the vast expanse of his private office and after the initial pleasantries, a glass of Scotch on the rocks and Cuban cigars,

Phobos cum Chang laid out the plan of destabilizing the banking system, carefully leaving Ares out of it. He indicated that this would be only the beginning of the turmoil that was about to be unleashed on the world and emphasized that Mr. Yu and his crime empire's help would be important in securing as much destruction as possible in the aftermath. The reward for Mr. Yu would be a once in a lifetime opportunity to become the true ruler of the world in the chaos that would ensue. Mr. Yu listened carefully with intense interest as he had no reason to doubt the intentions of Chang, knowing that he came recommended from higher up.

"I was sent here to let you know of this as a favor from someone who thinks highly of you and wants you, one, to prepare for the upcoming events, and two, to be his ally in the aftermath," concluded Phobos. "When the time comes, I will be on your side as well."

***

In the weeks that followed, the Hong Kong triad changed its business practices radically. The profits from the casinos they controlled were immediately converted into gold bullion. Similarly, the majority of their cash reserves were converted into gold, but at multiple locations around the world so no concentrated activity can be detected. Arms' sales were only conducted in gold payments. Buyers were sent out to all the main markets of the world and quietly, secretly, were buying as much gold as they could find. Prices of the precious commodity started creeping up by week two, but it was after a month or so that the Indians first started feeling the true strain on gold supply and the Arabs next; the price of gold shot up in the midst of all the uncertainty, as no one had a good explanation why that was happening. That uncertainty affected the stock markets around the world, which started recording daily drops of several percentage points.

As this storm took the markets of the world by surprise, the message from Mr. Yu arrived at Mr. Chang's office, with Ares standing in attendance.

"We are ready now. Unleash the Kraken, unleash chaos and mayhem."

SEVENTY-THREE

The sun, too, shines into cesspools and is not polluted. – Diogenes

It had been a stressful few days for Pia. She had flown back alone, worried about Pythi and his father. He had not texted her before his flight had taken off, and, while on some level she understood his pre-occupation with his father's accident, on another, she had felt like he was ignoring her and pushing her out of his life.

When she landed in Athens, there were several messages from him, and she felt some qualms about thinking badly of their relationship. "Things will work out," she said to herself, as she climbed on the bus to Lavrion. The bus ride had been uneventful, except for an incident when the bus driver had to swerve quickly to avoid an oncoming car, and the other passengers in the bus had become very excited, with much yelling and shouting on the bus. Pia, feeling tired and exhausted, had not reacted, knowing within herself that she was protected. The incident passed and soon she found herself getting off the bus at Lavrion and taking a taxi for the short ride to Sounion, back to YahYah's home.

YahYah was overjoyed to see her and after a quick refreshing shower and over a cup of coffee, with the fire burning in the grate of the small cottage, Pia told her all about her trip and the accident with Pythi's father. YahYah listened, then crossing herself prayed that Pythi's 'babas' would recover soon and that her daughter and this man she loved would be re-united again. They chatted on, YahYah telling her about the neighbors, and then going on to tell her about the strange night she had had while Pia was gone.

She had felt the presence of evil on her doorstep. Had lain in bed and heard voices outside her door, and had seen several men trying to break-in, but somehow, they had been pushed back. Through her curtained window

245

in the dark, she had seen the men being pushed around like skittles till they had run away and all was quiet again. She had tried to quietly pick up the black rotary phone she had in the house to call the neighbor, but the line had been dead. After the men had left, she had fallen asleep, afraid and exhausted, only to dream off a beautiful vision of beings in gossamer gowns floating through her home filling it with light, and big, strong warriors with spears and tridents in their hands standing guard outside her door.

She told Pia that when she woke up in the morning, nothing felt different and yet all was changed. She had called the neighbors to find out if they had heard anything; they had not.

Her neighbor, Giorgos, had mentioned over coffee the next day that a fisherman he had met in Lavrion had mentioned that there might be a haunted house or a witch living in Sounion. There were a couple of men in Lavrion who were spreading the rumor.

YahYah saw the concern in Pia's eyes as she recounted the incident and hugging her granddaughter told her not to worry.

"I know who was protecting me," she said.

"No man will be able to harm me if the Goddess is watching over me, and She is."

"I have lived through wars, occupation, famine, starvation, so many terrible times and through it all, my beloved Goddess has protected me. I know she was there that night."

Then smiling, she said, "And she protects you too, and your mother."

"The necklace you wear around your neck...that was passed down in our family to all the daughters. It has been blessed by the Goddess herself. No harm can come to us."

Then, getting up from the table, she kissed her granddaughter warmly, and went to take a nap.

Pia sat by the fire pondering her words. Why would anyone want to harm her beloved YahYah. She was old, kind, and so loved by everyone around her. Pia could not understand it. But she knew that YahYah's words were true. She had a deep and ingrained belief that she was the child of the Goddess Athena and that the Goddess, being her Guardian Angel, watched over her and looked after her, as she had her mother, through her long recovery from cancer. Her appearance during her meditation had confirmed it.

She felt safe and peaceful in the small cozy cottage she loved so much. It was a cold afternoon, and she sat by the fire, deep in thought, pondering her relationship with Pythi, thinking back and smiling to herself as she recalled the beautiful moments they had shared. It was already late night in the United States and she would wait to call him in the morning.

After YahYah woke up, they cooked dinner together, a chicken stew with okra and tomato sauce and baked fresh bread to go with it. They continued talking and discussing the events of the past few days, going back over and over again, to the night when the men had tried to break in to her home.

Then stopping, as YahYah was kneading the bread, she looked up at Pia and pondered, "If they were looking for money or jewelry, they would not have come here, they would have gone to the house at the top of the hill, where the Tonialides' live, everyone knows they are rich and everyone knows that I have very little. I have enough to live and I am happy with that. So, why would they come here and nowhere else? No one else saw or heard anything. I am not that old that I imagined something as scary as this. I saw them through the curtain in the dark. It was very terrifying."

Pia, hugged her trying to give her some comfort.

"YahYah, I am here with you now. We will try and find out if anyone in the Village saw anything. I will call the hotel and talk to them to see if they had any visitors that night," Pia responded.

They continued kneading in silence for a few minutes and then YahYah looked up again and said, "The only thing I can think of...it must have something to do with that evil man who came looking for you the day after you had left with Pythi."

"Evil man? YahYah, what are you talking about? What evil man?" Pia was astounded and she heard her own voice going up an octave or two as she asked the questions.

"I didn't want to bother you, but a man stopped by here the day after you left. He came to the door asking for you and told me that he was your boyfriend from America and that he had sent you a message to say he was coming to see you. I knew he was lying. He had a bad energy and I simply wanted him to go away. I told him you were gone and I saw him get really angry when I would not tell him where you were. I thought he was going to strike me, but then Giorgos saw him, walked up the hill and before he could meet the man, he got in his car and drove off."

Pia was completely aghast, "Why did you not tell me this YahYah? I called you every day. I have no idea who this person was, and I don't know of anyone coming to visit me. Did he give you his name? How did he look?"

Pia was almost shouting now, her worry and fear getting the better of her. Taking a deep breath she calmed herself. Then, lowering her voice, she asked YahYah again, "How did he look YahYah?"

"He was tall, an American, but he spoke a little Greek. Nice shirt, blue color, I think, and long pants. He had a hat on his head. It had American letters on it and when he got back in the car, he threw the hat on the seat in anger. I can't remember much more, but call Giorgos and Irini who saw him, they may be able to give you a better description. He was nice looking Pia, he just had a very bad energy."

Before she could finish, Pia picked up the black rotary phone and called Giorgos and Irini and invited them over. They came within a few minutes and as she made everyone coffee, she recounted the conversation she had with YahYah. They said they had seen the man and agreed with YahYah that he was American. He had been there for only a few minutes and they had watched him from their porch. Giorgos agreed that he had seemed angry when he left, but they all thought that it must be someone that Pia knew. How else would he know to come to Sounion?

Pia sighed. These were simple folk. The power of the Internet was unknown to them. They had no idea of modern communications, blogs, messaging, and so on. She made a mental note to check her blog and her messages to see if anything stood out.

They continued talking and Pia brought up the night when YahYah had seen the men at the door. They had a long discussion about it and Giorgos picked up the phone and called the hotel Aegeon. He knew the owner well and asked him to find out if anyone at the hotel had heard or seen anything.

Conversation moved on to Pia's travels and Pythi. They teased her about him and YahYah invited them for dinner. The meal was ready and they sat down together at the small cramped table, laden with food, the cottage full of the aroma of baked bread and the delicious chicken stew. They washed it down with some local wine and it was a hearty, satisfying meal.

Half way through the dinner, the phone rang and it was the owner of the hotel. He had just spoken with Dimitri, the receptionist who had night duty the night of the intrusion. Dimitri had seen a taxi pull up on the hotel camera and three men getting out of it. He had turned on the inside lights expecting them to come and check in. They often had late night travelers, and when he checked the roster had seen that no one was scheduled to check in that night. But, there was nothing unusual there either. Sometimes, people stopped by to see if there was a room available, tired from traveling. Dimitri had waited a few minutes, had watched the men pay the taxi driver, had seen the taxi drive off, and waited. The men were now out of range of the outside camera and he expected them to come up the stairs to the reception area and ring the bell. But they never did. He didn't know what happened to them…but, Dimitri, who lived in Lavrion, did know the taxi driver. Panos, the taxi driver who also lived in Lavrion, may have more information.

Giorgos, relayed the conversation, and promised YahYah that he would go talk to Panos in the morning. The rest of the evening passed uneventfully. It was always pleasant having Giorgos and Irini over and by the time they left, YahYah was ready for bed.

Pia checked her watch; it was almost seven in the morning in the States. She texted Pythi to see if he was awake. He was at the hospital and asked her to give him a few minutes to step outside. Cell phones were not allowed inside.

He called her a few minutes later and they had a brief conversation. He filled her in on his father's condition, they talked about missing each other and agreed to Skype when he got to his parents' home to change and rest.

"I love you," he said, "And miss you so much."

"I know baby, but I am with you, always," she responded, "Stay strong."

Pia did not mention anything about the happenings in Sounion. He did not need any more worries on his plate.

SEVENTY-FOUR

Fantastic truths perish slower…Sappho's moon will survive the moon of Armstrong.
Different computations are necessary. – Odysseus Elytis

The priestess entered Athena's chambers and in an excited, giggly voice announced that a handsome Sea-Guardian was waiting in the anteroom with a private message from his master. Athena raised her eyebrow, the right one; that was highly unusual.

"Show him in," she said with a smile, "And try not to act silly in front of our guest." Her girls, in spite of their superior spiritual development, were innocent and naive around men.

The Sea-Guardian entered the chamber with an air of power reminiscent of Poseidon that made her heart skip a beat. He bowed respectfully and addressed the Goddess, "Divine Lady, my Lord and Master Poseidon sends his respects and warmest greetings. He also extends a kind invitation to your Divinity to join him for dinner at Sounion tonight. He would like very much to see you and talk with you. He only asks your Grace, if you would be kind enough to meet him in a mortal body at the taverna 'Akroyiali' at the bay of Sounion, just below his Temple. He will wait for you there, also as a mortal man, at ten. May I tell him that you will join him?"

It was only eleven in the morning, plenty of time for her to prepare and look her best. She wanted to look perfect for this rendezvous, and she liked the idea that Poseidon had chosen the vulnerability of a human body; the divine egos would stay at bay that way. "Tell Lord Poseidon that I accept his kind invitation and it will be my pleasure to meet him at Sounion at ten. You may go now."

***

She arrived in a white sedan she chauffeured herself, as any common mortal would do. She had stopped at the top of the hill, before taking the steep road down to the bay and Akroyiali, to admire the serenity and beauty of the place under the veil of night, with the moon rising over the standing columns of the temple and reflecting into the darkened sea. Sailboats were bobbing in the light breeze. *Poseidon has chosen a truly magical place for his abode*, thought Athena to herself. Then, she took her position behind the wheel of the car and drove it slowly, carefully, down to the taverna. She parked it in the dark, unpaved parking area behind it and walked the short distance to the front, which was almost on the water. Dressed in a simple white dress with blue trim, golden sandals and her long dark hair flying in the light breeze, she was simplicity and beauty personified.

She entered the lit porch of the taverna which was buzzing with the chatter and laughter of happy groups around tables with checkered red and white tablecloths spread with food and drink. She looked around trying to spot him. At the far end, there was a semi dark table where a mature, long haired and bearded lone man, wearing a Greek sailor's cap, was sipping on his wine with his gaze fixed towards the sea. *Even as a man, he is a wild and handsome one,* she thought to herself as she started weaving through the tables to reach him.

It was the sudden quieting of the taverna buzz that brought him out of his reverie and he turned to see what had caused it, only to have his eyes filled with a vision in white that had taken the taverna goers' breath away. He got up to welcome her, took her hands in his, and kissed her tenderly on the cheek. "Thank you for coming. I thought we would attract less attention in human form, and was hoping that these simple surroundings would help us forget our lofty offices and be ourselves for a change." Then, looking around, he smiled, "You see, I didn't count on your stunning beauty to totally silence the place." She returned his kiss with equal tenderness, and teased him with a charming but crooked smile, "I'll take that as a compliment and I really like your fisherman's hat. You make for a convincing man of the sea."

She moved to take the chair opposite him with her back to the sea. "No," he touched her hand, "The good view is on this side. Besides, I want you next to me." He served her wine as she sat in the chair to his left. Nearly touching each other, they let a comfortable silence settle between them, tasting their wine, lost in the reflection of the water in the distance. "You look much less aloof and more approachable as a human," she broke the silence first, still looking out in the distance. "And you look much more beautiful and warm in flesh and blood," he countered, equally as absorbed by the night views. "Taking off your regal war helmet and letting your hair down, so to speak, may have been a good idea," he added as he placed his hand over hers on the table. Enjoying the warmth of his touch, she made no effort to pull her hand away.

"As well, thank you my divine fisherman for not bringing your mighty trident with you. It could be unnerving for an Athenian maiden having that thing sticking between her and her date," she said playfully, turning her head to look him in the eyes. His hearty laughter that followed broke any remaining tension between them and soon they were like any couple in the grips of a budding romance, full of attention to each other, flirting, lost in tender touches and stolen kisses.

"You've done very well so far as my charming date, dearest, but does this place have anything near to ambrosia with which to feed a starving mortal lady? I'm famished!" Complained Athena with a frown on her face. "Oh, I'm terribly sorry, my precious one, I was so lost in you, I forgot about your stomach," and with that he waived at the waiter. He proceeded to order appetizers, salads, home cooked dishes, and various types of the fried small fish everyone seemed to be enjoying.

"Fresh? They are virtually still alive," assured the waiter. "No fresher fish on these shores; our own fishermen brought them in this afternoon."

"You have ordered for an army and we are only two. Do humans eat that much?" Enquired Athena. "Sometimes they do and they surely enjoy sitting around a full table," responded Poseidon, "But, mostly, I wanted you to have a taste of everything since you don't do this often." They toasted to Pythi and Pia and they congratulated each other for their defensive successes with the Sea-Guardians and the priestesses. Then, they agreed that the next step would be to start dismantling Ares' offense, without letting down their guard. Having cleared the business part, they returned to each other. They kept drinking their wine and sampling everything, as carefree and happy as any mortal couple in love can be, until late into the night.

At midnight the taverna keeper informed them that they were closing for the night, the waiters were clearing and picking up the tables, but they were welcome to stay there and enjoy the night breeze. By 12:45, when they turned off the lights and the taverna keeper wished them good night and left, Poseidon had pulled her chair close to his and she was nestled in his arms, with her head on his shoulder, looking up at the hill, in the direction of the remains of his Temple, a contented soft calmness over her face.

"My dearest," she said in a low voice, "The physical look of your abode does not do justice to the grandeur of the ethereal one, but you have picked a spot of exceptional natural beauty. I am so glad you invited me here tonight." He caressed her hair, placed a gentle kiss on the side of her neck that made her shiver, and said with a mischievous grin. "The night is young, my Princess, and I want you to feel the full range of human sensations while you are in this body. I want you to feel the sand grains and roundness of the pebbles between your toes at the beach and the exhilarating touch of the sea water on your naked body under the moonlight. I want you to experience pleasure as only humans can do. Are you ready for a stroll along the beach?"

She threw her head back offering him her lips, "Only if you kiss me as if I am the only woman on this Earth," she whispered.

"You are to me," he said with a throaty voice, pulling her closer to him as they locked lips in a passionate kiss that seemed to defy time.

SEVENTY-FIVE

The descent to Hades is the same from every place. - Anaxagoras

G-Lover had had a bad few days. His was on a downward spiral. Anger suffused him, and hatred. As he sat in his hotel room, late in the evening, surrounded by luxury, his mind raced….pictures of his family, his parents fighting, his mother, whom he hated and loved, actually despised most of the time. She ignored him, while living the high society life, moving from one man to another, one plastic surgery to another, one more charitable event to another. She had no charity for anyone; it was all about herself and the drugs she abused. He hated his father, whom he never saw and with whom he had no contact.

He thought of his school friends. He hated them too. Privileged and pompous, he thought. He had not stayed in touch with any of them once he had finished school. And, in college, he had been a total misfit. The few weeks he had spent living in the dorm had been horrible. He hated sharing a room and bathroom, he had issues with his roommate, and his classes had been a waste of time. He had waited for the weekends to come back to his secluded room in the often empty mansion. No one bothered him there and after a while, the weekends had stretched into weekdays till he had quit college all together. No one had cared. He had a trust fund; it would carry him through his lifetime.

His life was full of hatred. The only people he liked and enjoyed hanging with were his friends in cyberspace. Until now. He was angry with them too. He had seen the message about the call-in, but had been too late to check in. Why were they requesting call-ins without him? He was the one who had been the master mind of this whole operation and he had done a great job. Hadn't he? He controlled the group and now they were meeting without him. They needed him, or did they?

And then, there was his beloved Greek Goddess, G2. He was obsessed by her. He followed and commented on all her posts. Sometimes, she replied, always upbeat and friendly. Through her blog he knew all about her life and the events that had transpired. He had been convinced that she was his and now here she was writing about this new found love in her life. The thought of it brought about another torrent of rage. She would be his. He was going to show them all, he was going to show the world.

He leaned over his laptop and sent an encrypted message to the others to log in for a call-in in fifteen minutes. Then going to the bathroom, he freshened up, did another toke of cocaine, wiped his nose to make sure there was no residue, moved his laptop to the desk by the window, his back to the room as he got ready for the call.

In a few minutes he heard the pings as each one logged in. They were all on. It was time, he logged on too.

"Hi guys, everyone good?"

They greeted each other, it was light hearted but he could feel an underlying tension.

"What's going on?" He asked, "I saw the call-in and sorry I missed it. What happened?"

The others were silent and through the grainy screen he watched them. Each one was waiting for the other to respond and for a few seconds there was silence.

It was Andrei who first responded.

"Z called in, man. He was concerned because money had been moved in and out of one of the Greek accounts."

"What the fuck, man, I move money in and out of accounts all day, you guys know that. What is so concerning about this one?" G-Lover asked.

Ziggy started to explain, his voice rising. "Dude, this was not the usual movement of money. Someone physically walked into the bank where I work and withdrew the money. It's a big deal, man, the account was flagged. The security team locked down the bank to try and intercept the guy. I didn't know what was going on but the teller at the counter is my friend and she gave me the name on the account. That's one of ours. Who the fuck would walk into a bank in Athens, Greece and withdraw money from my account?"

G-Lover felt his anger rise again. These dudes were weak. They needed to trust him. Now he was going to have to explain himself to them.

"Man, calm down, our accounts are secure. You know that. So what if the account is flagged. They can run every diagnostic they want. Our system is a hundred percent proof. You guys know that, we have done this enough times. The money just disappears…poof!" He laughed, trying to lighten the atmosphere.

They all laughed and agreed, but it was Andrei who interjected, "Yup buddy, we know our system is great but who would physically walk in to withdraw the money? I am here in Romania, Yuan is in Hong Kong, we know Ziggy didn't withdraw it, so who else?"

"I did, man, I am here in Greece to see my girlfriend. Needed some cash, so went to the bank and got some," he said angrily.

At this, the three erupted at the same time, "What the fuck?"

"It's okay guys, no one knows who I am."

Ziggy burst out, "Do you not know that they have cameras in the Banque? They have you man. They got your hat, your description, and that you are American. While they are not saying much at the Banque, I know they must be looking for you. If you are still in Athens, you better leave soon, you are too hot."

"Come on Z, don't be a pussy. I'm okay. No one is looking for me."

Ziggy could feel anger rising in him. He hated being called names, especially a pussy. It was really insulting and he had been insulted his whole life. He was going to stand up for himself now.

"Don't call me names, man, I don't like that. You know you broke the rules, and almost got caught. We could all be in jail because of you and I am not going to jail. No way man."

Now G-Lover was really angry. "Fuck off Z, you know that I am careful and that I take care of all of you. I am not some stupid asshole, trying to get caught."

"You are acting like an asshole, calling me names and putting us all in danger. Stop it, man."

G-Lover was really angry now, but backed down. "You are right, man. Won't happen again. Gonna see my girl and go back to the States. If you are around maybe we can meet before I leave," he said laughing, "But maybe the pussy thinks I am too hot?"

Yuan watched as the two of them argued. He quietly froze the picture of G-Lover and screen-shot it, listening to their conversation as he zoomed in and out.

At this point Andrei intervened, "Ok guys, stop it. It's done. Everyone needs to be careful. The world is looking for us. Lay low, disappear, and be invisible."

G-Lover started laughing, almost hysterically, "Yup, especially after tomorrow. Big operation going down tonight. Wait and see guys. This is going to be the mother of all takes."

Yuan, who had been quiet so far, spoke up, "What are you talking about? We are done. We have the money, let's take it and run. No more G, that's when the slip ups happen, let's not be too greedy. We all have enough."

"Guys, I know this was not in the plan but it will be okay. Trust me. You guys have a good night and remember to watch the news tomorrow. I'm out," so saying he signed off.

The others signed off too.

Yuan looked closely at the photo he had screen-shot. He enlarged it and moved the photo around. It was as he feared; on the bedside table, behind G-Lover, sat a bag of white powder.

Wow, thought Yuan, *He didn't care to hide it, or did he not care? Or was he slipping?*

He knew all about drugs and their effects, he lived on the streets of Hong Kong, he saw how desperate and crazy people could become in drug induced states or when they were in need of some. He had seen the worst side of human life and he was going to get himself out of the life his birth had wrung upon him.

A few minutes later, he contacted Andrei, and told him what he had seen.

"I'm out brother. It's too dangerous. Catch up with you someday. Stay safe."

Andrei walked the halls of the quiet orphanage. It was dark and cold. They did not have enough money for electricity and the nuns turned the lights out at 8:30. The heat too. The children cowered under their meager blankets trying to stay warm. It was not enough but it was the best the nuns could do.

He walked back into the small office, unplugged the hard drive of the old computer, put on his jacket, picked up the keys of the old van belonging to the nuns, and picking up the computer, he walked out of the orphanage without a backward glance. Turning on the van, he backed out of the driveway and drove as far away as he could.

Good thing he did too, because by the next afternoon, it was all over the news.

SEVENTY-SIX

It is frequently a misfortune to have very brilliant men in charge of affairs.
They expect too much of ordinary men. – Thucydides

It had been a busy but frustrating few days for Derek, Sam, and Tanya. Weeks sitting in the basement running diagnostics and programs had revealed few leads. All three of them were convinced that the Greek account was key, but the account had gone dormant and there was little they could do but wait and watch.

Derek lived on his computer, going back to the hotel to change, shower and take short naps. The Banque had installed a small couch in the basement and Derek had taken it over, too tired to walk the short distance to the hotel; he often fell asleep there. He was obsessed with infiltrating the hackers. It had never taken him this long and he had begun to take it all personally. He, Derek, was the master of breaking in and hacking accounts, he knew all the tricks and yet, somehow, this infiltration seemed to be fool proof and the answers eluded him.

Tanya and Sam were more balanced. While they spent endless hours in the basement, they took a few hours off to go walk around the city, eat at the local tavernas, and had even rented a car to drive to Piraeus, the city port to have dinner and explore. The evening at Piraeus had been a wonderful change of pace for them, and they had enjoyed it, strolling through the narrow streets of Faliron overlooking the port, which housed all kinds of boats and ships. They gazed at the blue water while they sipped ouzo and ate mezeh, consisting of fried kalamari, sundried and grilled octopus, fresh salad, a variety of cheeses, and barbouni, a delicious redfish native to the area.

Throughout the evening, Sam enjoyed a side of Tanya that he never had before. Gone was the closed, edgy, business-like professional that he knew at work. The walls had begun to come down and they laughed and talked exchanging stories, enjoying each other's company. As he watched her sitting across from him, he felt the urge to lean over and stroke the beautiful wild mane of hair that was flowing in the breeze or kiss her full mouth, which he had not really noticed before.

While she was in jeans, which was her daily garb, she wore a soft flowing shirt and her hair, which was always pulled back in a ponytail or bun, tumbled down below her shoulders. She laughed and talked with an abandon he had not known before. It had been a fun night and since then they had gone out several times.

"It's just friendship," Sam told himself, "She is not interested in a relationship, and I should not push for more. It would make things very awkward if she does not feel the same way."

And so far, she had not indicated otherwise.

Back in the basement, they had daily conference calls with Pythi, who was spending time with his father and who, they were delighted to hear, had come out of the coma and was recovering slowly. They all had missed Pythi and hoped he would be back soon. They understood that he was pre-occupied with his father's health but really needed his expertise to move forward. They really needed a break.

Then it happened…It was a desultory evening in the basement. Pythi had been gone several days. They were at their wits' end as to how to proceed when they got a phone call from the Bank in Dubai and then another. At the same time, all their computers started buzzing and flashing. It was late in the night there and only two members of the Dubai team were at work. Money was rolling out of the Bank. It was as if a giant hand had stepped in, flipped a switch, and had begun to wipe the Bank clean.

Derek, Sam, and Tanya jumped up running to their servers to access the security walls of the Bank of Dubai. Derek was yelling into the phone, shouting instructions. Tanya dialed Pythi. "Pick up, pick up," she beseeched the phone, and after four rings he did. He already knew.

Sam, trying to stay calm, did what none of the others thought to do in their panic. He shut down the entire system for the Banque Nationale. He knew that he did not have the authority to do it but he was going to take the chance. He would take the heat tomorrow, if he had to; at least the Banque was safe.

They watched helplessly unable to do anything remotely, till Sam, the engineering expert, grabbed the phone and called the team in Dubai, instructing them how to shut down the system, to stop the bleeding.

It had only been a few minutes since the beginning of the chaos but all three of them felt like they had run a marathon. They were gasping and breathing hard from the stress, their adrenaline pumping as they continued to look at their screens which had gone quiet.

And then, it started again….Derek, who was remotely connected to all their accounts started yelling.

"It's the Bank of Hong Kong now. Oh my Lord, it's the mid-morning there…no way to contain this one."

A few minutes later it was a Bank in Switzerland…and then one in Macau….and in London…..and so it went for about an hour. Uncontainable, unstoppable, just chaos, worldwide.

Within an hour it was all over the news. Every news network was carrying the news of the high jacking of bank funds. The talking heads everywhere on television stations, adding to the chaos with their inept commentaries and suppositions, did a good job of spreading panic throughout the globe. Alarmed depositors were already forming long lines at banks trying to withdraw their savings in fear that the money may disappear.

The only good news the team got that day was that Pythi was on his way back, being flown in on a company jet.

***

In his lair, Ares and his two sons were watching the panic spreading around the planet with cautious euphoria. This was unexpected but good, so long as Pythi's team couldn't pull an ace out of their sleeves to put an end to the spreading madness. The trouble was that G-Lover was acting on his own, on a whim, prematurely, uncoordinated, and without guidance from Ares or Deimos, who had not been given time to restore discipline to the Warrior team. This was it and there was no plan B to fall back on. It had better work!

SEVENTY-SEVEN

Badness you can get easily, in quantity; the road is smooth, and it lies closely, but in front of excellence
the immortal gods have put sweat, and long and steep is the way to it. – Hesiod

Pythi was on his way back to Athens. It had been grueling. His father was doing better, beginning the process to heal, and his mother seemed to be stronger and very supportive, ready for the long challenge ahead. His dad could still not walk, but at least he could speak, communicate, and had no paralysis from the injuries. It would take months for the broken bones to heal, for physical therapy, for the pain to recede and for him to resume somewhat of a normal life, that is, the new normal after such devastating injuries. Both Pythi and his mother realized that they were lucky to have him back and they were going to do everything in their power to help him in this process of recovery.

He had held his father's hand and told him that he had to go. Of course, his father understood. They had watched the news together as it broke on the TV in the hospital room. Pythi had been dumbfounded; his worst fears were now realized. Everything had faded around him as he focused on the news. He knew that his phone must be ringing off the hook, but he could not turn it on in the hospital room. He knew that he was needed.

"Dad, will you be okay?" He asked.

"Go," said his father, "I will be fine, you need to go save the world."

"Save the world? This is just a banking crisis. We will get them; hackers like this always leave a footprint."

His father smiled quietly, "It's more than that, son. Go, you are needed more than you know."

So saying, he closed his eyes, indicating he needed a nap.

Pythi kissed his forehead as he left the hospital room, praying that he would stay safe till his return.

His parting with his mother was more difficult. She didn't quite understand why he would have to leave before his father had fully recovered. She was petulant at first, but Pythi understood that it was her fear that was driving her. She needed his support and was reluctant to let him go. He hugged her and told her that he had made arrangements for their care, and he was only a phone call away, but there was a spreading world crisis that he had to handle. Mollified, she let him go.

He drove to the house, talking on the phone the whole time. From the messages on his phone he realized that it was no longer simply a case of corporate hacking; the FBI and Homeland Security were now involved, and after speaking on a conference call with his boss, the next call was to the Bureau. He had worked with them before and realized that a briefing was in order.

Once he got to the house he called a taxi while he packed, then made sure he had locked up, before jumping into the cab. He had a long ride to La Guardia, but he needed that time to make phone calls and do some damage control. He was proud of how Sam, Derek, and Tanya had handled the whole situation. Dubai was now under control. It was Hong Kong and Switzerland that worried him. But that would be taken care of soon; teams were already dispatched there as well.

Before he knew it, he was at the airport, at the private terminal, being whisked onto the corporate jet. He glanced around as he stepped in; he had ridden on it often, and knew the staff. They greeted him by name and made sure he was comfortable. A large mug of coffee sat beside him as they took off, and he already had his laptop on, submersed deep in the files that Derek had sent him. He worked on the files for a few hours, then, turning off his computer, went to the back to lay down. The plane was equipped with a small bedroom and he knew that he needed to get some rest. Once he hit Athens, he needed both feet on the ground, running.

At least, he would be closer to Pia, but given the circumstances, he had no idea when he would actually see her. He had texted her and told her that he was on his way back. She knew all about the crisis. Like the rest of the world, she was following it on television too. He knew that she was rooting for him and smiled to himself as he fell asleep. The Gods had been smiling on him when they had brought Pia into his life, he couldn't imagine life without her anymore.

***

G-Lover lay in his hotel room, on the rumpled bed, watching the news. Every few minutes, he would cackle with laughter. This time, he had really pulled one on the world. He did not need cocaine today; he was riding a high, a real high. He had spent the last few hours with the remote control in his hand, switching from channel to channel, and on every channel the talking heads were discussing the imminent collapse of the world financial markets. The New York stock exchange was about to open and he knew it was going to be a blood bath. He laughed gleefully. Life was good. He was the victor.

He wondered what the others were doing, but knew that, at least for the day, he had to lay low.

***

Andrei was about to board a plane to Argentina, when he heard the news on the television monitors at the airport. He smiled grimly. He hoped that Yuan had taken his advice. He was out, moving on. A new identity, a new life. His tracks covered. If in actuality it was G-Lover wreaking havoc on the world markets, he wanted no part of it. He had his money. Enough money for him to live in relative luxury for the rest of his life. He would make a new life for himself, maybe even find someone to love and have a family someday. That was all he wanted, a quiet life. He was out.

***

In Hong Kong, Yuan watched the news with some surprise. They had never discussed Hong Kong or Switzerland, or any of the other Banks. This was too large, if in fact it was G-Lover. They would get caught. He needed protection and, like his friend Andrei had suggested, he had protected himself. Enough money stashed away, but not too much. He had quietly made arrangements for fake passports for his mother and himself. When the time was right, if they needed to, they would steal away. But first he had to get ready for a very important meeting he had set up after receiving Andrei's warning.

***

Ziggy watched the news in horror. Things were going from bad to worse and he felt physically sick. He had been nauseous and felt like all eyes were upon him at the Banque. He needed to get away. It was the topic of conversation among the bank employees, and all the television monitors were carrying it. He could not escape it….he felt the world closing in, like he could not breathe and he needed to go home. He needed to do something, but he didn't know what to do. He knew he had to clear his head and find a way to protect himself. This was too large, and if in fact it was G-Lover, they would get caught. He had never thought of going to prison. It was not in his plan. He would never survive prison, he was physically too weak, plus he could only imagine the shame on his family. His parents would probably kill themselves from the agony of knowing that their son had behaved like a criminal.

No..no…no…the panic set in again, and he began to hyperventilate. He needed to do something and he needed to do it fast. But what?

He was leaning up against a door, his breathing raspy, his skin pale and sweaty, when his supervisor found him. He had one look at Ziggy and led him to a stool, gave him some water to drink and told him to go home, when he felt better. He had too much on his hands today; he didn't need to worry about a sick employee and having to call an ambulance to get him to the hospital. Let the boy go home and have his family take care of him. He needed to go to a meeting with the manager.

When the dizziness subsided and his chest stopped thumping, Ziggy clocked out, and began the slow walk to his apartment. The cool air made him shiver and, although he tried walking faster, his leg felt even worse and the heaviness in his limbs would not permit him to move faster. He walked laboriously to his little apartment and let himself in.

His roommates were at work, the little apartment quiet. It smelled of cigarettes and garbage. Ziggy complained to himself as he walked to his room. His roommates were pigs. He was the only one who cleaned this stinky little place. He would have to take the garbage out later, but right now he had things to do. He locked the door behind him and turned on his computer. All the screens in front of him began to light up, one by one. He began to feel better. Computers comforted him, they were his friends. They did not insult him, talk back or hurt him. They had an understanding, his computers and him, he found solace in that.

Soon all his screens were alive. He decided the first thing to do was to contact Andrei and Yuan. If indeed it was G-Lover who had wreaked this morning's havoc, then they - Yuan, Andrei, and him - had to stand in solidarity and protect themselves. He told himself that he had no reason to panic, they would figure it out. They were the geniuses, they would be okay.

He decided not to go into the Cloud group they had set up for themselves, secure as it was. He had an email address for Andrei and had sometimes used it. In fact, unbeknown to any of the others, he had cyber stalked them all. He knew their IP addresses, emails, gamer id's, skype aliases. He had hacked into their chats and read their emails....but only from time to time. He was not some sleazy stalker; he just wanted to find out what his friends were up to.

He sent Andrei a short email, very generic. "You good dude?" Was all it said.

He took a sip of water as he hit send. Almost instantaneously, he heard a ping.

He looked up; the email had come back undeliverable.

He was sure of that email address, he had used it often. He tried another one, undeliverable. He checked the Gamer ID....gone, Facebook page...no longer available. And on and on....and each time his level of panic went up a notch.

Finally, he decided to log into the secret Cloud chat room they had set up only for themselves. They had been very careful and he knew that this one was almost foolproof. He logged in, ready to send Andrei and Yuan a message to have a meeting so that they could discuss the happenings of the day. This time he began to hyperventilate. Neither Yuan nor Andrei were part of the group anymore. They had either removed themselves or someone had removed them. The only names left were his and G-Lover's.

A feeling of deep betrayal swept over him. How could they? They had been friends for years; they knew each other better than if they were friends in the real world. Why would they leave like this, without letting him know, he had been a good friend to them. He sat there at his computer, his body racked with tears, feelings of insecurity and inadequacy flowing through him, his mind racing, his heart thumping, full of fear and anguish. He had to do something to protect himself and his family. After all, he too had worked hard with the others to set up this operation. It was his expertise that had created the almost impenetrable firewalls and security blockades. He was the smart one, he would find a way, but first, he needed to make sure that his money was safe and that G-Lover was not moving it from one account to another. He just needed to log in to make sure that there was still a large enough balance in the accounts G-Lover had allotted to him.

It didn't take him long to run a sweep through a number of nameless accounts set up to filter the money. Then, knowing that it may be dangerous, given what had already occurred, he decided to log in and check the Greek accounts. He would make sure to be quick, just in case the account was tagged. It would be difficult to trace if he only took a few seconds. He just needed to know…

With shaky fingers, he logged into the Greek accounts, first one, and then the others. The money was all there. He began to feel better. He was just about to log out, when his phone rang. His cell phone rarely ever rang. He looked at it; the number was not one he knew. He answered.

"Yes?"

"Dude, it's Yuan….I won't be on long, so just listen. I'm calling from a number that cannot be traced back to me. Dude, you better run….lay low for a while. We are very hot. G-Lover made it go down big, now the whole world is looking for us. This was not how it was supposed to go down. We are out, get out too, now."

Before Ziggy could respond, Yuan continued, "We love you brother, take care of yourself. Hopefully, we will talk again one day soon." He hung up.

Ziggy looked at the disconnected phone and sighed, and in that instance he realized that he had not logged out of the Greek accounts. It had been almost three minutes since he had logged in. He logged out and turned off his computer system, even pulling the plugs out of the socket. Then, limping across the small room, he crawled into the tiny bed. He needed a nap and then he would wake up and decide what he would do next. There was no place he could run to. Maybe take some of the money from one of the accounts and go for a few weeks to Santorini. He always wanted to go to Santorini. He could lay low there. Spend a few weeks till things cooled down, then he would take all his money and go home. His parents would be happy to have him back. Feeling better and happier about his plans, he curled up and fell into a deep sleep.

***

At the Banque, Derek, Sam and Tanya huddled over Derek's computer. They had been in crisis management mode all morning, phones ringing off the hook. Things were moving very fast and they knew that Pythi would be landing in a few hours. Through the noise and the conversation, the yelling and the sound of the servers and computers whirring, she heard it. It was the sound that she had been waiting for, the soft "ping ping" telling her that the account she had tagged had been accessed again. This time she was ready. She yelled at the top of her voice…

Both Sam and Derek stopped talking on their phones mid-sentence and looked at her as if she had gone mad. She was pointing to her computer and gesticulating for them to come over. They ran as fast as they could. Derek stepped in and began his capture.

"Please," he begged the computer, "Stay on there, and give me thirty seconds, at least. Come on baby, we need this...ok, a few more seconds....please, please don't log off."

Tanya and Sam were standing behind him, in rapt attention, tension seeping out of them. Tanya had her fingers crossed and she was praying on the inside. They so needed this break. They got it....for three whole minutes. That was more than they could have hoped for and all three of them knew they now had enough information to be able to track down the person, or persons, involved with the Greek accounts.

Hi-fiving each other, they set to work. Each one had a job to do; IP addresses, phone numbers, location, emails, bank account numbers, photographs, etc., would all be tracked. Together, they would have this done by the time Pythi got off the plane and drove to meet them. They were elated.

SEVENTY-EIGHT

When strong, be merciful, if you would have the respect, not the fear of your neighbors. - Chilon

Pythi hit the ground running. As soon as his plane landed he heard the good news from Tanya, Derek, and Sam. They had even located the physical address of the computer and it was a few streets away from the Banque. They were waiting for him to get there.

On his arrival, they met with the Banque Managers and their security team. They had traced the IP address to a Banque employee and Ziggy's file was produced and scrutinized. The local police were called and updated and the Homeland Security specialist at the American Embassy was also dispatched. It was time to go get him.

***

Ziggy was woken up from his sleep with the knocking on the door. It was mid-afternoon, and still half asleep he limped to the door, thinking it was probably a friend of one of his roommates at the door. He was irritated and groggy when he opened the door to find at least a dozen policemen, and several others surrounding the doorway. He stepped back in alarm, but he had nowhere to go. There was only one way in and out of the apartment and it was surrounded.

The cops were yelling at him, to put his hands up and turn around, they pushed their way in and grabbed him. He lost his balance and began to fall face down. Someone caught him, but they grabbed his hands and pulled them behind his back and before he knew it, he was handcuffed. He began to cry. His worst nightmare had come true. He had been found.

He was taken to the closest police station where the cops and a couple of people in plains clothes began to interrogate him. It didn't take them long.

Ziggy was terrified, weak, and wanted this whole nightmare to end. He kept telling them that it wasn't him, it was the others. He told them that he was innocent, that the whole plan had been hatched by the American.

Behind a one way glass, Pythi listened. He understood Greek and listened carefully. When he heard about the American, he asked to go into the interrogation room. They let him. He found a shaking Ziggy, sitting alone in the room, a cup of coffee on the table. The whole room reeked of urine; Ziggy had wet himself when he had been arrested. He was still sitting in his soiled clothes.

"Do you speak English?" Pythi asked.

Ziggy heard the American accent.

"Yes."

"Tell me all that you know about the American, who is he and how do you know him?" He asked in a kind tone. Ziggy took a deep breath and started talking. All of a sudden, a light went off in his mind. He stopped midsentence and turned to Pythi.

"What will happen to me?" He asked almost in agony.

"You have committed a serious crime; probably you will spend time in prison. Then again, the judge may consider your young age and be lenient, I don't know, I'm not a lawyer," said Pythi.

At the hearing of the word 'prison,' Ziggy froze and he started trembling.

"I will never survive prison," he whispered whimpering, "I'd better die. I will tell you nothing, I need to see a lawyer; it's my right."

Pythi tried everything he knew to make him feel safer, but to no avail. The prospect of prison time had petrified Ziggy and his mouth remained closed as a clam. Pythi started feeling sorry for this unfortunate creature engulfed in fear, but he needed his information desperately and immediately, so they could go after the brain of the operation and stop the cash hemorrhaging from the banks throughout the world.

He stepped out of the interrogation room and walked to the office of the Captain of the Police in charge of the station. He found him in an animated conversation with the Athens Chief of Police who had just arrived. The Chief was quick to grab Pythi's hand and congratulate him in passable English on the success of his team. Pythi thanked him, settled them down, and using simple English he explained that the arrested youth was petrified at the thought of punishment and prison and he would not divulge his information.

"This is a small fish," he explained to the two policemen, "We need to find the big one now, and we have no time for lawyers, legal procedures and waste of time. Millions of dollars are drained from banks everywhere as we speak. We need to stop it now. You have to give immunity to the prisoner so he can talk."

The Chief of Police jumped to action and he immediately called the Justice Department and identified himself. "I need to speak to the Minister of Justice, immediately, it is very, very urgent," he said. Once connected, he started a lengthy explanation in Greek, which soon turned into an argument with the person on the other end. Finally, he hung up and turned to Pythi. "He will not accept total immunity, but he will accept to charge the felon with misdemeanor and hand him a suspended sentence, for full cooperation," he said. "That should be good enough," said Pythi, "Please come with me."

Back in the interrogation room, Pythi introduced the Chief of the Police to Ziggy. The Chief spent some time asking Ziggy in Greek about his hometown, which he knew well, discussing his family. Then, in a fatherly manner, he explained to Ziggy about the seriousness of his crime and the assurance from the Minister of Justice himself that he will be punished only with a suspended sentence, if he cooperated fully with the investigators and helped resolve this catastrophe. The high ranking uniform, the ministerial assurance, the fatherly tone, and the promise of freedom calmed Ziggy enough to think rationally. After a few moments of silence, he turned to the Chief, "You give me your word of honor as Chief of Police that I will not spend a single day in prison?" The Chief considered him, "If you cooperate fully with us, I do, son." Ziggy then turned to Pythi, "You are my witness that he promised. Now, what do you want to know?"

Ziggy began to tell Pythi all that he knew. He went back to the beginning, when they had first become friends playing games and then on to how the friendship had developed. He told him what he knew.

"He calls himself G-Lover, but I know that is not his real name."

Pythi mulled that over in his head. Why did the name sound so familiar? He knew he had heard it mentioned before.

"Where does G-Lover live?"

"Somewhere in the US, New York, I think."

"Have you ever seen him?"

"Yes, lots of times. We talked on our computers all the time."

"What does he look like?"

"Get me a laptop and I will show you."

Pythi turned around and looked at the one way glass. "Can someone get him a laptop?"

A few seconds later a cop came in with a large photo. It was the grainy reprint of the security camera from the bank.

He put the picture down in front of Ziggy.

Ziggy glanced at it. Then, looked up in surprise.

"Yes, that's him," he responded.

"Are you absolutely sure?" Asked the cop in Greek.

"Yes, that's him."

The cop and Pythi exchanged glances.

"This picture was taken in Athens, a few days ago. Do you know why he was in Athens?" Pythi asked.

Turning to look at Pythi, Ziggy responded in English, "He said he was in Greece to see his girlfriend."

"He has a Greek girlfriend?" The cop asked.

"No, no. She is American. She is here to see her family."

"Where is she, in Athens?"

"I don't know."

"Did he tell you he was coming to Athens?"

"No," was Ziggy's terse response.

"Is he still in Athens?"

"I don't know, maybe."

At this point another cop brought in a laptop. The laptop was put in front of Ziggy and his shackles were removed.

"No fast movements, no jerky actions," warned the cop. Ziggy nodded.

Pythi leaned over and asked him to pull up his email and any contact information he may have for G-Lover. Ziggy hesitated.

The cop got up and leaned over Ziggy, raising his hand. Ziggy recoiled.

"You will do what we say, or you will rot in jail for the rest of your life, dog," said the cop. In fear, Ziggy complied. He slowly began to show Pythi all that he knew about the man online, uncovering his history on the Internet.

Pythi sat quietly listening, but in his mind he realized that he was dealing with a kid with some phenomenal brain power. This kid could compete with the best of hackers. He was smart, quick, and very comfortable with the laptop in front of him. Instinctively, he also knew that the kid was holding out. He had more information that he was not sharing. They needed this information to crack this operation.

The room now had three cops and Pythi in it. They were listening and looking intently at the computer as Ziggy began to explain how they had infiltrated the Banque. He liked having an audience and he had seen the look of respect in Pythi's eyes. He had no idea who the American, Pythi, was, but he did know that the guy understood computers and security systems. It was he who was asking all the questions.

And so it went, till early evening and beyond. The questions were endless and Ziggy began to feel very tired. Cops went in and out of the room. Pythi stayed, except to leave and get coffee. Ziggy had mentioned the others in the group too, but they would be more difficult to find. They had cleaned out their history and there was only a faint footprint. It would take a seasoned team to uncover their whereabouts. It was G-Lover they were interested in. From the account narrated by Ziggy, it seemed as if he was the key player and finding him became imperative.

***

Back at the apartment, the cops cordoned off the area as a crime scene. Tanya, Derek, and Sam were allowed in and they removed all Ziggy's equipment and had it transported to the basement of the Banque, which had become command central of the whole operation. Pythi had sent them Ziggy's log in information, so they didn't waste time trying to find it. They didn't ask how he got it. They worked late into the evening to uncover information from the computers."Every computer has a story to tell, let's find out yours," Derek said to the computer in front of him as he started the diagnostic. Tanya and Sam, worked beside him. They knew that Ziggy had been involved with the Banque infiltration but were still trying to find out if the net he had cast was wider. How and if he was also involved with Dubai, Switzerland, Hong Kong and all the other banks. More than anything the team wanted to know how they had done it. These were smart criminals, they had created a system that had fooled all their security systems in place, and the team really wanted to know how they had done it.

***

At the police station, the cops had changed shifts but Pythi still remained. The security analyst from the American Embassy now sat behind the one way glass. They needed to find this G-Lover and he was collecting information to send back to the States. Pythi had learned a lot, and while he despised what Ziggy and his friends had done, he had begun to feel a sense of respect for the complicated, almost genius-like mind that sat in front of him. The kid was amazingly intelligent, but socially totally inept, riddled with insecurities due to his disabilities. He was completely introverted till you put a computer in front of him, then he came alive. He had a hard time making eye contact. With a computer in front of him, he spoke to the computer. This was his language, this is how he communicated, this was his comfort zone.

Pythi understood this. He had many members in various teams who would relate completely to Ziggy. In the world in which he worked, Ziggy would fit right in. He felt a little sorry for the kid who had said over and over again that he never meant to steal anything from anyone. His friend had talked him into it. After badgering him over and over again, Ziggy had finally come clean and told Pythi about the manner in which they communicated. He told him about the i-cloud communication room they had set up for their meetings and brainstorming sessions. He also told Pythi that he could not log in from the laptop in front of him. The security settings only permitted them to log on from the computer set up for it, which in Ziggy's case was the computer in his room at his apartment.

Pythi stepped outside, called Derek and asked him to bring Ziggy's computer to the police station. It had begun to rain outside and it was a gloomy cold evening. He had exchanged texts with Pia throughout the day but they were short communications. He really wanted to see her, to hold her and touch her. He wondered what she was doing. He stood outside in the cold, taking deep gulps of the fresh air, trying to release the rancid, smoke filled air that had filled his lungs for the past few hours. He talked with Homeland Security as well and was told they were trying to track down the real G-Lover. Then, taking a few more deep breaths, he went back inside.

Ziggy looked really tired and Pythi thought the kid might faint, he was so pale. He asked one of the cops to get him some food. The kid had not eaten all day. They had given him some coffee and allowed him to smoke from time to time. He had not been allowed to get up or move. He waited for some food to be brought in, then, he tried another tack.

"Tell me what you know about G-Lover's girlfriend," Pythi asked.

"Not much," responded Ziggy.

"He always talked about this girl who he cyber-stalked. He would tell us that he was going to marry her, but we all knew that he had never met her," Ziggy smiled as he said this, "He knew everything about her on line, though."

"How did he do that?" Pythi queried.

"Oh, he had hacked her email; he followed her on Facebook and Twitter. It's not that difficult to do," he responded.

Pythi smiled. He knew that. For a few minutes, he let the kid eat, watching him. He was even awkward eating in front of Pythi, holding the plastic fork in his left hand, shoveling the food in his mouth and chewing with his mouth open. There was an open coke can in front of him and he washed the food down with gulps of coke.

After a few minutes of silence, Pythi asked, "Did you ever hack into her email? What is her name? Do you know?"

Ziggy waved the plastic fork in the air as he spoke, his mouth full of the last morsels of food, "No, I didn't care too. I used to hack into his email and he never sent her any email. He just messaged her on Facebook or on Twitter. Mostly, he made comments on her blog."

Pythi looked up at this, "She has a blog?"

"Yup, I follow it too. She is a good writer, very thoughtful and sympathetic."

"What does she blog about?"

"Nothing…everything, life?"

He pushed the plate aside and pulled the laptop back toward himself. Then hitting a few keys on the keyboard, he turned it around to face Pythi.

"Here it is, her blog. She has a picture of herself in the top right hand corner. Cute looking, no?"

Pythi stared at the screen of the laptop, disbelieving. He lowered his eyes so as not to let Ziggy see the shock registered there. He was looking at Pia's face on her blog site. His blood turned cold.

Taking a breath to steady himself, he asked, "And he came to Greece to see her?"

"Yes, he wants to marry her, he is convinced that once she meets him, she will fall in love with him. He knows everything about her. He just has to meet her in real life. She had put on her blog that she was in Greece and he followed her here. He has a lot of money, his family is rich."

"If his family is so rich, why did he withdraw money from the account at the Banque?"

Shrugging, Ziggy replied, "I don't know. I don't know everything about him. Drugs maybe? Or maybe he was going to buy her an expensive present? He calls himself G-Lover, you know. Her blog name is G2 for Greek Goddess; he is G-Lover, Goddess Lover…cute right?"

Pythi could feel an anger building inside him. He wanted to smack the kid across the face and tell him to stop. Instead he asked, "Do you know when he was planning to go see her?"

"No, but he had said soon. He was only in Greece to see her. Maybe he has and already gone back. I don't know. He never told me he was coming, he never told me he was leaving, so I don't know," he shrugged. "But knowing G-Lover, he is probably stalking her right now, if not on line then in real life."

Pythi pushed his chair back. He needed to get away; he had to go to Pia. He needed to make sure she was okay. Wishing Ziggy a good night and waving at the cops he left. It was almost ten o'clock at night and the rain was coming down fast. The night was dark and the rain and moisture created a mist that enveloped everything and made it difficult to see. He found the little car in the parking lot and while the wipers were sweeping away the rain and the car heater was warming up, he called Pia. No response. His anxiety level increased.

He called the team and gave them an update. They were to bring the computer that belonged to Ziggy to the police station and then have Ziggy log into the i-cloud to request a meeting with G-Lover. Maybe through the i-cloud they could capture his physical location. Then he asked to speak with Tanya and told her what he was doing and where he was going. She asked if he wanted them to go with him. He replied that he didn't. He would stay in touch with them.

Then he tried Pia again; once more, no response. He swung the little car around and pulled out of the parking lot, driving as fast as he could, to Sounion.

SEVENTY-NINE

Let no man be called happy before his death. Till then, he is not happy, only lucky. - Solon

It was media frenzy. The BBC, CNN, FOX, Aljazeera; local channels were reporting on the unprecedented bank runs the world over. The news had leaked that banks worldwide were experiencing mysterious drain of cash and people were rushing to empty their accounts in fear that there would be nothing left. The lines at the banks were endless. The banks were out of cash to distribute and riots had erupted that necessitated the involvement of the Police and the National Guard in many countries. It seemed that the banking system was collapsing and no one appeared to have a good explanation for it. Curfew was declared in many of the big cities of the world to contain the unrest. The uncertainty had thrown the major stock markets into a downward spiral and the words "crash", "1929" and "hyperinflation" were in everyone's mouth.

The one exception was gold, which was not being traded any longer, as the holders of the precious metal were not willing to part of the safe haven in the face of collapsing currencies. Rumors were that its black market value had quadrupled and it was going higher by the hour. Lin Yu, sitting comfortably at his mansion on his private island, was rubbing his hands with satisfaction, feeling his wealth multiply as the clock was ticking, but mostly tasting the additional power his gold reserves would afford him. After he enjoyed the show of panic that his TV monitors were bringing him for a while, he leisurely enjoyed his tea and finally picked up his secure line receiver and dialed the personal number of the Chinese Premier. The exchange was short and to the point, they both agreed that this financial turmoil presented a wonderful opportunity for the ambitious dreams of China.

"It is a great time for China to reclaim her glory of the past and assert her dominance over a collapsing world," said the Premier, "And it is time for you and me, my friend, to take charge and lead that transformation. For China, for the Chinese people, for us," Lin Yu completed. They agreed to monitor the developments closely and meet secretly soon to discuss the opportunities that were opening up. They wished each other well and hung up.

Satisfied, Lin Yu smiled a wide smile, then, he pressed on his intercom to his secretary, "Please show this young man, Yuan, in; I've heard so much about him. He has been waiting for a while and it is high time we met. I'm very curious to see what he has accomplished with that laptop I gave him so long ago."

EIGHTY
Small opportunities are often the beginning of great enterprises. - Demosthenes

G-Lover drove like crazy in the blinding rain, his mind in turmoil, thoughts racing through it, though his eyes were fixed on the narrow road. He needed to make it to Sounion as fast as he could. He had hacked into Pia's email; it was easy to do and sent her a message as Pythi asking her to meet him at the Temple, telling her he couldn't wait to see her in their special place. He had told her that he was going to be waiting for her, and then signed off.

He hoped that she would be there. It was his tryst with his destiny. Everything else had gone well that day and now his time had come to make things right with his girl, his love. He was going to take her away to his hideaway and they were going to live together far away from all the craziness in his life. He was filled with excitement and trepidation. He couldn't and wouldn't allow himself to think of rejection, she would love him, she must.

Pia had read the email. Frowning, she wondered why Pythi had not called her or even texted her saying he was on his way. *Maybe, he was surrounded by people and couldn't,* she thought. Looking out the window of her YahYah's home she saw the rain beating down and again questioned why Pythi would want to meet her up at the top of the hill, at the Temple. There was very little shelter there from the rain and the cold. But then, she remembered the wonderful date he had taken her on, when he had planned the amazing dinner at the Acropolis in Athens. She wondered if he was planning something like that tonight.

She got dressed in warm clothes, jeans, a thick sweater, a waterproof jacket and comfy boots. Then she wrapped a long, bright scarf around her neck, and put on a little make up. She was excited. She was going to see Pythi again. She had missed him, it had been very hard for her and she couldn't wait to see him and feel his arms around her again, even though she questioned his choice of meeting place on a stormy night like this one. But, Pythi, her Pythi, was romantic and maybe he had a surprise in store for her.

She stepped out of the little bedroom and told YahYah she was going to take the car to see Pythi. She was careful not to tell her exactly where she was going. She knew that YahYah would not be happy if she knew that she was going up to the Temple in the middle of a stormy winter night. Then kissing her beloved grandmother, she picked up the keys and let herself out before YahYah protested too much.

It was dark outside, really dark. The wind howled and she could feel the spray from the angry ocean as she walked to the car. She unlocked the door and sliding in, shook the water off her face and hands. Then saying a prayer for protection, she turned on the car and the headlights so she could see the road before her as she began driving.

"Maybe Pythi doesn't know how bad the weather is here," she said aloud. "Maybe, I should call him and let him know. It may be better for him to simply come to YahYah's house." She reached into the pocket of her jacket to find her phone and realized that in her haste she had forgotten it. It was still at the house.

She decided she wasn't going to turn back now. She would just drive up to the Temple and wait for him there. The road was wet and frequently flooded and the rain was coming down very hard. On clear, bright days, one could see the beautiful Temple from miles away as it towered over the landscape. On this rainy night, the mountain was covered in rain and mist and she could hardly see a few feet in front of her. She was going to have to talk with Pythi about his crazy schemes.

This definitely felt dangerous and not right, but she pushed on, driving slowly, her face pressed as close up to the windshield as it would go, the wipers working as fast as they could, but doing little to clear the windshield and provide her with a clear view of the road. It was nerve racking, and in spite of the cold, she felt that she was sweating from the anxiety of driving in these terrible conditions. If she could turn back, she would have, but that was impossible on this narrow winding road. The only turn around was at the top of the mountain, in the small parking lot of the Temple.

Driving at a really slow pace, the little, old car stalled several times but she managed to make it up to the parking lot at the top of the mountain. She pulled into the lot, the only car there.

No one in their right mind would come up here in this storm, she thought. She tried to peer out of the window of the car, but all she could see was darkness. The clouds hung heavy and low, the rain and wind seemed to intensify at the height, whipping around the little car and shaking it. The old car had no heating and she sat there in the cold, blowing on her hands to warm them, and putting up the hood of her jacket to keep her head warm.

Of all the things I have done for love, this one is the craziest, she thought to herself.

***

Pythi, tried calling Pia for the seventh time, or was it the eighth, he wasn't sure. She was not answering her phone.

"Pick up, pick up," he beseeched. He really needed to warn her.

He was driving as fast as he could but he knew that it was not fast enough. He had a bad feeling and it was getting worse. Pythi relied on his inner instinct and it was sending him a very bad message right now.

***

He called Tanya, and gave her Pia's number and asked her to try calling as well. Tanya and the team were at the police station. They had taken the computer to Ziggy and were seated in the room with him, along with several police officers.

Ziggy was allowed to get up from the chair and set up the computer. Then, moving it to an angle so the others could see, he showed them how he accessed the i-cloud. He also showed Tanya, Sam, and Derek, the encryption system they used to ensure the security of the cloud.

The kid is a genius, all three of them thought to themselves.

Tanya asked him a lot of questions and he answered them, patiently, happy that someone understood his "language." Derek and Sam sat enraptured, listening to him. The police officers were bored. He sent a message on the cloud to G-Lover, requesting a meeting, but, he told them, he could tell that he was not on line.

"Do you have his email address?" Derek asked.

"I have all of them," Ziggy said, then as if he was showing off for them, he said, "I hack his email all the time, to check out what he is doing."

"Can you hack into it now?" Sam asked, "Will it take you long?"

"A few minutes," responded Ziggy, and they watched as he proceeded to hack into G-Lover's email.

Derek asked that he slide over so he could take a look. Ziggy explained how they had learnt to use covers for their email, to send emails to people pretending to be someone else.

"It's our technology," he said proudly. "We use it when we play games with players all over the world to confuse them, it is easy to do."

"Amazing," thought Derek, "This kid is far beyond us and we thought we knew every trick in the book."

Derek was scrolling G-Lover's email as Tanya and Sam continued to ask Ziggy questions. Not a whole lot in his incoming mail. In fact, it seemed like he hardly used email. He scrolled through the inbox, mostly offers from stores and email solicitations, not much personal information here. He then went to his sent mail. He had sent emails to some lady, letting her know he was vacationing, and that he would be home soon. Derek presumed that it was either his mother or his housekeeper. There was no thread there, no response.

He almost missed it…an email to "his Love."

"My sweet love," the email read, "I am back in town and will meet you at our favorite place tonight. The Temple, and all that it holds, is waiting for us. I will see you there at eleven o clock tonight. I hope that you are up for it. I love you and can't wait to hold you in my arms. P."

Derek turned the computer to Tanya and Sam and let them read it. It took Tanya a few seconds to read it, then, grabbing her phone, she rushed out of the interrogation room. It was 10:50. She hit the speed dial for Pythi's phone number as she tried to find a private space to speak with him.

He answered on the second ring.

"Boss," she said, "This is trouble," as she proceeded to tell him about the email. That he had signed off with the letter 'P' really scared her. "We all read G2's, I mean Pia's blog, and everyone who reads it knows that she is at Cape Sounion. He is going to meet her at the Temple, hurry. I'm going to go back inside and let them know that the police need to be on their way too. This man is dangerous," so saying she hung up and raced back inside.

Back in the interrogation room, she filled in the others and the police. She was told that there was no police station at the Cape. The closest one was at Lavrion. One of the police officers stepped outside to call the dispatch at the Lavrion station, to send a couple of squad cars up to the Temple. He came back a few minutes later to let them know that no one was answering at the dispatch desk; they would try again in a few minutes.

***

As she sat shivering in her car, Pia could see the headlights of the only car in sight as it wove its way over the mountain, at first at a distance but gradually getting closer, till finally she could see it at the bottom of the hill, moving up toward her. It was still pouring rain, and in her excitement, she had forgotten an umbrella. Well, she thought, I will just wait in the car till he comes to get me. The car made slow progress as it continued its way up the steep mountain road, its headlights throwing the falling rain into relief as it inched forward. Pia looked at her watch, it was almost 11pm.

EIGHTY-ONE

I'm not afraid of an army of lions led by a sheep;
I'm afraid of an army of sheep led by a lion. – Alexander of Macedon, the Great

The Goddess flew above the storm and the rain clouds watching, her lips grim, tension seeping out of her. Where was Poseidon? He was supposed to be here, helping control this situation.

It was all getting out of hand and her beautiful ward, her little angel Pia was in terrible danger. She knew Ares was close by, she could sense him, but given the raging storm, the heavy cloud cover, and the ocean that was dark and angry, she could not spot him. Of course, this was going to be an advantage for her as well. High above the clouds, she watched the lone car make its way slowly up the hill and, as she watched its slow progress, resolved that she would do whatever it took to save her child. If she had to pick up a sword and fight, she would, she was ready...

Under the cover of the storm, Poseidon was ready and watching too. The austere God, in all his glory was an ominous figure, huge and powerful. Undaunted by the storm raging around him, trident in hand, he was ready for war and whatever the night may bring. His Guardians were ready too, armed and under cover of the night, they stood behind him, quietly, in silence waiting for a sign from him.

He saw the beautiful Athena in the distance and his love and affection for her grew stronger. She had come to face this foe and stand with him, to help him, this time. He could feel her tension, but he could also feel her strength. She was a strong one, his Athena, and she feared very little. With her by his side, they would be victorious. It was time...

EIGHTY-TWO

All men's souls are immortal, but the souls of the righteous are immortal and divine. – Socrates

As he drove up the mountain, G-Lover contemplated what would happen next. His hands were shaking and he needed a quick snort to boost his confidence. His emotions were swinging from high to low, in one moment he felt immortal and unbeatable, and in the next he felt miserable and defeated. He realized that all the actions he had set into motion were going to come to a head in a few moments. He was going to come face to face with his future, whatever that may be. He touched the pocket of his jacket and took a deep breath….the gun was still there. She would be his one way or another, no other man was going to have her.

Pia watched the car pull up to the parking lot with bated breath. She could only see the headlights in the blinding rain and, when the lights were turned off, she was left in utter and complete darkness, the sound of the pounding rain and the darkness making her feel almost panicky.

He turned off the lights and waited for his eyes to adjust. In the darkness, he reached into the glove compartment and found his stash of drugs. Quickly, he rolled out a line, snorted it and wiped his nose with the back of his hand. He felt his jacket again, making sure the gun was still there. Then, he opened the door and stepped out into the pouring rain. It had begun to thunder and the lightning strikes seemed to light up the entire sky. He saw the car parked at the other end of the parking lot and ran toward it ….she was there, waiting for him.

Pia sat waiting in the car, wondering what to do next. The rain was coming down so hard she did not see him till he pulled open her car door and the rain poured in. She looked up, a smile on her face…and froze.

This was not Pythi, she was looking at the face of some strange man who was yelling at her in the rain and she could not hear what he was saying because of the downpour and the thunder. She tried to pull the door shut on him, but couldn't because of the wind and his body standing between the door and her. She pushed her booted leg out and kicked him hard to dislodge him from the car. He yelled in pain and grabbed her hand. When he reeled back from the power of her kick, he took her with him. They were now lying on the wet, hard stone and she struggled to get away from him.

Pia was terrified but her instinct to protect herself kicked in and she fought him hard. G-Lover fought back but he was surprised at her strength. She got up on her knees trying to crawl away from him. He caught her legs and tried to pull her back to him, all the time yelling at her telling her that he loved her.

"I love you; I am not going to hurt you. Please stop and listen," he yelled, but she had either not heard him or she wasn't having any of it. She managed to scramble away and getting up on her legs began to run toward the Temple. He got up and tried to follow, slipping along the way. She was getting away from him and he knew that if he lost sight of her, he would never find her in the dark. She was approaching the turn to the pillars as he got a more steady footing and began running after her.

***

Pythi was almost there. He pushed his rental car to go up the mountain at top speed, paying little attention to the rain and the horrendous storm. It felt as though the heavens had opened up. The rain seemed to get stronger the higher up he went, and the wind pushed against his car.

He pulled into the parking lot. In the light shed by the car's headlights he saw two cars and his heart felt like it dropped to the pit of his stomach. YahYah's old car stood at the other end of the parking lot, the door wide open, in the pouring rain. The other car was parked a little distance away. In the beam of the headlights he saw a movement and, when he looked in that direction, he saw the distant figure of a man scrambling up the mountainside toward the pillars. He grabbed his phone as he unbuckled himself and called Tanya, yelling at her to send the police to the Temple, before he stepped out into the pouring rain, leaving the car running, and its headlights on, so the light beam might help him.

He ran as fast as he could knowing that Pia was in danger, wondering where she was, chasing after the figure he had seen but which had disappeared. He had on a light jacket with no protective rain gear and was completely drenched, the cold seeping into his bones, but he was unaware of any of it. All he could think of was Pia. He blamed himself. He should have warned her. Thoughts raced through his head as he ran, making sure not to be seen and to stay out of the beam of light from the car.

Pia ran as fast as she could. Where she was running she did not know, she prayed for the Goddess to protect and save her and called her name. She felt Athena's ethereal shield deploy around her. She was at the top of the mountain running toward the pillars when she heard the first shot. It hit a large rock a few feet away from her and shattered it. She was completely terrified now, convinced she was going to die; the shield was not meant to stop bullets. She was being shot at and she had nowhere to run. She zigzagged through the pillars as she heard more shots. He was behind her and she could feel him getting closer, she needed to hide.

She remembered the rock, her rock, the huge boulder that sat on the western edge of the hilltop. The very rock that she had clambered on as a child and hidden under to get away from her brothers, the rock where she and Pythi had first made their peace. She knew where it was and began her descent toward it, praying that there would be no more lightning strikes and that in the darkness she would be able to find it and hide. She slid, the wet soil and pebbles giving way under her, as she ran toward it. She could hear him yelling now. He was shouting her name, telling her he was going to find her. He was still telling her how much he loved her, shouting at her to stop and show herself.

Pythi was gaining on him; his instinct was leading him in the right direction. He could hear the man yelling in between the shots he was firing and knew that he would have to take him by surprise or they would both be dead.

He was a few feet behind him when he saw the man lunge. At that same moment, lightning lit up the sky and he saw the man launch himself onto Pia who was cowering and screaming as she ran. He landed on her and both of them rolled a few feet down the mountain.

It was an instant, but in that instant Pythi felt rage from somewhere deep within him, he felt a huge well of anger gush out. Anger at this man for harming his beloved, anger that he would dare hurt Pia, anger that he had put her in this situation, and this anger propelled him.

In a rage, he grabbed G-Lover, and with a force he did not know he possessed, he pulled him off Pia, hitting him as hard as he could. He got the man's shoulder and G-Lover grunted in anger as he turned and began to fight Pythi. Pia was screaming now, yelling and screaming for help. One part of her knew it was futile, but some other part within her hoped that someone would hear them or else Pythi and she would surely die here on this hilltop.

She was crying, asking the Goddess for help, as before her the two men fought each other. They were sliding around in the mud and the rain, the pebbles giving way under their feet as they grappled with each other. They had slid south of the rock, almost to the edge of the mountain, while Pia cowered behind a pillar. She picked up a small rock and launched it at the man, it hit him, and he turned with a surprised look on his face. It gave Pythi the opportunity to hit him square in the face and G-Lover flew into the dirt. Pythi moved toward him to hit him again when he heard Pia screaming.

He heard her a split second too late, the bullet grazed his shoulder and the impact made him fall back. Pia thought he had been shot. He fell back with a thud and she knew that she would remember that sound for as long as she would live. To her ears, it was the sound of Pythi dying. She ran out from behind the pillar toward Pythi. She needed to get to him and she didn't care if she got shot doing it. She saw G-Lover from the corner of her eye, standing now, just below her rock, the gun swinging in her direction as she ran in the rain toward Pythi, who still lay on the ground.

"I hate you," she screamed over and over again, as she ran toward Pythi.

"I love you," he yelled back, as he pointed the gun at her.

"I love you, and have for a very long time. I am going to make you mine, forever."

She did not see him raise his hand and point the gun at her like he was zeroing in on his target; she was so focused on getting to Pythi. She did not see the sky open up or the lightning that poured forth. She did not feel the air turn very still for a moment and then begin to churn as the pebbles and rocks around her were picked up and swirled as if a vortex was picking them up and discarding them. She did not feel the vortex building around her.

At the moment she reached Pythi she looked up, lightning was still creating its fiery display in the sky, and she found herself looking straight into the eyes of G-Lover. The lightning making his blue eyes look ghostly and translucent, as he half-smiled, still telling her that she was his forever. She saw the look in his eyes and knew that he was going to kill her.

In a split second everything changed. She heard the loud crackle, she felt the movement, as if the earth shifted under her feet, and she saw the look of alarm in his face as he turned, but it was too late. The rock, her rock, which had stood in the same spot for thousands of years; on which she had played as a child, her rock that had been lodged into the earth since time immemorial had dislodged, and was hurtling toward him. There was nowhere for him to run, it was too late. He saw the huge boulder bearing down on him and before he could react, it hit him with a force and a speed that pushed him over the edge of the high cliff. Pia watched in horror as he disappeared from view, hearing his scream fade as he vanished into the rocks below.

She thought that the huge boulder, her rock, would follow, as it had such great momentum. But when it reached the edge of the cliff, it stopped, abruptly, as if someone had simply held it back, and then giving itself another shudder, it seemed to settle into the very edge of the cliff.

She knelt down beside Pythi, crying his name, touching his face, seeing the blood seep out of him.

"Pythi, please don't die on me, please," she beseeched. She felt his hand move and looked at him startled. He was looking at her, he was alive.

She began to cry again.

"I think I am okay, injured and bleeding, but okay. Help me up, let's try and find some shelter."

He winced as she helped him and together they stumbled to the shelter of one of the largest pillars which had a small overhang. They slid under it and, holding each other, they watched the immense vortex swirling around them. The air was fine and felt very pure and clean, they saw the rocks and pebbles swirling around them. It was as if an immense force had opened up from the center of the Temple, pouring out the most pure, clean energy. As the storm subsided they felt the energy increase and continue to swirl till the vortex grew wider and wider, first encompassing the top of the mountain, then moving across the way to cover the town and the surrounding mountains, then spreading across the ocean and continuing to grow....moving, swirling, expanding...

How long they sat there, they did not know. The police found them some time later and Pythi was whisked off to the hospital. The bullet had grazed his shoulder but not shattered any bone. His flesh wound was stitched, dressed, and he was allowed to leave. Pia brought him back to YahYah's home, where together, they clambered into the soft bed, laying side by side, whispering quiet words of love as they fell into a deep sleep.

***

It was five in the morning when YahYah woke up and, as she did every day of her life, rain or shine, she made her cup of coffee, bundled herself in a long coat and stepped outside to drink it, watch the sunrise, and pray. As the soft rays of the sun began to appear over the horizon, she glanced up at the Temple as she did every morning, sensing a peculiar lightness and power that she had never experienced before.

Her eyesight was not as good as it used to be, but she always looked up and prayed to the Goddess. In the soft early morning light, she glanced up. There, high above the mountain, looking down on the Temple, she saw the diaphanous image of the most beautiful woman she had ever seen, floating on the clouds, dressed in a gossamer gown, her hair flowing behind her. The beautiful lady looked down at her and smiled the most beauteous smile. An owl flew beside her. And above them, she saw him. She had seen him many times in her dreams, the Lord of the Temple, beloved Poseidon, strong and so handsome, holding his trident and gazing out at the ocean, the Guardian of the World as she knew it. He turned, approached Athena, and placing a caring and protective hand over her shoulder, he looked straight into the old woman's eyes from the distance and spoke for both of them without uttering the words:

"Many blessings to you and your loved ones, Pia and Pythi; they have given us a lot of joy. We will always be with them. This old temple will be their place of peace and tranquility in the years to come, as they grow more sensitive to the energy of the vortex that has just opened, and, we hope, they will be curious enough to find ways to interpret and dispense its wonderful promise in a spirit of service to humanity."

YahYah closed her eyes and gave silent thanks with an almost ecstatic smile. She knew now, no matter how many storms may come their way, no matter how fierce they may be, her beloved Pia and her love, Pythi, were blessed, and, eventually, all would be right with the world.

EPILOGUE

Tanya, Sam, and Derek, with the help of Ziggy, managed to recover most of the stolen money. Some of it was gone forever, as was Andrei, whose trail had turned cold. Ziggy was sure he would reappear someday, probably at a time and place that no one expected him. The world would be looking and waiting.

No sign of Yuan, either, or his money. Rumors had it that he had become the trusted advisor to the Head of all Triads, who had used the temporary crisis to enrich himself beyond measure and consolidate his undisputed now power by mercilessly crushing his competition.

Tanya and Sam had begun to date each other. It was an easy relationship. Sam adored her and they had planned to visit her aunt in England soon.

The Professor, Pythi's father, was healing slowly, and his mother had truly retired so she could be with him full time and help him on his path to recovery. They were talking about selling their home and moving to a place with only one story, to make it easier on the Professor. Actually, it was Pythi's mother who kept bringing it up. The Professor loved his home and was happy to stay in the guest room till he was able to walk up the stairs again.

Ziggy had spent long hours working closely with the team. They all liked him and noticed that he worked tirelessly without complaining. After some bargaining and discussion with the Greek Police, the FBI and Homeland Security, due to all the help he had given the team, he was given a full pardon. The team was overjoyed and he was soon asked to join them as a team member. He was on his way to New York for training. He couldn't believe his good fortune and promised himself that he would make them all proud of him.

Pythi closed out the operation in Athens, and Pia and he headed back to the United States. YahYah was sad to see them go, but was so happy they had found each other. When Pia was not around, she made Pythi promise her that when it would be time to marry Pia, it would be in Greece, at her beloved Temple, at Sounion. He agreed. The couple was looking forward to spending Christmas with his parents, who were anxious to meet the girl that had won their son's heart.

Ares had retreated to the consoling hospitality of Hades to lick his wounds and regroup, and both of them, in-between self-reminders that there will be other opportunities, were casting a watchful eye towards the East, towards China.

***

In his lair, Poseidon sat on his favorite rock, perched at the edge of the cliff, on the hilltop of Cape Sounion, a faint smile on his lips, looking out on the beautiful and calm, azure sea. Beside him sat his lovely cohort, the beautiful Goddess Athena. Fingers linked, they sat in silence, content, both smiling in agreement. The world was right again; for now at least. Together they had been triumphant; this time. Ares had been vanquished; for the time being.

Above them, the beautiful Temple shone bright in the sun, its white marble pillars reflecting the sun's incandescence. The air was crisp, the birds were chirping loudly, the olive trees were swaying gently in the soft sea breeze.

All around them, spreading outward, wave upon swirling wave, they watched the portal energy expand and intensify. It was clean, clear, fresh, and full of the strength of the Divine Lord. It was pure and radiant. The vortex had finally opened and it was flowing at full-force. The long-awaited vibrant light was ascending and spreading across the world to join with that of other such centers in forming a network that would help condition the planet for the new dispensation. Nothing could stop that any longer, not Ares, not anyone.

Poseidon had arisen indeed, and the seeds of his promise were already finding fertile ground in the hearts and minds of the people. It had been a long time coming. It was now.

ABOUT THE AUTHORS

PETROS ZENIERIS was born in Athens, Greece, where he put together his first writings in his native Greek. After completing a University education in Engineering, his philosophical tendencies and insatiable curiosity, desire for graduate-level education and applied research, and need for Self-discovery brought him to America. There, he completed his graduate Civil Engineering studies and satisfied his desire for research in his field. He developed a professional engineering career, found his teacher and wayshower in kriya meditation, and met his Twin Flame. Petros calls Florida home and Greece his endless, self-renewing love affair. The Middle East is where he currently lives, works, and writes. The Garden of the Beloved is his inspiration.

JER ZENIERIS was born in Mumbai, India where her love of reading and writing was nurtured. She moved to the United States to pursue a higher education and received her Ph.D. from the University of Oklahoma. There she met her beloved husband and together they have raised two great kids, explored the world, and pursued their spiritual growth. A former College Professor and grant writer, she now runs a real estate business in Jupiter, Florida, where the family lives. When she is not writing, she enjoys long walks on the beach, yoga, and meditation.

Made in the USA
San Bernardino, CA
22 December 2015